Troublesome Creek

Charles McRaven

A Wings ePress, Inc.
Historical Fiction Novel

Wings ePress, Inc.

Edited by: Jeanne Smith
Copy Edited by: April Bennett
Executive Editor: Jeanne Smith
Cover Artist: Trisha FitzGerald-Jung

Wings ePress Books
www.wingsepress.com

Copyright © 2021 by: Charles McRaven
ISBN-13: 978-1-61309-552-2

Published In the United States Of America

Wings ePress Inc.
3000 N. Rock Road
Newton, KS 67114

Dedication

For my five children, who were young pioneers

* * *

One

The campfire illuminated a tangle of laurel bushes deep in a cove on the west side of the Virginia Blue Ridge, showing in an unreal glow the tethered horses and the man's sidelighted face. Behind them, now in darkness, lay the foothills east of the mountains, and nearly three years of his life along one of its creeks. Ahead, still touched by the faint, deep blue of the Appalachians rimming it, lay the Shenandoah Valley.

Stephen Davis stirred the embers under the roasting grouse and remembered. Three years, and he'd meant to make that place, those people, that work in wood and iron, his life.

Wasn't meant to be; simple as that.

And the five years before that, trudging the mud and dust and blood of the war with England, his deadly skill in high demand. The dreams rarely came lately, of the dead faces of the men he'd killed. The events of that life along that creek had worn them out in demanding work, unrequited love, the fresh raw violence that had overtaken him.

But there'd been the good of it all, too: his friendship with Tom Logan, whom he'd rescued from slavery. The high adventure that always seemed to accompany his old comrade-in-arms, Ned Drake. The fine furniture he'd crafted, much of it now in plantation parlors. The good friends he'd made, who'd stood with him against the smooth-mannered outlaws there.

And the woman he'd loved too late, and lost.

Maybe.

Kentucky. Her family had said she'd joined a wagon train of missionaries on the way to work among the settlers in Kentucky. Well, he'd been headed that way himself, right after the war, when he'd caught sight of that other, stunningly beautiful girl at the plantation on the creek. Turned his head, she had, and he'd thought he'd finally won her. Till the blood and all. And that slick preacher...

No, that turned out the way it was meant to. It was the other...

About two women too many, seemed like.

He guessed he'd go on beating himself over the head with it all, and none of that would help any. Time to put it all in the past, now: plan his next moves better. So far no clear course, except to find Anna. Then try to make it up to her for the way he'd treated her.

Take some eating crow, that would.

Stephen was largely self-educated, being a voracious reader. His father, a miller and gunsmith from England, had insisted that even a man who worked with his hands need not be illiterate in this new land of largely unschooled settlers. And five years of close association with Ned Drake, the witty but penniless planter's son, had taken more of the rough edges off.

Didn't matter, he reflected; out in the border territories an education didn't build you a better cabin, or grow you a better corn patch. Or make you a better rifle shot, either. Probably a lot of men out there as good as he was.

No, there weren't.

But just how he'd fit in, with backwoods settlers or in the few towns that'd sprung up since the Revolution, he couldn't predict. Again, it didn't matter much. He'd just have to take life out there as he found it, the way he'd handled the years on Buck Mountain Creek.

One major difference, he reflected, between his situation now and the one he'd been in that late fall of 1781 just weeks after the surrender at Yorktown: he'd been dirt poor then, and now he had money. Sewn into his clothes, in a doubled leather belt, in his saddlebags, even in pockets in his boots. The gold coins were noticeably heavy, but he'd grow used to that, he was sure. It was a good feeling, being for the first time in his life able to buy the things he needed—would no doubt need—in the new country.

Wouldn't be much demand for a furniture maker in wilderness Kentucky, he realized. But he could always go back to dressing millstones. Millers and blacksmiths were usually the first craftsmen in a settlement, and yes, he could do both those jobs, if necessary. But depending on how things worked out with Anna, he'd want to secure a good piece of land first. The old saying was, "All it takes is two people and a piece of ground."

And he'd made the mistake of letting her get away from him.

He shook his head impatiently; *no use going over that again.* First he had to find her, find out where he stood. If he still stood, which didn't seem likely, the way she'd just gone off. Him away two weeks with Tom over in Caroline County at Ned's wedding, and she'd just vanished. Even her family up little Lynch River had been shocked.

But when Anna Compton made up her mind to a thing, her father had told him, it was as good as done. Tall, part Indian, the striking girl had been their farm's right hand until her brothers had grown. Not that pretty, Stephen remembered, till she smiled, and that made her beautiful. But the smile was rare: a serious young woman, that one.

"Give me something to smile about," she'd told him when he'd clumsily brought the subject up. And he'd been so blinded by the planter's daughter, he'd...

Just let it go; all that's over, and a good thing, too. Look ahead, not behind. Nothing in the past to hold you; it's all out front.

~ * ~

Morning found him descending the west slope, down from Brown's Gap. The leaves of late summer were still on and he couldn't catch sight of the winding Shenandoah River ahead. The way looped into hollows, came out of them onto spreading meadows, some of which had log cabins, small fenced fields, hastily-thrown-up barns and sheds. The plantations would be down along the river, where the topsoil was deep, the land flatter. German settlers had come down from Pennsylvania two generations before, to stake prosperous farms.

The country was filling up, Stephen had noted before, traveling to sell his woodwork. Here, the rich Valley land began to show patchwork fields almost touching each other as the land leveled out. No wonder people were traveling further west, now that England no longer ruled them, forbidding settlers from escaping that country's imposed heavy taxes.

Here was prosperity, despite the drain of the recent war. Millwheels turned lazily under the reduced flow of creeks and river before the fall rains. Farmers forked hay onto rising haystacks, interwoven around tall poles set deep in the ground. Fat cattle and sleek horses grazed the streamside fields. *Maybe this next generation can grow and live in peace, now. Surely that can happen, after all we did to get free.*

He envisioned the next days, weeks of travel, up the winding river, southwest between the ridges, toward Kentucky. The lush farms would give way to stony slopes, scattered cabins, crude settlements. He'd have to get through those mountains to the west, into the deep hollows and fast streams he'd heard about. Maybe he'd even be able to catch up to Anna's wagon train, although he didn't know which route they'd take.

More likely, finally reaching the limestone country he'd heard about near Lexington, in Kentucky Territory, they'd stop for a while and he could search for her. But that would be many, many weeks ahead, even into winter, and the chances of finding her would diminish with the distance.

Too many rivers to cross.

But from what he knew, they'd head not for those settlements, but the raw untamed wilderness perhaps nearer, down in the mountains south. Where the few people there lived far from civilization, from villages, from churches and the Word of God. That'd be their mission.

But there was the lawlessness of the new country. Drifting ex-soldiers like himself, disenchanted farmers, tradesmen lured by the prospect of unspoiled country, would be joined by those desperate to escape debt, legal troubles, their sordid pasts. Best to plan for his defense, a man traveling alone.

Well, nothing new there, he guessed, remembering the recent violence along Buck Mountain Creek.

The inns and ordinaries of the region were a mixed offering. He passed the poorer of these, knowing the flea-ridden accommodations would provide little rest and unpalatable food. The better ones would be expensive, and while he had a sizeable share of the gold he, Tom and Ned had recovered, he didn't want to waste it. Better to camp most of the time, with perhaps a good bed and a cleanup every week or so.

So he followed the roads of the Shenandoah in the generally southwest direction, looping as they did from village to mill to plantation, traveling many miles farther than a straight line. He met solitary riders like himself, wagons of farm produce pulled by nodding, somnolent mules, groups of families headed for market. The women were red-faced in sunbonnets, the men lean under slouch hats, all bearing the mark of the soil they worked.

Sometimes he'd meet or overtake a carriage, drawn by matched horses, purposefully making its way no doubt to or from a town, its occupants dressed finely, the men in tricorner hats, the women in voluminous dresses. Or a briskly trotting official of some kind, intent on arriving at whatever law office or courthouse or new manufacturing concern a prosperous area always generated.

~ * ~

The wagons were well-fitted, financed by organizations of churches in the East, and progress had been good once in the Valley.

Anna Compton, who'd never been west of the Blue Ridge, was surprised and pleased at the miles covered by the five conveyances, tan-topped canvas covers like ships' sails on this flattened land. At this rate, they'd be in Kentucky well before cold weather and, she hoped, set up in some sort of accommodations.

Didn't matter, she told herself; they could minister to the needy from tents, if necessary. She knew there were towns from which the missionaries could venture out into the wilderness, but suspected they'd actually be out among the scattered cabins and camps themselves most of the time. The backwoods settlers, the Indians they were planning to live among, would be deep in the uncivilized areas, away from schools, churches, settlements.

This was exciting, and she looked forward to the work, which she now saw as her life's calling. After having grown up on the family's riverside farm, toiling alongside her father and brothers, the tall girl felt she would and could be of more help to humanity with this group of believers. God would use her, as He had back on Lynch River, at the new church there among the children. She'd even planned a school there, but now saw that hadn't been meant to be.

No, she'd had to give that course up, with the disappointing events surrounding her relationship with Stephen Davis. Or, more accurately, her non-relationship. She remembered now, driving this team through the Valley, the humiliation of his blindly pursuing the dazzling Abigail Thomas and slighting her. But she'd borne it, as she'd always borne the grueling labor of the farm. Tall, unsmiling, she knew she'd had no chance with the brooding ex-sharpshooter from the Continental Army.

Not with Abigail around.

But afterwards—and she gripped the reins harder, stiffened her back against the jolting wagon—Stephen had actually expected her to open her arms to him after Abby had eloped with the handsome Philadelphia preacher.

Second hand, second rate, second choice, to be condescendingly considered only after your real prize escaped.

A hot flush of shame reddened her face. Not so much at the insult, but at the memory of how close she'd come to forgiving Stephen, opening not only her arms, but her heart to him.

No, he'd been just like the others Abby had attracted, and expecting more of him had been foolish, but she'd done it for some reason. And he'd fallen into that schoolboy worship of the girl, and that was his measure. And, un-Christian or not, she just hadn't been able to swallow her pride that much, no matter the life it might have led to with him.

Because she would never know just when another pretty face might come along, and whatever she and Stephen could have built between them might evaporate in that shallow streak he'd shown her.

So here she was, traveling toward another life, a life of service, albeit with a hard lump of regret inside her. The new land, the new challenges, the new faces, would surely in time erase the bad memories, the longing, the emptiness.

No, they wouldn't.

Like Othello, she had loved not wisely, but too well. Shakespeare: she and Stephen had read Shakespeare together. And he'd seemed to share her love of literature, of learning. At least with that part of his mind not preoccupied with another spoiled but attractive face.

No more of this; it's all behind me now and my life's ahead, whatever that life is supposed to hold. And it's not going to hold Stephen Davis.

The miles unfurled before them, the wide farms, the villages, the mills, the bustling life of the Shenandoah. Toward the westering sun the wagons creaked, the wheels measuring the days, the weeks until her new life would begin.

~ * ~

Stephen journeyed on, his mind on the probable situation in Kentucky. Surely just a more primitive version of the Piedmont: more wilderness, more game, fewer farms. Less law. Soldiers from that region had fought alongside him and his comrades in the war.

Their towns, like Lexington and Frankfort and Bardstown, were surely prosperous by now in that bluegrass country rumored to be as rich as the Shenandoah.

So no, those wouldn't be the missionaries' destination. Not along the well-traveled routes west from Lexington in Virginia and on across the Jackson River past the few settlements to thread into the high mountains. From word at inns and campgrounds on the way, he was able to trace their travelings; perhaps then, Big Stone Gap, well down toward Tennessee, was their route.

Leaders among the settlers, like Daniel Boone, had first opened up the Kentucky land in defiance of the English. Now, a generation later, the missionaries, the traders, even some manufacturers, were probably getting established along the rivers. To the west, the Ohio River encountered falls at the fledgling settlement of Louisville, and that would no doubt become a major trading center. But the caravan wasn't headed toward towns with churches. Nor toward the other settlements in the territory, apparently.

The letter Stephen carried, from the aging Reverend Carson at Charlottesville, told of three possible locations for the missionaries traveling ahead of him. But, the cleric had pointed out, the purpose of their work was to reach into the back country, away from towns and churches, to bring the Word to the lost and forgotten. Just where his friends would actually go in their quest was a question in God's hands alone, he'd said.

Not much help. But of course, with only a few weeks' lead, surely other people along the way would remember the wagon train of missionaries and help point him on their way. And also, he'd certainly gain on them, providing he wasn't on the wrong track.

Perhaps he'd best pray for guidance, here. Attendance at the new church where Anna had taught the children and the overly-slick preacher had held forth had made him more aware of God. It might help if...

No, a man who'd killed so many, both in the war and in that bloody business on the creek, could hardly expect any God to direct him on a personal quest. And even if that God did forgive, the accusing faces of the dead in his dreams would never shift their tortured eyes from him.

He had only his purpose, and the shame of the way he'd mistreated the finest woman he'd ever know, to drive him onward. And if he failed, it'd be after the fight, as he'd told Tom Logan.

~ * ~

The Shenandoah Valley narrowed, then disappeared as Stephen rode into the mountains. The roads were worse here, and the taverns and inns predictably shabbier, the travelers rougher in appearance. He rode with his long rifle sheathed but within easy reach. And he had two pistols concealed in holsters under his untucked shirt, and a long knife. Barring an attack by a whole band of outlaws, he felt certain he could defend himself. And of course, the wagon train ahead of him would be a more formidable target for highwaymen. He knew from Reverend Carson that there were able men accompanying the missionaries, men who were no strangers to the rough life in the new country.

Stephen had always been withdrawn, except in the company of close friends. Now he merely nodded to those he met or traveled near, preferring his own counsel. A cheery salesman of printed cloth leading a packhorse laden with samples wanted to talk as they rode alongside. But the man's vocabulary consisted mostly of the details of the mills in New England that produced his wares and his sales potential.

"Going to be a hefty trade with these new cotton farmers of the South," he confided. "And these farm women'll buy, no matter the cost. Tired of homespun fabrics, they are, and these samples will bring in the orders." He opened a flat display case to show Stephen small swatches of fabric, which were indeed colorful. But they only reminded him of the bright dresses Abby Thomas had worn, as opposed to the sober grays and browns Anna owned. He rode on ahead.

Eventually, after many days' travel, the only settlement of note on his path still in Virginia was Saltville, a bustling center devoted to the mining and shipping of that commodity. Long known to the Indians for its natural deposits of the mineral, this outpost was at the edge of the remote country, not far from Kentucky Territory. Stephen theorized that the missionaries might stay over there, to resupply and refit before launching into the high Appalachians to the west. He pushed on, riding late and early, intent on making up the miles to that outpost.

Just what his strategy would be when and if he caught up with Anna Compton, he hadn't worked out yet. But he'd make certain she knew he wouldn't give up on her, no matter how far she traveled or how deeply she immersed herself in her work. He aimed to be the man in that woman's life, whatever it took. And he also meant to be strong competition to any eligible men she might meet in the new country.

And wrapped in one of his saddlebags was a carved hand mirror he'd meant to give her that time he'd found her gone from her parents' farm. It was an oval, with vines and leaves cut into the cherry wood, a gift he'd labored long over. He also remembered a small sewing cabinet he had presented to her, back at the beginning of their friendship. She hadn't wanted to take it without trading him, feeling embarrassed. *Well, she'll get the mirror this time, no matter what.*

If I ever find her.

He'd thought Anna had understood how sincere he'd been in his suit, and had felt certain he could win her, given time. But that hope had evaporated when he'd found she'd disappeared, along with any chance to ingratiate himself with her.

Deep one, that. I always knew it, but fancied I'd be up to the task with all we'd shared. But a man who understands a woman is a liar, Pa always said. Took it a lot harder than I thought, she did. Probably a lot gone on between her and Abby I didn't know about, before I knew them.

Yes, he could picture the two girls, growing up just a few miles apart. The pampered plantation daughter with her head-turning looks, and the tall, probably initially awkward farmer's daughter, hands hardened in labor, quiet by nature, her own head buried in books early on. Abby claiming every young man she met and Anna lost in the background. Tom Logan had been right in his appraisal. "Anna's what Abby would like to be." Stephen had laughed at his insightful friend at the time, but no more.

He was roused from these musings late in the day by the arrival of two men on horseback coming into the road from a dim trail. They appeared suddenly from between steep sides of a narrow draw, where huge boulders had hidden them. The hair on Stephen's neck rose. Both men were roughly dressed in greasy buckskins and their faces were heavily bearded, though the taller of them had a carefree air about him. Both had rifles on their saddles and holstered pistols.

As they fell in beside him, Stephen shifted to the far side of the road to forestall any attempt to flank him. He'd transferred his horse's reins and the packhorse's rope to his left hand at sight of the men, and now had his right on the butt of one of his own pistols.

"Headin' t'Saltville?" the tall man asked, not unpleasantly. He had an open face, appeared to be about thirty years of age. The other man, older, heavier but a head shorter, shifted his eyes constantly. Looking for advantage? Stephen wasn't about to give that.

"That way, all right. Guess I won't make it by nightfall, though."

"No, not on th' main road. We know of a shortcut'll git y'thar though, you ride hard."

"Don't reckon so. My horses are tired. Find a farm, spend the night." Stephen wanted these men gone. If both drew down on him at once, he'd have to move fast to survive. He hadn't had time to unsheath his rifle, and while he could easily drop one of them with one pistol, the other might be too fast for him.

"Don't know of enny farms ennywheres near, stranger. We're gonna take th' shortcut up ahead. Welcome t'jine us."

"Thanks for the offer. But I've a few friends should have caught up by now. Guess I'd better wait for them." He didn't really think they'd believe this, but it seemed worth a try.

The men exchanged a brief look and the older one glanced back up the road. It was empty, and a straight stretch showed nothing but Stephen's faint dust. Then a quick nod from the taller man signaled their intent, and Stephen caught it.

Easy-going one's the bigger threat. I'll gamble the other one's slow, will follow his lead. Best guess I can come up with...

The first man's hand snatched his pistol. Stephen dropped the reins and lead rope, spurred his gelding and whipped out his own gun, fired. His ball caught the man full in the chest, and the unfired pistol fell. The other man, gun out, couldn't get a clear shot as Stephen wheeled his horse, pulled his other pistol, cocked it.

"Drop it!" he commanded. "I don't want to have to kill you, but I will." It had happened so fast, the tall man was still upright in his saddle, a confused look on his face, and the other robber hadn't fully realized his partner was dying. He steadied his hand, trying for a shot.

Stephen shot him in the head, flinging him from his saddle, arms wide.

And then without pause or reflection, he caught the packhorse's lead rope and rode away, reloading his guns with powder and ball. He was outwardly unmoved by the shooting, turning over the facts of it in his mind. Men who drew down on a traveler could as easily kill him as not. Matter of survival.

Whoever discovered the robbers would no doubt get the word to whatever lawman of the district, and he knew he'd best put miles between himself and them. With their guns and whatever possessions still on them, the discovery would be confusing enough to gain him some time, so he rode briskly ahead, despite the hour.

There were enough tracks in the road that even a sharp lawman, or any other outlaws, should have trouble figuring out what had happened, and Stephen knew he stood a good chance of being out of the territory before any sort of pursuit. Have to push his horses a bit, but then he'd stay over at a distant place, let them and himself rest.

He reflected that it had been the killing of some of the sophisticated robbery ring back on the creek that had pushed Abby

Thomas over the edge, as it were, along with getting abducted by her former suitor. And his blood on her when Ned Drake had shot him to rescue her.

Well, I've never looked for trouble, but it always seems to find me.

These men here, now. Just highwaymen, seeing a lone man on a good horse, and they'd tried to rob him. At least that. Surely would have killed him too, since he could otherwise identify them. Didn't see any other way he could have handled it. He'd given the second man a chance, but he hadn't taken it.

Mistake, that.

"Men just seem to die around Stephen," Abigail had lamented to her mother...just before she'd run off with the minister. Yes, he guessed that was true. Men who wanted to kill him first, but that hadn't mattered enough to her, apparently.

And perhaps the new land would demand that he defend himself, too.

So be it.

Two

Stephen didn't stop long in Saltville, reasoning that anyone seeking the killer of the two robbers would inquire at this closest village. He did stop at a prosperous inn, late as it was, to buy provisions, and to learn also that the wagon train of missionaries had stayed two days there, resting their horses and resupplying.

And that they'd moved on just three days before. So he'd almost caught up with them, down the long Shenandoah. But he'd have to stop, too, so no chance of catching them soon. He put aside his impatience and rode on, seeking a place to stay far enough beyond Saltville to evade suspicion.

He found it after a chilly, uneasy night's camp along a small stream well off the road. The morning mists lifted as he moved on, revealing a well-tended farm on a flat a few miles farther where two creeks merged. Tall haystacks from the last-of-season cutting stood along the creek bottoms, and sturdy barns reminiscent of Pennsylvania flanked a two-story clapboard dwelling. Chimneys wafting smoke at each end reminded him of the house he'd built along Buck Mountain Creek just the year before, with the help of the entire community there, for his intended bride. He shook off the unwelcome recollection.

A young man on horseback, leading a brown cow, greeted him as he splashed across one of the shallow creeks.

"Howdy." The boy reined his horse, taking in the lines of Stephen's black gelding.

"Mornin'. Been travelin' some, and wondered if y'all could put me up for a day or two." Stephen had developed the habit of rural speech when around country people, although he and his sisters had been strictly tutored by their English father to speak as the gentry.

"Should be able to. G'on up to th' house; Mama'n th' girls'll likely take care you."

"Much obliged. Nice horse y'got there."

"We raise 'em. This'n come f'm up th' Valley though, Winchester." The horse in question was a striking sorrel stallion, well-muscled, with an aristocratic bearing. He looked fast. Obviously breeding stock.

"Looks like good land here, too. Oh, I'm Stephen Davis, couple years out of th' Army."

"Lige Baker." The young man extended a work-hardened hand, shook. "We been here since b'fore I'se born. Daddy, he'n Mama come down f'm Pennsylvany on back. Said there was too many people settlin'."

"Was up that way a year or two ago, tryin' t'sell furniture I was buildin'. Didn't have much luck."

"You a woodworker, then?"

"Was. Lookin' at new territory; don't know just what I'll end up doin'. War kind of left me restless, y'know?"

"Heerd that f'm some others was in it. M'brother, he got killed at Cowpens."

"Oh, sorry to hear that. We fought there, too. Was a couple Bakers, as I remember, but don't know of one got hit."

"Name of Willis. He was th' oldest of us. We shore do miss him." The boy's face showed pain.

"War's hard, every way you look at it. Just glad it's over with. Man's free now to go anywhere an' get set up anyway he can, since."

"Yeah, I might go West m'self, year or two on. Well, you g'on up t' th' house. I'll git this cow back to th' lot. Bad t'jump an' run off, she is."

Stephen thanked young Lige and steered his horses toward the farmhouse. As he neared it, he saw a plump teenage girl hanging clothes on a line, with the sun just well above mountains to the east. Beyond her an older woman tended a scrub board near a cast-iron washpot over a stick fire. He waved a greeting.

"Hello, there," called the woman. "Light down, sir, and stay a bit. You a soldier?"

"Was, ma'am. Your son Lige told me about y'all losin' Willis. Sorry to hear that."

"Well, wasn't enny stoppin' him once he made it up to go t'that war. We's pretty sure we'd be outta it, this far away, but he just *would* go. I'm Trudy Baker, an' this's Lessie." She indicated the girl. Stephen tipped his tricorner hat, introduced himself.

"Pleased t'meet y'both. Lige said y'might be able to put me up for a day or two. Been travelin' far."

"Can do that, shore. M'man, Theodore, he's out with our other two, bringin' th' cattle down outta th' high fields. Frost up there already, an' th' grass scarce. Lessie, you tend th' clothes here, an' I'll just take Mr. Davis to th' house. You et yet?"

"Did, and thanks. Got supplies at Saltville last night." He didn't volunteer why he hadn't stayed there, but she seemed to know.

"Ain't but th' one good tavern there, you prob'ly saw, an' it's high-priced. Don't blame you fer comin' on. Lotta folks travelin' through, on down t'ord Tennessee er into Kentucky. Y'aimin' t'settle?"

"Maybe. Friends gone on ahead, some missionaries headed for Kentucky Territory. Catch up to them soon, I reckon."

"Was some wagons passed t'other day. You a preacher?" She eyed him closer.

"Oh, no. Was a woodworker, grew up on a mill over in Goochland. Just got to know those folks since th' war."

His hostess showed Stephen to a small room up in the loft of the house and filled a pitcher of water next to a washbowl. He thanked her, deposited his pack, then went to stable his horses.

"Jist turn 'em out with ours, Mr. Davis. Good grass down by th' creek," she assured him. He did just that, noting the lush meadow, which the family had obviously kept the stock out of till now.

Everything about the place was neat and efficient, he observed. Typical of Pennsylvania farmers, even this far out. Good; he'd be able to rest and refit without being a burden, then. And be beyond inquiring lawmen too, he hoped. If indeed anyone investigated the deaths of the two robbers.

~ * ~

"Here's what we know," the portly man in the powdered wig stated. He and three others were gathered in his study in a townhouse in Philadelphia. They all appeared to be prosperous merchants, here for a strategy conference. And they were, after a fashion.

"Horace Weston was killed, and money taken from his house in Caroline County. This was in addition to the chest of gold our Mr. Hayes was taking west. Lawyer Eddins was the last to see Weston alive, and he's now in custody down there. Rawlins Butler was also killed, along with the entire Virginia organization. Now, we know the money Hayes had hidden, which we suspected this ex-soldier Davis of taking, was recovered and supposedly turned over to the court in Charlottesville."

An exclamation rose from the others seated in the room, and looks exchanged. The speaker resumed. "No, I'm afraid, whatever disposition is or has been made of that money, we cannot make any legitimate claim to it. It will just have to be written off as a regrettable loss. But I'm convinced Eddins neither killed Weston nor took that other chest of money he was holding there; he's been with us too long for that. From what we've found out, the massacre—yes, that's what it was—of our associates there was the work of this Davis. We've learned he was a sharpshooter in the Army under Greene. Hayes ran afoul of him over an escaped slave, or something of that sort.

"Anyway, I feel this man not only destroyed our operation under Dr. Weston but took our gold. Probably turned the Hayes chest over to the court to cover himself. If what we believe is true, this man is highly dangerous to us and to our interests. If we're ever to consider rebuilding our operations in Virginia, he must be eliminated. Now, any questions?" He looked to the leader of the group, who'd remained silent.

These four men were, despite their legitimate appearances as businessmen, the core of a well-established network of mercantile theft. They had cultivated contacts within many of the manufacturing and commercial enterprises throughout the East, who provided steady streams of stolen goods and cash to them. The referred-to Dr. Weston had set up the organization before the Revolution and had run it out of his plantation in Caroline County, Virginia. While this group in Philadelphia oversaw the collection of the funds, taking a hefty percentage off the top, Weston had seen to it that most of the money was invested, scattered, distributed so that none of it could ever be traced.

Now the doctor was dead, money missing, their organization in disarray, and a shadowy, violent man threatened them, if at a distance.

"What's happened to Weston's place?" a tall, cadaverous man asked. He had a bent-forward stance, as if squinting over ledger sheets.

"His widow remarried soon after the doctor's death, a young planter. We know nothing of him beyond his family roots in the Tidewater. As I understand it, she knew nothing of our operations."

Another, a wrinkled, gnome-like man with piercing eyes, asked, "Do we know how to reach this Davis?"

"We know his general location. Eddins had sought to have him jailed after he killed Hayes back in late winter, but failed. It was ruled self-defense, that."

"Ah, Hayes always was hot-tempered. A risk, that one. Probably a good thing he's gone. To endanger the syndicate over a mere slave."

"Yes, well, his indiscretion apparently started the whole unraveling of our affairs there. But yes again, we can find Davis."

After this report, the host looked to the fourth man again, a handsome, brisk, decisive type, who had always advocated bold action. The others counted on him for leadership, in whatever operation they ventured into.

"Thank you, Codington," he said, "for your information. It's obvious that we must remove this Davis first, then we can go about rebuilding. I'm in favor of keeping the location in Virginia, because it's far enough from here to shield us, and because Hayes was doing a good job building up plantations west of there, even if they hadn't produced much profit yet. We must also keep control of those, to ensure the return on our investments."

"Do we have the right man for Davis?" Codington asked.

"We did. The man Dinkins, and his wife, whom no one ever suspected, who'd done several jobs for us. But they've disappeared. Now, I don't think that's a coincidence, given the other mayhem among our people. I wouldn't be surprised to learn that Davis found them out, too, and killed them.

"So, our usual resources no longer available, there is another man I've used before, who's proven himself effective. You recall the Higgins Mercantile affair? Our man inside was Ellsworth, old Higgins' assistant, our pipeline to that profitable source. But Higgins began to suspect, and we had to act quickly. The man I refer to, Justin Ames, removed the old man within an hour of my instructions. Made it look like an accident, and as you know, Ellsworth is now in charge. And I've had other occasions to employ Ames also, to good effect." He sat back, eyeing the others.

"Then let's get it into motion," the diminutive member declared.

"Oh, I already have, anticipating your agreement." The others looked at each other in surprise, then all of them burst out laughing.

~ * ~

They were here at last, Anna Compton realized: Kentucky. There was no definitive line between Virginia and this attached territory yet, but the people who lived here knew where they were, and were aware that the distant government in Richmond had little to do with them here. This was near-wilderness, the ages-old hunting ground of several Indian tribes, but home to none of them. Now the stream of white settlers had increased since the war, and the land was rapidly being taken up along the rivers and creek bottoms.

Kentucky: fertile ground for evangelism, Reverend Carson had told them back in Charlottesville, a place to do God's work. The aging minister had only regretted his inability to join this mission.

"But go forth, children, with His blessing. You will be God's hands and His voice among the remote holdings there, His only presence. And may He guide and guard you in your holy work."

Yes, His hands and voice. Certainly a high and demanding life's work, Anna reflected. For one who had failed to fit into the mold of housewife and mother, this was not just an alternative, but a calling. *He* worked in mysterious ways, she knew, and wondered if this journey had been ordained from the beginning. It would seem so, her driving this wagon team as naturally here as she'd driven the horses on her father's farm. And no matter the hardships they'd encounter, she was sure they'd be little different from hacking out a homestead from the forest, as they'd done in Virginia.

Her only regret—well, a major one—was not having room for her precious books. And there wouldn't be many to be had up ahead, she feared. Encouraged by her mother, a part Indian child raised and taught by Reverend Carson, Anna had read everything she could find from early childhood on.

That had been a strong link, she'd believed, between her and Stephen Davis. They'd exchanged books, discussed ideas, shared so much. Such a disappointment, that man: the veneer of his self-education had not made him wise.

But then, I was not grown wise, either. It has taken this jolt to awaken me to my real life...

If only she could rid herself of the memory of him.

~ * ~

Theodore Baker was a bearish man of fifty, red-faced, hearty. He, with another son and daughter, drove the small herd of cattle down a trail between steep hills to the creek fields that afternoon. The boy Lige opened a gate for them, spoke to them, then closed it after.

Stephen was repairing a pack strap at the main barn and stepped out to greet the farmer as he rode up. He introduced himself, learned the names of twelve-year-old Jeremiah and his sister Julie, fifteen.

"Well, you're surely welcome, Mr. Davis. Fall comes early in these mountains, and we're hustling to get set. Don't suppose you'd care to stay a bit?" He eyed the black gelding in with his own stock.

"Thanks, but I'm trying to catch up with friends heading for Kentucky. Just needed to rest the horses before moving on."

"Fine horse you got there. Do any trading?"

"Not much good at that, I'm afraid. Did trade for that one, back in Albemarle County, for some of the furniture I made in my shop there. But no, I'm not that sharp about horseflesh."

"Lige was just starting to tell us you'd been a soldier."

"Was. He told me about your son at Cowpens. Bad, that."

"Well, we couldn't tie him home, any more than your folks probably could with you, I'd wager." Stephen noted that the man was well-spoken, and saw the parallel with his own father. *A man needn't be an ignoramus just because he works with his hands...* But this manner of speaking hadn't rubbed off on his family, he observed. Here environment apparently had most to do with one's habits.

The buckle on his pack strap riveted again, Stephen joined the family at chores. Julie departed for the house with the pack that had held the food they'd taken into the mountains with them. Jeremiah helped his father extend a rail fence, and Lige claimed the traveler to help hew timbers for another barn.

This was work Stephen was good at, and the two of them made rapid work of the newly-felled chestnut logs. Lige regaled his new friend with stories of the deep snowdrifts that would drive them all indoors before Christmas, and of the good hunting thereabouts. But he was also intrigued by the idea of going on into the new country and asked many questions.

"Well, I was headin' to Kentucky myself three years ago, but got sort of...sidetracked at a plantation out of Charlottesville. Just now gettin' back on that track. I really don't know much about the territory, other than it's not all filled up yet. Did know a few men in the Army from there, sure liked it."

"Pa says ever'body just wants t'be somewheres else," the youth mused. "Y'git tired of th' same thing all th' time. But he says places is all about th' same, once y'git settled in."

"About right, I've noticed. Folks about th' same, too, though some're meaner than others, no matter where they come from." He was thinking of the two robbers, and the supposedly respectable outlaws he'd tangled with back on his creek place.

And he knew he wouldn't be able to escape people like that, no matter how far he traveled.

It was not a good feeling.

Three

Justin Ames was an ex-soldier who'd made a name for himself as a fearless and resourceful warrior against the Redcoats. This in large part because he'd grown up as an orphan in the streets of Philadelphia, becoming of necessity a skilled pickpocket and thief to keep himself alive. He'd known and worked with several of that city's robber barons, supplying them with stolen goods and favors in return for a sort of purchased immunity from the law.

That had all ended when a supposed friend had informed on him to police, who'd stepped up their efforts to clean out what was his livelihood. The "friend" had disappeared, but Ames had then found it convenient to join the Patriot army, which effectively removed him from the area.

It was there he perfected his skills at assassination, which was the specialty his superiors required of him. He could slip into a British tent past sentries, slit an officer's throat without a sound or struggle, then escape without detection. And did, often. That this method of crippling the enemy did not have the sanction of any official whatsoever did not mean it wasn't done.

So Justin Ames became a valuable asset during the war. He regarded his work as a sort of calling, and all for the good cause of liberty.

Only then the war ended, and he was right back where he'd started: older, harder, better at what he did, but without any sponsor for his talents. Until he'd chanced across Reginald Cabot in Boston, where he'd gone to escape recognition.

Cabot was that selfsame leader of the robbery syndicate out of Philadelphia, and soon learned of Ames' skills. And while the organization already had in place an assassin in Virginia, there were occasions in the capital when it was deemed necessary to eliminate competition, or a troublesome obstacle to their operations.

So upon his return to Philadelphia, Cabot had arranged for the ex-soldier's presence when needed. And found cover employment for him in his own legitimate business, that of carriage-making, in a part of the sprawling city where he could keep a low profile. Ames wasn't expected to produce much at his 'day job,' just assist wherever he was needed and learn the business along the way.

An engaging fellow by nature, the assassin further ingratiated himself with all he met, making his real profession completely out of the question in the minds of his acquaintances and fellow workers. That this amiable, smiling young man was capable of slipping a knife between the ribs of an enemy was unthinkable. Surely.

Now he listened to his employer's instructions gravely, planning his strategy as the details were received. As he learned of the extent of this Stephen Davis' destruction of the syndicate's Virginia operation, he realized he wouldn't be up against any ordinary adversary. Sharpshooter in the war. Had killed one of the principals with a hammer, against a loaded pistol. And apparently bested the organization's own assassin, plus his capable wife, if the evidence were to be believed.

A hard man, no doubt. And if there was one principle Ames lived by, it was never to underestimate the opposition.

He learned that the man was ostensibly a furniture-maker, situated up a creek out of Charlottesville, Virginia. Good: as a passable carriage craftsman, he could possibly insinuate himself into the man's business, enough to get close to him. At least be able to talk shop to a certain extent.

He also learned that Davis had been acquitted of several legal charges brought against him, and that he had the support of the community as an honest, valued citizen. That was due no doubt in part, Cabot told him, to his having turned at least part of the money he'd stolen over to the court.

Smart move, that. So no, I can't just shoot him down, with the whole settlement probably looking out for him.

Or maybe he could; what with the general movement of displaced soldiers, settlers all over the territory, who'd notice one more stranger? Well, just have to see how the land lay once he was there.

"And here's your advance money," Cabot was telling him. "There'll be more on your return of course, as usual. Now, it's probable this Davis had help, given the extent of the damage he's done. So see who else might be part of our problem. Understood?"

"Completely." So then, he'd have to plan to stay around, discover the true situation, and whoever else might become targets. More complex, but he was certain he could handle it.

~ * ~

It was time to move on from the pleasant farmstead, and Stephen was anxious to make up for the two days he'd spent with the Bakers. Besides, he'd started getting coquettish glances from daughter Lessie, which made him uncomfortable. He said his farewells early and splashed his horses across the shallow creek to the road west.

The random, almost offhand nature of the attempted robbery played on his mind; in the past he'd encountered situations that demanded action, true, but there had always been some agenda involved. A soldier had to kill to avoid being killed. Likewise, the intended victim of an outlaw plot had to defend himself. But for a man of apparently scarce means to be casually accosted on the road drove home the fact that he was getting into lawless territory. The accepted rules of the more civilized sections of the new country just didn't apply here.

That meant he must be on his guard every moment, then. He'd relished the quiet of his little shop on Buck Mountain Creek, and at night had been jolted awake at longer intervals by the nightmarish re-living of wartime violence. Until even that haven had erupted in gunfire reminiscent of the war itself.

But surely, once settled on a place of his own, among other decent landholders, he'd be able to go about making a living without always having to look over his shoulder. Yes, with a good wife and children, he was sure he could finally find the peace he'd sought ever since Yorktown.

And the good wife had to be Anna Compton. But first he'd have to find her again, then prove to her he was worthy of her. Looked like two fairly big jobs, unless he could catch up to the missionaries and locate near their base. The other part would be harder; a woman didn't just pack up and leave her family, the country, unless she felt she'd been wronged greatly. And he guessed she had.

But he'd have to leave that part of the job till he could see just what he was up against. He felt sure Anna hadn't formed any attachment to anyone of the missionaries. Reverend Carson had told him of the others: two young married couples, other older pairs, and some young children. But of course there were the two ex-soldiers he didn't know, traveling with the group partly to provide protection.

But Anna wouldn't make any decisions hastily; that just wasn't her way. And she hadn't had a beau back home, her six-foot height and bookishness having intimidated the local youths. He needn't worry, on that score.

Still, he remembered the way her rare smile lighted up the room around her, the way she was so ready to give herself to any need... *Dammit, I've just got to win that woman...my life won't be worth living without her.*

So, just stay the course, here. Five days behind them, and he was traveling probably twice as fast. He didn't know how far they'd go, although Carson had told him the goal would probably be to reach some settlement, then decide which way to branch out into the wilderness.

That would mean they'd get through the highest of these mountains first, which were hardly inhabited at all. So, into real wilderness, with no towns he'd ever heard of near. No way to know which way, yet. And the way the primitive roads wound around, going from mill to blacksmith shop to settler's cabin, there'd be multiple turnoffs. He'd have to catch up, at least to be able to ask after them. Five wagons together shouldn't be that hard to trace.

He hoped.

~ * ~

It was several days later that Justin Ames rode into Stanardsville, on the principal way west over the Blue Ridge. He knew from directions Cabot had given him that Davis' shop was south ten miles or so, not close to any village. But a furniture-maker's place of business shouldn't be hard to locate. He reflected that the syndicate's man Hayes had traveled this way, on his ill-fated confrontation with Davis over that business about the slave.

Well, Hayes had apparently been short-tempered, and that had gotten him killed. Still didn't seem likely, a man with just a hammer against that loaded pistol, but that's the way Cabot had understood it. A sharpshooter: that could be dangerous too, of course. But Ames had already planned to scout out the area thoroughly before acting, and when he did act, it would be well-planned and would not fail.

He asked directions to a road south, and was told that a well-used one lay a mile west. That led south and forked east again, eventually to Charlottesville, the farrier who was shoeing Ames' horse said, about the only village of any size that way. The man wanted to talk while he worked, and recounted the capture of that settlement during the war.

"Almost got Guv'nor Jefferson, Guv'nor Henry, an' th' whole passel of delegates," he recounted. "Brit name of Tarleton had a bad reputation fer burnin' folks out. Did git Dan'l Boone, was here f'm Kentucky fer th' session. Let 'im go, though: don't reckon he looked like nobody important."

"I heard something about that. Didn't he lead an ambush on Tarleton at the Blue Ridge?"

"Did, with a young feller named Jack Jouett an' his pa. Got aroun' a thousand militia up in th' rocks, opened fire f'm cover on Tarleton's cav'ry, turned 'em back 'fore they could cross over to Staunton, where th' delegates had run off to. Drove th' lot of 'em all th' way to Yorktown, they did, an' you know whut happened then." The man shifted a chew of tobacco, let go a stream of juice, reached for another hoof to shoe.

Ames wandered about the village, which was little more than a stop on the road northwest from distant Richmond. He imagined life here would be insanely boring, and apparently strapped by poverty. There'd been no plantations much since the Potomac, only the rare one at the rich river bottoms he'd crossed, and only primitive settlements. He'd be glad to get this assignment over with, and back northeast.

The centers at Georgetown and Alexandria did have some culture, he'd noted, and yes, he might stop over longer on his way back to the capital. The standard of living his profession had allowed had made him come to appreciate civilization. Might be good to have another base, too, in case his activities back home gained him too much notice.

His horse shod, Ames rode to the junction of the Charlottesville route and turned into it. Ten miles to Davis' place; he should be there by mid-afternoon, find a place to stay. He'd use the story of looking for a farm to buy…no, he didn't look like a farmer. Well, he'd just say he wanted to see some of the fine furniture Davis made, having heard of him from friends further north. Yes, that'd do nicely: prospective customer. Be easier to kill the craftsman that way.

But if he *had* been only a part of the group that had destroyed the operation here, he'd have to get the rest of them, too. Be too hard to do until he'd found out who they were. So hold off on Davis; go see him after he'd learned the gossip about the four men who'd been killed. Six, if you counted Dr. Weston and the assassin Dinkins. Or eight, since Dinkins' wife and brother had also disappeared. Surely be a lot of talk about what had happened, this soon after the fact. And the right names would come up; no way they wouldn't. He smiled at the dirt road ahead, cresting the low hills toward his quarry.

~ * ~

The brothers of the younger robber Stephen had killed had sworn to track him down and exact revenge on him, but they'd had little to go on. First of all, they didn't know which way the killers had traveled. They were certain no single adversary could have outgunned both men. But there were too many hoofprints in the dirt track by the time they'd been told of the shooting for any clues. And no help coming from the local constable, who was probably glad to be rid of the two.

The MacNaughtons, two generations in the mountains of the new country, were a close-knit clan, and a perceived wrong to one of them demanded retribution by all the men of the extended family. They were a scraggly lot, except for Ansted, the pleasant-mannered one who'd been killed. An affable sort, this cousin/brother had always been able to allay any suspicion on the part of an intended robbery victim until it was too late. The clan now greatly mourned his lucrative absence. And not a few of the young frontier women would miss one of their favorites.

More puzzling was the fact that Ansted and his sometime partner Luke Kane had been gunned down and nothing apparently taken. Obviously, a planned robbery by them gone bad, and whoever had killed them hadn't been interested enough even to take their horses and guns. Certainly outside any of the family's experience with enemies.

But that didn't matter. It was the principle of the thing, and whatever these hard-eyed men could do to avenge this one of their own, they would. It was decided that two of them would ride north on the main road, asking at inns, taverns, settlements, about strangers. Two more would ride on toward Kentucky on the same errand, and two more would ride south toward Tennessee, that territory connected to North Carolina. The rest would inquire around Saltville itself, in case the killer or those who'd helped him, might just be local. Bad blood in several directions nearby, certainly.

That only two men would try to apprehend the killers reflected the obviously-disproven belief that any two MacNaughtons could handle whoever'd done the killing. It also showed the family's belief in their own invincibility. Shortsighted perhaps, but in line with their code.

The clan hoped for any loose talk that might shed light on the shootings, and all were prepared to act on the slightest information. In addition to the motive of revenge, they felt it necessary to reassert the perception that the MacNaughtons were not men to be reckoned lightly with.

But each effort yielded no information. No group of desperate men, or even men who'd talked about any confrontation, came to light. The only possible lead came from the inn in Saltville, where the host remembered a lone rider buying food. He'd been struck by the fact that this man had come after dark, declined to stay over, although his horses were clearly tired, and had ridden on. This even after the innkeeper had informed him there were no more accommodations for many, many miles.

Couldn't have been their quarry, the MacNaughtons agreed, even though it might have been a man intent on leaving the territory for some other suspicious reason.

"He say ennything 'bout maybe runnin' into our cousin an' Luke Kane up th' road?"

"Never said a word, no. Quiet young feller, just wanted provisions, asked th' way t'ord Kentucky an' left. Paid in gold, which I 'preciated."

Again, not likely to be the man. The clan steadfastly refused to believe a single man could outshoot both experienced marksmen. Still, it turned out to be the only possible lead. After their return from their various pursuits, the men gathered to pool their non-information.

"Ain't but th' one possibility," old Abner MacNaughton concluded. "An' when all th' others don't work, that'n's most likely, no matter how it don't fit." He expelled a stream of Virginia tobacco juice and waited for a response.

"Wal," one cousin finally spoke up. "Been sorta hankerin' t'ride on out t'Kentucky territory, m'self, see whut's thar. Might jist do it now, seein's thar's a chancet t' learn sump'in. Enny of you wanta come along?"

No one did, especially, the pickings having been good around this home territory. But they soon all agreed that with Ansted gone, that might well change. He'd had more nerve than any of the rest, and had contributed heavily to everyone's welfare up the hollows of the MacNaughtons' environs.

So one other unattached cousin, a Caleb, having thought it over, eventually reached the conclusion that yes, maybe that'd be a good plan.

"I reckon I c'd see goin' with you, Shelby, seein's thaings might git a mite lean around here, winter not bein' that fur off. An' mebbe Kentucky'd be a good place t'start over, kinda, make a name fer ourselves thar."

"Wal, all right, then. So we'd best git on with it, while thar's a chancet t'ketch up with whoever done this. Y'don't mind thar might be a bunch of 'em?"

"We knowed that t'start with. No, reckon th' two've us kin handle 'em, we git th' drop on 'em. Hafta use our haids, not go chargin' in amongst 'em, git kilt. B'sides, if this feller's our only clue, might jist be him by hisself. Though I don't b'lieve thet fer a minnit." More tobacco juice, followed by a general bestirring of the assembled council.

So it was that the two cousins, mounted on the best horses they'd been able to steal, set out west on the dubious trail, provisioned lightly, armed heavily, financed only with the scant contributions of others of the clan. They figured they could acquire food and money the usual way, from better-possessed fellow travelers on the road.

~ * ~

Deep in the high mountains of the territory, the wagon train of missionaries wound its way ever westward over passes, down twisting creeks and rivers, up other creek valleys, narrow and dark in sun-shielded days. Stops at night were often at impromptu campgrounds, sometimes in the company of other travelers. Invariably the group inaugurated hymn-singings, devotionals, and Bible readings. These were received with varying degrees of acceptance or tolerance among the others, many of whom were occupied with axle-greasings, wagon repairs, or imbibing spirits.

Well, Anna Compton surmised, nobody'd ever promised them this work would be easy, and she supposed it would be the same at their destination. So, do all the good they could, even here on the way. God didn't differentiate among His people; all of them deserved to hear the Word, wherever and whenever it was presented, and by whom.

After weeks on the road, everyone was weary of the travel, and the group often speculated on just how far into the frontier they wanted to venture. It was soon agreed at one stop in the mountains that the next village would offer enough surrounding wilderness for their efforts to bear fruit, given their information that there weren't that many settlements to begin with.

So it was that they reached a place called Ketchum's Mill, on a creek improbably named Troublesome, which none of the group had ever heard of. It was barely a village, with only the combination gristmill and blacksmith shop, and not even a tavern. But inquiry revealed that nothing lay beyond but backwoods, with no roads for many miles, so yes, this seemed in reality the end of this one.

A council ensued, at which it was decided to claim land up the creeks for cabins, to be begun immediately. They'd camp meanwhile, all hands to concentrate on shelter first. Then they'd locate and acquire, by whatever means, a spot along the mill creek and begin a log church, with any luck well before cold weather.

Not all the nearby land had been claimed by the sparse homesteaders, and they were directed to steep hollows unsuited to farming. But yes, small plots could be grubbed out for eventual corn and potato patches. And agreement was soon reached with the miller, a pleasant sort, to donate a site for the church from his holdings.

There would of necessity be the need for hunting and trapping to survive the next few months. Little trading or purchasing was possible here, so getting through the first winter and spring would be hard, but the little group was optimistic, trusting in God to provide for them.

And they'd honor and worship that God beginning with Sunday services in the open, in a circle of their wagons. All were to be welcome, and the hopeful missionaries prepared to begin their new lives in earnest. They knew few would join them at first, but the natural inclination of people in remote areas was to gather for news, gossip, food, and yes, whatever else these new people could provide.

~ * ~

Stephen was confused. None of the little-used branching roads seemed to lead to any destination; all were reported to peter out in the deeper hollows west. That could mean he'd missed a major route, or that the wagons were virtually at the end of one of these tracks, which would necessarily be their destination. But which one? There were few cabins here, where people would have noted the passage of the missionaries. Lone hunters could have missed them entirely. Settlers off the roads would also be ignorant of them.

It'd be a matter of asking everyone he met and digging out any nearby settlers to see if they'd heard of the travelers. Take time, any way he went. And of course he might already have come too far. But no, the owner of the last farm he'd stopped at, miles back, had said this was the way, against all reason.

"Dunno whut they 'spects t'find, up in them hills," he'd puzzled, "but they was dead-set, fer folks shorely lost, like they was. Ain't nothin' on ahead of 'em but woods an' Indians, fur as I know. Some cabins here'n thar, but mostly hunters, few places with mebbe a horse an' a cow, but no settlements. Could be they'll turn back, be back by in a few days."

Stephen doubted that; if their zeal had led them into the true wilderness, that's where they'd be. But the land was vast, and no telling how far each faint track led before the last hovel or camp.

There were just enough wagon tracks to make it impossible to tell which would have been their route. So again, where to start?

But wait, they must've asked someone the way, or been pointed to a likely location. He'd just have to try that, too. Find them somehow.

He couldn't help thinking how ill-prepared the group probably was, going to the end of some road where they could neither buy provisions nor maintain any contact with the rest of the world. But he'd seen religious bands before, so sure they'd thrive anywhere despite poverty, lawlessness, lack of resources, sure their God would protect and provide for them.

And well, maybe He would.

So, try the most-traveled road first.

~ * ~

Justin Ames too, had hit what could be a dead end. He'd learned that Stephen Davis had left the country, supposedly for Kentucky Territory. Missed him by a few weeks, it seemed. And that might or might not be good news for his employers. With their nemesis gone, they could begin to rebuild their lucrative organization: problem solved.

Unless Davis had been just one of several determined citizens who'd wiped out their operations. Which would mean the rest of them were still here, and would be doubly suspicious of new people at the old activities.

Davis' improbable partner, a free black man named Tom Logan, seemed to have known nothing of the recent carnage, which wasn't surprising. Blacks kept a low profile all over the new country, he'd learned, considering such happenings as "white man's business." Logan only confirmed that Davis had gone and didn't plan to return.

For his part, Tom Logan had indeed been right at the center of the action, but he wasn't about to tell this stranger any of that. He'd known from the day Stephen had taken him in, starved and footsore from his escape from slavery, that he'd have to continue to bow and scrape to survive. And, free or not, he'd keep his own counsel. He had a good trade as a blacksmith here, and that's all he'd aspire to.

Besides, this man inquiring after his friend was just a little too friendly, too smooth, in his questions. Tom guessed correctly that they hadn't eliminated any of the robber ring beyond just this territory, and logically they could expect others. So it seemed the "others" had found them. He and his new bride Molly, late of the adjoining plantation but freed, would just hide and watch.

Ames called on Hezekiah Thomas, the prosperous planter nearby, for more information. Here too, he gleaned little, the planter and his wife being reluctant to relive the recent events. Having lost their last child in her elopement with the Philadelphia minister, they were withdrawn, even resentful. Ames sensed that whatever involvement Thomas might have had in the bloodletting, it had left a deep scar.

Next, he visited the plantation of the late Rawlins Butler, back a few miles the way he'd come, and down a creek called Swift Run. He met the guardian of the two young Butler children, a relative of the late member of the local organization. Wesley Beadle and his wife were more forthcoming.

"Davis and his partner Drake killed Cousin Rawlins in cold blood," the planter averred. "He'd been courting Hezekiah Thomas' daughter when Davis came along and the two of 'em squared off from the beginning. They say 'twas Drake did the actual killing, but he's gone clear out of the country somewhere. And now Davis is gone, too, so I guess justice will never be done." The man was angry, even though he'd come into an evidently prosperous plantation. Ames pressed for more details.

"Fellow named Hayes confronted Davis over a runaway slave and Davis killed him. Lot of money involved some way too, rumor has it. Anyway, turned out the slave wasn't the one Hayes thought he was, but the money being gone, a Doctor Weston from over in Caroline County had Davis arrested and tried. Got off.

"Then some more men got killed, and Davis apparently found the money, or had it all along, and just turned it in to the court in Charlottesville. Or maybe just some of it. Anyway, the man packed up and walked away from his furniture business. Way I see it, if he'd been in the clear, he would have stayed, but he didn't. Got too hot for him, apparently. Probably more to it all than what I know, but that's the gist of the situation.

"These children are orphans, and the wife and I run the plantation in their interest, all legal from the court. That's all I can tell you."

So this Drake had been in on it. Who else? Ames rode into Charlottesville, called on the local constable, Jeb Barnes.

"Who wants to know?" was the first question from the taciturn lawman.

"I'm an old army friend. I served with Stephen Davis at Cowpens. Heard he'd settled nearby, but now I find out he's gone out of the country. Sorry to've missed him. Thought maybe you'd know if he'd left any word where he was headed."

"No, don't know a thing. You might've heard there was a big to-do with some outlaws operatin' hereabouts, got Stephen hisself caught in th' middle of it. Accused of murder, an' a bunch of other stuff. Nothin' to enny of it, an' seems like justice was done, all told. Stephen in th' clear, no doubt of it, which you'll be glad t'hear, bein' friends an' all. But yeah, he's gone, an' don't even his old partner Tom Logan know where."

"I see. Yes, I came down by way of Nicksville, and did hear some things. Guess every place has its bad apples. What was it, a vigilante group wiped out the outlaws? Citizen's militia?"

"No, t'was Stephen hisself did most of it. They thought he had some money b'longed to 'em, and went after him. Pretty much ruined his plans with Squire Thomas' daughter, but that's another story. An' when it was all over, Stephen found th' money, turned it over to th' court here, Judge Edgerton." The constable reflected a moment. "Sure hated t'see Stephen leave. Good man, had fine prospects. Trouble just seemed t'find him, no matter whut."

So, Ames reflected, Davis had indeed been the big man who'd crippled the very profitable workings of his employers. And he was gone. End of story?

No, this Drake had killed Butler, and probably some of the others. But Wesley Beadle had said he'd left the territory, too...

"One more thing, Constable, if you don't mind. Stephen often mentioned a man named Drake he'd known. I heard he'd been here, too, about the time of the...trouble. Any idea where he might be?"

"Ned Drake. Yeah, he was th' one cleared it up 'bout a runaway slave th' late Doctor Weston claimed, er his friend Hayes did. Wrong man, turned out. Ennyway, Drake's up in Caroline County now, married th' doc's widow. Possible he's heard f'm Stephen, though I doubt it. 'Less y'know him well, he ain't that open 'bout his doin's. But y'd know that, I reckon, since y' fought b'side him."

Barnes was not sure this man was actually a friend, but he had nothing to go on but the feeling. Affable enough, easy-going, but there was a glint behind the eyes. Could have come from the war, of course. Stephen had that too, sometimes. And yeah, Drake did, too, in spite of his generally good cheer.

Ames bid the lawman good day and departed. He'd just call on this Drake on his way back to civilization. He knew the location of the late doctor's plantation, now Drake's, and yes, there was too much here for coincidence. Just a friendly call then, and perhaps something else Cabot had told him about Weston...

Four

"Damn, this ain't gittin' us nowhere, Shelby," his cousin complained. "We ain't found a trace of ennybody, an' don't really know who we's after. So whatta we do? Jist keep on keepin' on?" It was late in another day in the near-wilderness, and the two were facing another barren camp, and almost the end of their provisions. They hadn't met or caught up with a single likely robbery victim, and the armed occupants of the lone cabins had eyed them with suspicion. And offered no information.

The cousins set about camping alongside a small stream. There was almost no grass for their horses, the forest shade allowing little to grow. Have to find someplace tomorrow, they figured, some farm that had graze, or maybe some grain. Couldn't keep on this way, and they had no idea how far it was to any settlement.

It was upon this threadbare scene that two men rode, on fine mounts and leading packhorses. The MacNaughtons looked at each other as if they'd been delivered, then welcomed the other travelers.

"Howdy. Be glad fer you t'jine us. 'Bout finished off a turkey we kilt a ways back, but reckon it'd feed us all some," Caleb offered.

The riders looked about, and at the setting sun. Then they took in the two MacNaughtons, exchanged a look, and decided.

"Reckon we'll push on a bit," the older of them replied. He had white hair wisping from under his slouch hat, and a faintly military air about him. It was clear from his answer that he didn't relish sharing a campground with the cousins. The other man was younger, about thirty, with a nervous eye that never seemed to stand still. Shelby MacNaughton immediately suspected he might be ex-military too, and maybe had what folks called "war nerves." Might even be dangerous, get the drop on a man.

"Suit y'selves. Don't s'pose y'd sell us a bit of grain fer our horses, would you? We're plumb out." He indicated their lean mounts.

That got a reaction. Possibly because the two men rode excellent horses themselves, and noted these obviously poor men's hungry animals.

"Could spare a bit, I guess," the older one agreed. "Looks like they ain't been eatin' regular." He dismounted, moved to one of the packhorses.

"No, thaings a mite lean back t'home. Grass all gone, an' me'n my cousin thar, we d'cided to head on west, see if 'twas better. Sure 'preciate it."

The other rider turned his horse to watch the men, his hand near the butt of a pistol he carried holstered at his belt. The shifty eyes went from one man to the other constantly. It gave Caleb MacNaughton the feeling that they'd better go easy here.

The grain changed hands, and the cousins expressed their thanks.

"Whatta we owe you, friend?"

"'S'all right. We been short ourselves, time t'time. Hope youl find what you're lookin' for, on ahead." The white-haired one swung into his saddle, and the two rode away, to the repeated thanks of the others.

"Now whut?" Shelby asked, his eyes showing he knew this wasn't the end of their dealings with the prosperous riders.

"Wal, th' young one's sorta creepy, an' we'd best make shore he don't git th' drop on us. But I'd say this's our one chancet t'git ourselves some more good hosses an' a stake. Dunno whut they got on 'em, but them hosses'd bring a price, we git to a settlement." He asked this question also with his eyes.

"'D say so. So pack up, you'n me, an' we's off on thar trail. Won't go fur, this late, but we gotta slip up on 'em, take 'em by s'prise. Knock over th' scary one first; I'll take him. You aim fer th' ole man, an' we's that much richer."

It was soon done, the scant packing. The cousins set off on the little-used road, following the fresh hoofprints. But dark was coming on, and they guessed their quarry must know of a place to camp. Be harder to find one, come good dark.

So they pushed ahead in the failing light until yes, they spotted a campfire well along. They stopped, conferred.

"Th' young'un, he'll keep watch while t'other man gits 'em set up," Caleb said. "Cain't trust him not to. So you scout out th' place, git him located. Soon's you shoot him with yore rifle, we'll rush th' camp, take th' other'n. Won't be no match fer th' both of us." Shelby nodded, dismounted, slipped off into the woods that bordered the stream. He reasoned the lookout would be on the same side, since he could see a high, steep hill just outside a bend in the stream across. Heavy brush there, but more open among the trees this side. He moved carefully, rifle ready.

Cousin Caleb tied the horses well back, then slipped closer, trying to see if both men were at the camp. He couldn't see the younger man, so stationed himself behind a big fallen log, ready to charge when the time came.

So it was that when the man appeared, having been alerted by something in the deep woods, he passed not three yards from the crouching Caleb.

So, th' hunted man's bein' th' hunter, looks lak. Smarter'n I thought. But not smart 'nuff: I'll jist git him m'self.

He could just make out the shape of the stalking man, a darker outline against the faintly lighter trees. He leveled his rifle, sighted. Fired.

The man grunted, staggered, fell. Then Shelby crashed forward toward the campfire, letting go a bloodcurdling yell. Caleb paused an instant to grab the fallen man's guns, then joined in the charge.

The older man dumped water on the campfire from a kettle, which instantly went out. In the relative blackness, the robbers couldn't see where he'd gone. They both stopped, listened to a scrambling at the campsite. The man called out.

"Jamie! Jamie, you all right?" No answer from the form lying in the woods.

"Got to git around 'm," Shelby whispered, motioning. "You stay here an' pin him down, he shoots at ennything. Thet'll give him 'way. I'll g'on past, then make some noise, draw him out."

Caleb nodded, although the other couldn't see him. He was trying to accustom his eyes to the darkness, detect any movement. If the man would stay put, their plan would work. If not, well, they might just be able to free the horses and leave him afoot in the dark, ride hard clear out of the territory before morning.

Which is almost exactly what happened. Shelby managed to get upstream of the camp then, hidden behind a large boulder, threw a stick that made a sound.

Nothing happened. He waited, then threw another larger one. Again, nothing.

So, th' feller's either waitin' fer one of us t'show ourselves, er he's lit out. Dunno which. Reckon we'll jist wait a spell, see who moves first.

Then there was a sudden pounding of hooves from the camp back toward the way they'd come. Both cousins fired at where they thought their target should be, but they couldn't tell if they'd hit anything. They came out of cover, ran to the campsite with the one object: get the other horses and supplies and ride away.

The rider sped past the tethered horses of the outlaws, not seeing them off the road. He was almost certain his companion was dead, and that he'd have little chance against his attackers. He didn't know what lay beyond up the road, but he did know there were remote cabins they'd passed.

The only problem, other than that the outlaws now had their other horses and all their supplies, and that they'd surely killed his friend, was that they'd managed to wound him, too. It was in the flesh of his side, but it hurt like hell. He'd have to bandage it somehow. He felt under his blood-soaked shirt. Good: it'd gone clear through, leaving a ragged hole. He clamped a hand over it, pressing the cloth hard against the blood flow and the pain.

~ * ~

Stephen Davis met the white-haired man early the next morning, leading his horse unsteadily toward him, his side bandaged with his torn shirt, his eyes glazed with pain. He'd been unable to remount. Now he held up a bloody hand, seeking help.

Stephen reined in, reaching to steady the wounded man.

"Outlaws got th' drop on us," he managed. "Killed my partner, got our horses and all of it. You got anything t' keep down infection?"

"Let's get you settled, sir. Looks like you got it cleaned out, but with the walking, it's not stopped bleeding. Yes, we can burn it if you can stand it, or I've got a little whiskey, should do it."

"Don't know which'd be the worst," the man replied, with an effort at grim humor. Stephen laid him on a mossy bank at the stream's edge. Then he took the whiskey from his saddlebags and soaked the bandaged side with it. The white-haired man groaned.

"Worth it, though," Stephen told him. "Now, you'll need to hole up somewhere for a while, get somebody to bandage that better. Cabin back about a half mile, where I asked for directions. I'll get you there, but I'm behind time, and will have to ride on."

"Appreciate it, young man. Oh, my name's Archie Nolan, out of Winchester, goin' on into Kentucky. Th' robbers tried to get us to stop with 'em, and when we wouldn't, they must've followed us to our camp. My partner Jamie was on lookout, but they got to him. Reckon they're pretty good at robbin'."

"I'd say so. Usually try to find a lone man. I was jumped back beyond Saltville, myself, couple of hardcases. Sorry about your partner. Where'd this happen?"

The man told him. He'd ridden hard, then the weakness had almost made him pass out, so he'd stopped, cleaned the wound as best he could, bound it. Then led his horse deep into the forest to await daylight.

Nolan could sit his horse after Stephen had helped him mount. The two rode back to the lone cabin, where the settler Henry O'Neil and his wife agreed to take care of the man. Another huge man there helped get him settled.

"I can pay my way; robbers didn't git to my saddlebags," he promised.

"Reckon we c'n take keer you till you're mended," the woman told him. "Ennything you c'n spare, we'd 'preciate it, but we'll help, jis' th' same. We ain't been bothered much by outlaws, not recent. Folks knows not t'push m'man Henry, an' George, m'brother here."

George Wellerby was the giant, and he and the woman's blocky husband were a formidable pair. They had a small holding, subsisting mostly on hunting, with a side-hill corn patch and kitchen garden. They remembered the pair of outlaws, who'd stopped to see if they could buy feed for their horses. Of course the settlers hadn't had any to spare.

"Like to try m'hand at goin' west, m'self," George confided, "now that Sis an' Henry's all settled. Reckon there'd be a way a man c'd make somethin' of hisself out thar?"

"I don't know the territory, George, but I'm going to see for myself. I imagine you could make it anywhere I could. And I'm sure we'll meet again, this being on about the last road to the new country. I'll surely be back for provisions before long, and I'll stop by then. All right?"

"Shore. An' y'll know whut's out thar by then. 'Preciate it, Mr. Davis." Stephen and the giant shook hands.

"I'll go on, then. Oh, if I could, I'd like to buy a shovel from you, to bury Archie's partner." Stephen didn't want to leave the body for the wild animals.

And as he took his farewell, he slipped gold coins into the woman's grateful hand. He didn't know the man Nolan's real situation, only that he'd lost most of what he'd owned, and it was no strain to help. Nolan thanked him again, saying they'd meet again, somewhere in the territory, and he mentioned a small settlement well ahead.

With a description of the robbers and the horses firmly in mind, Stephen then rode the trace again, and within two hours had reached the Nolan campsite. He buried the body, then set out again. Only the newly turned soil and campfire ashes marked the spot, and a few hoofprints.

The robbers would ride hard, he guessed, but then slack off, feeling safe. He didn't plan to hunt the men, but if he ran across them, two men with three mounts, extra guns and two packhorses, he just might inconvenience them a little before riding on. Not to borrow trouble, but he guessed the new country could do without such non-citizens as that.

~ * ~

Anna Compton's first impression of the settlers here at the end of the road was, they just weren't very clean. Back on Lynch River in Virginia, her neighbors had been mostly small farmers, with the odd plantation dwellers, but they were quite civilized. She herself had often come in from the fields drenched with sweat from haying, plowing, tending the cattle or hogs, but her family had always stressed staying presentable. Here, the hunters, hillside cabin dwellers, just didn't seem to care.

The children ran ragged around the mill, the only place anything of interest was happening, and they were a scruffy lot. She remembered the bright, scrubbed little girls and boys she'd taught at the church back home, and knew she'd have to plan some way to improve the lot of these waifs.

And that job would be bigger than she'd realized, from the aromatic gathering of them and their parents at the missionaries' first worship service. Perhaps most of the people who'd come were just curious and had no appreciation for appearing their best for the Lord, but this was almost embarrassing.

Since these newcome people of God and the children among them moved among the settlers in their best clothes, clean and pressed, they reasoned that their new parishioners would take the hint. If not, maybe it would be part of their mission to help clean up the people, as well as the dusty, horse-manure-scented place itself. They agreed that whatever course was required, they'd take it on, in the spirit of serving God.

It was evident that no one in the community had any medical knowledge, and with the usual mishaps of frontier life there were unattended wounds, sores, evidence of ailments. Two of the missionaries had limited nursing experience, and knew that keeping bodies clean was often most of cures. These two, Harvey Campbell, one of the ex-soldiers, and Tildy Driscoll, the buxom, no-nonsense wife of Elder Hiram Driscoll, therefore undertook to explain that if the sufferers wanted to get well, they'd have to submit to frequent scrubbings. Presented in those quasi-medical terms, they hoped to influence the entire settlement positively.

With their doctoring, ministry, land-claiming, cabin-building, planning ahead and working toward subsisting through the winter, the missionaries had their collective hands full. They all pitched in for the first cabin-raising just days after arriving, and had a rough structure up in three days. The fireplace and chimney would take more time, of course. None were accomplished joiners, but all had done this work before, and they made use of every glimmer of daylight for the job.

The women and children would all crowd into this first shelter, and work would begin immediately on another for the men. After that, the married couples would build their own houses, with everyone's help, and pair off as the structures were completed. Besides Anna, the two ex-soldiers were the only single people in the group, and they planned to lodge individually with any of the other families that had room.

Maybe in a year or so, Anna speculated, she'd be able to manage a small cabin of her own, near neighbors but private enough for what reading she could manage, and suitable for her future as a spinster. And no doubt this would be her fate, and she was resigned to it. Besides, serving God was a higher calling, and she'd chosen it gladly.

Well, not as gladly as she probably should have, with the memory of Stephen Davis still in her life.

Inevitably, she'd observed the two single men in the group, not with any pairing in mind, but perhaps idly. Harvey Campbell was short and stout, his head coming up to her shoulder. He chewed tobacco constantly, and punctuated every communication with at least one expectoration. He was totally unlettered, if at the same time zealous in his devotion to his faith.

The other, Todd Epsworth, was missing an arm from the war, but had demonstrated an impressive ability to shoot a gun, chop a tree and, back on his family's farm in Buckingham County, to plow a straight furrow and fork hay. But at twenty-one, Todd had an almost childish outlook, and couldn't hold a conversation without a deal of blushing and stuttering. He seemed to hold no bitterness at losing his arm, which was admirable, but then he wasn't bitter or overly concerned about anything. He believed in what the group was doing here, but left the impression that he'd as soon be elsewhere, maybe fishing.

And certainly none of the hunters or other single men here in the wilderness held any appeal for Anna. The few here seemed to prefer horses and dogs to women, anyway. So no, no need to pursue any speculation in that direction, she decided.

She *had* allowed herself the fleeting concern that Stephen might awaken to his faults and just possibly decide to follow her West. Almost certainly not, but there remained the thought, which she would not permit herself to call a hope. And if that should, against all odds, prove to be the case, she wasn't sure just how she'd handle that. She hadn't been able to accept the humiliation of his spurning her, or his audacity at expecting her to swallow her pride and embrace him.

And while all her religious training had taught her that pride was the deadliest of sins, she knew she had to cling to that shred of it.

So, humble before God, yes. Humble and pride-free among these souls who needed her, certainly, even in their unwashed state. Accepting and of service to her fellow missionaries, yes.

But in no way could she see putting herself into the role of taken-for-granted object of a fickle man's fancy. That would just have to remain her unforgiven sin, she supposed. *And all have sinned; all fall short of the glory of God*, according to the Apostle Paul. And yes, she'd work on that, given time for the hurt to heal.

Given time.

Meanwhile, there was so much bone-tiring work to be done. Scrubbing clothes in the kettles of creek water, putting up logs and timbers, cooking, cleaning, helping everywhere she could. *Just as I've always done, really. Less to work with here, but human need is the same, whatever its social setting.*

Each night she collapsed wearily onto her sleeping pad, at first in one of the wagons with a minimum of at least one other woman, then in the crowded first cabin, with all of them and the children. At least she slept well, even if dreams of her former life kept intruding. And too often they included Stephen.

Five

The assassin Ames turned his horse into a long lane of boxwoods leading to the neat plantation house that had been Dr. Horace Weston's. Well, before that it'd belonged to his cousin John Logan, of course, and yes, there was still a suspicion that Weston had perhaps hastened the demise of the late colonel. So now it belonged to the twice-widowed Constance and her new husband Ned Drake, the mysterious friend of Stephen Davis the spoiler.

Ames didn't know what to expect, but wanted to gather as much information as he could. And if indeed this Drake proved to be a danger to his employers, why he'd just have to remove the man. He'd know soon enough. It was late in the day, and he fully expected to be able to ingratiate himself into an invitation to stay the night, claiming as he did his Army service with Davis. *Let's see, where was it they soldiered together? Oh, yes, at Cowpens, then at the siege at Yorktown. So many there, surely that'll work. And almost no privileged planters like this Drake must be, in the ranks with us foot soldiers.*

And there was another reason to get inside the house. Cabot had told him of a hiding place in Weston's study, where he hid the gold shipments for the organization. It was just possible the last, unrecovered one could still be there. It'd been unclear just what might have happened to that cache.

He was met at the door of the house by an ancient black butler, who looked him over critically, all the while smiling a welcome. But with his expensive clothes and the air of gentility he'd cultivated since the war, Ames felt he could fool any mere black.

"Justin Ames, an old army friend of Stephen Davis, whom Mr. Drake will know."

"Sho'ly, Mr. Ames. Jist you set here a bit, an' I'll go fetch Mistis." The man slipped away, with that smooth deference of the career house slave. That he was no longer a slave didn't occur to the visitor: they'd be rare here in the South, anyway.

In a moment, a quite attractive woman appeared, dressed as he imagined a plantation chatelaine would be, as fashionably as any lady in Philadelphia. He rose, bowed.

"Welcome, Mr. Ames. I'm Constance Drake. Ned will be here shortly; it's his habit to oversee the work of the place till almost dark. Can I offer you refreshment?"

"A pleasure, Mrs. Drake. Why yes, I'd have a touch of cider, thank you." He reasoned that temperance might be an attribute of this fair lady. So he'd be temperate, at least till Drake appeared. Actually, he'd welcome a good planter's punch, or other whiskey-based beverage. The lady sent the butler on this errand, and settled herself prettily, a lace fan in her hand.

"So you're a comrade of Stephen's. Ned will be so glad to meet you. May I inquire where you two served?"

"Well, at the surrender at Yorktown, primarily. We were shipped around so much we may have been unknowingly in each other's company before. But, his being a sharpshooter I, as a lowly private, wouldn't have come into direct contact with him before." *Be careful, here; keep it simple so she doesn't ask too many questions.*

"Yes, and I know Stephen is still somewhat withdrawn, except with his close friends. I know the war still troubles him."

"It troubles all of us, ma'am. War is a terrible thing, and we paid a high price for our independence." He didn't know which way to steer the conversation, but apparently Constance Drake was adept at this.

"Are you a family man, Mr. Ames?"

"Not as yet, unfortunately. I'm in business in Philadelphia, a demanding position in a trade organization, and have not as yet met the right woman. And, again unfortuntely, I was orphaned at an early age."

"Oh, I am sorry to hear that, but in such a city, you will surely find your destined love, and will have the family you lost."

Just then Ned Drake entered. He was a cheerful-looking man, freckled, with red hair. He looked younger than his wife, but had the easy manner of one born to plantation life.

"Ned, dear, this is Mr. Justin Ames, a wartime comrade of Stephen's. He was at Yorktown."

Drake gave a searching look at the other's face as he offered his hand, and the first warning signals went off inside Ames. Could this youthful planter suspect something? This no-doubt-spoiled scion of some other plantation? *But better go doubly careful here.*

"Delighted to meet you, sir. Any friend of Stephen's is a friend of ours. Welcome."

"Thank you, Mr. Drake. I must admit to knowing our Stephen only slightly, but was traveling over in Albemarle County anyway, and thought to look him up. His reputation as a furniture maker has spread. Finding that he'd left, I was returning East and recalled that someone had mentioned your name and this plantation."

"I see. Yes, my old friend has gone out into the wilderness, I fear. Sudden decision, and one we all regret." Drake was thinking, with his not ever having met this man, supposedly Stephen's friend, there was something wrong here. The fellow was just a bit too smooth. He resolved to draw him out. "So you were at Yorktown. I suppose most of us were there, at the last."

"Oh, were you in service, too?" It seemed so unlikely, this fresh-faced lad.

"Yes, for the duration. Stephen and I served together for five years." The clear blue eyes were on Ames, who felt a touch of inner panic. "Under whom did you fight?"

"Well, I was all over, you know. Mostly under LaFayette. But I prefer to dwell on the war as little as possible; had a bit of the war nerves there for a while. Don't like remembering it."

"Of course, sir. Well, you're welcome to dine with us, of course, and stay over. Are you familiar with plantation operations, perhaps?"

"Thank you, sir, for your hospitality. As to your other question, not really. My work has been in Philadelphia, trade organizations, mostly. I'm currently with a carriage manufacturer."

"Really? Then perhaps we can do some business, sir. We have need of a good carriage here. We're just building up from a period of neglect, while the late Dr. Weston was engaged in his practice. I'm afraid the place has gone without the amenities, except for the house, of course."

In fact, Constance had retained the doctor's fine carriage at his death, but Drake wanted to find out as much as possible about this reputed friend of his closest comrade. There was more than the man's smoothness to consider: a flicker of intensity in his eyes in unguarded moments. Drake knew he and Stephen had not eliminated all the members of the outlaw band, since the money had come from East somewhere, and yes, this could well be one of those shadowy figures, bent on discovering what had happened in that bloody few weeks earlier in the summer here.

For his part, Ames knew he was in a battle of wits with the pleasant planter, and now suspected the man to have been vastly more involved in the recent massacre than anyone had thought. A deceiving countenance and manner, the man had, which could conceal a deadly bent. Again, he wanted to know more, and the way to do that was to stay and investigate.

Perhaps the beauteous Constance would be of help.. He'd noted a certain steely resolve in that lady, beneath her manners. She *had* been married to the doctor, after all. Would surely know a great deal, if one could get it out of her...

The pleasant but inconsequential talk went on through supper, late as it necessarily was, with the planter's commitment to his chores. Afterwards, Drake invited Ames into his study for a drink, and further conversation. *Ah, this is exactly where I want to be,* he realized.

And Drake wanted him there, also. He'd learned of the secret compartment from Tom Logan, the freed slave who was the third member of the tight friendship he and Stephen had. Tom had been the late Colonel Logans' body servant right here, and had been sold West by the devious doctor.

And unknown to Ames, he'd been the one who'd recovered the last chest of gold from this very room. Drake knew this, and wanted to observe his visitor, see just what the man was after.

Watching his eyes move about the room as he accepted whiskey, Drake felt strongly that the visitor wasn't what he pretended to be. *So, just send him on his way, none the wiser? Or force his hand?* The planter had a loaded pistol in the drawer of his desk, and of course Ames was unarmed at the moment.

Drake decided to let the man have some rope with which to hang himself.

"Just make yourself at home, Mr. Ames. I'll just say goodnight to Constance and be back with you in a moment. Feel free to refill your glass." And he was gone.

What luck! Ames sensed his mission was falling into place as he quickly ran his hand over the wainscoting he knew concealed the hiding place.

And there it was: just a slightly loose section he knew to press, then slide quietly.

Ned Drake had secured another loaded pistol, and stood hidden behind the partly open door, watching. A grim smile spread as Ames slid the panel open, reached for a candle to light the interior. And yes, there was the chest, inside once more, where the new plantation master had replaced it, containing most of his third of the recovered gold. That treasure represented the path to reviving the rundown plantation, without which the nearly penniless planter and his bride would have to labor for years toward that goal.

Ames was breathing hard in excitement. He glanced about, then pulled the chest out, opened its unlocked lid. Gold coins reflected the candle's flickering light. Then he closed it again, slid it back into place, and was closing the panel when Drake accosted him.

"Very slowly now, Ames, replace the candle on the desk and keep your hands in sight. I'd say we have a few things to discuss, wouldn't you?" The planter's voice was pleasant, his smile seemingly genuine. But Ames felt, rather than saw, the deadly intent of the man. He knew there was no way out of this, now. Then his eyes caught the partly-open desk drawer, and the glint of a pistol butt inside as he set the candle holder down.

"Well, it seems you've caught me snooping, Mr. Drake. I must confess to a strong curiosity. I was just..."

"Who *are* you?" The voice was suddenly harsh, as was the sound of the rigid pistol being cocked. The blue eyes had gone hard.

"Oh, no need to jump to conclusions, here..." *If I can just distract him, I can reach that gun...* "I can explain. You see, I'd heard of this place, and..."

Then Ames shifted his eyes to the hallway behind Drake, and his mouth opened in horror.

"*My God! What's that behind you?*" and he pointed a shaking finger, while slipping his other hand to the desk drawer.

But Drake did not shift his gaze from the man, nor acknowledge any supposed presence behind him. Instead he stepped forward, shoved the man backwards onto a chair, pushed the pistol close to his face. And removed the other pistol from the drawer.

"Now, again, who are you and whom do you work for? Last chance to answer before I blow your head off." Ames could tell the man meant every word of it. And he had only one weapon left.

"Who I am is not important, Drake. Because there are many of us, and if you succeed in killing me, which is not going to be easy, another will take my place. You have our gold, or what's left of it, and we'll take it back, no matter what that requires." He sat back, letting his hand fall alongside his leg, where a keen knife was concealed in his boot. He knew Drake would feel confident, with two guns on him, but he hoped that would allow an instant's inattention, and that's all he'd need.

"So you're part of the East Coast operation Weston put together. We knew we'd never find you or your cohorts, but since you've found us, I guess that'll do, as far as you're concerned. Now, I need names and places, please." The planter's eyes stayed on Ames' face.

"Which you won't get from me. You know I can't betray my employers and ever expect to surface anywhere again. No, I'm afraid this is the end of the road for me, since I perceive you'll have no qualms about killing me, even in cold blood."

Drake considered for a moment. He'd no doubt this man would, if allowed, kill him, and perhaps Constance also. He was undoubtedly on a mission to right the supposed wrongs he, Tom and Stephen, and yes, even Constance, had done the outlaw band. But killing him here, now, while the man was unarmed? That was plainly not the...well, gentlemanly thing to do.

"I'll make you a sporting proposition, Ames. Shooting you outright doesn't appeal to my sense of honor, somehow. I'm laying this pistol on the desk, and you have just enough time to get your hands on it. If you're fast enough, you just might get off a shot. If you're not, of course it'll be self-defense on my part. Agreed?" And he laid the pistol he'd taken from the drawer on the desk.

A trick. Gun probably isn't even loaded, or its prime gone damp. No, I'll take my chances with the knife...

"Done." And as he shifted carefully in the chair, he was astonished to see Drake lower his pistol. *All right, that proves this's a trick.* He smiled, reached slowly for the gun, while pulling the blade from his boot with his other hand. This time the other man's eyes did flick toward the pistol.

Ames lunged up and forward while dodging to the side, the blade out front, going for the arm that held the gun. And in that instant, he knew he was faster, would slash his way free, would...

An explosion engulfed the room, and Ames felt the shock of being hit full in the chest. The knife dropped as his hand went desperately to the wound, and he felt his knees crumple.

"Thank you, my dear," Ned Drake said to his shaking wife, who held another smoking pistol. Her other hand was over her mouth, eyes wide. "I didn't see the knife." He retrieved it and the gun, kicked Ames' lifeless form, then went to her, held her.

"He might have cut you," she sobbed.

"And would have and worse, but for you. You are an admirable woman, Constance." He kissed her repeatedly until she calmed. She even smiled up at him.

"I like you whole," she said.

~ * ~

Following first one branched road then another, Stephen finally learned from a hunter that yes, the five wagons had passed that way earlier. They'd inquired as to any village ahead, and he'd told them of the scant grouping of cabins called Ketchum's Mill, on a creek at the very end of the road.

"Dunno whut they'll find thar," he wondered. "Last time I was t'thar, warn't but old man Ketchum's mill he was puttin' up, an' mebbe half a dozen cabins up th' hollers. Been a year or so, though, so mebbe more thar now. Sat'day was a week ago I seen 'em, so reckon they's settled in. Nothin' but high mountins on a-past, an' no road ner a way t'cut one."

The days he'd lost didn't matter now, Stephen realized; the missionaries were bound to have found their wilderness. And he'd find Anna there, who'd be the unknown quantity. Well, free country, and he'd just settle in himself, get set up for the long work of convincing her of his sincerity. If that meant a veritable siege, so be it; he wasn't giving up on the girl.

But of course, if she rejected him outright, wouldn't even speak to him, it could get awkward, being in the same settlement. In that case he'd make himself useful to the community anyway, surely in helping build the inevitable new church. And Miss Anna couldn't fault him for that kind of effort, he was sure. So she would either relent or not, given time.

Yes, time. He had plenty of that

~ * ~

As coincidence would have it, the cousins MacNaughton had also chosen the way to Ketchum's Mill. There was no road beyond that settlement, they were told, but yes, a man could ride up and over the steep mountains on a faint trail west. Though for what reason, nobody could imagine. Oh yes, hunting was sure to be good, if this pair was after that, but nobody to trade pelts with, much. Folks there, they'd heard, just scratching out a living, and no store or any supplies to be had.

"Mebbe oughta pick 'nother road," Caleb had suggested. "Don't seem th' place ennybody'd go, he had th' choice."

"Wal, way I see it, th' fellers done in our cuzzin might be lookin' fer jist such a place t'hole up, stay hid, case of kin like us comin' after 'em, wouldn't y'say?"

"Good a guess as enny, I reckon. Though I still cain't see why they didn't take nothin' off th' boys. Oh, I reckon Ansted 'n Luke, they jumped 'em, prob'ly had th' drop on 'em outta that blind gulch. An' somway th' others was better shots, er quicker, but still seems they'd of took th' guns, an' mebbe shore th' hosses. Ansted's was as good a hoss as enny around."

"Mebbe jist didn't care. Y'know, they mighta been lawmen even, come t'thaink of it. After somebody else, coulda been, an' jist didn't want t'take th' trouble."

"Naw, lawmen'd stick around, ast questions. Coulda jist been th' one feller, though it don't figger. I say we jist g'on t'this mill place, an' if nuthin's thar, we head on over th' hills, git on to whutever's ahead."

"I reckon. Don't look like we got a lotta choice, 'less we do stumble on th' man, which ain't a bit likely, this fur 'long."

And so the two rode into Ketchum's Mill, leading the two packhorses and the fine sorrel gelding they'd stolen. They inquired at the blacksmith shop, at which an elderly man hammered iron, if there might be lodging. The mill was silent, the creek flow being down in the dry weather, and only the smith's house built onto the mill, one other near upslope, and a gathering of wagons a distance away, showed life.

"Naw, ain't nobody got enny room. Th' church folks there, they ain't got but th' one cabin up, all crowded in, an' ever'body's scratchin' t'git set for winter, too busy t'build ennything like a tavern." He took glowing iron out of the forge, set to hammering it.

"Wal, shorely somebody's got a little whiskey, ain't they? We're a mite dry f'm th' road."

The smith returned the iron to the fire, pulled twice on the bellows handle.

"Oh, reckon we c'd take keer of a little thirst. M'wife, she's in th' mill there, an' keeps a thing er two fer sale. G'on in. I might even jine you in a minnit, I git this wagon brace done."

The men tied their horses and entered the dusty mill. An older woman sat in a crude rocking chair, sewing quilt patches.

"Hidey," she greeted, putting aside her work. "Kin I he'p you fellers?"

"Yes, ma'am," Caleb said, removing his hat in an attempt to appear as deferential as possible. "We'd like a drink of whiskey, please ma'am."

"Whiskey it is, then, young man." She rose, eyeing the two scruffy men. They didn't look like good, solid citizens, she reflected, not like those nice people in the wagon train. If this settlement were to become a respectable village, she doubted this type would contribute much toward that. But, not to judge, as the church folks had said Sunday at the open-air worship service. Most of the settlers here weren't all that proper either, she knew.

"You boys come far, I reckon," she observed, by way of starting a conversation. Wouldn't hurt to find out all she could about any new arrivals. Sort of her duty really, so the community could know what to expect. "Ennybody comes here, bound t've rode pretty far."

"Fer shore," Shelby answered. "We heered this wuz 'bout th' end of th' road, too."

"Is that. Oh, folks has rode on up a trail west over th' big mountain there, on into th' territory, but cain't no wagon git over. Y'uns set on stayin', er goin' on?"

"Dunno, yit. We're sorta huntin' a friend of our'n, headed this way. Feller ridin' with a packhoss. Er mebbe moren' one of 'em, by now. Tryin' t'ketch up with him, see which way t'go, after."

"Well, ain't but th' church folks come in lately. Been here some over a week. They aim t'stay, build us a meetin' house an' all. Whut's yore friend's name?"

Shelby had realized, as soon as he'd said it, that the woman would ask just that question, and he simply did not have a name in mind.

"Wal... thet's th' funny part, I reckon. We've rode with him, but never heered his name, actual. Got on th' road ahead us outta Saltville. That makes it hard t'locate him, an' we might be on th' wrong road, I know."

"I'd say so. No, ain't been ennybody new, like I said. Mebbe m'man'd know." She stepped to the door, called the smith, who'd just banked his forge fire. She knew Killebrew Ketchum, smith and miller, wouldn't know as much as she about any travelers, but she wanted him to get a good look at these men. Something about them she didn't like.

"Killy, you seen ennybody new 'sides th' church folks here'bouts?" She cut her eyes toward the two inside.

"Naw, don't reckon so. I'll have me a nip of that whiskey, too, Belle. You fellers doin' all right?" He settled himself at what was a counter and bar combined, but also eyed the two, cued by his wife's look.

"Doin' good, now," Shelby answered. "Good draink of whiskey'll do that fer a feller. But don't look lak we'se on th' right road t'ketch up with our man."

"Road don't go no futher'n this. But there's a trail up an' over..."

"What I tole 'em, Killy. Reckon a man coulda rode through, mebbe at night, an' we wouldna seen him?"

"Could shore been thataway. You'ns headin' on?"

"Don't rightly know, now. We was goin' t'team up 'th this feller, g'on west, git some land some'ers, settle down. Now, reckon we done lost him, so we got t'set an' figger, some."

"Wal, nothin' goin' on here. Ain't 'nuff folks here t'keep m'mill runnin', even when thar's water in th' creek. I'd say, iff'n you wuz plannin' to settle, on over th' mountain fur enough, thar's river bottom land, not all rocks like this."

Ketchum's wife wasn't ready to let her suspicions go, just yet.

"I see y'got an extry hoss an' saddle. Lose somebody?"

"Oh, that." *Another problem*; Caleb thought fast. "Naw, feller we's talkin' 'bout, he said was 'nother man gonna jine up with us, an' did we have a hoss fer him. So yeah, we reckon now we'd trade er sell that'n, ennybody wants him. Folks back home raises hosses, y'see, an' that's whar we lost our man, goin' back fer this'n." *There, that sounded reasonable*, he hoped.

"Don't say?" the miller was interested. He swallowed the last of his whiskey, rose, and went out, followed by the cousins, to inspect the horse. Killebrew Ketchum knew horses, and this one was a fine creature. Maybe too fine for these two ragged men to have offered it to a stranger to ride. His wife was right; something was wrong here.

"Problem is, don't ennybody 'round here have money t'buy a hoss," he went on. "An' dunno whut y'd take in trade." He was going over the animal carefully, noting his points.

"Dunno, either. But we're gittin' a mite low on money, so yeah, we'd like t'make some sorta deal roun' here iff'n we could. Might jist stay a day er so, see whut turns up." Shelby nodded in agreement. The prospect of riding away from even this tiny village didn't appeal to him much. Like he'd observed, they probably shouldn't have taken this dead-end road in the first place.

~ * ~

"I've been rethinking this whole business of the western plantations," the carriage-maker Cabot told his second-in-command Codington. "Hayes was convinced that was the place to put our money, but the initial returns aren't good. Seems the best land has long been taken up in the valleys, and those creek-bottom places he bought and homesteaded are the leavings."

"So what are your conclusions?"

"That we should now look elsewhere for our investments. There have been discoveries of iron deposits further south and west, and the demand is high for that. We haven't heard from Justin Ames, so perhaps we shouldn't go about rebuilding the network as it was, since we'd have to begin from nothing, anyway."

"But you arranged for him to clear the way, remove that fellow Davis and any others responsible for our losses."

"Admittedly, and that's still the plan. But given the meager returns from the plantations so far, it looks as if that entire endeavor needs modifying. I see iron and steel as the future, and if we can get in on its mining and milling, we can't lose." The robust man rubbed his hands together. Codington, accustomed to proceeding on safe and tested routes, was skeptical.

"But Hayes' operations were far away, and if I understand you, this iron is even further. Won't that present a transportation problem? The maps show only a few rivers big enough for transport in those mountains, and I doubt if there are many roads suitable for heavy hauling."

"The method being tried there is to smelt the ore right at its source. That way only the finished product need be moved. And there are already routes to the heads of navigation in that region, I find. But here's the best part: that is an impoverished area, southwest Virginia, on into Kentucky. We can get mining labor, teamsters, all the laborers we require, very cheaply. Keep the overhead low, and we'll profit mightily."

"But we'll have to reach the mills, and there aren't many in the South. I see Richmond and perhaps Harper's Ferry, but they're very far from the known sources. I fear it would be a complicated arrangement."

"I've thought of that, of course. We'll need to transport our product only for a short time, until we can build our own mills nearby. We can turn that region into a manufacturing center, much like they've done at Fort Pitt, and we can be in on its very beginning, when the real fortunes are made. And…" he thought a moment, "we really do need to get the investment phase of our operations away from here again, before the authorities get too nosy."

"But that's wilderness, Cabot. We can't just turn it into an industrial complex overnight. That'd take an army of engineers, roadbuilders, specialists."

"Where's your thirst for adventure, Codington? I recall you were skeptical of Hayes' plans too, at the time. And perhaps you were right in the long run, but what has it cost us, really? We'll continue to receive whatever those holdings bring in as they grow.

"And we must remember this: This capital that keeps coming in isn't our money we're investing. We stole it, plain and simple, and if ever we're to gamble on developing anything new, we should certainly do it with someone else's money. How can you argue with that?" The man laughed.

"I suppose you're right," the other reluctantly agreed. "We *have* done well these years, and with the expansion West, yes, I agree we should get in on it. Why don't we talk with the others?"

"As soon as possible. I was going to wait for Ames' return, but this plan need not have anything to do with that region. Let sleeping dogs lie, I say. If he can avenge us for our losses, perhaps even recover some, so much the better. If not, we just bypass that whole chapter."

And that was the course of action the others agreed upon at a meeting later that night. Questions were raised, of course, but the general idea of the iron mining and smelting evidently appealed to the group: new land, new *legal* business, no possible repercussions from old enemies. Altogether a sound proposal. Surely.

"We'll need to scout out the territory," Cabot proposed. "Find the best central location, vis a vis source, shipping, labor. Gentlemen, this could well be the beginning of an industrial surge that will make us all rich."

"But who'll we send?" asked the ever-cautious Codington. "The man will have to know the business, won't he? Have a firsthand knowledge of just what's there, how rich the ore is, what's involved in digging it out, transporting it, processing it. We can't just send anybody, but of course you'll have thought of that."

"I have, yes. And contrary to the course anyone would expect, that of bringing in an outsider, much as we could use the expertise, I just don't think we want another finger in our pie." He looked around the group, smiling. The others were puzzled. If not an expert, then...

"Yes, I intend to go myself. There are independent prospectors in the region, no doubt planning to return East seeking investors, backing. I shall save them the trouble, by going directly to them. I have locations in mind, and a few names. So, unless any of you can come up with a better suggestion, I'll take the proverbial bull by the horns and lead this adventure."

The men were visibly taken aback at this plan, muttering to each other as Cabot beamed. He was their leader, the one who held the organization together. His going out on such a venture would leave them to man the details of their illegal efforts themselves. But yes, they could do that.

But there was a further consideration. If by chance the authorities he'd mentioned *were* getting close to them, he'd be conveniently and safely out of the country when the axe fell.

On them. Was he planning the whole business this way? Was this talk of the iron venture just a blind? Less savory characters would certainly see it as such. So, it came down to whether his co-conspirators trusted him or not.

And men who made their livings beneath the law seldom survived if they trusted anyone, even their compatriots. But then, he was a Cabot, of that respected Boston family, even if he was the black sheep. Surely...

And none of the others wanted to question his judgment. Word was, he'd been a dangerous brawler in his younger days, and nobody wanted to see how he'd react to insubordination. So let him have his fun, going out to the end of the earth. They could keep the money coming in here, with him or without.

And just maybe his scheme *would* pay off.

Six

When Stephen Davis rode into Ketchum's Mill on the creek called Troublesome, the first thing he saw were the two MacNaughton cousins, with the extra riding horse and the two packhorses that fit the description Archie Nolan had given. They were hanging around the silent mill, watching the blacksmith at work. He had not a shred of doubt that these were the robbers who'd killed the partner Jamie and wounded Nolan. He had a strong urge to shoot them on sight.

But that wasn't the way to start out in this settlement that he knew held Anna Compton and her church people. He'd just watch the men, find out what they were doing here. He'd been told of a trail on over the mountains, and if they took that, he could follow them and dispense some needed justice beyond anyone else's knowledge.

Just now he wanted to find a place to clean up before seeking out Anna and finding out just where he stood. He rode up to the mill. The two cousins eyed him shrewdly, but he gave them a pleasant nod, addressed the smith when that man pushed the iron he was working back into the fire.

"Hello, sir. Heard there wasn't an inn here, but where might a man set up camp?"

"Oh, ennywheres 'long th' creek, I reckon. I'm Killy Ketchum, th' miller, only ain't 'nuff water in Troublesome t'run th' wheel till some rain. An' who might you be?"

Stephen swung off his horse, looped the reins and the packhorse's rope around a post. He kept the corner of his eye on the others.

"Stephen Davis. Yessir, I've done a mite of milling and smithing myself, back in Goochland where I'm from."

"Don't say? Wal, ain't a whole lotta need 'roun here yet. Few folks up th' hollers, an' th' new miss'naries settlin' in. These fellers come in few days ago, ain't decided whether t'stay er ride on," indicating the cousins.

"Well, I've got friends among the missionaries, so I suppose I'll plan on staying around a while. Any decent land to be had, up a stream somewhere?"

"Some, though it's mighty steep, mostly. Th' church people, they don't seem t'mind. Reckon they're gittin' some help f'm wherever they's from, t'keep 'em. Oh, these is th' MacNaughton cousins, f'm close t'Saltville, they tell me."

Stephen nodded to the two again. They didn't seem inclined to speak, so neither did he. A ragged pair, despite their good horses. Probably all stolen, he reasoned. *Good men to watch close.*

"Well, I don't need much either. Did woodwork after the war, and might put a hand to that again, but like you said, not much need here. Good hunting hereabouts?"

"Tolerable. Ain't all hunted out by a sight, but y'got t'do moren' stomp th'u th' woods nowadays. That's a fine-lookin' rifle y'got thar." Eyeing the long gun.

"My pa's a gunsmith, along with his milling. Carried this one through the war. It'll hit a target."

"Say so. I like a long barrel like that, myself. Done a few locks an' sich, but never tried a barrel; ain't that good a smith."

"Neither am I. I do make a few tools: mill picks, saws, axes. Barrel's just too much work, and you can spoil one easily, after days of work on it."

For their part, the MacNaughtons were a bit wary of this stranger. They'd expected the man they'd heard about to be ahead of them, and not necessarily on this road, but their natural suspicion kept them from ruling him out. Friend of the church people, though… didn't sound like a killer, even if he had been a soldier.

"Wal," Shelby announced, mounting, "reckon we'll g'on down t' our camp, seein's nobody kin work a trade fer this hoss we's stuck with." The two rode away, leading the three other animals. Stephen noted the neat packs, out of keeping with the scruffy men.

"Y'hungry, Mr. Davis? M'woman, she allus cooks up a big dinner, 'case enny of th' settlers drops by. I'se about t'bank th' fire an' have a bite, m'self."

"Be obliged, sir. Been a long road, and sorely tired of my own cooking."

"Wal, yer shore welcome." He turned toward the mill, called. "Belle, we got comp'ny. This here's Stephen Davis. He's a miller, too, an' a smith. Now how 'bout that?"

"Come on in, botha you. Glad t'meetcha, Mr. Davis." Peering past them at the retreating backs of the MacNaughtons. "Good, they're gone. Not t'throw off on ennybody, but them two jist ain't all they 'pears t'be." She bustled about the hearth, where a stew bubbled, and the smell of biscuits in a Dutch oven wafted.

"Now, now, we cain't go jedgin' folks, like th' church people say, Belle. But you're right, those boys don't set well atall."

"How long have they been here?" Stephen asked. He was calculating the time Nolan's attackers would have spent on the road.

"T'was three days ago. Said they was s'posed t've hooked up with 'nother two fellers, only one didn't have a hoss, so they went an' brought one. Lost track, they said, an' ended up with th' hoss." He didn't sound as if he believed that story.

"Hmm. Well, perhaps they'll travel on. Don't look like the type would settle, to me." Stephen wasn't about to share his suspicions with these people, although he'd liked them instantly. *Wait and see.* If the two planned to ride on, they might try to rob somebody here first, too.

He accepted a steaming bowl of the stew, two hot biscuits and a mug of cider, cool from the mill's springhouse. The three sat at a rough table, after Belle Ketchum removed her quilting from it. He looked about the mill's interior, noting the small set of stones, the belting, shafting, the quality of the woodwork. It was rough, but sound.

"Nice place you have here. Where'd you mill before this?"

"Oh, aroun', here'n thar. Was in th' Valley fer what, Belle, ten year? Then th' young'uns left out, an' we jist said why didn't we g'on too, see some new country. 'Fore that, we's in Buckingham, whar th' slates is. Growed up on in th' Tidewater, but didn't do no millin' there. Learnt from th' feller south of th' James, whar I met Belle here. How 'bout you?"

"Born and raised out of Goochland. Pa came over from England, married soon after. Sister's husband wanted the mill, and when I came home from the war, didn't feel ready to settle yet, so I moved on."

"Didn't find y'self no wife, then?" Belle's keen eyes were on him.

Stephen laughed. Seemed as if every older woman he'd met wanted to pair him up. He didn't resent it; women were like that, even his mother.

"No. Thought I'd found the right girl, but she ran off with a preacher. So I just picked up where I'd left off almost three years later, and here I am."

Belle Ketchum's mind was working; she'd been intrigued by that tall part-Indian girl with the church people, the only single one, except for the two ex-soldiers. This boy was tall, too, and spoke well, like the girl did. And where'd she said she was from? Couldn't remember. Maybe more'n chance to these two? Belle liked a little spice in her life, and this...

"Wal, if y'settle in here, more folks likely t'show up, way they's comin' West these days. Th' missionaries git their church built, next thing'll be a tavern, er mebbe at least 'n ordinary. Folks'll come, fer sure. Man won't hafta stay single long."

"Not in any hurry, I guess, though I did know Anna Compton, a young woman supposed to be with these folks." Belle Ketchum smiled. *Yes.* "Hope to get to know her better. Maybe help with the church, or something. Now though, where'd a man look for a piece of ground not too far out, Mr. Ketchum, would you say?"

"Hmm. Downcreek's mostly took up. Up a ways there's a little holler, but hard t'git to. Don't reckon a man'd ever git a road in to it, an' that's likely what's kep' it open. Got a good spring on it, an' nice buildin' timber. Lightnin' fire burnt a bunch of big trees, oh, mebbe fifty year ago, an' th' young stuff's right. White pine, an' they ain't no better, I'm shore you know."

"Sounds good. Anybody troubling to go patent land around here, or is there a courthouse anywhere near?"

"Oh, s'posed t'put in a claim, all right, but all th' way back t'Saltville's th' closest. Most of us jist marked out our lines, figger t'git it all legal sometime. Nobody worries 'bout it much." The subject didn't seem too important to the miller, either.

"May ride up to it, then. Do want to look up the missionaries first, though. You say they're building up some of the branches close?"

"Are. Worked it out with us t'put th' church jist down th' creek, but wanta git cabins up first. Got one fer th' wimmen an' little'uns done, an' on one fer th' men. They wanta git set 'fore winter, with th' fam'lies in, 'fore then."

Stephen thanked the old couple, paid for his meal, and followed directions to a spot he could camp for the night. It didn't look like rain, for which he was grateful. He unpacked the essentials, scrubbed up in the creek, shaved, and donned clean clothes. It was by then mid-afternoon.

Stephen wasn't nervous, he kept telling himself, but he also kept finding reasons to postpone his visit to the missionaries' construction site, to which he also had directions. Would it look bad to interrupt their work? Should he wait till day's end? Should he pitch in and help, as if that were the most natural course? He had no doubt his effect on Anna would be a jolt, this many weeks and this far from their last meeting, but that'd be the case no matter what.

He finally repacked his possessions, led the packhorse back to the mill, tethered it, and set out for whatever the meeting held for him. He didn't want to leave anything at the campsite, with those two hard-eyed men around.

~ * ~

"Thet stranger Davis, now," Shelby said, "he looks an' talks like he'd have money on him. Good hosses, an' I'd wager they's valuables in them packs."

"Could well be. Y'figger we'd oughta jump him, 'fore we head out?"

"Don't see whut it'd hurt, none. An' even if 'tis a long shot, he jist *could* be th' feller done in Ansted an' Luke."

"Don't see that atall, him bein' in with th' church folks an' all. But yeah, even with th' stuff we got offa th' two we hit, we need a better stake. Druther come into th' new country over th' mountains flush, 'steada broke. How you figger we'd oughta do it?"

"Wal, we dunno whut kinda feller he is, er how hard he'd be t'kill. Don't fool m'self we c'd git his stuff 'thout shootin' him fust. So I'd say we jist pay him a visit at his camp, late like. I seen whar he's set up."

"So y'don't wanta stay 'round here enny longer? Figger we cain't sell nothin' t'these pore folks?"

"'Bout th' size of it. An' whutever we git offen Davis, we gotta carry on west with us 'fore we c'n sell er trade it, too."

The two planned their attack for that night, and their getaway to follow immediately. With just the lone man, they'd use the same strategy as at the last robbery, without fear of being slipped up on. They saw no way their scheme could fail.

~ * ~

Anna Compton labored along with the other women at the men's cabin-raising, peeling bark from the logs, whittling pegs, minding the children, helping cook the midday meal. And being tall and strong, she even helped the men at the log-hewing, notching, lifting the logs into place, their having laid the puncheon floor the previous day. Her thoughts were on the building of the church, to come after these initial shelters.

She remembered the community house-raising she'd been a part of at the big structure Stephen and his intended, Abby Thomas, had hosted the previous year. Everyone in that rural community had shown up, dozens of them, in wagons, on horseback, on foot. It had been a festive occasion, with Abby's father the squire providing food and whiskey, each family bringing something to share, all working at the framing-up.

Stephen had been a great favorite there, she admitted. And by that time, she'd accepted the fact that he'd valued their friendship so little he'd courted and won the other girl. Seen her as just that, a friend, not in any way to be desired as a wife, although the two of them surely had more in common than he and Abby.

And she remembered also Tom Logan's wise insight into the situation. The ex-slave knew Stephen had chosen badly, and seemed to know Anna's heart. Thinking back on it now, sadness, regret, and still a little anger came with the images.

Where could I have handled it differently? When could I have been more forceful, asserted myself, made it all turn out better? No, no use going over that again, here and now. Given the circumstances, she realized, she'd done the only thing she could have: She'd been gracious, embraced Abby, visited her, cheered her when the shock of the killings threw her into depression and doubt.

I was who I've always been; there to help, to lean on, to nourish, to heal. Yes, and to be by-passed, disregarded.

Her hands did the cabin-building chores automatically, having done them often enough before on her father's farm, that house-raising, the building of that other new church back on Lynch River. Her mind was free to roam at will, but she must curb it, keep it from those memories.

But she could almost see Stephen Davis even now, riding the black gelding he'd traded her father for, coming to see her, to share books, to bring little gifts, to be a...friend.

Yes, only that.

She straightened at the approach of a horseman, amid the chopping, hammering, sawing, the exchange of words all around her. There was something familiar about that figure, lean, purposeful.

And the black gelding...she'd helped raise that horse, she was sure of it.

Anna shook her head to clear it. *Memories taking over here. Thinking too much. That can't be...*

That *was.*

That horseman reining in, tipping his tricorner hat to the lot of them, acknowledging the men on the wall, the women, the children.

And her.

He dismounted, looped his reins over a low limb, walked toward her. She'd risen, dropped the work she'd been doing, and was aware that she'd stepped toward him.

No. Stop. You can't welcome him now. Here. Not after...But oh, my God am I glad to see him! He's come all this way, and there's only one reason for it. Dear God, help me to steady myself, hold onto my sanity, here. He's nervous, and well he should be. But yes, I am in control. I am...

"Hello, Stephen. Welcome to our future settlement. You seem to have found us." Foolish words.

"Anna. Could you doubt that I would?"

"I didn't know what to think. I guess I thought there was an ending, the...right one." *Oh, too harsh.* And his face registered her words.

"Never an ending. I hoped you'd realize that, even though I caused our parting."

The others were staring. With an effort, Anna turned, forced a smile, and began introducing Stephen to her friends.

"Stephen Davis was our friend and neighbor in Albemarle County," she began, and she gave everyone's name, realizing he'd never remember them all. It gave her a moment to collect herself, though, with the greetings, smiles, handshaking. The children shyly appraised this tall stranger who had a holstered pistol on him, and a very long rifle on his saddle. Anna reflected that Stephen had been forced to be always on his guard, and must continue to be, perhaps for the rest of his life.

"I heard of your venture here, folks," he was saying, "I'd intended to come west just after the war, but got sidetracked, I guess you could say. Now, having had the benefit of my church experience with Anna's family and others, I'd like to help here in any way I can. I've done a sight of building, smithing, woodworking. And I like the land here. So, very much to the point, may I join you?"

Oh, my God, he's serious. He's come all this way, and he means to keep after me, weaken my resolve, undo my pride. But I can't refuse his offer, not with our situation here.

"Why, we'd be more than happy to welcome you, Mr. Davis," Elder Hiram Driscoll said with a glance at his wife Tildy, "wouldn't we, brothers and sisters?" They all expressed their approval, and Anna realized Stephen's eyes were on her. She nodded, smiled as graciously as she could.

"Then," Stephen said, glancing at the westering sun, "I'd say I should get a hand on one of those broadaxes, since my arrival has meant burning daylight." He strode over, hefted a big axe, and without another word, began to hew an already-scored log with precise strokes. Appreciative chuckles erupted, then the work resumed all around him.

Anna felt weak inside. Later, she told herself, she'd take time to assess her feelings, which were now a jumble: part resentful, part glad, part betrayed, part yes, hopeful. No, surely not...*hopeful.*

Not now.

It was soon evident that Stephen far excelled all of the men at this work, and he shaped the cabin logs with near-perfect ease. He cut the dovetail notches by eye, again with the confidence of long practice. Very quickly, the other men deferred to him as to such puzzles as notch depth, corner height control, the inevitable drifting off-square of the structure. Stephen had the answers to all their questions, but avoided any possible air of condescension. And worked harder than anyone, earning the respect a master craftsman was due.

The women cooked, the day's light lessened, the men called a halt to progress. Tomorrow they'd be ready for the two top plate logs, then the roof framing. They'd cut out the window and door openings then, and begin the chinking of the spaces. This men's shelter, following the earlier erection of the women's, would be ready before Sunday's worship service, which would be outdoors before the mill, barring the scarce rain of the fall season.

Anna and Stephen had been polite to each other, but there was no breakthrough, no joyful reunion. If the others thought this odd, they did not comment, although speculation naturally ran high among them. They would, of course, talk about what the relationship between these two had been, could be again—human nature.

Curiosity. Nosiness.

Anna needed time to think, time to sort out her emotions. Here he'd come, unannounced, into her world again, into her *life*. Unbidden, unexpected.

Unwanted?

No, don't think that way, but don't open yourself to hurt here, either. Do not let his being here tear you apart. You have a life here, a new life, and you'll stay the course, no matter this man's presence. And if it becomes intolerable, well then, one of us will just have to leave.

Again.

For his part, Stephen knew he could not have expected her to open her arms to him, not after the extreme course of suddenly disappearing from his life and her home and everything she'd known. He'd understood he must prove his devotion to her, his sincerity, and yes, that it'd take time.

Time, that was the healing factor for both of them. And here at the end of the world, time would be all they had in abundance.

He took his leave of the group, promising to come again in the morning, and accompanied the women and children by torchlight to their cabin in the next hollow. Then he followed the starlit trail back to the settlement to retrieve his packhorse and make camp.

He'd learned the hard way that men like the two he'd met earlier weren't to be trusted, even if he hadn't already had the conviction that they were the robbers and killers at the Nolan camp. He'd take precautions then, camped alone as he was.

~ * ~

"Been thainkin'," Caleb MacNaughton announced, poking at their own campfire farther down the creek. "If we's gonna rob th' stranger, thet means yeah, we gotta leave outta here, like we said. But I got th' idee we c'd have us some fun in th' bargin, we play it right." His face wore a malignant grin in the flickering light.

"Whut kinda fun?"

"Wal, a couple them wimmen in th' church bunch, they's fine-lookin', wouldn't you say?"

"An' married, all but that tall thaing. You thainkin' we c'd git next to enny of 'em? Don't rightly thaink so."

"Naw, but don't nuthin' say we couldn't grab us a pair of 'em, haul 'em off into th' woods, git us some of thet. Thar cabin's over th' ridge, too fur f'm th' men's camp fer enny hollerin' t'be heard. I'm thainkin' thet fust, then hit th' Davis feller, an' ride on outta this hole with all of it."

"Yore shore a bad rogue, Caleb, shore are. Only thaing missin' f'm yore plan is us some good whiskey. An' the' miller, he's got some. But I don't reckon it'd do t'git th' whole place all riled up at oncet. Might git t'be too many t'fight ourselves through."

"Now, thar'll be a way t'git that done too, we figger it right. But either way, I'd say yore right: we need t'study on it more, make ourselves a plan. So whut I'm thainkin' is, we don't try fer it t'night, but sorta scout it out better. Them folks ain't gonna git all scattered out in thar own cabins fer a spell, way they's goin'. Whyn't we git some sleep on it, an' study out jist how we'll git it done tomorrer?"

"Prob'ly a good idee. But I shore do like yore plan, Cuzzin. Shore do."

~ * ~

Stephen slept away from his dying campfire, in dense brush. Rolled convincingly in plain sight was the shape of a man, consisting of his packs, covered with blankets and his tricorner hat over one end. He always slept lightly, and had his pistol near at hand. He also knew the tethered horses would warn him of any intruders.

But dawn found the camp quiet, and he roused, went about his chores after a mostly-untroubled sleep. Relief at having found Anna mixed with his concern at the situation between them, but that hadn't robbed him of much rest. It would work itself out, he knew, just as not rushing into any action had worked out for him in the past. Just hide and watch, his friend Tom Logan had counseled more than once.

So he fed his horses and himself and set out for the building site for another day of work. After this cabin was completed, he planned, he'd scout out the rough hollow Killy Ketchum had mentioned. Need to get his own place built before winter, and make some provision for feeding his horses then. What little grass grew hereabouts had been claimed by the settlers for their animals, of course.

Anna hadn't slept well, with her own private demons to contend with, but she resolutely set out with the others for work, determined to be of service. She wouldn't let her own demands keep her from her duty, and would, with God's help, get through this. Nothing was changed, she kept telling herself—*just stay the course.*

But she couldn't suppress a tingle at seeing Stephen, already at work with the big broadaxe on one of the long poplar top plate logs. She'd heard his steady strokes before she saw him, and already knew that signature. He straightened, smiled a greeting, which she returned as she went about helping the other women set up for the day's activities. She couldn't know that her smile had been something Stephen had come to live for.

Yes, just stay the course.

At the empty women's cabin, the MacNaughton cousins examined the lay of the land, as it were, planning their attack.

Confronted with loaded pistols, they had no doubt the women would be no threat, and that they'd be able to seize two of them easily. Then they could take them back to the creek, where first one then the other could keep watch while the other ravished his captive. The prospect delighted both men, who then speculated on which two they'd abduct.

"Little young thaing, 'thout no kids, thet's th' one I want," Caleb announced. "Y'reckon you c'd handle thet long tall one?"

"Be somethin', wouldn't it? She's 'bout as big as me, but yeah, with a gun t'her haid, I reckon she'd go peaceful like. Might hafta slam her 'round some fust, but don't reckon wimmen t'put up much of a fight."

The two counted what remained of the money they'd stolen from the Nolan camp. They decided it would be wise to buy a jug or two of whiskey from the miller, rather than take the chance of robbing them, too. No sense in creating more problems than they could handle.

This they did then, obtaining only one jug, the miller being low on supply. And of course they sampled some of his wares on the way back to their camp, just to make sure of its quality. With the result that the rest of their day was spent in total idleness, their plan becoming fuzzier with each drink.

Seven

Two days later, with the roof of split shakes on, fireplace and chimney partially complete, and the new cabin livable, Stephen decided to move his camp to his proposed homesite. On checking in with the Ketchums, the old man drew him aside.

"Jist wanted t'warn you, Stephen, them two drifters been drinkin' heavy, an' I got th' feelin' they's up to no good. They finished off a jug of whiskey, then come fer more, which we hadn't much of. Belle, she heard 'em sayin' they reckoned that'uz all right, then, since they had thar work t'do. They wasn't all th' way sober, but both of us s'spect they're plannin' somethin' ain't right. Hangin' 'round here don't make sense neither, an' I plain don't believe thar story 'bout that extry hoss."

"Thanks, Killy. I've got my own suspicions about those two, and just how they came by all those horses. Man was killed some days back on the road here, and another wounded. I helped the one man, buried the other, and learned they'd been robbed of just two packhorses and the one saddle horse. Now, I've got no proof, but these are almost certainly the same men. And the first move they make that's out of line, I think we should deal with them.

"But there's no law against their being here, and they just might not be the ones I suspect. Their story's full of holes, but I'd want to be sure. What I don't want is for them to pull something like that around here. Now, I'm going up to that little hollow you told me about, and if you and maybe a couple more men could keep an eye on those men till I get back, maybe we can keep that from happening. I'd planned to stay over there, make camp, but I guess I'll come on before night. I don't think they'll try anything in broad daylight."

"S'spect yer right on that. Thar's n'ole bachelor feller, Daughtry, makes our whiskey, lives jist up yonder, ain't got a lot t'do. He c'n watch 'thout nobody catchin' on. An' I'll jist ride on down little later, natural like, m'self. Meet you back here jist b'fore dark, then."

Stephen rode away with some misgivings. If those were the robbers, or any robbers, there was so little here to tempt them it should be safe. But perhaps they thought the missionaries had money to finance their venture. He couldn't see the cousins trying to rob the whole encampment, but then they'd be divided at night. And yes, with the women and children unprotected, and out of hearing of the others. He envisioned an attack on the women, on those young wives.

On Anna Compton.

Surely these God-fearing people, especially the women, wouldn't be armed and ready, given who they were. And the robbers would know that.

Stephen resolved to return early, just to be prepared. And his already-closeness to the miller told him that man could and would handle any violence in his village. He felt Ketchum could be depended on.

And this bright day belied any evil, with just the first leaves turning after a cool night. The trail wound upcreek a mile, where the rough side hollow showed as just a blind little draw up the mountainside. A small stream trickled among giant boulders, and there appeared no way up. But riding past this, Stephen found an old game trail leading back the wrong way, but upward. He followed this and found that it switched back some distance up the hollow itself.

Here the dim trail branched, and he followed it back and up still farther, around a bulge in the wall of the mountain.

This was heavy timber, and high above the main trail and creek. But as he rode, leading the packhorse, a narrow bench widened, the trail curved out of sight from below, and a meadow opened, boggy with seeping springs and lush grass. He guessed there was bedrock beneath the thin layer of soil that could not support trees.

He dismounted, and let both horses graze. They'd had nothing but grain for days in this sparsely cleared land of steep slopes and narrow ravines, and went at the tall grass eagerly. He took his rifle and scouted the hollow on foot, finding it wound behind what had appeared to be the back bluff wall, to open again into another meadow. This area was out of any north wind, sheltered but sunny, a pleasant, hidden retreat of maybe five acres. There was good building stone broken from ledges above, and plenty of good timber, second-growth from that fire, so not all of it huge. Cabin material, for certain.

He found the source of the small stream at a spring coming from a split in a sheer bluff face. Just off to the side was a more or less level bench that would do nicely for a cabin site. He continued around the back of the hollow, keeping to the edge of the meadow, finding it not as steep as he'd imagined. Eventually he reached his horses again, concluding that this was perhaps the perfect site for a hermit to hide himself in. Whether a woman—Anna—would like it was another question.

The settlement would grow, he was sure of it, here at the end of the road. A tavern soon, to join the mill and the new church, and more people. Only a mile out was really just next door. And while this would never make a farm, a small corn patch, room for some vegetables, well-watered, could be created. Yes, this would be the Davis homestead, he decided, his base for the near future, while he cleared things up with Miss Anna.

~ * ~

"Y'say he's gone?" Shelby MacNaughton wasn't sure he'd heard right. Yes, Belle Ketchum repeated, Stephen Davis had ridden out early, taking his packhorse with him. She didn't bother to explain that he'd be back that evening, wanting to see the reaction from these scruffy questioners. She had them pegged as derelicts, probably dangerous, and wanted them gone, too.

Now she watched both men, who exchanged worried glances, nods, before turning and riding off toward their camp again. They'd evidently had some plans that included Stephen, and she was glad her partial information seemed to have prevented whatever they'd been. That tall young man was likable from the first, and these men weren't. She went back to her quilt piecing, rocking in the worn hickory chair on the mill porch.

"Now, don't git yerse'f all riled, Shelby," his cousin advised. "This don't change a thaing. We'll jist g'on 'th our plan up at th' wimmen's cabin t'night, then light out after Davis, ride hard. Shore t'ketch up 'th him soon, an' he'll be easier to hit out in th' woods than here around folks. An' that'll put us on past ennybody comin' after us."

"Wal, then. Mebbe us gittin' a little drunk an' losin' a couple days wasn't so bad, after all. I'se some worried ennyways, tryin' t'do it all right chere under ever'body's nose. Yeah, reckon yer right, Caleb. Y'allus was better at figgerin' thaings than me. An' I've 'bout stood it long's I kin 'thout no woman. Git caught up quick, though, I reckon, git my hands on that long tall 'un. Allus liked a woman'd put up a little fight, an' reckon she will. Git t'enjoyin' it, though, an' she'll prob'ly be right good."

The cousins failed to note the old settler Daughtry slipping through the woods far behind them, and wouldn't have been worried if they had.

~ * ~

This was Saturday, Anna noted. A good week's work, with the new cabin done and plans laid for beginning the church building. Time now to prepare for the morning's service, with her teaching the children. Elder Driscoll would be in overall charge, and she'd join the others in hymn-singing before the sermon, taking her small charges down by the creek for their Bible lesson afterwards. The other women were glad for her role, since it gave them a respite from the constant demands of the little ones.

She loved children, and had actually enjoyed helping raise her younger brothers and sister back in Virginia. Most of the time, at least. That she might never have any of her own had concerned her often, in this role of spinster she'd chosen. She tried not to think about that, instead accepting, or trying hard to, the fact that she could enjoy more of them this way. Yes, and for longer, as more younger ones came under her care.

The bright day wore on, with all the women catching up on household chores neglected during the rush of cabin-building the days before. Anna reflected that this would have been market day back home, although their farm had been many miles from the nearest village. A day for hauling grain to the mill on Buck Mountain Creek, a day for a visit to the blacksmith shop on the Thomas plantation, a day to visit friends.

She must get to know the other settlers here better. The women had come to the first church services hesitantly, bringing their barefoot children to stand and listen feeling, no doubt, totally out of place. She and the others had made a special effort to mingle with them, talk to the shy children, assure them that God welcomed them, no matter how they were dressed.

Of course the missionaries would stress the congregation's looking their best as the church became more organized, and they believed they'd have a positive effect on the whole community. Eventually, they hoped, some of the men other than Mr. Ketchum would join them. *Just a matter of time, surely.*

Late in the day, Anna helped gather the dried wash from the lines, joined the others for supper. Somehow, this catching-up had tired her more than the work of the building. She guessed it was the repetitiveness of the household work, as opposed to the exciting labor of creating new shelter from the primitive woods. She liked being a pioneer, turning her capable hands to shaping wood, seeing the results.

That got her to thinking of Stephen Davis again, the consummate woodworker. And the little portable cherrywood sewing cabinet he'd made for her two years before. She'd been so embarrassed by the unexpected gift, she'd insisted on trading him and Tom a pair of pigs for it. Her mother had believed Stephen was courting her, but she'd known by then that was not to be. But she cherished the gift nonetheless, and it was among the few possessions she'd brought West with her in the crowded wagons.

She had by now reached a place in her mind from which she could continue her duties efficiently, having put Stephen securely out of the forefront of her life. Things would work themselves out, if she trusted in God, which she did. Or if they didn't, that could well be God's will, too. Not to trouble herself, either way.

If only she could truly accept that.

Anna Compton had no way of knowing she was to be the planned victim of a sadistic beating and rape that very night. Neither did Sissy Blair, the pretty young wife of Herbert Blair. The two were eager in their missionary work, seeing it as their life's calling, with many years of God's service ahead of them.

Sissy was just a little childish at nineteen, giggly, but completely good-hearted, and devoted to her young husband. Even here in this wilderness, she believed completely that nothing would, or could ever, mar their happiness.

The men had come for supper also, and the married couples managed to stroll off into the gathering darkness for some time together before parting for the night. Anna kept the children at games in the cabin, alone with them, hearing the occasional voice from outside. She was grateful that this group housing arrangement would be for only a little longer. High time the families had their own spaces again, and she hers.

~ * ~

"Them boys is packin' up," Killebrew Ketchum had told Stephen on his return from his exploring. "Belle said they was some disappointed you'd done left, an' they've no doubt got somethin' on thar minds. Don't see 'em leavin' in th' dark, though, bad's th' trail is up th' mountin. Ole Daughtry, he didn't see nothin' unusual, but when I slipped down t'have a look-see, thar they was, gittin' th' camp broke. What you make of it?"

"Been my experience you can't ever let yourself underestimate the enemy, Killy, and that's what we have to think these men are. No, they shouldn't try the trail at night, unless there's a strong reason to." He thought a moment. "And what could that reason be, do you think?" He squinted at the older man, a thought solidifying in his mind.

"'Cept fer robbin' somebody here, don't make sense. Now, Belle 'n me, we'd be th' likely ones. Daughtry an' th' others, they ain't got a thing, and I 'spect they know that. But...say, y'don't s'pose they think th' church folks has money, do you? Reckon that's why they been hangin' 'round this long?"

"I was thinking that, myself. But here's a worse thought: they know the women are off in the other hollow—everybody does—with no men near to protect them. I wouldn't put it past those two to try to get to the women, just before they run on out.

"The women won't have a lookout, and there's probably not a one ready to fight, with the possible exception of Anna Compton. I know she's seen some violence in her old community, and she didn't flinch. But men like that'd figure on easy takings, I'm afraid."

"By God, yer right! Been tryin' t'figger what they're up to, an' that'd fit. So what'll we do?"

"I'll leave my horses up at Daughtry's, slip on down and follow them, no matter which way they go. If it's on out of the country, so much the better. If they plan to rob you or the missionaries or worse, I can handle them."

"Y'ain't goin' by yerself, Stephen. Me'n Belle, we feel sorta responsible fer folks here, knowin' 'em all since they come, y'see. I'll jist go with you. Ain't a bad shot, m'self."

Stephen did not relish the idea of more killing. The two robbers he'd had to shoot back beyond Saltville still weighed on his mind, as did every one of the others from his past. But then he thought of the wounded Archie Nolan, whose young partner Jamie lay in his grave, and his resolve hardened. More so when he momentarily envisioned one of the outlaws with his dirty hands on Anna Compton.

~ * ~

Anna lay on her pallet, with two of the little girls close by. The day, despite her resolve to let things work out, hadn't been easy. And now sleep didn't seem to want to come. The sounds subsided around her, the restless movements of bodies settling for sleep, the deep breathing, little sounds of tired women and children.

She was aware of a sort of responsibility she'd taken on for these in this cabin. The other women were older, with the exception of young Sissy Blair, but none seemed concerned for the fact that they were unguarded here, secure in the belief that as God's children, no harm would come to them. But at twenty-three, Anna had seen enough of human evil to know that men did not always play by the rules. There'd been the men who'd gone after Stephen back on the creek in Virginia, when he'd done absolutely nothing to provoke it.

And she'd had no sympathy for weak Abby Thomas, horrified by the sight of the blood of her attacker. Or perhaps the girl had just used that excuse to draw away from Stephen, having already met that dashing minister. Whatever, she'd been too much like other women who couldn't handle the harsh realities of pioneer life. Anna knew blood must flow sometimes, despite one's best intentions.

She supposed she had a long way to go toward the ideal of turning the other cheek. She certainly wouldn't turn hers if some attacker threatened these children, these other women.

Which was why she kept the pistol her father had pressed upon her at her leaving those weeks ago. Primed and powder dry, it was within reach under her blanket, where it lay every night. Some of the other women had clucked their disapproval, but she ignored them. She was who she was, and that included being a woman who'd fight, if and when the situation demanded. So far it hadn't, and yes, maybe it wouldn't.

Still...

The sound was of a small branch cracking underfoot outside. She eased to a sitting position, her hand on the pistol, listening for more. Nothing came. She rose quietly, moved to the shutter, open now that it was past mosquito season. No moon illuminated the space around the cabin, but the stars were bright. She thought she saw the shape of a man, motionless after that sound. She focused a little to one side to clear the image.

A man and carrying something. As she watched, pistol ready, he knelt, fumbling. Sparks flew from flint and steel and a small flame sprang from a tinder box. He lighted a splintered pine torch as she moved to slide the wooden bars across both the doors. As she turned back, she didn't see or hear the second man at the open back window, easing himself into the room.

As the flare of the torch lighted the outdoors, sending weak shafts of light into the cabin, she saw the tall figure of Stephen Davis beyond the first man, gun drawn.

"Turn around slow, MacNaughton," he commanded in a low but deadly voice. "Killy, you go around to the back, get the other one." The miller moved quickly.

But the man with the torch tossed it away, whirling, drawing his own pistol. Stephen shot him, the gun flaming, roaring, the man dropping like a sack. Then, inside, someone grabbed Anna from behind, twisting her toward the back window. He hadn't seen her gun, and she held onto it desperately, feeling the prickle of the man's whiskers, smelling his foul breath. If she could just twist free...but he held her arms immobile, pushing her toward the back door.

The room was suddenly chaos, with women screaming, children crying, bodies everywhere in the dim, flickering light from the torch out on the ground. The man let go with one hand, reached past her for the door bar, slid it open. Anna wrenched free, jammed the pistol into his stomach and pulled the trigger. The gun bucked in her hand, the sound deafening, and the man staggered backwards, trying to hold against the blood gushing from his front.

"Bitch," he snarled, and fumbled for his own gun. In that instant Killebrew Ketchum slammed the butt of his rifle into the back of the man's head, and he went down.

"Bring th' torch, Stephen!" he called. Anna, blood on her from the dying man, stepped to the front door, opened it. "Now, you ladies jist calm down," the miller soothed. "We got ever'thing under control. Jest you stay still now, an' we'll clean this mess up proper." The women cringed, holding their children, whether from fear or numb obedience, he wasn't sure.

Stephen brought the torch in. Anna threw wood shavings on the fireplace embers, and the flames lit the scene further. Ketchum dragged the dead outlaw out the back door while Anna worked at quieting the women and children. Stephen saw the blood on her.

"My God, Anna, are you all right?" He held the torch close, anxiously searching.

"It's not my blood, Stephen," she told him, strangely calm. "The man had me...I had to shoot him."

"I know. We weren't fast enough. But you're sure you're all right?" He was starting to brush at the blood on the front of her nightgown, then realized what that might look like, and hastily drew his hand away. "Oh, I didn't mean to...sorry..."

"It's all right, Stephen. And so am I. I saw what happened out front and didn't hear the other one come in the back till he grabbed me. Who were they?"

"The two men camped on the creek who'd robbed and killed one man, wounded another back on the road a few days ago. I got the other victim to a cabin where he's recovering. Suspected these two, but no proof. Learned they'd packed up to leave tonight, so knew they planned something. Ketchum and I followed them, but evidently not close enough."

"No, you were in time. The other man would have had us; we had only the one shot." She paused a moment. "Now, you men go outside for a bit. I need to get into something not all bloodied, and we'll mop up in here. But don't leave yet, please." She was willing herself to remain calm, although she knew a reaction could set in at any moment.

The two men nodded, filed out. Dragged the bodies farther from the cabin.

"Women all tore up in thar," Ketchum observed. "Don't blame 'em much. Helluva way to wake up, coupla hardcases comin' t'rape 'em. Bad on th' little'uns, too. Miss Anna though, she's a cool one, y'notice?"

"Did. I've known she has steel in her for some time, Killy. Wouldn't many women have the nerve to shoot a man like that. Our society's lied to them about being safe among men."

"Ain't th' time t'bring it up, Stephen, but Belle, she thinks you'n Anna oughta git together." Stephen could almost see the older man wink.

"Don't think I haven't considered that, my friend."

The door opened, and Anna came out.

"Now, you men come in; kettle's on for something to drink. And be assured we're so very grateful for your protection. Stephen, walk with me a moment?"

"Surely. Be right with you, Killy."

Practical Tildy Driscoll seemed to have everything under control inside the house, and the sound of children sniffling had gradually ceased. Stephen and Anna heard the women talking excitedly among themselves until they were out of hearing in the starlight.

"Stephen, I..." Anna didn't know just what to say, but knew she must explain, somehow.

"Don't feel you have to say a thing, Anna. I know why you left home, and why you couldn't allow yourself to be insulted, and...used, I guess, the way I treated you. But you'll remember I was aware of that the last time we met, and promised you I'd prove my love to you. I'll never get over my shame at being blinded by Abby Thomas, when all along you were there. And I'll do everything I can to convince you that you're the right woman for me, no matter how long it takes.

"It'll be my penance, working here, doing whatever I can to help. And no, I don't expect you to welcome me now, if ever. I'll just have to live with that if you continue to reject me. But I won't leave you. I won't try to build a life without you. I've been blind, but my eyes are wide open now, have been for months."

It was a long speech for the taciturn Stephen Davis, whose thoughts turned inward most of the time. He waited to see what she'd say, but suspected he'd said it for both of them.

He was right.

"Stephen, I don't know what to tell you. But I do know I'm so very glad you've come, and not just because you've protected us. But I'm so unsure of you—us. I thought I knew you back in Virginia, then found I didn't. That hurt, but you know that. And you also know I must work this out myself, to see if I can trust you. And myself. But we've always been friends, at least that. So let's just let that grow, if it's meant to. All right?" It was almost a plea, but a controlled, even determined one.

"Dear Anna. No man could deserve you. But know I'll try."

They returned to the cabin, entered, and partook of hot cider with the others. Ketchum threw Stephen a questioning look, which he ignored.

The two took their leave, with Stephen promising to set up camp along the one trail below this cabin.

Eight

Two weeks later, white-haired Archie Nolan rode into the settlement, still stiff and somewhat sore. Stephen had been helping build the rising church that day, a timber-frame structure near the creek and mill. He welcomed the man at the mill, led him to his dead partner's horse and the two packhorses.

"Yep, those're ours, all right. Guess you took care of those men for me, didn't you, Stephen?"

"With some good help, yes. Oh, this is Killebrew Ketchum, the miller and smith. These others are missionaries, putting up a church here."

"I know Mr. Ketchum. Hello, Killebrew. How's Miss Belle?"

"Wal, Archie, glad t'see you. Stephen didn't tell me you was th' one he found all shot up t'other week. Y'back fer more prospectin'?"

"Some, yes. Man I've been in touch with wants to know more about the iron ore I found. Seems he has a lot of backing and wants to see how profitable it'd be to mine hereabouts."

"Seems a bit far f'm ever'thing, but you'd know more 'bout that than us. Oh, here's Belle. Archie's back, girl. Seem's like th' late outlaws we took keer of sorta helt him up some."

Belle Ketchum joined the men, and they walked down to the church site to greet the missionaries. Nolan was impressed with the structure.

"Somebody knows his building business, I'd say," observing the tight mortises, knee braces, timbers.

"That'd be Stephen," Killebrew told him. "He's a reg'lar wizard with wood. Wouldn't doubt he's a better smith an' miller than me, too, but he won't own up to it."

"Y'don't say? You suppose you could maybe build a stamping mill, Stephen? And maybe a smelter?"

"Maybe a mill, but I don't know a thing about smelting ore. So there's iron around here you say, can be mined?"

"There is. And well, we'd need labor too, and a way to get it to market. The distance is a problem, of course, but there's such a demand, th' men with the money will find a way to move it. And this's just one of the locations they're looking at, so we haven't decided anything definite yet."

"Well, back to your question: farther downcreek, after some others join it, there's ample water for a mill of any kind. Not enough to float iron downstream, though...too steep and too many rocky rapids."

Belle and Killebrew Ketchum were visiting with the missionaries, who were stopping work for the day. Each family had claimed land for itself, and both the men and women were clearing, beginning to build, along with work on the church. Belle, of course, had to hear about each project, and spend time with the children, with whom she was a great favorite.

Anna too, kept an eye on the young ones, having to pull one or more out of the creek as necessary, or break up a squabble. Stephen noted the easy way she had with the children, as he had back in Virginia. *Natural mother, as well as able to protect herself,* he observed, and not for the first time.

On that note, the missionaries were somewhat in awe of Anna's having shot her attacker, but to a person, no one felt she'd done wrong. After all, it'd been Killebrew's smashing the man's skull that'd actually killed him. And she hadn't appeared troubled by her act at all. The violence of it all was still with her, but she dismissed it with the realization that there'd been no other way.

I know God will pardon me for helping take a life: His forgiveness is from everlasting to everlasting. And all of us are sinners; all fall short of the glory of God, as the Apostle Paul wrote. Besides, I was protecting the other women and children. With of course, Stephen's and Mr. Ketchum's help. God sent them too, I'm certain of it. He provides, in every situation, for those who believe.

And she'd found that, unlike Abby Thomas, the blood, not unlike that of a butchered hog or steer, hadn't unnerved her at all: a significant difference between them. Another one…

"Where you staying, Stephen?" Nolan asked. "I just camped along th' creek last time, myself."

"I've got a little hollow staked out up the mountain a mile or so. You're welcome to join me there if you like. There's still some grass for the horses there, which you surely know is scarce around these woods. The community will have to clear more land or haul in grain, or both, just to feed the stock."

"Might just do that, then. I'd like your ideas on some aspects of the iron processing. Not many men in this region qualified, since most of it's up at Fort Pitt or all the way to Massachusetts."

"Not my field, but the water power is something I can help with, certainly. Good stone around for a diversion dam, and not hard to locate a forebay, despite the drop. Yes, let's talk more while you're here. By the way, was your partner Jamie a foundryman?"

"He was, and that makes losin' him that much worse. For a valuable specialist like him t'be casually shot down for whatever he might own by scum like those men makes me more'n just mad."

"Well, they'd planned more outrages here, till we stopped them. That sort seem to drift to the frontier, no matter where it is. No law, no organized resistance among new settlers. But that'll change, as this place grows."

"I certainly hope so."

Stephen talked with the men at the church site about the next steps in the building, and what each could do to speed progress, in case he got to the site late. He then tipped his hat to Anna upon leaving, who rewarded him with her gracious smile. He noted that whatever remorse she might have felt at shooting her attacker, she didn't show it. *Woman won't hesitate to do what's necessary, a real pioneer.* And his admiration for her continued to grow.

He and Nolan rode upcreek toward Stephen's claim, talking of the iron ore plans. The money for the venture would come from a group of businessmen and traders in Philadelphia, who aimed to develop this region as a counter to the Fort Pitt interests. They apparently foresaw a future in which iron and steel would be the key to an age of industrialization similar to that in Europe. Iron plows, ship's hardware, cannons and rifles, wagon iron, hand tools, kitchen hardware—all would require more of the black metal as the new country grew.

"As long as the iron industry stays north," Nolan told him, "whoever controls it can set th' prices as high as he wants, and the people will have to pay it, or do without. If we can get some competition going, it'll benefit everybody, from the smallest farmer to the biggest shipbuilder." Stephen couldn't argue with that. He'd known firsthand the shortage of iron and the rare dependable steel in his work back in Goochland and at his woodworking and forging work on Buck Mountain Creek.

But he'd also heard of limited mining and processing up the Jackson River, which flowed into the James well north up toward the Valley and then west. Just how extensive that effort was, he didn't know. Conversation with Nolan revealed it was a one-man-run operation, literally a monopoly in that region, but growing slowly.

It seemed a near-miracle would be necessary to turn this wilderness into a productive source for the needs of the nation, but he knew it was just a matter of sufficient finance. Enough money poured into any venture would yield a return of some size, and the only limitation would be how much that return would profit its investors.

They made camp alongside one of the springs up in Stephen's hidden hollow, and he was glad for the company. Not since leaving Virginia had he been able to talk at length to anyone about more than building, and Nolan was articulate, experienced in business and the affairs of the new country. He liked the man.

For his part, Nolan was discovering that this young fellow was skilled in several areas, all of which could be of benefit to the venture. Given a knowledgeable smelter-foundryman, the three of them could form the core of a sound enterprise. And not incidentally, they could also become the leaders of the region's new settlements, being in on the ground floor, so to speak. The prospect intrigued him.

~ * ~

Anna had watched the two men leave, while also rounding up the children for the walk up to their cabin. Stephen hadn't pressed her at all these several days, and she'd been grateful for that. And she had to admit, some of the knot of resentment was dissolving inside her as he worked among the missionaries, skilled, helpful, polite.

Of course, the entire settlement had already paired them up in their minds: the tall, quiet ex-soldier/craftsman and the one single woman. *As if I had no say in the matter.* But she couldn't resent that, either. They were good people, if a bit nosy, and she was coming to realize that here she really had the best of both situations. That is, she caught herself, if she and Stephen *were* meant to be together.

The revival of the old attraction for him returned, and she realized she was blushing. Fortunately, no one noticed. But well, she'd chosen this life over having a man—the only man she'd ever wanted—and now here he was, so...

Now stop this! We've been over this so many times. But she couldn't begrudge him the occasional appreciative smile when he was obviously trying so hard, and that made her remember: he'd said he always treasured her rare smiles for him.

And now he'd found a location to settle upcreek. She was curious about that place, and wanted to see it in spite of herself. He was surely beginning a house there in the few hours he wasn't here helping. A tiny cabin, like the one he'd had on the other creek? Or would he begin a big house, as he'd done later, when he and Abby Thomas were engaged? Surely not that, yet. No, patient Stephen would put up minimal shelter to get through the winter, keep on helping here, making himself indispensable.

Taking her for granted? Again? She tried to summon anger at that thought, but it wouldn't stay.

"Annie? You're looking up that creek like a statue." Tildy Driscoll's voice cut into her thoughts. "We're most gone already, an' you're standin' there holdin' those young'un's hands like you plan to stay here all night. You feelin' all right?"

"Oh. Yes, I'm fine, thanks. Just thinking...how far we've come on the church, Tildy. We'd planned just the simple shelter, and now we're well on the way to a real sanctuary." She hoped the woman would believe that.

"Thanks to Stephen Davis, girl. None of our men are that good at buildin'." Then she glanced shrewdly into Anna's face. "Just how well did you know him back home?"

"Oh, he and my father traded. He came to our church some, with his friend, the slave he'd rescued, set free. He was...actually, engaged to another girl at the time, Tildy. Just a friend of the family, I guess you'd say."

"Well, whatever happened back there, he's here now, and thank the Lord for it. I won't pry into your affairs, Annie, but he seems a fine young man, and..."

"You're right, we've let the others go on ahead," she interrupted. "Come, children, we must be going. No time for daydreaming." And she hurried them along. Tildy Driscoll smiled...she knew there was more to this than the girl let on.

Busy at the evening chores, Anna let her thoughts return to the little hollow Stephen had mentioned as his homesite. He'd be camped there with the man Nolan, no doubt deep in speculation about the iron ore plans. He'd said there was grass there, rare in these woods. Surely a good spring, and yes, he'd build close to the water. She saw again her man—no, not *her* man—swinging the heavy broadaxe almost effortlessly, hewing the timbers for the church. And fitting the curved knee braces exactly, boring the auger holes, driving the pegs she and the other women had cut of the seasoned locust so they wouldn't shrink and loosen.

She'd stolen glances at him often, she realized, and wondered if the others had noticed. Probably had, the way they seemed to want to push the two of them together. *Well, not till I'm ready—no, not unless I'm ready. No, put that thought away, now.* But another thought took its place: she'd speculated about a little cabin of her own, somewhere near, hadn't she? And two people in two little separate hovels...no, that must be Tildy Driscoll putting that idea in her head.

But if she'd admit it, the prospect of working day after day beside Stephen Davis on a home of their own was intriguing.

Not that it'd ever happen.

~ * ~

A lawyer named Samuel Eddins emerged from the courthouse in Charlottesville, Virginia, into the sunlight of fall. He had been detained for many weeks while the legal system tried to build a case against him for the murder of his client, Dr. Horace Weston. He had apparently been the last person to see the doctor alive, but had not killed him. On the contrary, Eddins had actually been a part of Weston's circle of illegal activities operating in Virginia to invest much of the stolen money that came from the Cabot group in Philadelphia.

Eddins had been the prosecutor against Stephen Davis in an aborted attempt to convict him and recover the money Jacob Hayes had carried west with him. Now, stripped of his position as Commonwealth's Attorney, but retaining his license to practice law, the man was again free. Only the hearsay dying word of one of the band, at the hand of Davis, had implicated him in the affair, and no corroborating evidence had ever been discovered.

And there was his ironclad alibi, that he had left the doctor's house while the man was still alive and well, had been witnessed by enough people at the plantation house and at a nearby tavern, to result in that murder charge having been dropped. But not until a suspicious Judge Amos Edgerton had pursued it to its end.

Eddins had heard that the entire band had been killed or had fled the country, and he felt that he must not stay in the area in case additional information came to light. So he'd go to Cabot and see how he could fit in with whatever else the man's group might have planned. With his legal standing, he was sure there'd be a place for him.

So it was that he journeyed to the capital city and met with Cabot at the man's carriage-building establishment office.

"Glad to see you free again, Eddins. Nasty business, losing Weston and the whole operation."

"Yes. We underestimated Stephen Davis and his friends. I'm afraid we were swayed by both Weston's and Rawlins Butler's emotional attachments to the case."

"I knew of the doctor's vendetta, but Butler? How so?"

"Oh, he was pursuing the same young woman as Davis and apparently lost his suit. Clouded his judgment, and I'm afraid that influenced us unduly also."

"I see. But we've heard nothing of Davis since or, for that matter, from the man we sent after him. What have you learned of him?"

"Well, word is that Davis has left the country. And it would seem that your man Ames confronted a friend of his at Weston's plantation and was killed."

"Really? Ames was good. Who was this friend?"

"Army comrade of Davis' named Ned Drake. Testified at Davis' trial, which we unfortunately lost. Married the doctor's widow, now owns the Caroline County place."

"And he obviously beat Ames, dangerous man. And so we've lost him, as well as Dinkins and his wife, our other assassins. I'm afraid that section of Virginia has become too hot for us, Eddins." Cabot felt he'd been more than justified in abandoning any idea of reviving operations there.

"I agree. So I'm here at your service, sir. Whatever legal aspects of your other operations I can assist with, I stand ready."

"Yes, and there is something we've begun looking into that will require deeds, corporate work, other legalities. It'll be technically in Kentucky, but of course that's a territory of Virginia, so you'd be the logical man to handle that work. What do you know of the area south and west of where Hayes was setting up plantations?"

"Very little. Poor country, full of mountains. Hayes had searched out the good river valleys for our investments, and the land gets rougher on past there."

"Precisely. But that rough country is full of iron ore, it seems. I've connections to prospectors there, and the others and I agree that we should explore possibilities, with an eye to establishing a virtual monopoly on the industry in that region to rival Fort Pitt's." He sat back to watch the lawyer's reaction.

"Iron. Yes, there's no doubt the demand will increase, now that westward expansion is a fact. But the distances...what about transportation?"

"That is the major hurdle, admittedly. The best concentrations seem to be beyond the navigable rivers, so I've engaged engineers to work on just that problem. And you'd be amazed at their suggestions, Eddins. There are some quite good minds at work here, now that England no longer has our hands tied."

"Really? I suppose we could blast roads down out of the mountains, to the heads of navigation by bateaux. Is that their suggestion?"

"Not really. You may not know this, but the iron mines and smelters at Fort Pitt and in Massachusetts utilize hand cars on rails to transport their ore and processed iron. Limited distances, of course, but the engineers see no reason these rails could not be extended, the cars pulled by mules, as in canal traffic, to any necessary destinations."

"Down out of those steep mountains? I'd say that would be a monstrous feat."

"Well, several interests are negotiating with French black powder manufacturers for their canal operations, and their superior explosives have proven themselves. You'll recall how undependable our own product was during the war: no two kegs alike, too many misfires." Cabot led the lawyer to a map of southwestern Virginia, including the eastern reaches of the Kentucky territory.

"Here's where our contact Nolan has discovered rich deposits. There's a spot at the end of a wretched road, where the mountains west of there are a real barrier. But that very road can be widened, a grade established, he tells me, for either a usable highroad, or even the installation of rails."

"But rails? That would require a great deal of iron, would it not?"

"Exactly. So the initial output of the foundries would be for those very rails. They spike them upon rot-resistant timbers on a crushed stone bed, and they're very stable.

"But here's the best part, Eddins: our iron ingots would be transported almost all the way, *downhill.* The natural law of gravity is with us on this venture. The mules would be necessary only on those stretches where it's impossible to establish the desired grade. Our operating costs, once the rails are in place, would be minuscule." Again the carriage-maker leaned back in his chair, triumph on his face.

Eddins thought about this venture. There'd be a limitless volume of deed work, rights-of-way documents, operating agreements. A veritable gold mine of legalities, even if the plan ultimately failed. He couldn't lose here.

"Excellent venture, sir. How far along is it?"

"Not far enough. I've heard back from Nolan that his smelter operator was killed in a robbery, and we must find another to send. The plan is to employ local labor to dig the initial ore. We'll construct a small smelting plant to see the quality and get a better idea of the potential before we invest in a mill or the rail plan, or failing that, a better system of roads for transport. We'll also need a foundry operation, but that too, can start small. There are limited such operations at Richmond, where we found Nolan's man, and we feel we can locate other talent there or at Fort Pitt.

"We see this as perhaps the greatest opportunity of the century, Eddins. Despite the initial difficulties, we can supply the needs of this new country, and of course, become rich in the process. What do you think?"

"I think, sir, that you have, as usual, found the ideal venture for our interests. And as I stated, I'm ready to serve in whatever capacity required." The lawyer was thinking that, as a member of the core group, he would surely profit greatly, and ride the crest of the inevitable industrial wave that would follow. Then a new thought intruded.

"But surely others have begun to prospect into this country; it can't have remained completely undiscovered." Settlers had after all been trickling into the western regions for two generations.

"There's only one small operation which I plan to visit. I'm told only one man's the head of it, and given the same difficulties we'll encounter, I'm certain we can buy him out. And of course, that production will give us a leg up on the operation, so to speak."

Eddins nodded. *And be well away from the searching eyes and ears of that bloodhound, Judge Amos Edgerton, as well as the innocuous-appearing but deadly Ned Drake. New country, new opportunities, relative lawlessness.* Except, of course for his own brand of law.

~ * ~

Archie Nolan led Stephen downcreek a short mile from the settlement to his prospecting site of a few months earlier. The fresh soil was reddish in color, and the rocks, curiously heavy, also bore that hue.

"Iron, and I'd say a good quality," he pronounced. "And I've scouted across that ridge, where we can join the road without going back to the mill. Is there enough water here, you think, for power?"

"No, but you probably know there's another creek beyond that next slope. Let's ride that way and I'll show you a damsite." They guided their horses along the narrow bench alongside the creek, still low before the fall rains. Sure enough, the even larger one merged with Troublesome, fed by springs and melting snow from the high mountains above. And here also was a narrow rapids with low, rocky bluffs on both sides.

"Dam site here...anchor the stone where the sides narrow, in a concave shape, a horizontal arch, for strength. Close-fitted stones, there'd be minimal leakage. Cut a millrace into the stone face from the forebay, feed an overshot wheel for maximum power. You said the primary work would be a trip-hammer to knead and process the hot melt? If the smelter is close, that should be no problem, given this location."

"Excellent. I took samples from this entire area, and I'm convinced there's sufficient ore for the operation. And of course, we'll expand later, following the veins of iron. This has washed down off the slopes, so we can also begin tunnels into the hillsides to extract as much as possible close by."

Both men could envision a network of rails and handcars bringing the ore to the top of the stone smelter, thence to the mill itself. After that, the ingots would be loaded onto wagons for the trip to the headwaters of the major streams. Although that would be a formidable distance, it was an exciting prospect, one wholly removed from the hunting and limited farming possible in this remote wilderness.

Nine

With fall well advanced, the settlers at Ketchum's Mill realized the need for a contingent to travel back to Virginia for supplies, not the least of which must be feed for the livestock. No hay had been harvested from the meager fields, and only limited grain. With the framework of the new church up and ready for roofing and siding, Stephen knew the settlers could finish it without him. So he and the other ex-soldiers Harvey Campbell and one-armed Todd Epsworth agreed to take three wagons for the trip. They'd also lead several more of the horses for sale, since they couldn't feed them through the winter.

Stephen had no illusions about returning to the Saltville area, even unaware as he was that relatives of the slain robbers were there. It was an outpost, the beginning of the wilderness, and it was quite clear that outlaws hid among the steep hills near there, preying on travelers. The wagons loaded with provisions would be a tempting target, and he aimed to defend them forcefully if necessary.

They left on a fine autumn morning at daylight, with frost on the carpet of fallen leaves. The horses were a bit lean, but the empty wagons were no load, so they made good time. They'd spend a few days in the farming valleys near Saltville gathering grain and what odd pieces of iron they could find for the smithy so they and their teams would be fresh for the return trip.

Archie Nolan had sent letters with them to be posted to his contacts in Philadelphia, telling further of the prospects here, and the need for a smelter builder and operator if the new venture were at least to make a start anytime soon. He was anxious, but had little expectation that his backers could move that fast. This far out, even their considerable money would have its limitations. Still, he'd continue to dig, analyze, and prepare the way.

Stephen stopped briefly at the O'Neil homestead to report that Nolan was well and settled at Ketchum's Mill. Again the giant George Wellerby told him he wanted to travel west, and it was agreed he'd join them on their return.

"I'll find me sumthin' t'keep me eatin'," he assured the travelers, "even if't ain't nothin' this winter but puddin' an' wind." Stephen was certain the settlers would welcome the help of this man and see to it that he had food and shelter.

Eventually reaching Saltville, they inquired at the same prosperous inn Stephen had stopped at those weeks before. Who among the valley farmers would have grain to sell? And of course, salt, leather, and perhaps cloth.

The innkeeper directed them to a newly-opened store that might or might not have woven cloth, and mentioned several established farmers who would welcome the sale of produce.

A knot of idlers noted the travelers, and heard of their quest. Among them were two of the ubiquitous MacNaughton clan, ever on the lookout for victims. These reasoned that travelers seeking supplies would no doubt be carrying money to pay for them and resolved to watch for an opportunity to rob them.

Stephen had also noted this pair who were faintly familiar in appearance. But more obvious was their studied indifference to the new arrivals, while managing to stay close. He mentioned the men to Campbell and Epsworth, who nodded in agreement, eyeing the two. It'd do to watch them, they affirmed, heading their wagons toward the nearest of the large farms.

There they negotiated for grain and salted hams. At another farm they found more grain and potatoes. Eventually they returned to the village store, where they noticed the same two men loitering near. Stephen posted Epsworth at the door to keep an eye on the wagons while he and Campbell looked over the goods inside.

There was a limited supply of cloth all the way from the New England mills. It was expensive, but Stephen wanted the women, especially Anna, to have some of it. He knew from growing up with his two sisters how this fabric was treasured. More so when it was beyond reach. They also bought spices and a few cooking utensils. There was leather too, from a tannery farther up in the Shenandoah Valley.

Iron would be scarcer, they knew, since every farmer and hunter and settler needed horseshoes, harness hardware, plow points, nails and a hundred other items. But here there was a surprise. It seemed that further up the valley, west up the James River, those iron deposits Nolan knew of had been discovered, a few smelters built, and a limited supply was available. Again for a steep price, they noted.

Well. The name Clifton Forge was mentioned and other locations. Stephen would certainly talk this over more with the prospector. Meanwhile, they bought a few pieces, per the smith Ketchum's order.

Stephen wanted to stay at the inn that night, partly to guard against attack by any robbers after their loaded wagons. Another reason was to learn whatever news they could of the doings of the new nation, always of interest to remote settlers.

The money for their purchases had come partly from the missionaries, Ketchum, and from Stephen's own pockets, as well as from the sale of the extra horses. Unfortunately, the lean animals hadn't brought a good price.

They'd spent more than he'd anticipated, but realized the law of supply and demand was at work here, and there was no help for it. Soon enough, he imagined, the settlers back at the mill would expand their steep fields and be able to produce more of the necessities themselves. One man among them had begun terracing to hold the steep soil, something he'd learned from his native Italy, and others would do that also.

Whether their iron venture would succeed or not, he knew the settlement would expand to a point at which the effort could survive, then sustain itself at that locally-needed level. Off the main roads, Ketchum's Mill on Troublesome Creek would probably not become a trade center unless that iron industry did indeed prosper.

And he began to feel there might be something awry about the whole plan. If the Clifton Forge iron had to be this expensive, no doubt because of its remoteness, that would be more so from Ketchum's.

Well, not his concern. If Nolan and his backers wanted a mill built, he could do that. If the venture fell flat, no harm done, as long as he and the laborers got paid. He resolved to make sure that if things did go forward, everyone would be paid as the work progressed. No promises, no being put off.

The men took turns watching their wagons at the inn that night in two-hour shifts. Stephen doubted that anybody would try to raid them at such a public place, but he was taking no chances. And indeed, when he turned the watch over to Stephen, Campbell reported seeing the two loiterers moving among the horses around midnight.

There was no moon that night, and an overcast cut visibility almost completely. Stephen concealed himself beneath one of the wagons, where he could dimly see the horses in the corral against the slightly lighter skyline. He had his rifle, two pistols, and a long knife. Confident he could raise help from the inn, he was not overly worried, but one never knew. A quick attack and escape by a band of robbers could succeed before others came.

Epsworth relieved Stephen well before dawn, with no disturbance noted. Then at good daylight, the three gathered inside for food. The innkeeper spoke to Stephen.

"Been thinkin' I remembered you from somewheres," he began. "You was through here some weeks back, got provisions."

"That's right. Heading on to Kentucky."

"Reason I remembered, there was some of th' MacNaughton bunch in, next day. They're a no-good clan, hide out in th' hills around. Askin' did anybody know about a couple of 'em gittin' killed up th' highroad. Figgered it'uz a bunch, since t'was that devil Ansted MacNaughton was one got shot. Him an' Luke Kelly, was about as bad. Told 'em you was th' only one not from here through that night either way. Hoped they didn't make nothin' outta that, but it got t'worryin' me." The man's eyes asked the question.

"No, I've no idea who you mean. I rode on with no trouble. These men are part of the missionary group who came through a few days before that I asked you about, and they're settled in now, on west. We've been fortunate to be left in peace."

Both Campbell and Epsworth glanced at Stephen. They'd recognized the name MacNaughton. But at a nudge from his boot, he managed to convey to them the need to keep quiet.

Afterwards, still gathering supplies, they questioned him.

"No need to get that bunch after us again," he told them. "They're probably missing those two we had to take care of, along with whoever else they've lost. Men like that don't ever forget what they see as a wrong. We don't need that kind of attention."

The former soldiers nodded in agreement. They both suspected that Stephen had been involved in the first killings, no doubt in self-defense, but they knew firsthand of violence, whether in warfare or on the frontier. They were somewhat concerned that this man who'd joined them was evidently a skilled warrior, however.

But just as both of them had found forgiveness and security in their faith, they reasoned that Stephen was on that same journey, and theirs was not to question. That he had saved the women and children at the cabin from the outlaws was enough.

~ * ~

"Thar ain't nuthin' but some of them mission'ries," the MacNaughton men had reported to old Abner, their clan leader, the night before. "Be easier'n fallin' offa a log t' rob 'em."

"Shoulda done it 'fore they spent thar money. But yeah, we c'n use ever'thaing we c'n git, winter comin' on. How many y'reckon y'd need, boys?"

The two were brothers named Paul and Silas, from their mother's dimly-remembered childhood church experience. They resembled most of the rest of the clan, with black hair, sallow skin and the blue eyes of some of the transplanted Scots and Black Irish who'd settled in these mountains. They hunted, worked a little when it was unavoidable, and were becoming more adept at robbing the travelers on this main road south and west.

"Don't reckon we'll need but one more," Silas averred. "One of 'em ain't got but one arm. Easy 'nuff t'lay up fer 'em, git th' drop on 'em, leave 'em afoot, then jist take off with th' wagons an' our hosses, on back here. Three wagons, three of us." He punctuated his statement with a stream of tobacco juice.

"Sounds right. But we done lost ourselves four good men here recent, y'know. Dunno if we'll ever hear tell of Shelby an' Caleb." The old man had some misgivings.

"Oh, they'll turn up agin, like as not 'fore winter. Don't reckon they's found who done in Ansted an' Luke, but they'll be back."

"Wal, whyn't y'take little Carver, since y'don't need nuthin' but 'nother wagon driver. He's all hot t'git in on ennythaing he kin."

"He ain't but what, fourteen? A mite young, Ab."

"T'drive a wagon? You two kin keep 'n eye on him, keep him outta trouble. Reckon his ma'll worry, but he's gonna slip off, git hisself in trouble ennyways iff'n we don't take him out some."

It was decided that the MacNaughtons, who had by then found out which way the three wagons would go, would leave ahead of them, then ambush them far enough along the way that they'd be beyond detection. Young Carver was excited at the prospect, even though his mother absolutely refused to let him have a rifle.

"Boy'll git hisself kilt," she stated, with arms crossed in defiance of the men.

"Oh, all right, Ma," Silas agreed. "Won't be no danger, way we got it all planned out. He'll be safe 'nuff, with us."

They left before dawn, the frost heavy on the ground, and rode past Saltville just as the first light was coming up. Young Carver had managed to steal a pistol from a hiding place, concealing it under his coat.

"We'll go on a fur piece," Silas told them. "Case thar's shootin', folks'd hear an' might come runnin' in on us. Right big farm on out, whar two creeks comes t'gether. On past that, ain't nuthin' fer a stretch."

On they rode, confident that the missionaries would drive their laden wagons right into their trap, and they'd become that much richer. With the horse sales they'd seen, they felt their quarry still had money, and that, with the supplies and their wagon horses, would be a good haul.

Stephen and the others had, however, arranged for pasture and hay for the teams for two more days before starting out. They'd stay on at the inn and eat and sleep well, with the hardships of camping ahead of them on the road.

The MacNaughtons passed the Theodore Baker farm Stephen had stayed at and set up their position well beyond, only to wait out the entire day. One party of five hunters rode past, but the robbers let them alone. Hunters rarely had money, and that was too many guns to face.

They were forced to camp in the cold that night, having brought little in the way of provisions and no shelter.

"Reckon they's took 'nother way?" Carver asked. He didn't want to doubt his brothers' information, but something wasn't working out here.

"Naw, they's prob'ly jist goin' after some wimmen er somethin', stayin' over 'nother night," Silas guessed.

"Mebbe gittin' drunk?" Paul speculated.

"Mission'ries? Wouldn't thaink so, but off away frum th' others thisaway, could be. I ain't likin' this bein' out in th' weather, though. Looks lak t'might rain 'fore mornin'."

And it did. A slow drizzle began at midnight, and continued past dawn, while the three shivered around a sputtering campfire. They were wet to the bone, frustrated, cold. And angry at their targets for not showing up the way they should have.

"Might jist oughta shoot 'em all, fust off," grumbled Silas. "Be quicker that way, an' no danger one of 'em might git off a shot."

"Wal, jist you keep yer powder dry, best y'can, an' ain't nuthin' fer us but t'wait 'em out. They'd oughta be 'long 'fore dark. Y'wanta try t'shoot us a rabbit er somethin' t'eat? I'm that hongry."

"Try, I reckon. Mebbe a couple squirrels, ennyway. Whyn't you keep watch, an' Carver'n me, we'll see whut we c'n git us. We'll shorely be back 'fore ennybody comes 'long."

The two took the rifles and began to still-hunt. Their boots made no sound on the soaked leaves, and some distance from the campfire they spotted two squirrels playing tag up a big chestnut tree. Others scampered around, finding the fallen nuts in their split-apart burrs on the ground.

Carver loved squirrel hunting. And he was a good shot. Both hunters bagged their targets, sending the rest scurrying up trees out of sight, while they reloaded. But this time the dampness got into their priming pans, and their next attempts were misfires. Cursing, Paul tried to wipe his pan dry, but moisture condensed on it almost immediately.

"Reckon thet's it, then, boy. Two ain't much, but it's moren' we had. Let's us go on back, now. Hope Silas's kep' th' rest of th' powder dry."

Their brother had, setting his pistols close to the fire so the heat would keep them dry. Dangerous, that, if he got it too close, but sheltered under a piece of canvas, the weapons had fared well enough. The others set the rifles close also, and proceeded to skin and clean the squirrels.

"All we c'd git, powder gittin' wet an' all. Reckon it's gotta do us," Paul told his brother. They spitted the meat on sharp sticks and roasted it, at least partially, before gnawing at it.

The rain slacked, then stopped in midafternoon, and the three re-primed the rifles and pistols. Carter showed them the one he'd smuggled, and the others grinned.

"Knew you'd do somethin' lak that, boy. Won't need it, 'less we git into a fight, but we got it figgered not to, way we got th' drop on 'em."

Meanwhile, Stephen, Harvey Campbell and Todd Epsworth explored the village of Saltville further, learning what they could of the outside world, the availability of supplies, generally letting their horses rest and feed. Then they spent another night at the inn, one man again keeping watch over their wagons and horses. There were no incidents, however, so at dawn of the next day they set out on the long road to Ketchum's Mill.

That meant another cold, damp night out for the MacNaughtons, who by that time were less sure they were on the right road. They were tired, hungry, cold, and still wet. An impromptu council ensued, at which they decided this just wasn't going to work out. So they began the ride homeward, empty-handed.

Stephen hadn't forgotten the two older brothers, and since there'd been no attempt at robbery at the village, he concluded that an ambush was highly possible. He reasoned that such an attempt would be beyond the nearby farms but kept his eyes keen and his weapons near anyway.

The miles passed, and they were nearing the Baker farm. Since they hadn't stopped on the way in, Stephen decided to spend a few minutes in a visit this time when they reached the place.

So it was that the three wagons topped a rise to confront directly the two older MacNaughtons, whom they recognized immediately. With them was a younger boy, and the three stopped at sight of the wagons, mouths open in surprise.

Stephen didn't hesitate. He drew both his pistols, telling both his companions to do the same.

"Get your hands up, all of you," he called. His lead wagon was within twenty yards of the men, easy range. And behind him he knew the other men had their rifles out. The MacNaughtons never had a chance.

But young Carver, cheated of his great adventure, wasn't about to let this opportunity, as he saw it, pass. Even as his brothers raised their empty hands, he clutched his pistol, aimed.

Stephen shot his horse out from under him, and the boy's gun exploded harmlessly into the air as he fell. Silas looked down in horror, thinking his brother killed.

"He's not hurt," Stephen told them, holding his rifle rigid at his hip and the other pistol steady. "Now, you two get down and lay your weapons on the ground. All of them. Slowly, or you die."

They did as told, even restraining the angry Carver, who'd gone for his fallen gun again.

"Now back off, all of you." Harvey Campbell came up, collected the guns, put them in Stephen's wagon. "Now, drag that horse out of the road." Campbell helped the others accomplish that chore, then without asking, led the other two horses back, tied them to his and Epsworth's wagons. The three then drove past the huddled would-be robbers. Campbell leaned out, keeping his rifle on the three.

"You got yourselves a walk, so best be starting off," Stephen told them. "And if we see any of you on this road again, we'll shoot you down. Do you understand?" The three, heads hanging in shame, shuffled off back toward Saltville.

The wagons turned in at the Baker place later, where they were greeted by Theodore as he rounded up horses.

"Well, Stephen, glad to see you again. Looks as if you're provisioning for the winter."

"We are, at least for the first part of it. These men are with the missionaries: Todd Epsworth and Harvey Campbell, Mr. Baker. We've located at the end of a long road into the mountains, place called Ketchum's Mill."

"Think I've heard of it. I see you've extra horses."

"And there's a story attached to them. Robbers named MacNaughton from beyond Saltville tried to waylay us, and we sent them home on foot. Now, we can hardly feed the stock we've kept, so would like to make you a present of these horses. I wouldn't doubt they're stolen, anyway."

"I've heard of the MacNaughtons, yes. Ugly clan, but numerous enough that no one's gone after them. I expect the local constable to act eventually, if enough of us push him. But yes, we can always use another horse or two. Much obliged, but we can't just take them. Now, I know it's not a good trade, but why don't you folks come by in the spring for a few cows? Won't have to feed them over the winter, and you'll have milk and beef later on."

"We'll take that trade." The other men nodded in agreement. "I know the women would like that, too. And with some clearing we're doing, there'll be grass by then. So thanks, sir. And how's my young friend Lige?"

"Well, Lige thinks he wants to go west, seek his fortune. I tell him he's a mite young yet, which he is, but he'll be glad to see you. Come up to the house now for a drink. Can you stay over?"

"Afraid not this time but yes, we'll stop for a short spell. Long road ahead of us, and we want to get more cabins built before winter. I haven't put up shelter there myself yet."

The men tied the teams, joined the farmer at the house. Mrs. Baker was glad to see Stephen again, and so was young Lessie. She kept glancing at Todd Epsworth, who, despite his missing arm, was a handsome young man.

"So you two're missionaries?" the housewife asked.

"We are that, ma'am," Campbell answered. "Todd and me, we soldiered together durin' th' war, an' both of us have felt called to join in th' Lord's work."

"Well, that's good news. I hear most've those frontier settlements're sort of, well…Godless."

"That's what set us off on this mission, fer sure. Not many settlers where we are, but they come to our services, and once th' church is finished, we c'n expect more."

It was a pleasant visit, and Stephen was glad to strengthen ties with this family. Young Lige came in from herding cows and joined in the talk. It was obvious he thought the whole idea of the new settlement was a grand adventure. The visitors assured him it was just like any other new place, and very raw at present.

"Not good farmland like this," Todd explained, his earnest face reddening somewhat in the presence of the women, "but we're gittin' set up quick, with Stephen's help." Lessie smiled at him, and he looked at the floor.

"Bet th' huntin's good, though," the boy pressed.

"It'll have to be," Stephen assured him, "if we're to get through this winter."

They took their leave then, wanting to get as far along the road as possible before camping. Baker assured them in parting that the cows would be ready by spring, two fresh with calves. That would be a bonus for the missionaries.

Days later, the trio stopped at the O'Neil homestead, where big George joined them. Knowing there would be little feed, he didn't take his horse, but climbed into Stephen's wagon for the trip. He'd brought only his rifle, an axe, knife, and a small pack containing blankets and clothes.

"Figger that's all a man needs, if he's willin' t'work his way. I c'n hunt, trap some, mebbe trade fer things I need. Cain't do that, I'll just hafta do without; done that b'fore, a buncha times."

"I'm sure the folks there will be glad to have you," Stephen assured him. George was good-natured and, given the evident extensive building and clearing he'd no doubt done at his sister's place, he could and would work. Yes, he would be a great help at the cabin-raisings, land-clearing, wood-cutting. He could also envision the women feeding this man, who'd surely make them proud of the quantity of their cooking, if nothing else. Stephen envisioned the big man as being available everywhere, and surely he'd be on hand to help with the house he planned up in the hidden hollow off Troublesome Creek.

Then there was also the possibility that they could all find jobs at the iron works, if that venture saw the light of day.

Ten

"And you're most welcome. Now, is that roast goose I smell? You must know we're tired of our own cooking, dear lady."

"It is, and we'll feed you to foundering, as you once said of my family's fare." She started to turn away, then seeing that no one was watching, impulsively gave him a quick kiss on the cheek.

Stephen was stunned. He realized that as long as he'd known Anna, they'd never touched, except once or twice at a dance. And here she was, giving him that magnificent smile, clutching the roll of cloth to her, dark eyes glowing. He wanted to take her in his arms, right there before everyone, but she turned away, stepping quickly into the church. He stood there staring after her, while the others began to gather at a long table for the meal.

He was aware of the clean scent of her, the warmth of her kiss, that momentary nearness that left him tingling. And remembered again her *Give me something to smile about,* from those years ago in Virginia. And he resolved to follow this opening in her reserve as strongly and as quickly as he could.

So after the feast of goose, Stephen approached her casually.

"I've been meaning to invite you to see the place I've chosen for my cabin," he began. "Would you come with me now?" *Be bold, be direct: don't let this opportunity pass.*

"Oh, I...well, but there's so much to do here..."

"Now, you go on with Stephen," the ever-present Tildy Driscoll spoke up behind her. "Plenty folks here t'handle things." Anna looked from face to smiling face among those at the church, and realized they were delighted that Stephen had asked her. She tried for a fleeting moment to feel the victim of a conspiracy.

It didn't work.

"Well, of course then. Thank you, I will." And she handed a kettle she'd been holding to Tildy, turned, and retrieved her coat. She walked beside Stephen to the settler Daughtry's cabin, where he'd left his horses. Stephen tried to appear calm, as did Anna, although she distinctly felt that a line had been crossed somewhere. She resolved not to analyze it away, though. *Just let it happen...perhaps it's time now, anyway.* They greeted the old bachelor, borrowed his one saddle from him for the packhorse, and readied the mounts.

It was a short mile to the trail up to Stephen's little mountainside hollow, and they set out side by side, where the beginning of the way was wide enough.

"I've wanted to get your thoughts on the cabin site, Anna. That place I built on the creek in Virginia sort of hung out off the hill, if you remember, not a good location."

"I remember it well. You and Tom had our whole family to dinner there once. You had so little to eat on, Tom was using pot lids for plates with all the dignity of a plantation butler." The memory made her smile, and Stephen felt a fullness in his throat as she went on. "I hope he and Molly aren't being excluded there. So few free blacks, I don't know how far our old neighbors' goodwill extends, now that you're not there to smooth the way."

"I sent him a letter from Saltville, along with yours to your folks and those the others sent. Maybe someone from there will come this way soon, and we'll hear some news."

They talked of mutual friends they'd known, and the awkwardness began to melt between them. Very soon, it seemed, they were at the steep trail up to Stephen's claim. He'd begun the homesteading process legalities for this place and the missionaries' holdings back at Saltville, and whenever a surveyor came to the settlement, they'd be able to record their claims properly.

As they dismounted in the grassy meadow Anna glanced around, but something was on her mind.

"Stephen, Harvey Campbell said you were stalked at Saltville, then later encountered outlaws. And there were those two men here…" She paused at the memory of the violence and her part in it. "Are we, here at the end of nowhere, to be preyed on by such men?" She realized that she'd actually been worried about Stephen while he was away.

He hadn't told anyone about the two others who'd ambushed him earlier, and added to the other incidents, it did seem this lawless region would be dangerous.

"I'd say yes, this wilderness does seem to attract that type, although I've learned those we've had trouble with here seem to be part of just one outlaw clan. A substantial farmer I stayed with told me the settlers around Saltville will probably go after that bunch soon, though.

"But in all honesty, I do think we'll all have to be on the watch here, at least until the place grows, and we can afford some sort of constable. I notice you carry your pistol, and you can use it, and I'm glad. We like to pretend that women are safe in our civilized society, but that's a myth where there are men who break all the rules."

"Yes. I never thought I'd have to use my gun, but I'll not hesitate again if the need arises." It was not a boast, nor did her face show regret.

Just the plain fact: if a man's fool enough to attack her, he'll die.

"You are an admirable woman, Anna." He was remembering the hysterical Abigail Thomas, at the killing of her abductor. Tom had been right: this girl was worth any number of spoiled plantation daughters. A silence then inserted itself as they stood, and he hastened to fill it.

"Now, there are several springs above this meadow, and there was plenty of water even back when it was so dry. There's obviously solid rock under the grass here, so the soil's thin. A little bench over beyond those first trees could be a kitchen garden, perhaps terraced a little to hold the soil, which I can add to, then another small meadow. But I'm afraid that's the extent of the possibilities for growing anything here."

"Not a farm, by any means. So how do you plan to survive, if I may ask?" There was just a hint of a tease in her eyes. Yes, she'd come from a prosperous river farm.

"Well, as you know, I'm not a farmer anyway. And Ketchum's already got the mill and smithy, my two major vices, since there'd be no market here for my furniture-making. Archie Nolan is sure there'll be a boom in the iron ore down the creek and is talking about my working with them.

"But Anna," and he faced her, took her hands, "we both know I didn't come here to make my fortune. I'm here because you're here, and I've already admitted I was a complete fool to hurt you the way I did. We talked about just letting things work themselves out between us that night of the shooting. But I want to plan my place here, and I want you in those plans. No, don't shake your head just yet, please.

"I'll build myself a hut here, but I've been thinking: why don't I make it half a dogtrot cabin, adding the other half later, with the brazen hope of dragging you off up here to live with me as my wife, if and whenever that can happen." He hurried on. "I want to know what you'd like here. Or anywhere else. I can live in a cave, but you..." Her smile stopped him.

"Dear Stephen. To borrow from our mutual favorite, Shakespeare: 'Methinks the (man) doth protest too much.' You won't be dragging me anywhere." Were her eyes teasing, or was that anger? He couldn't tell. He'd never known what was in her mind...

"You're saying I shouldn't presume..."

"I'm not saying anything, except that when and if I'm ready, I'll certainly come willingly, no dragging required." That *was* a tease...

"So...this place? My...plans...?"

"Oh hell, Stephen Davis, for a normally quiet man sometimes you just talk too much." And she reached, shook him, then drew him to her in a powerful embrace and kissed him hard, long. He felt her lean body against his, moving a little, as if trying to melt into his. *Oh, my God! Oh, my God! this woman, this incredible woman, she's...*

Then she drew away, looked him directly in the eye.

"And as for your wilderness mansion, if there *is* a cave here, I'm ready to chase the bears out and set up housekeeping in it with you."

"You...you mean that? You really do?"

"When have you ever known me to play games, Stephen? You know I say what I mean. Now, your mouth is hanging open, so close it before a bee flies in and let's plan that house." She took his hand and led him up toward the tree line above the meadow.

~ * ~

When Stephen and Anna rejoined the missionaries at the church much later that day, they did so hand-in-hand, and it was plain to everyone there what the situation now was. And so they announced their engagement to all, including Killebrew and Belle Ketchum and bachelor Daughtry, who were present. The general delight warmed them both.

"Now, we'll need to find ourselves a minister," Stephen said to Elder Hiram Driscoll. Anna had told him the leader wasn't authorized to perform marriages.

"Well now," that man began, "It happens that letter you carried to Saltville had a request for a pastor for the new church, Stephen, so let's pray that God sends us one sooner rather than later. And congratulations, both of you."

Anna was hugged, made over, blessed and slyly advised by all the women. Stephen got his share of backslapping from the men. All the children laughed, shouted, chased each other at this good news. This was followed by a celebratory supper and a deal of good cheer. Then George Wellerby approached Stephen.

"Looks like y'll need that cabin fust thing now," he told him. "Reckon you'n me c'n git it up, we git right onto it."

"Thanks, George. Yes, that can be your first job here. I can pay you, of course, and I know all the folks here will have work for you, too."

"C'd use a bit of help 'round th' mill," Ketchum offered, "an' at th' forge too, yer willin'."

"Moren' willin'. Oughta find m'self a place t'stay, though."

"Wal, if y'don't mind th' comp'ny, I got room up at my place," Daughtry volunteered. "Figger we c'n stay outta one 'nother's way, all right."

So it was arranged. The following morning, Stephen, George and Ketchum set to work at the smithy forging two broadaxes, a froe, chisels and a felling axe. The miller had a store of cured hickory for handles, and the trip to Saltville had yielded a few pieces of blister steel for the cutting edges. These were forge-welded onto the wrought-iron axe heads, then hardened and tempered. Working steel had always been Stephen's smithing specialty, and Ketchum gained a few pointers from him. He'd borrow a crosscut saw from the missionaries to speed the basic construction of his cabin, but additional finishing tools would have to wait.

By late afternoon, the axes and other items were finished, and Stephen helped Ketchum adjust the pitsaw at the mill for cutting boards. The church was ready for its flooring, the siding having exhausted the supply of boards on hand, and the demand for lumber would continue to prove high. With the creek flow back to normal after the dry months, the saw could work away all day, its slow strokes not overly demanding of power.

The missionaries' cabins had been floored with puncheons, split logs adzed to more or less smooth surfaces, then rubbed with creekstones and sand. Stephen wanted flooring lumber, but knew he'd have to wait months for it to season to avoid shrinkage. He resolved to resort to the puncheons in his cabin for the time being, to overlay them later with tongue-in-groove boards.

The next day, he and George Wellerby began setting the blocks of stone up in his hollow for the foundation corners of his first log pen. With no idea when a minister might make his appearance, Stephen had decided to go ahead with the single pen, leaving the rest of the house for later. He'd need to get inside before winter, which wasn't far off.

The missionaries had offered a house-raising, but with their own hurry to make their cabins livable, he'd declined. He figured a week or less for the log work with George's help, then another for the roof framing and shakes.

Ketchum was busy making nails for the entire community, now that he had a supply of iron, and Stephen could always go help with that chore. George wanted to learn smithing too, so it seemed an ideal arrangement.

At night, the big man walked or rode Stephen's packhorse the mile to the village, to be fed by Belle Ketchum, then sleep at Daughtry's. The old man was mostly deaf, but George's booming voice could always reach him, along with whoever else happened to be anywhere near. For his part, Stephen elected to camp on the site, although he did accept frequent invitations to have supper at the women's cabin with Anna.

That young lady, having laid the last of her reservations to rest, began working toward the necessities of a new life with Stephen and their soon-to-be household. She spun, wove, quilted bits of salvaged cloth, sewed and patched. Theirs would be a frugal home, although Stephen had assured her he could afford whatever utensils and other items beyond their hand-making that she'd need.

It was an active heady time for both of them, busy in the face of winter, but when together planning, sharing, both treasured their rediscovery of each other. Stephen had learned from necessity to be a patient man, and Anna, too, was content for their wedding to occur whenever God decided on the time. Not that they weren't anxious to be together. They still joked about finding themselves a cave, or dashing off to Saltville on two fast horses, but they knew they could wait. At least for a few weeks, or they hoped, maybe just a maximum of a month or two.

Archie Nolan had been out prospecting most of the time until cold weather came, then he arranged for a tiny room in the attic above the smithy for his lodging. Belle agreed to cook for him, and he settled in. He hoped for word from his backers about the proposed iron venture, and that soon arrived, in a more tangible form than he'd expected.

Reginald Cabot himself arrived one windy day in November, muffled against the cold, obviously weary from the long ride. He'd brought a packet of mail from Saltville, which was welcomed by the entire settlement. Nolan joined him and the Ketchums for a hot dinner before the fireplace in their house, which was built onto the mill.

"What a wilderness," the Philadelphian declared. "I thought Saltville the end of the earth, but it appears you've discovered that here." It was said not unkindly, because the man had known his opportunities lay beyond civilization as such. He had, however, expected at least an inn or a rude tavern here, neither of which existed yet. The matter of his lodging could wait, however. He was anxious to exchange information with Nolan and plan their venture.

The rhythmic sound of the pitsaw gave a reassuring background to the men's conversation afterwards, as they caught each other up on developments. Ketchum went regularly to check on the progress of the squared log that was working its way through the blade, driven by a ratchet device he and Stephen had perfected. He was in and out and heard only parts of the talk.

"I've located a smelter operator, Nolan. Had to practically steal him from Fort Pitt, but he likes the idea of getting in on the ground floor, so to speak, of our operation. Wrong time of the year I know, but with whatever preparations we can make here, we should be ready to proceed in the spring. That's why I came on, to avoid wasting part of another year."

"Well sir, I've found what I'm reasonably certain are ample ore deposits on down this creek and up side draws. There's some that's washed down, and rich pockets of it in the rock of the region. Of course we can't speculate on the real extent of it until we dig into the hillsides more. Be aware that it is possible there won't be enough to justify your plans.

"And from my experience, I'd say we should perhaps start small, not count on a huge lode. But of course, if the nearby ore does play out in time, there's more, even if we must go a bit farther for it.

"So I'd say, if your man can have the smelter going by summer, we can have the mill and possibly even the foundry ready by then, too."

"I haven't found a millwright yet, but there's time for that. Do have a line on a foundry operator, though."

"There's a fellow here, former miller, who's quite good at construction. Worked with the missionaries here on their cabins and on the new church. Quite a craftsman, and I feel certain he can construct anything we need."

"Really? And here at the end of the world? I'm surprised our friend Ketchum built this mill, no more people than are here to support it. What's your friend's name?"

"Stephen Davis. He's also a smith, and has..." Nolan stopped, seeing the expression on Cabot's face.

"Davis? *Stephen Davis?* Surely not. Where's this man from?"

"Goochland. Grew up at his father's mill, knows millwrighting well. What's the matter, sir?"

"Oh, Goochland, on down near Richmond, yes. Nothing, I guess...common name, surely. Just thought...no, go on. So you think this man can work with us? That's excellent. He might even be able to get a start in any good weather this winter, put us that much ahead. Surely cut timbers, have them ready." Cabot dismissed any idea that this Davis could be the furniture maker from Albemarle County who'd decimated his operation in that part of Virginia.

And when Nolan went on to recount his own ambush by the robbers and Stephen's subsequent rescue, Cabot's suspicions vanished. Obviously a sound man, not the bloodthirsty, devious character he'd pictured that other Davis to be.

The Ketchums offered Cabot space to sleep in their house since he'd be there only a day or two. After eating Belle's cooking, the man suggested she open an inn here, since he expected an influx of people once the iron mining began. She was intrigued by the idea.

"In fact, with what I expect to be the increased need soon, I see this as an added business opportunity. Yes, I'd say that'll be a certainty." He thought it over for a few minutes. "Say, what would you say to my hiring your builder, Davis, to put up such a structure over this winter, have it ready for traffic in the spring? Since our operation would require lodging, we'd actually depend on the place. If you'd be interested in running it, we could make the arrangements now, Mrs. Ketchum."

"Might work out," she mused. This place had been lonely enough since their arrival, and the mill was silent most of the time. Now though, it was constantly working, turning out the lumber the new people needed. Yes, maybe an inn, to make this a real settlement. And if this pleasant man was willing to pay for it, why not?

The day was ending, and Nolan planned to take Cabot down to the iron mining and milling site the next day. As it happened, Stephen Davis and George returned from the cabin work, responding to an invitation to eat with the missionaries. Nolan led Cabot to the church, where they had joined the others, who were finishing for the day.

"This is the man we were talking about, Mr. Cabot: Stephen Davis. Mr. Cabot is from Philadelphia, Stephen. And this man is George Wellerby, who's helping Stephen with his cabin."

Cabot shook both men's hands, noting Wellerby's size and approving: he'd be a good hand at mining, and there were surely others here.

"Pleased to make your acquaintance, both of you. Archie tells me you're a master builder, Mr. Davis."

"Hardly a master, sir, but I've done a deal of timber framing, and grew up at my father's mill. I'm not a professional millwright but can and have built the machinery necessary for sawing and grinding."

"Well, there's apparently little difference in the drive mechanism for our iron-working. I'd say, if we can work out terms, you'd be able to construct what we'd need." Cabot was observing the tight mortises and the exact work in the church.

"I'd like that, sir. When did you have in mind to begin?"

"Oh, if it weren't almost winter, we'd go ahead right now. But if you could assemble a crew to hew timbers and stack them, we'd have a head start next spring. We don't intend to waste time."

"In that case, George and I could begin within two weeks. We're finishing work on my cabin now. And some of the other men here would welcome the work, I know."

"Fine, just fine. A labor force is a necessity, and it'll be much better to use men from here, rather than bringing them in. I have the plans for the mill with me, prepared by a knowledgeable wright in Fort Pitt. Since Archie's vouched for you, I have no hesitation in hiring you."

Terms were soon agreed upon for the future mill, and also the immediate construction of the inn. And to his surprise, Stephen was given a substantial cash advance toward the work. He'd actually planned to ask for a token, not wanting any of the settlers or himself to do any work not paid for, but this was generous. Cabot seemed to have plenty more with him, and the others remarked that he had been lucky to escape robbery by himself on the long and lonely road he'd traveled.

"Oh, I can take care of myself, always have." The man dismissed the subject with a chuckle and patted the pair of pistols he carried. "Now, Mr. Davis, I'll leave it to your discretion whom to hire, and how to direct the work. I believe in delegating responsibility where appropriate, and you seem to be the right man in the right place for us."

Whereupon Cabot also met some of the missionaries. He expressed appreciation at their plans, and praised their efforts, here in the wilderness. He was a personable fellow, and they took to him. And if his eyes stayed on the tall now-smiling Anna Compton a bit too long, no one noticed.

"I'd say what you're doing here with this church is vital to a new community, folks. And I want to donate a sum to help." Which he did, to the profound thanks of elder Hiram Driscoll.

"Tomorrow we'll inspect the site," Nolan promised as the others departed. By now, other cabins were finished, and only three of the women still shared that original structure, where the two others fed their husbands and children and Anna provided for Stephen when he could visit. George liked to eat wherever there was food, usually with the Ketchums and Nolan at the mill.

Stephen came to the settlement more now that the first half of his cabin was nearly done. What remained was the finishing of the fireplace and getting on with the chimney, and the few pieces of furniture he and Anna planned. She'd stressed the need for a raised hearth for cooking, something he'd seen only in the German settlements in Pennsylvania and other areas of the North during the war.

"Even if I weren't so tall, I'd want the hearth at a reasonable height, Stephen. I'd say there weren't more of those because the men don't do the cooking that often, but it just makes sense." She'd come up to help him and George begin the chimney stonework. Anna was no stranger to any phase of farm or country work.

"Well, yes, it does, now that you bring it up. And in my years of bachelor food butchering, I never thought of it. Just figured those German places I'd seen were some sort of culture thing from the old country."

At her direction, they also built in an oven, encircled by a part of the main flue.

"I can bake in it or, with a low fire, it'll be ideal for bread-rising or even drying wet gloves and socks," she told him.

Stephen had also scouted out seasoned dead trees for furniture wood, and planned to work on those projects inside during bad weather.

Now back at the settlement, the two of them walked hand in hand up to her cabin, which would be taken over by the last of the others. Both were quiet by nature, but they always found a lot to talk about between them, and they looked forward to a lifetime of sharing everything from Shakespeare to planting beans. Both of them also regretted only that they couldn't begin their life together sooner.

Reginald Cabot was excited next day at Nolan's findings when he accompanied the prospector and Stephen downcreek. He completely dismissed the possibility that the ore might be limited. That which Nolan had separated out looked good, and the millsite was promising. The great hurdle would be, as they already knew, building a serviceable road out of this mountain fastness. That it must also be graded to accept the future installation of the rails made it a harder obstacle, but Cabot again refused to be daunted.

"Engineers can handle it," he promised. "Some of those fellows I've talked with are like wizards; the harder the challenge, the better they like it. Why, I've heard of plans to construct a canal up the Potomac River from Georgetown, despite those incredible falls. It seems nothing is impossible for them, given enough backing. And with the money my associates and I can bring to this project, rest assured we'll succeed."

His enthusiasm was easy to share, and each man could envision the completed complex: the water-powered mill, the smelter, the tunnel mining. The picture would transform this lost outpost to a bustling, profitable center. Stephen privately worried about the already-established works west of the Lexington village, but said nothing. He knew little of this business and was glad simply for the chance to use his skills in helping put it together. He did wonder at Cabot's seeming unlimited wealth and his generosity, but supposed that in the postwar centers of the Northeast, commerce and trade must be booming.

Eleven

As winter closed in, Anna raised the subject of a school with the other settlers. She'd taught the children at church back in Virginia, and was doing so here, but felt the need for more education for them. The immediate problem was books, since there had been so little room in the wagons for them on their trek west. The new church was the ideal place for a school, being empty most of the week, although the women had already formed the habit of gathering there one day a week for quilting sessions. She could work around that.

And since the community was getting low on everything again, she put in a request for school supplies. There was some discussion about who should make the trip this time. Stephen was busy with the new inn, and so was George. The two single missionaries, Todd and Harvey, volunteered again, having no family ties there. And with the prospect of staying the winter, Archie Nolan agreed to drive the third supply wagon.

Stephen warned the men to be on the lookout for robbers, of course, and was somewhat surprised that Nolan would face that likelihood again. All felt, however, that the three of them stood a good chance of survival. After all, the MacNaughtons hadn't actually robbed them last time.

"Just be ready to take some pre-emptive measures, men," Stephen advised them. "Any of that clan show up, I'd contact the constable in Saltville for help this time. Mr. Baker's idea of getting the community together to put that outfit out of business was a good one, and perhaps it's time for that. And," he added, "I'd stop by Theodore Baker's farm again, and see if he'll swap horses with you for the return trip. That way you'll only be in town for a day and can travel faster on the way back. Here's a bit of money to encourage him, although I've the feeling he'll do it out of goodwill."

"Oh," Elder Driscoll remembered. "I had a letter that Mr. Cabot brought, telling of a minister the Presbytery people had located. They didn't know when he'd be available, but you might inquire at Saltville at the church there, see if they've heard anything."

Stephen and Anna shared an eagerness to learn of this development as soon as possible. Indeed, they'd considered joining the trip themselves to be married in that village. But that would exclude all their friends here so they decided against it. Also, they agreed that the privacy they wanted following the wedding wouldn't be available on the wagon trip. Soon enough, they told each other, as long as it was imminent.

~ * ~

Reginald Cabot hadn't wasted his money in Ketchum's Mill. He hadn't told the others in his circle in Philadelphia before, but there really was trouble brewing for them there. A group of merchants who'd been robbed too many times had employed a former tradesman named Mason, now a private investigator, to find out who was stealing from them. And the man had made significant headway, catching minor members of their own organization who'd been less than careful. He was finding out names, and Cabot wanted a place to go, very far from home, when it got too hot.

And he could foresee becoming a sort of ruler of the new settlement, with all its possibilities, well away from law enforcement, away from enemies. Given some improvements such as his new inn, he could see being very comfortable there. His society-minded wife would never consider the move, and that would just have to be her lot…he'd go without her, maybe find himself another woman, in time. The prospect made him smile as he rode the many miles back north.

And Codington and the others? Well, let them know the situation, then let them react however they would. This business was all about looking out for oneself, and that was his priority. Time to draw in their tentacles, he guessed. They still had a good thing going, despite the two chests of gold lost in Virginia, possibly both to that other meddling Davis fellow. That got him to wondering what had happened to the assassin Ames. Could the marksman have killed him, too? Stephen Davis. Coincidence then, his having the same name as the engaging young builder at Ketchum's. Well, a lot of Davises, as he'd noted before.

~ * ~

Young Carver MacNaughton had fumed almost constantly since that humiliating encounter with the missionaries that had cost him his horse, his gun and his pride. His brothers had given up without a fight, and he was ashamed of them, too. A man made up his mind to a thing, he oughta go through with it, he reasoned. And all right, one or two of them might've got hit, but that was gonna happen when a man made his living with a gun.

So he was excited to learn from brother Paul, who made it a habit to hang around the inn in Saltville, that the missionaries were back for more supplies.

"This time we'll git 'em," the youth vowed. "Shoulda took 'em last time, but you two was yeller, give up 'thout a fight."

"We'd a got kilt," brother Silas declared. "You didn't git a look at thet tall one's eyes, boy. Cold killer, that'n. Soon's shoot you as look at you. You's jist lucky he shot yore hoss 'stead of you when you pulled yore gun thataway."

"Still say we coulda took 'em. Ennyways, you said that'n wuzn't with 'em this time, din't you, Paul? Others of 'em be easy, Bible folks an' all."

"No, he wuzn't, but th' other two wuz. Feller with one arm, an' t'other'n. Old 'un with 'em this time. Naw, reckon they ain't thet dangerous, if we wanta jump 'em."

"Wal, let's git goin'," the boy urged.

"No hurry; they laid up extry last time. Hosses porely, an' I reckon they'll feed 'em up some 'fore they sets out. Didn't like campin' out in th' rain waitin' fer 'em last time, m'self."

"Hosses porely, y'say?" Old Abner MacNaughton reflected. "Thet means thar ain't been much graze fer 'em wharever they's settled. All steep an' woods on west, not good fer nothin'. Wonder whut th' bunch is doin' in a place lak thet?"

"Wal, lak th' boy sez, they's r'ligious, so reckon they settin' up a church an' all, mebbe in with th' Indians thar."

"Damn waste of time, thet. Only good Indian's a daid one."

"Thaing is," Paul continued, "they gonna keep comin' in fer supplies, we kin lay fer 'em, git ourselfs plenty, ever time, we plan it right."

"I reckon so," the old man agreed. "But we's lost us some men of late, one way or t'other. Could be thet hard-eyed feller you saw last time, he's done kilt our boys. Wouldn't doubt he's th' same one we's after fer shootin' Ansted an' Luke Kelly, back then."

"We dunno as Shelby an' Caleb er daid, Paw," Carver pointed out. "Could be they jist kep' on west, see whut they c'd find."

"Naw, I got th' feelin' they's daid, all right."

It was agreed that the MacNaughtons would go into Saltville the next morning, wait till the wagons left, then trail them to a suitably remote campsite for the robbery. Carver felt excitement rising inside him. He'd get the chance this time to show the clan what he was made of.

~ * ~

The missionaries loaded supplies while Archie Nolan went to the local church and inquired about the new minister.

"Well sir, you're in good time," the pastor informed him. "Reverend McKnight and his family just arrived yesterday. We were debating whether to send word on to you folks or provide an escort for them. This is fortuitous, indeed: God's providence."

"Well then. Have they a wagon?"

"Yes, with all their worldly possessions. I hope there's lodging for them there?"

"That'll be no problem, sir. The new inn's partly finished, and any of the settlers would be glad to take them in."

"Fine, fine. As I said, the Lord provides."

The Reverend Armistead McKnight was a slightly stooped, black-clad man in his fifties, almost gaunt, with silver hair. His wife Ella was round, red-faced, and pleasant where her husband was reserved. Their two children were girls, one about fifteen, the other two years older. Nolan couldn't keep their names straight, but one was Alice and the other Marina. He'd met them at the Saltville inn, and announced that they'd be leaving within two hours.

"Good, good," the reverend intoned. "The sooner our travel is over, the better. I hear it's a long way."

"Several days, yes, sir. But I'm certain you and your family will like th' new church, and th' settlement. It's small, but will grow mightily in a few months, with th' plans that're in motion."

"Ah, and what might those be?"

"Iron mining and processing. Our backers in Philadelphia are prepared to develop the place beginning in the spring."

"Well. Seems a long way from markets, but I'm no judge of such things. We shall be ready in two hours."

And they were. The four wagons rolled out of the village, laden with most of what would be needed for the winter. The horses were tired, but they'd reach Baker's farm before nightfall, where they'd negotiate the trade or, worst case, rest the animals there a day or so.

Lige Baker greeted them at the horse barn, and sent the family on up to the farmhouse, while he and the others unhitched the teams. They fed the horses well, then joined the others.

"Well, I'm sorry Stephen isn't with you this time, Harvey, but we're glad to have you," Theodore Baker welcomed them. "And we're glad you've decided to go to Ketchum's, Reverend McKnight. That promises to be a thriving center, from what I hear."

The minister was impressed with Baker's library, and the man's evident education. The two, along with Archie Nolan, spent hours after supper in discussion of the prospects for the new nation while their wives visited and the young people played games. Harvey Campbell was the only one not drawn into any group, but he drifted from one to another, enjoying the company, listening, occasionally offering an opinion or taking a hand in a game. Altogether a pleasant evening.

Marina McKnight, who turned out to be the older daughter, spent some time talking with Todd Epsworth apart from her sister, Lige and Lessie Baker. That young man, despite his war experience, was by nature shy, but was obviously taken with Marina. Lessie cast longing glances at Todd, who was almost unaware of her.

In the morning, the negotiations for the temporary horse trade complete, Baker expressed his gratitude for the sum Stephen had sent but insisted on accepting only half of it.

"I figure I owe him anyway, but there'll be those cows in the spring, so yes, a good exchange." He also cautioned the travelers.

"Those MacNaughton scoundrels have been active here lately," he warned. "I'd travel far today to get out of their territory. I'm afraid they'll steal anything they come across, and they're downright mean." Campbell assured him that they'd keep their eyes open for trouble, and the wagons rolled out.

The trio of Paul, Silas and Carver MacNaughton rode into Saltville around noon, to discover that their quarry had departed the previous afternoon, laden with supplies.

"But we'll shorely ketch up with 'em," Paul was certain. "Hosses prob'ly porely, an' they won't've got fur yestiddy."

They also learned that the minister and his family were with the party, and that gave them some pause. Another possible gun to face. But hell, Carver pointed out, a preacher wouldn't likely even have a gun, nor know how to use it if he did. The others eventually agreed, and the trio set out on the road after them.

~ * ~

"We disarmed that bunch last time, Reverend," Harvey Campbell had told the minister after they'd left the Baker farm. "Was two grown up, and one boy, looked t'be brothers. But we was told there's a whole clan of 'em, so no tellin' how many might try to rob us. Now, with these fresh horses, we c'n drive on in the dark, t'put distance behind us. Or we can find a place well off th' road somewheres to camp, where they won't find us. I'm open t' suggestions."

"Well," Archie Nolan put in, "I got sneaked up on back in the summer, farther along than this by those other two. I'd say we should find a farm we can stay at. Doubt if they'd try anything against a bunch of us. Problem is, there aren't many on this road."

"I'd say God will protect us," the minister offered, "but I've learned He has His own plans and schedules, and expects us to help when necessary." And he produced a pair of loaded pistols, which he appeared to know how to use. "Since you men know the territory, I'll defer to your judgment as to which option is best. Trusting, of course, that we won't encounter bandits in the first place."

The drawback to the off-the-way campsite was that in these steep hills, there just weren't any hidden places the four wagons could get to easily. And as Nolan had said, there were few settlers along this stretch of wilderness road until the Wellerby sister and brother-in-law's place, except hunters' cabins up steep trails. That left the choice of pushing on as far as possible, perhaps even all night, to hope to outdistance potential marauders.

"If we don't push too hard, the horses can manage it," Todd speculated. "Then, come daylight, we can post guards along the road and rest up. With luck, we'll be beyond their range. But they may know we're on this road, since they seem to keep watch at the village."

"In that case, they'll trail us, knowing we'll have to stop soon," Nolan reasoned. "So one plan's as good as another. But yes, posting guards, traveling at night makes the most sense. Too easy for a camp t'get surrounded when it's dark. I hope our leaving soon has worked, but perhaps not. I also hope the Bakers and some others can clean that nest of vipers out soon."

So the wagons rolled on, into and past the winter afternoon, twilight, and finally, darkness. A half moon lighted the way somewhat, and a cautious pace let them negotiate the rough places in the rough road. They stopped only briefly and only when necessary, then continued the journey.

~ * ~

"Damn people's gotta stop soon," Silas MacNaughton griped. "Hosses gotta be near 'bout wore out b'now. Too many tracks t'tell if they's ahead of us, er mebbe turned off at somebody's farm. Thet's rat likely, since they gotta rest them hosses."

"Naw, we'll ketch 'em up, an' rat soon," Carver averred. He didn't want to miss the chance for the robbery, even though his brother's reasoning made sense. "Jist 'nother mile er two oughta do it, don'tcha thaink?"

"Mebbe so," Paul agreed. "But I don't fer shore wanta camp out in this cold agin, waitin' fer 'em. We shoulda gone on in yestiddy, trailed 'em right off."

"Couldna got thar in time," Silas pointed out. "No, reckon they's tricked us this time. An' we cain't hardly ride up to ever' farm lookin' fer 'em. Git ourselves shot thataway."

They rode on in silence for another hour, then reined in, agreeing reluctantly that the missionaries must indeed have taken refuge at a farm on the way. And no telling when they'd venture out again, or from just where.

"Damn, this outlaw bizness ain't gittin' us nothin' here lately," lamented Silas, eyeing the sinking sun. It would be late and cold when they got back to clan territory, again empty-handed. "I figger if I'd been able t'work some'ers, I coulda made more'n we has all this year."

"Ain't nobody'd hire enny of us," Paul pointed out. "Mebbe thet's whut cuzzin Caleb an' Shelby done, rode on outta th' country, whar nobody knows us."

"Pa thainks they's daid," Carver reminded him.

"Could be. Man keeps on, he's bound t'meet up 'ith 'nother feller, better'n him with a gun. Look at whut happened to Ansted, an' he wuz th' best 'mongst us." He turned his horse for home, and the others followed.

Carver didn't like his brothers' defeatest attitudes. Just turned fifteen, he had that adolescent belief that he was bullet-proof, and wanted to prove it. He was doubly bitter at not getting his chance at the missionaries for the second time and began to formulate a plan.

Just as soon as winter was over…

~ * ~

Stephen and George and the other men were making good time on the new inn, despite the cold. Hewing timbers was hot work any time of the year, and they welcomed the task. Fitting the mortises and tenons was slower and more tedious, but Belle Ketchum plied "her boys" with hot soup and drinks often, warming them. She was looking forward to operating the inn come spring and was actively involved in its design. She was determined that this should not be just another flea-ridden hovel travelers encountered so often along the back roads but a comfortable, clean lodging.

She had Stephen locate the kitchen in one section of the house, with a future summer one in the stone basement, which would use the same fireplace flue as the main one. This instead of in a separate structure out back, which was customary to safeguard against fire. It would be warm in winter and cool in summer, and she could deal with the stairway, since it'd be used only in the busiest season. Especially later, when she knew she'd be able to hire girls to help.

Stephen missed no opportunity to see Anna. Her school was operating in the church despite the scarcity of the few ordered books, and all the men supplied firewood to keep the place warm. George was always shy around the tall girl, but plainly almost worshipped her and Stephen. Anna had learned that he could not read, and had promised to work with him, away from the children, which would have embarrassed the big man. Stephen was grateful, remembering how long it had taken him to teach his friend, the ex-slave Tom Logan, even with her periodic help.

So the two of them went often to the little cabin, where Anna lived with Sissy and Herb Blair, for supper. There were other invitations also, and the two bachelors fared well.

But both Stephen and Anna were anxious for the arrival of a minister, and the consummation of their planned wedding. The little cabin up the hollow seemed especially empty to him, and he worked there too, as he could, beginning the second half of the dogtrot house.

Belle urged the men to finish the inn as soon as possible, pointing out that the minister would need a place to live whenever one got there, and would also probably have a family. But she also knew the place would surely be otherwise empty till spring. One day she'd push the two men on its construction, urging the completion of at least some rooms, and the next she'd insist that they go work on Stephen's house. All in all, she was a pleasant pest.

The men among the missionaries, as well as the other settlers, hunted the mountains that winter, bringing in turkeys, deer, and the occasional bear. It was their custom to share the meat, and community hog-butcherings and scaldings were frequent. The earliest to arrive there, including the Ketchums, had let hogs run wild, feeding them a little corn to keep them coming around. So hog-hunting was another activity, the animals fattened on chestnuts and acorns from the woods.

~ * ~

Reginald Cabot had taken a side trip up the James River tributaries toward the iron mines on west of Lexington, Virginia, on his return trip. He wanted to see how their operations were doing and, frankly, to check out the competition. He was aware of their iron being supplied to merchants and small manufacturing concerns, and that worried him. Their transportation obstacles were less daunting than his would be, and that spelled a situation that could and would undercut his profits, if he let it.

He did not plan to let that happen.

At the outpost of Covington, he soon learned the power behind most of the iron industry centered around a man named Lester

Cummings, a transplant from Saugus, Massachusetts. The man knew iron, and apparently was a sound businessman.

Cabot made discreet inquiries, then determined to meet the man himself. He'd try to buy him out, if possible, always the first approach. Failing that, he'd have to resort to other tactics to neutralize what was essentially a monopoly of the black metal in this region.

He could do that.

Cummings was a brisk New Englander, almost begrudging the time Cabot's visit took. He heard him out about his plans for the Ketchum's Mill works, then shook his head.

"Doesn't matter what contraptions you devise, Cabot, it's still just too far to markets. I can float my product down the Jackson River at high water, then on down the James to Richmond, but I'm not making much at it. This is the limit for operations, at least for another generation or two, when more people will create a market nearer. I admire your spunk in attempting such a venture, but I fear you'll go broke on it. Especially since you appear to have little knowledge of the business. No offense intended, of course."

"Oh, none taken. But as for knowledge, I control a number of enterprises, and have employed good and experienced men to run them. And that works for me. So that part I can handle. I realize, too, that I'll have to take a loss at first, but my other ventures can offset that. Until now, I had no idea the extent of your operations here, and speculated that the ore might possibly be running out. Not true, apparently."

"No, from our prospecting, we expect supply well into the next century."

"Well then, my planned offer to employ you, at a very high figure, would be a waste of both our time."

"I'm afraid so, sir. Good day."

Cabot spent another day determining that Cummings ran almost a one-man operation, overseeing, tending to every detail of his mining, smelting, foundry work, himself. If something were to happen to that man, the entire production would suffer a severe setback, until and unless another wizard could be found. And this was a wholly-owned venture, so there was no board of directors to take over in the event of the top man's...indisposition.

He'd pay Mr. Cummings another visit, but not till his own operation was up and running. That was the way to handle competition, he'd learned, growing up in the streets of Boston and now headquartered in the capital.

The memory of the Massachusetts city caused him to think of his society-minded cousins back in his hometown who'd disowned him early on. And now that brought a smile.

Twelve

Well out of MacNaughton territory, the wagons stopped briefly at the O'Neil farm to report on George's becoming a valued member of the Ketchum's Mill community. The husband and wife fed the travelers and promised to visit when the crops were next laid by.

"Sounds like a likely place t'be," Henry O'Neil speculated, eyeing his own limited acreage.

"Now, we ain't more'n got dug in here, mister," his wife cautioned. "Steep 'nuff hills hereabouts, 'thout needin' mountins straight up t'try to farm." Henry shrugged, subsided.

The remainder of the trip was uneventful, with only light snows twice and a slow pace to spare the teams. Mrs. McKnight remained cheerful, the girls flirted with Todd Epsworth, the reverend read from his Bible as he drove his team, and Nolan and Campbell kept a sharp eye out. The MacNaughtons wouldn't be the only highwaymen set to prey on travelers, though this was now far from the best pickings.

They arrived in time for Christmas at the settlement, to the joyful welcome of Belle and Killebrew Ketchum, the missionaries, and just about all the settlers, among whom were Anna Compton and Stephen Davis, with a noticeable glow about them.

Realizing the need for the inn would be light through the winter, Stephen had hastened to complete just a pair of rooms with double-facing fireplaces, opening into the flue from the basement kitchen. That should lodge the McKnights, he reasoned, until the structure could be completed. Interior lathing was in place, though the plaster would have to await warmer weather and the necessary lime for mortar. No matter, the minister's wife assured him, they could hang blankets on the walls.

A tour of the church complete, with the minister's appreciative approval, a community meal of huge proportions capped that day's arrival. There was venison, goose and pork, along with the potatoes, corn dishes and preserves from the settlers' fields and the forest.

And there was mail, brought from Saltville, to be read and exclaimed over. And gifts the men had been commissioned to purchase. The minister and his family were warmed by all this fellowship and stated that God had evidently led them to the right place. Anna and Stephen nodded in agreement, their smiles wide.

"And so you two are the prospective bride and groom," the reverend intoned. "You must converse with Ella about arrangements, whenever you choose. Afterwards, we can send the certificate of marriage to Saltville for registry at the courthouse there. And just when had you planned the ceremony?" He paused a beat, then, "tonight's too soon." The entire gathering erupted in laughter. They'd feared the somber-looking minister had no sense of humor. And both Stephen and Anna blushed.

Christmas day was agreed upon, a week away. The bride would have liked her family to be present, but that was an impossibility at any time of year, given the distance. Besides, this was her home now, and she was already as close to these people as any she'd known outside her family back in Virginia.

Stephen had letters from both Tom Logan and his old friend Ned Drake, from the Caroline County plantation. Tom was doing a good trade in the fine tool-making he'd learned, and he and Molly seemed accepted well enough in the community. Ned reported the encounter with the late Justin Ames, who he was sure had been part of the illegal operation headed there by the late Dr. Weston.

"One more gone then, it seems," he wrote. "I trust you've avoided such confrontations wherever it is you are now. Since nobody knows just where, you should be able to lie low and be anonymous. And hurry up and settle things with our Anna. Connie sends her love, but wants you married to that delightful woman, who just might be able to civilize you, given a miracle."

Good old Ned. They'd had a merry five years of it in the Continental Army, despite the hardships. Ned had always found something to celebrate, be it a stolen bottle of the general's wine, or a chicken that had been resting uneasily on its roost at a nearby farm. A ladies' man, he had finally found his destiny with Constance Weston. No mention of imminent offspring yet, but it'd been only what...five months? Stephen could picture a herd of redheaded children populating that plantation in years to come.

Anna had received a letter from her family and learned of events among them. She missed them, of course, and knew that someday she and Stephen would make the trip back for a visit. Someday.

~ * ~

Christmas Day came, and with it the gift-giving so much a part of the celebration. Stephen surprised Anna with more than the minimal pots and pans and kettles she'd ordered from Saltville. There was a tiny silver crucifix on a chain, and a pieced double wedding ring quilt he'd ordered sewn when he was there earlier.

She'd already fashioned her wedding gown of fabric the missionary women had somehow brought with them. Tildy Driscoll smiled mysteriously when asked how that had come to be, saying only that she'd prepared for developments. Stephen wasn't allowed to see the bride beforehand, even during the exchange of gifts, that being the tradition the women insisted upon. She had ordered him a new pair of boots and a warm coat, which he received gladly, albeit not in her presence.

That afternoon, with the sun low over the surrounding mountains, everyone gathered in the church with the minister and the nervous groom. George Wellerby stood beside Stephen, grinning happily, clutching the ring that had come also from Saltville. Sissy Blair was matron of honor, and entered the church followed by the missionaries' daughters. There was no harpsichord or other musical instrument, but the group sang hymns of joy for the couple.

Then the church door opened again, and Anna walked toward Stephen on the arm of Elder Driscoll. Her eyes never left his, even as she took her place, holding a bouquet of dried flowers.

"Dearly beloved," Armistead McKnight began, and the familiar words rolled out over the heads of the company. Stephen blotted them out, as did Anna. Both felt this culmination of those years of knowing each other, of the rocky parts of their relationship, and this completion of each other's lives as they'd known them. Her dark eyes held her soul, Stephen felt, and he was ready to give this wonderful woman everything he was or could be, forever.

Then there were the vows, the placing of the ring on Anna's finger, the declaration. Then silence.

"Ahem. A kiss is customary, Stephen," the minister prompted.

Stephen obliged, to the applause of all present. A hot flush ran through him as she ran the tip of her tongue around his lips. *Brazen woman*...he clutched her harder.

Then they were walking side by side down the aisle, past the smiling faces, the clapping hands. At the doorway, Anna turned and tossed the dried flowers, which young Marina McKnight caught, to cheers.

Stephen set his bride on his horse, handed her up her coat. He mounted the other animal, took the offered package of prepared food Tildy Driscoll passed up, and they turned, waved, and were off up the path to their cabin.

~ * ~

The fire of seasoned locust logs had subsided into red coals by morning, but the snug cabin still held its warmth. The lovers stirred, kissed, looked into each other's eyes as the light came up around them. Neither wanted to move from this place and so they drew closer, and gently made love again. Anna was so responsive, moving with him, that Stephen's joy overflowed, as did hers. Neither of them had ever imagined that such ecstasy existed.

Much later, they washed, dressed, cooked. The fireplace flames danced around the kettle hung on the swinging crane, and the little room smelled of good food bubbling. A Dutch oven sat on coals, its lid covered with more of them, and the baking bread inside sent its aroma up also. The two of them felt as if they had their whole world right there, with no need to venture out, ever.

Two days later, George appeared, ready to continue work on the other half of the house. Stephen was out already, setting a short log between a corner and a window space. With no hurry for this part of the house, he'd elected to use short lengths instead of the full-length logs that would have to be cut later for openings. That also let him work alone although, with Anna's help, few of the hewn logs were too heavy for them to slide up skid poles.

Stephen had installed the one glass window he'd received from Saltville in the original log pen, now their entire living quarters. Another would go into the opposite gable end next to the chimney when that loft space was completed and flooring boards, currently stacked for seasoning, were installed. Glass was scarce, but the order was in for additional windows, and Stephen aimed for the house to be well-lighted inside. Most log cabins were dim on the brightest days. Meantime, the openings would be fitted with tight shutters, to be opened in mild weather.

Soon the woods were ringing with the sound of the men's axes, and Anna was peeling bark from the logs, helping carry them to the house. The three of them were strong, and the hewn white pine logs they'd chosen were the smaller trees that'd grown up where older ones had fallen, letting in the required sunlight for their growth.

Anna fed the men at midday, noting how much George consumed. Well, they all did, working hard this way. She was grateful for the deer Stephen had killed the day before, which they'd cut into strips to dry. They'd be all right this winter with the abundant game, and by summer they'd have a corn patch, some vegetables. Yes, this was to be their own little paradise.

By late afternoon, the second cabin logs were half up. They'd located a big chestnut they'd felled for roof shakes and had used the treasured crosscut saw Stephen had borrowed to cut blocks to split. He told George he'd rive shakes the next day, knowing the others at the settlement wanted the big man to work with them on their various projects.

"Couple of days, we'll get back on the rest of the logs, George," he said. "You take your time…we'll live in this end all winter just fine." The big man left, taking a cake Anna had baked to share with Daughtry and Nolan, among others.

The truth was, neither Stephen nor Anna wanted company just then. They'd go back to the settlement when they were ready, but for now, their new life together was a kind of enchantment, and they wanted it to go on forever.

Among the treasures they'd been able to get on the supply trips were a few books, and both eagerly devoured them by candlelight and the flames from the hearth. They began reading to each other, lying on blankets before the fire, listening also to the winter wind singing around the eaves of their little house.

They knew that life couldn't possibly get any better than this.

~ * ~

Samuel Eddins spent the winter in Philadelphia, tending to some of the legal aspects of Cabot's enterprises. In the spring, he was scheduled to travel down to the Saltville area to begin the process of acquiring land, claims and mineral rights to the iron-rich areas Archie Nolan had discovered. Both he and Cabot agreed it might be prudent for them to leave the capital permanently, with that relentless Mason moving closer in his investigations, which would inevitably lead to their group unless they were very careful.

As part of that circle, Eddins had managed to put away a sizeable amount of gold over the years, and he wanted to be able to enjoy it. Cabot had been a good man to tie to and promised to continue providing well. But another aspect of the Kentucky venture was that, if anything went badly wrong down there, it'd be easier for Eddins to disappear, to desert the sinking ship, as it were.

It never hurt, he knew, to have an escape plan.

Cabot had considered simply having this Mason killed, thereby removing the threat of discovery. But the man didn't run things by himself; he had a staff of what had become known as detectives helping him. Financed by a score of merchants, these men probably knew as much as Mason himself, and any one of them could continue his work. So yes, it was high time to move to greener pastures.

Cabot himself had returned quietly to Philadelphia that winter, cautioning his associates to tell anyone interested that he was still off somewhere out of reach. To make his anonymity more believable, the man had not returned to his house, taking lodging in another part of town and staying inside. Even his wife didn't know where he was, and he liked it that way.

"We'll be ready to travel by late March," he told the lawyer. "I've been in contact with the engineer, the smelter operator and the foundryman, and we'll go together with their families. You'll have to work to keep the legal side of things up with our operations, because we'll begin in earnest just as soon as we arrive. I plan to collect workmen soon, to add to whatever labor force is available at Ketchum's Mill. We'll hit the place like a small army and be in production as soon as we get a good road out of there."

This all sounded exciting to the lawyer, and he resolved to make sure all the legal angles were covered. The temper in the new country was for development anyway, and he knew they'd actually be setting precedents along the way, where legalities were still murky. No matter: possession was still ninety percent of the law, and there should be no one to challenge them out in that wilderness. The necessary land would be free, a luxury not available in the civilized areas of the new states.

Like Cabot, Eddins pictured himself in a position of power once established in Kentucky. The two of them would be the founders of the industry, settlements, whatever society grew up around them. Why, they'd become legends out there...in charge, sought after, dispensing favors and even a kind of justice, as they saw it.

Yes, altogether a heady prospect.

For his part, Reginald Cabot was preparing to leave the city with his fortune intact. His money would travel with them, divided among the several wagons of the group. There were loose ends to be tied up before spring and he went about that task methodically, transferring management quietly, withdrawing cash, placing others in charge of this and that. And ensuring that his share of the spoils of this operation continued to flow to him.

To Codington and the others of the circle, Cabot explained simply that he was going ahead with their plans for the iron venture and would of course work out a way of sharing the profits. He advised the others to have escape plans in case the Mason investigation got too close, but assured them the man would probably back off once he, the obvious principal suspect, had left. Privately, he didn't care a fig how any of them fared once he was clear, but he did want that money to continue, so urged them to take extra precautions.

But one thing nagged at him. Growing up off and on the back streets of Boston, he'd always managed to even any score against him. That of course was what had really been behind sending Justin Ames to Virginia. And now this Mason thing was becoming a personal affront.

He knew he must not leave that insult unattended to.

~ * ~

There was little activity on the road north of Saltville during the winter and the MacNaughton clan had less luck robbing travelers. For the most part, they stayed holed up in their mountain hollows, hunting, living off their earlier takings, and waiting for spring. They grew quarrelsome among themselves with cabin fever and it was not a pleasant time.

Carver MacNaughton had formulated his plan, and he was forcing himself to wait until the winter broke to carry it out. He was sure he was old enough to go out on his own and he'd do it. He'd simply leave home and head west by himself with whatever he could carry. He'd steal what he needed along the way, using stealth instead of bold robbery, which hadn't worked out well for the clan of late.

That meant patience, and he'd had to discipline himself during the cold time.

Like his brothers and cousins, Carver was a hunter, and had learned to wait long hours for game. So when the need arose in his traveling, he'd hide and watch, then take food or a horse when it was safe. Far away somewhere, when he came upon the right place, he might or might not settle. Probably not...the idea of roaming this broad country with his gun appealed to him.

And there was another side to his plan. He'd find out where the missionaries had gone, and he would find a way to settle what he considered a legitimate grudge against them. That hard-eyed fellow who'd shot his horse owed him, and he aimed to collect. So he'd go there, wherever it was, and use the hide-and-watch strategy until the opportunity presented itself. Then he'd even the score, provision himself at their expense, then ride on over the mountains toward the new settlements West, free and his own man.

Carver had observed what he had to admit was a worthless streak in his kin. Sure, it was easier to steal than to work, but their successes were now fewer and often brought in little. Figuring it over a period of a year, he knew if the men had worked during that year instead of robbing, as his brother had reflected, they'd have made more money. Labor didn't exactly appeal to him but having money did.

His conclusion was that if he were ever to make anything of himself, he must first get away from here, where the community of hunters and farmers were hostile to the MacNaughtons. Sooner or later, he knew, these good citizens would act, and some of his tribe would probably hang.

None of the men in his family had education beyond the simplest basics; most of them couldn't read or write. The late cousin Ansted had seen to it that he learned all he could, realizing he could more easily mix with potential victims that way. He'd even courted a local schoolteacher and persuaded her to help him with his reading and general knowledge. That he had later deserted her had not troubled him, and the lady had gone back North sadder but presumably wiser.

Ansted had taken a particular liking to his cousin Carver, who'd seemed to be a bit more inclined to use his head than the others of the clan. Oh, he had the same hot temper as the rest, the same aspirations to become a latter-day Robin Hood, and yes, sometimes he acted rashly. But Ansted had spent time with the boy and encouraged him in learning everything he could.

The result had been Carver's attaining a certain superior feeling over his cruder relatives. The more he learned, the more he considered himself cut out for better things than they. He could often talk his way out of trouble, manipulate his slower cousins, and oftener than not, come out ahead on any exchange.

He admitted that trying to draw his pistol against the missionaries that time had been a mistake, a hot-headed product of his frustration, and vowed never to let anger blind him again. He and his brothers should have been able to pass on, then follow the wagons to a suitable ambush site. But both Paul and Silas had told him those people had seen them hanging around Saltville, which was why they'd accosted them.

Carver knew, upon reflection, that the hard-eyed man in the lead had acted first, because he'd known somehow who they were and what they planned. How he'd known was a mystery, but he supposed there were men like that. Perhaps, like the MacNaughtons, the man viewed everybody as his enemy until proven otherwise.

But in that case, what was he doing with a bunch of churchy people? Nothing he'd ever heard about missionaries included having killers among them. And Carver had no doubt whatsoever that his enemy was a killer. He remembered the cold shivers that had run down his back at the sight of the rock-steady rifle held on him as he lay on the ground.

For that matter, the other two didn't seem like church people, either. Maybe they were just hired guards or something. Even the young one-armed one had a hardness about him, and all three brothers sensed that they'd been lucky being let go to walk home.

That didn't dull the thirst for revenge inside Carver, but it did make him more cautious. Yes, he'd wait out the time till spring, then prove to himself that he was as good as any man. Better than his kin, and yes, better than the man he was going to find a way to kill.

~ * ~

Archie Nolan was well aware of the flow of iron from the Jackson River area. He'd been in on some of the original prospecting there, and indeed had directed Lester Cummings to the area. Not a businessman as such, Nolan hadn't insisted on a share of the industry that followed his discoveries, but had been well paid.

Now he was older and wiser, and was determined to profit from his findings on Troublesome Creek. If Cabot and his backers had the means to handle the difficulties of transportation, there was a great deal of money to be made there. But Nolan also knew, much better than the Easterner, the near-impossibility of his plan for the road and the rail idea. He suspected that Cabot put too much faith in the abilities of the engineers he was so fond of referring to.

But it wasn't Nolan's money the man would spend. And yes, if by some miracle it could be made to pay off, he'd be right there in on it. Privately, however, he felt Cabot would be wasting gold, biting off more than he could chew, as it were.

There was another aspect to all this, too. Not only was there iron in these mountains, there was coal. The more he prospected, the more Nolan found of the black substance. And that could make the difference in the iron production, coal being a far more efficient heat source than wood. He hadn't mentioned the coal to Cabot, not having found much until recently, but now that opened up a lot of possibilities. Rich deposits of coal here could feed the industrial East, with less competition than that for iron.

And, the iron venture aside, it was much easier to mine coal than to go through the mining, smelting and foundry work to produce iron. Of course, coal wasn't worth as much as iron, but if it could be transported in volume, it could be quite profitable.

He debated whether to confide in Cabot about this discovery, sensing there was something too free and easy about the way the man spent money. That led to speculation about how he'd come by his fortune. And that train of thought brought up whether he wanted to be closely associated with what could be a man not wholly on the level.

In the end, Nolan decided to cooperate with Cabot on the iron venture but keep the coal discovery to himself. If and when the man's ambitious plans worked out, he could always then introduce the coal aspect, to produce the iron more efficiently. And yes, he'd be certain to have his own legal claims to the coalfields in hand before that time.

Thirteen

Samuel Eddins and Reginald Cabot both stayed largely out of sight for the remainder of that winter. Their group of 'businessmen' met periodically, but the general understanding was that they would continue with their illegal operations and replace, one by one, the men beneath them, the actual thieves. That would eliminate the contacts Mason was undoubtedly establishing and help keep them safe. Also, if each man at the top could invest in more legitimate trades, he could thereby protect himself further from the dogged Mason and his men.

Cabot informed the others at first that he would welcome their money in the iron project, but that this was his venture, and while they'd receive a return on their money, by then he didn't want them any further in on it. For one thing, the more they stayed apart, the safer all would be. For another, Cabot was full of visions of success, and he just didn't want to share.

Eddins was sure he could wrangle his way into more than just legal fees and didn't worry overly. He'd have to know as much about the business as Cabot, and the man needed him. He'd broach the subject of a partnership with him after they'd made some headway.

No use getting tied up early on something like that which could crash from poor planning, that transportation problem, shortage of manpower, or any of many other reasons new business ventures failed.

So as winter finally turned to early spring, Cabot wrapped up his last business involvements. Then he set in motion his final Philadelphia activity.

He sent an assassin to kill one Jedediah Mason.

"And if you are successful, with nothing to link you to the execution, I'll have more work for you," he told the man, an ex-soldier named Hiram Garst. Cabot had collected a share of Garst's fee from the others of the circle, which they agreed was only fair. Once Mason was gone, all felt they could continue quietly, safely.

Cabot didn't wait for confirmation of the kill. He had no intention of staying around, allowing the possibility of being linked with another assassination. As for his plans to lessen competition on the Jackson River, he'd deal with that Lester Cummings another way.

Cabot and Eddins, accompanied by the smelter operator John Leslie and the foundryman Sedgewick White and their families, made preparations to leave for Kentucky. They had four wagons among them, and the convoy set out from Philadelphia on a windy day of clearing clouds for Baltimore, Georgetown and down the Shenandoah Valley.

It was to be a long trip over roads less than ideal. But as much in a hurry to begin as he was, Cabot knew the high country they were headed for would be some weeks behind in warming up. So they'd travel at a leisurely pace, stopping at the better inns and camping only where necessary. The women were somewhat apprehensive, having heard the tales of Indians on that frontier, but the men and children were looking forward to the adventure.

"Our contacts there report absolutely no danger from the savages," Cabot assured them. "Kentucky has always been mutual hunting ground for the tribes, who live elsewhere. We won't endanger them, and they'll leave us alone."

Sybil Leslie, sixteen, and her brother Sam, twelve, did not share their mother's concern, nor did Amelia White, a cheerful ten-year-old, her sister Anne, eight, nor their brother Patrick, six. So Sarah Leslie and Aurelia White, who was nursing her youngest boy, hid their concerns as best they could, and prepared for the ordeal of the long journey. The party was well-armed, so when they reached the wilderness, they'd be a match for highwaymen or any other threats, Cabot again assured them.

As a final gesture, the man had sent his wife a note informing her of his leaving the country for destinations unknown and giving her access to a considerable sum of money to keep her indefinitely. He wrote her that if she wanted to dissolve their marriage, he'd arrange it. In his eyes, Cabot felt he had disposed of that complication nicely.

For the first days, even weeks, the travel was not unlike trips they'd all taken before. The four men tended to most of the driving, and at stops along the way farriers shod the horses as necessary, wagon wrights serviced the conveyances, and all went as smoothly as any such trip could.

Past the Potomac, which the party crossed on the ferry at Alexandria, civilization thinned considerably. There were a few plantations, smaller holdings, but fewer villages of any size. The quality of the inns and taverns diminished, and the women insisted on inspecting each potential lodging for vermin before they'd agree to stopping there for the night. That necessitated a few camping sessions, where the travelers slept on blankets in their wagons.

As Cabot and Eddins knew, the broad Shenandoah was rich farmland with substantial German, Scottish, Irish and Scandinavian settlers. It was abuzz with plowing, planting, all the activities of farmland being awakened from its winter sleep. Provisions were good and with care, clean inns could be found. There seemed to be no end to this valley, rimmed by the Blue Ridge to the east and the Appalachians on the right as they traveled.

The trip was boring for the children, but the stops at inns and stores were breaks in the monotony, and they held up as well as six stair-step young ones could. Sybil was not unaware of the young men they met and passed, although most were rougher in clothing and manners than she was used to. The planters wore tailored clothes by contrast, rode magnificent horses, and these young men were, to her eyes, dashing. She hoped there'd be eligible men like these in Kentucky.

At long last, the wagon train reached the village of Saltville, which Cabot informed them was the last outpost they'd pass. Here they stocked up on supplies and rested the horses for two days. Eddins made himself familiar with the legal structure of the place, introducing himself to the local judge, county clerk, and two other lawyers, who were both actually part-time, being primarily farmers.

Cabot told him to start preparing the way for homestead deeds and rights-of-way, as well as outlining the legal structure of the operation. He was to stay in Saltville for the present, awaiting details of the land descriptions, et cetera, which would be sent to him by courier soon.

And now being short a driver on the roughest part of their road, Cabot asked about and eventually employed a single young man to drive, work at the mines, and act as that courier. Abe Holloway was a lanky specimen, given to cheerful comment on just about everything he saw. *Not an unspoken thought in his head,* was Sybil Leslie's evaluation of this buckskin-clad youth.

Reginald Cabot informed his party that their destination lay less than two weeks away. That knowledge was received with some dismay by the wives, eagerness by the children, and anticipation by the men.

"Here's where we must be on the lookout for danger," their leader told them. "There's a band of outlaws who rob travelers, but they've never accosted this large a party. I'll take the lead wagon, and if you'd bring up the rear, Leslie, I think we'll be safe enough. Do have several loaded guns close and of course, keep your powder dry."

Thus sobered, the travelers began the last leg of their journey, into just what situation no one except Cabot knew. The mountains they'd been winding through grew higher, the creek bottoms narrower, the farms quite distant from each other, the pace necessarily slower.

There would be no more inns until Ketchum's Mill, but he assured the others that the new convenience there would be worth the trip.

"We've the makings of quite a civilized village there," he assured them. "The Ketchums are the soul of hospitality, the missionaries there are wonderful people with their new church, and the other settlers hardworking and honest. One young lady has by now begun a school, too. Altogether, I believe you'll find the place and the people quite to your liking."

The women hoped even a part of the man's cheerful bolsterings would prove to be true. There was still something off-putting about a place on a creek called Troublesome.

~ * ~

Hiram Garst planned the assassination carefully, with the promised future work for Cabot in mind. This Mason would simply disappear down a dry abandoned well outside town, with no clue and no recriminations. One complication was that the man always traveled with a bodyguard, a mean-eyed specimen Garst knew would have to be eliminated first.

He tracked the investigator's movements, seeking to establish a pattern he could exploit. Experience had taught him there would come a time the guard could be distracted, or simply shot from a distance. Then he was sure he could handle Mason easily and afterward cart the two bodies away for disposal.

Accordingly, Garst armed himself with a long rifle and two pistols and devoted his time to following the pair discreetly. To avoid drawing attention to himself, he altered his appearance often. A false mustache, different clothing, an affected limp, all transformed him. And no one thought it odd that a man carried a rifle about town; out-of-town settlers were in that habit.

Jedediah Mason was a former tradesman who, after having lost a great deal to mercantile thievery, had begun hunting down those responsible. His successes had attracted the attention of others in the thriving capital, and soon he found he could charge fees that let him ease out of his former business.

The work was not without its hazards. He'd been wounded once in a shootout with a gang of robbers who'd been working with an inside employee at an import warehouse. The outlaws hadn't known that Mason had discovered their in-house member and after severe threats, had turned him to his purposes. In time, such a man would be referred to as a double agent. In the firefight the contact had been killed, along with one robber, and Mason still carried a pistol ball under his collar bone.

That event had resulted in his designating one of his men, the fearsome Leighton Chiles, as his personal bodyguard. And as the work uncovered more elaborate, bigger operations, the danger increased. Mason was a good shot himself and had once acquitted himself well in a knife fight. But he realized he was, after years at his work, probably the target of more than one well-financed illegal operator.

This caused him to take further precautions; he limited his travel, especially to distant locations requiring using lonely roads. Chiles accompanied him everywhere, even sleeping in a spare room in Mason's house.

That had almost horrified Letitia Mason, who knew enough about her husband's work to fear some of his less than savory companions. However, Leighton Chiles' nature belied his stark, forbidding demeanor. The man was positively gentle, polite, and devoted to his employer. Soon he was treated as one of the family, something Letitia wouldn't have predicted at all from the man's appearance.

Another member of Mason's staff, one Clem O'Malley, also moved in with the family in their large Georgian brick house off the main downtown section. This man had a number of duties in the operation, but one specialty: since he looked much like Mason himself, he often accompanied Chiles on business trips, posing as his employer when Mason was safe at home. He and Mason wore identical clothes and affected similar mannerisms. And since the Mason children were grown and no longer at home, the double came and went undetected.

So when Hiram Garst stalked his quarry, he was ignorant of the actual identity of the man. He also found it very difficult to get the two targets away from public places where witnesses would be everywhere. No matter, he counseled himself, a hunter always had to have patience; his chance would come.

And it did. Weeks after Cabot's departure, the investigator and his bodyguard mounted horses and rode toward the home of an industrialist near his musket works just out of town. As it happened, the real Mason was at the time riding in his carriage in the opposite direction, with yet another of his staff accompanying him.

Garst followed the men to a wooded section of the road, keeping just out of sight behind them. Ahead, a straight stretch would give him his shot at Chiles, then he'd mount, ride Mason down, and the deed would be done. Since it was daylight, he doubted he'd be able to dispose of the bodies as planned, so he'd make the killings look like simple highway robbery. With luck, no passersby would happen along.

Chiles was not happy at accompanying O'Malley, feeling his place had been beside his employer. But he also sensed this was a vulnerable stretch of road and kept a roving eye on the forest, the curves, checking often behind them for any signs of trouble.

O'Malley was to handle the business with the musket manufacturer as a trusted representative of Mason's organization. He had his report of progress, Mason's plan for the rest of the operation, and was going over these as he rode. With Chiles, he felt perfectly safe. The man had an uncanny sense of danger and had proven it often.

He bent, retrieved papers from the leather case strapped to his saddle, intent on perusing them one more time before meeting the client. And it was in that instant that he felt in his shoulder the impact, then heard the rifle report from behind. He reeled, but managed to hold onto his seat, instinctively spurring his horse. But the horse's lunge ahead did topple him, and he fell face-first, stunned, into the roadside grass.

Garst had decided at the last moment to shoot only his main target, reasoning that with the distance, he could disappear before the bodyguard could reach him. The man would no doubt stay by his employer's side to help, but of course there wouldn't be any help possible.

And that's what Chiles did—leap out of his saddle, searching the road behind them, finding nothing but a cloud of black powder smoke, seeing only a dim shape galloping away.

He knelt over the fallen man, examining the wound.

"High, so it didn't hit anything vital," he pronounced. "Here, hold this cloth tight over it. I'm going to try and catch the shooter." He was up and mounted in an instant, pounding after the distant horseman.

Garst hadn't seen his target leaning over just at the moment of firing through the puff of smoke from the weapon's pan, but when he fell, he was sure he'd killed the man. He raced for cover, or for a good ambush spot. He wouldn't go far, giving himself time to hide, reload his rifle if the bodyguard rode after him. From this distance he couldn't tell whether the man had stayed or was coming on. If he came, that should mean Mason was indeed dead.

Chiles cursed himself for not being more watchful. Whoever that had been, he'd been a good shot; long distance, and now he was further still. He rode hard, catching sight eventually of Garst around a curve, closer than he'd thought, just turning off into dense brush. He caught a brief look at the man's face, but was certain he hadn't been seen clearly by him. Immediately Chiles reined in, taking to the woods himself to stay out of sight, but moving up.

Garst dismounted in deep cover, reloaded his rifle, tied his horse, and crept back to the road. It was empty. So had the man stayed with Mason, or was he stalking him, even now? Given even a glimpse of him, the assassin knew he could drop the other man, but perhaps he wouldn't have to. He'd accomplished his mission: Mason was undoubtedly dead, and he could just ride away, now that he was sufficiently armed again. Or was the target actually dead? Time to find out.

He mounted, rode briskly out of cover, and spurred his horse ahead. He looked back just as Chiles emerged from the woods, dismounted, and took aim at him. He swerved, dodged, flattened himself against the horse's neck. Then back again, presenting a fast-moving target.

He heard the report of the other's rifle but felt nothing. That convinced him he was free, so he continued at a high gallop, back toward the city.

Chiles, frustrated at having missed the fleeing man, turned back to the fallen O'Malley. It wasn't far to their destination, so he resolved to take the wounded man there, then send for a doctor. He reached him, heaved him up onto his horse.

"Can you ride?"

"I think so. Painful as hell, though. Who was it, you think?"

"Don't know, but you know Mr. Mason has a boatload of enemies. Surprised it was just the one man. Couldn't catch him or hit him, I'm afraid. But let's get you to safety, send for help."

He rode close, supporting O'Malley in his saddle, on to the industrialist's home. Once there, a serving man helped get the wounded man down and into the house. The master sent a helper riding for a doctor who lived nearby. Chiles stayed, presented the report, waited for the doctor.

Luckily the man had been at home, having just arrived from delivering a baby. Examining O'Malley, he pronounced the wound not that serious.

"Inch lower, it'd be a different story, sir. Rifle must've carried high."

"No, I bent down just then. Can I ride, you think?"

"Shouldn't, no. I'd say rest here for a day or two, if that's all right with Mr. Coulter, here." He looked to the musket maker.

"Certainly, Doctor. These men's employer has already saved me a deal of money, and he's welcome. And I'll send him back to the city in my carriage when he's fit."

That arranged, Leighton Chiles left them, full of anger at himself for his lapse, and rode toward Philadelphia, thinking. Obviously whoever had shot O'Malley had indeed mistaken him for Mason, and would almost certainly believe now that he'd killed him. That could be worked to advantage, he thought. *Have to get with the boss to discuss that idea.*

Garst decided it would be best to leave the city, now that he was convinced his duty had been done. He'd learned that Cabot had left town, and managed to find out where he was headed from a Mr. Codington he'd tracked down. With the story that he'd missed catching his boss, the assassin was able to assure this man he was an employee, and that Cabot had more work for him.

But unfortunately, before he could leave, Garst let himself be persuaded to join in an all-night high-stakes game of chance. Word was, a fellow from New York with more money than gambling sense, wanted to indulge his habit here. The assassin's cronies assured him they could all fleece this neophyte, and the idea appealed to him.

So it was supposed to go, but the New Yorker turned out to be much sharper than any of the locals, and instead took them for what they had. Garst found himself with most of his fee for killing Mason gone forever.

So he rode out of Philadelphia considerably poorer on the long road to Virginia, then Kentucky Territory. Be new country, at least, and no, this Cabot wouldn't be so easily rid of him. Man had money, he needed money, and he meant to earn as much of it as he could.

~ * ~

As winter had softened, young Carver MacNaughton had quietly slipped provisions off to a hiding place in a hollow tree far from home, had his replacement horse shod as a trade for helping the blacksmith on recent trips to the village. He collected blankets, rifle, pistol, gunpowder, lead and a bullet mold, and a waterproofed piece of canvas stolen by one of the clan from a traveler. He was careful to space his removal of these items so that no one would suspect his intent.

He was some days ahead of the Cabot party then, when he followed the forest road toward Ketchum's Mill. He had a little money he'd managed to steal from various members of the extended family, and none had caught him at it. As he rode, he reflected that he'd actually enjoyed working with the smith, who seemed something of a wizard, creating useful, even decorative pieces in iron, just by heating it and hammering it. *Might 'prentice m'self to a smith, som'ers on down th' road, I git to whar they ain't heered th' name MacNaughton. That feller in town shore kep' his eye on me, th' whole time, like I wuz gonna steal me a nail er somethin'.*

Carver was able to shoot a rabbit, then a turkey along the way, and only slipped up to a root cellar once to take some potatoes while the family was out in the fields. So he still had food to eat when, after many miles, he eventually reached the settlement at the end of the road. His plan was to stay well back, camping deep in the woods, going on foot to spy on the people there, see what the situation was. Then he'd decide on his course of action, which had as its uppermost goal to remain uncaught.

From his selected vantage point atop a cliff face where few trees impeded his line of sight, he was able to observe most of the goings-on of the village. In view were the mill, the church and the inn, as well as Daughtry's cabin up the slope, and various wagon tracks off up the hollows and downcreek. He noted the trail on west, making this, as he'd learned, truly the end of the road.

He could hear the rasping of the pitsaw up from below, as well as the hammering on the inn, the broadaxe strokes of the men hewing beams nearby. Most of the work seemed to be done by a huge man and a tall, spare one. He wasn't sure, but the tall one looked a lot like the hard-eyed guard, or whatever he'd been, who'd shot his horse from under him.

Carver couldn't hear voices from this distance, but could follow what was happening fairly well, just from the movements of the people. For instance, an older woman was in and out of the inn and appeared to be directing the men there. So, the innkeeper or his wife. The smith worked the open-fronted forge, and Carver was interested to note that he had no helper. Now and then the tall man would spend some time with the smith, then leave with a batch of nails, or some tool or piece of material for the building work.

The church seemed to be also a school, with a tall young woman herding children about. It was too far for a good look, but once in a while he could hear a shout or scream from the students at play. There were two swings, a wooden slide, and a seesaw visible.

Other men and women came from the roads and trails from time to time to visit the mill, the smithy, or the school. Smoke came from the large inn chimney, and several of the community gathered there at midday, obviously for dinner. Carver could smell the food from his perch, and it made him hungry.

He eyed the remains of his travel provisions, and decided he'd have to replenish them very soon, one way or the other. Be hard to do, though, with all those people around. Maybe sneak into the inn at night. Or follow one of the roads to a remote cabin to raid.

He considered working his way closer and shooting the tall man, then riding on west. But that hunger made him cautious; have to provide for himself better than that. Whole place be after him once he made such a move. No, just wait, and something would work out.

But it didn't that first day. He noted the children leaving the church, then the teacher walked to the inn where the men were inside working. Nothing happened for a while, then the woman emerged, went into the mill. The big man came out, took boards from the mill and carried them into the inn. Carver waited.

Finally, the teacher left the mill with a bag of meal and met the tall man outside the inn. It was late in the day by then, and the two of them mounted horses and rode off up the creek trail. They passed closer to the boy's lookout, and he could plainly see that the man was indeed the one who'd humiliated him and his brothers those months before.

So, they were the only ones who'd gone up the creek, which should mean they lived on the only place that way. All the others had gone in other directions, so these two probably had a cabin somewhere nobody else had wanted to settle. They weren't farmers, then. Steep mountain that way. A builder and his wife the teacher. Cabin would be hidden, probably up a ravine or little hollow.

Carver decided he'd wait for them to return to the settlement next morning, then find their cabin and rob them of food and whatever else he could take. He'd be on the trail on west and out of the country then, well ahead of any pursuit.

But that wouldn't satisfy his thirst for revenge. The man had bested the MacNaughtons, not even giving them a chance to fight it out. He aimed to bring that man down, and a plan soon took shape.

He could wait for them at their cabin, shoot the man with his rifle and hold his second gun on the woman while he escaped. Have to be sure to be ready to ride, with his horse hidden first.

Yes, he could do that.

Carver slipped from his hiding place and made his way back to his camp. He'd no grain for his horse, and that was getting to be a problem. Well then, he'd just take one of the couple's horses. Or two. The man owed him a horse. Or maybe he'd keep his own and take one and feed for them. Yes, either way would work. Use one of theirs for a packhorse.

He'd like to slip back to the mill and steal some grain now, but that was a risk. There were dogs in the village, and it'd be hard to evade them. Well, his mount would just have to wait; it'd all be better tomorrow.

Clouds had moved in, and it smelled like rain. Carver didn't like the idea of that, but the canvas would shelter him. He'd eat the last of his food, then steal enough tomorrow to see him well away. He remembered the good smells from the new inn, and also the activity around the place. The smith seemed to be the miller, too, the way he'd kept checking on the pitsaw and fussing about the machinery. Clear that they were short-handed in this place. Wasn't for that tall fellow—killer, his kin had guessed—he might find a way to fit in here. No, they'd sooner or later learn who he was: one of those MacNaughtons from back near Saltville, and it'd all be over.

He found himself cursing his shiftless relatives. If a man *was* to try to make somethin' of hisself, he'd hafta go clear outta th' country to do it. Well, didn't matter...he was bound for the road anyway, seek his fortune some other place.

A slow spring rain set in around midnight, and the leafing-out world was dripping and chilly next morning. Carver broke camp early, led his horse a long way around the hill between there and the settlement, and struck the creek some distance above it. He didn't know how far the man and woman lived upstream, but guessed he was between them and their work. He waited, well back from the creek and the trail that followed it on the other side.

Not long afterwards, the two rode into view, oiled rain gear covering them, but easily recognizable. The man sheltered a long rifle as he rode. Carver had never seen a woman that tall. They passed, and he waited a few minutes, then waded his horse across the rushing creek at a shoal and headed up the trail.

He almost missed the steep path up into a boulder-jumbled hollow. The fresh tracks came from there, still pooling rainwater, so this must be the way. He led his horse up the twisting trail, around outcroppings, through woods, eventually to a meadow with new grass already up. This was a south-facing slope, sheltered from the cold, a good spot. Past this was woods again, then another open space, with a double log cabin at woods edge above it. Smoke wisped from one of two chimneys, but there was no movement anywhere. Carver turned his horse loose in the grass and began his approach.

He went right up to the cabin, although with pulse racing, and called out.

"Ennybody home?" No answer. He rapped on the door of the section that had the smoking chimney. Again, quiet. He tried the door, but it was latched from the inside. He tried the door to the other section, finding it also locked. He went around to the rear of the house and tried the first door there. Locked, too. He saw no keyhole and wondered how the people got inside. The last door had a lock, but it was intricate and he couldn't figure how it opened. *Never seen a thing like that.*

There was a root cellar and he opened it, finding potatoes, onions, turnips. He'd have to find something to put them in. Then the smokehouse, in which were hams and sides of bacon. Yes, need that packhorse for sure if he loaded up.

The house had wooden shutters, latched from the inside like the doors. This place was as secure as it could be made, it appeared. Oh, he could find an axe, chop his way in, but he wasn't that sure nobody'd come along. *No, best just wait.* He took food, and found grain for his horse, which he then fed. There was an outside fire spot and an iron washpot, and he sheltered the place with his canvas, kindled a fire and proceeded to scorch ham and potatoes with onions.

This was a prosperous-looking place, he observed as he ate. Above was an open garden patch, newly-plowed, fenced tightly with rails interwoven with small saplings. Grass enough in the meadow for a little hay, and he reckoned the people traded or worked for whatever else they needed. He thought begrudgingly that this would be an ideal location for a man if he was to try to lead a normal life.

But that kind of thinking didn't fit with his plans. He'd let his horse graze the day while he stocked up. He found a packsaddle in the small barn and stuffed it with provisions and grain. Then he saw to it his powder was dry in both his rifle and pistol, and took shelter in the barn to wait.

Near the end of the day, he'd saddle his horse, hide him, then wait in ambush above the trail. If the man came first, he'd simply shoot him, take one of their horses, put the packsaddle on it, and ride away on his. The wife would no doubt scream and cry but he was sure he could handle a hysterical woman.

If she came first, he'd wait till she passed, then shoot the man. It should be a simple matter, either way. And he'd be avenged, well-supplied, and on his way to a new life. Yes, away from bumbling kin, mean-eyed settlers, and all the trouble his clan had endured. That they'd brought it all on themselves he more than suspected, but that didn't matter. He was about to make himself a new life, with a clean slate to start with and yes, even up an old score in the bargain.

The rain lessened, stopped, then began again. Twice more that day it looked like clearing, but clouded over again. Carver waited, judging the time the two should arrive.

~ * ~

At the village, work continued inside the inn with Stephen, Ketchum and George shaping and hanging interior doors, framing up beds, putting together chairs and tables. Belle Ketchum bustled about, delighted with her new place of business. The McKnight family and Archie Nolan were in residence, and everyone expected Reginald Cabot and the first of his iron-mining people soon.

A third trip had been made to Saltville earlier, in a rare time of thaw. So now the inn was stocked, bedding was being fashioned, weaving sheets and blankets was under way. The missionaries were earning some money at these duties, financed by Mr. Cabot's advance payment.

Stephen had letters from his family in Goochland, where he learned he had another young nephew; from Ned Drake in Caroline County, where he had a godchild on the way; and from Tom Logan, with the same news.

"They're getting ahead of us," he told his bride.

"All in God's time," she replied, smiling and lighting up the air around them. "They've been married longer."

And indeed, Stephen was glad for the time he and Anna had been alone in their new home. Children would be welcome, but the months of discovering only each other, sharing, loving, were as near paradise as either could have imagined. Now, with spring, everything would be moving faster, stealing time from them, drawing them more into the life of the village. But it was all an adventure, this beginning a new life for them and the others, and both of them were excited to be part of it.

Anna emerged from the church with an oiled cloth sheltering her, sending the children on their ways home. She went to the inn, into its warmth, and greeted her husband and the others. The minister's wife and daughters were at work quilting with Belle, the frame hanging from the ceiling of a room as yet without furniture. The scraps of sewn cloth, still bright even in this second use, gave the room a festive air. The women stood around the edges of the quilt, chatted, laughed, stitched. They invited Anna to join them, which she did for a while, drying out from the short walk from the church. A fire crackled at the hearth, and the tightly-built room was warm and inviting.

But the days were still short in the shadow of the mountains, and she needed to get on home, build up the fire, have her own home ready for her man's return. Indeed, her thoughts were already there.

"I'm going on home, Stephen, to dry out and get an early start on supper. You're welcome too, George, as you know." She smiled at the big man, who was always shy in her presence.

"Thankee, ma'am, but wet as 'tis, I b'lieve I'll just sup with th' Ketchums here. But y'all let me know when y'need more farwood."

"We will, certainly, and thanks for all you've done already." She kissed Stephen, retrieved her horse, and set out up the creek trail. Shielding herself from the rain, she checked her pistol to make sure it was dry, then tucked it back into the waistband at her back, under her cloak.

The rhythmic sound of the horse's feet and the swaying ride on the wet trail lulled her; the sound of the rushing creek was a song in counterpoint, and the soft patter of the rain a constant, soothing background. Anna had never been so content, and thanked God for her lot in life and His direction.

And I almost denied myself all this with my foolish pride. So glad Stephen came. So glad we both...well, grew up, I guess.

Fourteen

Carver MacNaughton decided it was time to find the place to ambush his quarry, so he slipped from the barn and around the house just in time to see the woman riding around the last bend in the path. He ducked back, peered around the corner of the cabin. She was alone. He shrank back, trying to decide what his next step should be.

He could just let her go into the house, go down and wait to shoot her husband, then come back... No, she'd hear the shot, perhaps have a gun in the house, be able to pick him off if she was maybe any kind of a shot. Probably not, being a woman, but that was a chance he needn't take.

All right then, he'd just let her get into the house, and he'd hold her hostage till the man came home. Maybe tie her up. That way he'd take the man as soon as he walked in the door, and he'd also see if there was money in the house. Daring plan, he knew, but he had the advantage of surprise, and...

Oh, my God! Never r'membered m'hoss. Reckon she seen it? Don't seem so, way she's jist comin' on. Rain, mebbe she didn't. Wal, don't matter. Jump her at th' back door, 'fore she kin git inside an' git a gun. If she saw th' hoss, that's whut she'll do, ennyways, so guess it don't matter. Slip up on her when she's undoin' thet lock thaing, go in with her, gun on her. T'won't be hard atall.

He was excited, his blood racing as the woman rounded the house, he staying beyond the other end. She dismounted, led the horse inside the barn, unsaddled, fed him grain and some hay. Then she emerged, walked to the back door, a strange-looking key in her hand. Carver moved silently around from his hiding place, right up behind her, the rain covering his approach. His heart pounded, but he remembered to keep the pistol dry under his open coat. *God, she's tall...*

She pushed the door open and Carver was upon her. He shoved her inside, slamming the door behind them, pistol out. She stumbled, turned, eyes wide, but did not cry out. He thought that was strange... women always screamed. She took in the pistol, his face.

"Git over thar," he ordered, shoving the pistol at her. "An' light some light, so's we k'n see in here." She moved slowly, deliberately, not wanting to startle this boy. She could see he was trembling, unsure of himself. She'd have to calm him, then she'd see just what was to be done. She herself was calm, somehow. She remembered that man months ago at the women's cabin, and how she'd dealt with him. The pistol was under her coat within easy reach if she distracted him, but she didn't want to kill this young intruder.

She lit candles from the smoldering hearth fire, set two logs on it, stood back.

"Now, we gonna wait fer yore husbin t'git here. An' when he does..."

She'd been trying to fit this boy's appearance into anything that made sense of the recent activities. Or was this just a random robbery? Not likely, hidden off the road this way. He was talking.

"An' shot m'hoss f'm under me. Nobody does thet to a MacNaughton, an'..."

So that was it: another of the outlaw clan. Apparently alone, or was he? In the rain, she hadn't seen a horse, but his—or theirs—could be hidden in the woods. She must take into account another man, or more. If—no, when—she subdued this boy, she'd have to barricade herself inside, drive them off with rifle fire.

Oh, no! Stephen will ride right into them. Must find out if he's alone.

"Have you had anything to eat?" she finally asked.

"Whut? Oh, yeah, I got me some taters an' ham 'while ago." And he just let it slip, "Thankee."

"You're welcome. We don't turn travelers away. You don't need that gun here. What was it you were saying about my husband?" She hadn't really registered it.

"He done us wrong. Drawed down on us, me'n m'brothers, when we wuz jist...wal, we wuz gittin' back f'm bein' out..." He stopped, realizing that whatever he said, he couldn't make himself or his brothers sound innocent. And somehow he sensed this woman already knew the story from the man, his side of it.

"Wal, don't matter none. We got somethin' t'settle, me'n him. M'paw thainks he wuz mebbe th' one kilt our cuzzin Ansted an' his partner Luke, too. An' we ain't heered f'm Caleb an' Shelby, wuz trailin' whoever done that."

Anna had no trouble remembering the two attackers. So this boy was bent on revenge, even without the facts. Well, that was the way of most enmities, she'd found...lack of knowledge, of communication.

"I'm going to start supper," she announced. "You can keep an eye on me however you want." And she moved to the kitchen area, ingnoring the weapon in his hand.

"Now, you stay rat thar, lady," he commanded. "Ain't gonna let you git yer hands on nothin'. We's jist gonna wait fer yer man, quiet-like." He moved with her, keeping the pistol trained on her.

"Have you really thought about this?" she asked. "How you'll be hunted, hounded, caught, hanged? You've got a life ahead of you and you're about to ruin it if you do what it seems you have planned."

"Whut I got planned ain't none of nobody's bizness, lady. I got me a plan, all right, an' yer murderin' husbin ain't gonna be around t'mess with it." He tried to sound menacing, but it came out in almost a falsetto.

"Well, in that case..." She knew she had to act quickly. Stephen could decide to come home early, since working by candlelight wasn't the best way for the fine finishing he was doing. It was obvious from his talk that the boy was alone—that about just himself settling with Stephen—and even if he weren't, she had to resolve this.

She reached toward the kitchen table. His eyes followed her movement, alert for any weapon. If she got her hands on a big knife, or...

Her other fist came out of nowhere, and struck hard against his gun hand, hurting badly. He grabbed that hand in his other around the weapon, then she had her hands on him, lifting him bodily, dizzyingly off the floor as if he weighed nothing. He was suddenly high up, then flying, being slammed hard against the log wall. Stars exploded in his head, and pain shot through him. He fell limply, the pistol going somewhere.

She retrieved it, took off her coat, removed her own gun, and watched him try to focus again. He was in a sea of pain, the woman indistinct before him. As his eyes cleared, he saw the cocked pistol she held, and saw his own weapon in her other hand.

"Now, we'll talk," she said calmly, although her heart was racing from the exertion. "Whoever you are, you've no score to settle with my husband. He's a fair man and doesn't invite trouble of any kind. Now, from what I know, it seems some of your clan stalked him and the supply wagons last fall, and from what the villagers at Saltville told them, you intended to rob them. The two others of you were seen, and our men were on the lookout. When they saw you, they covered you.

"You must have been the one who tried to draw his gun. My husband didn't want to kill you, although you must know this; if he'd wanted to, he could have shot all three of you before you could blink. He shot your horse out from under you to spare your life, young man, and don't you ever forget it."

Her voice was low, but the deadly seriousness in it penetrated his brain. He found he was deeply, inescapably, afraid of this woman.

Who *was* this? Not like any woman he'd ever imagined. Strong as a bull, nervy. And as likely as not to pull that trigger, he knew in his bones. She was talking, again:

"And when he comes home, we'll decide what to do with you. Right now, the choices would seem to be shooting you or hanging you. You've obviously taken on the role of a grown man, but you've gotten yourself off on the wrong track. Probably what we'll do with you is leave it to the others in the village. And oh, by the way, the two you mentioned: Caleb and Shelby? They were killed assaulting the missionary women one night late last summer.

"I'm telling you this so you'll know for certain what to expect. Now, I doubt that at your age you've been as evil as some of your clan, but we'll see what the other folks decide about that. Meantime, if you fear God, you should be praying to Him."

Whereupon Anna laid the guns well aside, and hauled the boy up and sat him in a straight chair. She kept her steady eyes on him, as if daring him to move, fetched rope, and began tying him up. He tried to push her hand away, but she struck his arm so hard the pain blinded him again. *Damn, she's strong.*

Then she went unconcernedly about preparing supper, filling a pot, setting it on the swinging crane in the fireplace. The fire crackled, warming the house.

"Do you want water?"

He was angry, defeated, humiliated. But he sensed that being sullen wouldn't work, with what he had facing him.

"Yes'm, please," he answered. She filled a cup and held it for him. He drank.

"Now, let me guess: I think you've left home, haven't you? Going out on your own now that you're almost grown."

"Wal, yes'm, that's rat, I done that."

"And I'm guessing also that there was a reason for that, beyond some idea you've had of evening a grudge. I can imagine that, from what I've heard of your family, life with them wasn't...pleasant. Am I right?"

Her voice was soft, even understanding. He found it difficult to remain angry at the way she'd disarmed him, handled him like a sack of potatoes. And she seemed to know some of what was in his mind.

"Yes'm, all th' men wanted wuz t'rob an' steal, an' git outta all th' work they could. Most th' work got done, us young'uns an' th' wimmen, we done it."

"I see. And I also see that you have something in you that wanted a better life for yourself. You can't have wanted to turn out like your cousins or brothers, seeing the trouble they were probably always getting into."

How did she know that? What could a schoolteacher know about growing up with nothing, being constantly bossed around by the men, whipped if a feller didn't move fast enough, always having to do twice the work around the place?

Carver wasn't letting go, changing his mind. Not by a long shot. But he also knew this woman could easily have killed him, might still kill him if he tried anything. And just now, tied to this chair, there wasn't much he could do, anyway. And what was gonna happen when the man got home? Instead of killing him and robbing the pair, his life was now in their hands.

And the boy had no doubt the man wouldn't be as easy-going as this woman. He could see those hard eyes over a cocked pistol, with him tied like this, and it scared him more than anything he'd seen or heard of in his life.

All right, then, it was time for him to use that brain of his. Time to try to talk his way out, if he could. And he damn well better be able to, or he was dead. But this teacher...she knew things. Could he lie to her and make her believe it? Or her husband? Part of him said he could, but the rest of him knew they'd see through any story he could put together.

Just then he heard a horse's hooves through the rain out front, and the sound went around the house toward the barn. And his young heart sank like a stone. He was gonna die; he knew it in his bones. *I tried to be better'n my kin, an' here I'm 'bout t'die fer it. Damn, I had th' chancet t'do rat, an' I din't take it.*

Just then, Carver MacNaughton would have given anything in this world to be that apprentice blacksmith he'd thought briefly of. *Ansted dead. Luke Kelly dead. Caleb and Shelby dead.* His brothers—and yes, himself too—foiled in their attempts at robbery. *If they wuz jist a way outta this, I c'd still do rat, I reckon. I'se s'posed t'be smarter'n th' rest of 'em, an' if I c'd jist git 'nuther chancet...*

The woman was quiet, cooking. It was just moments then, before the back door opened and the tall man entered. Carver MacNaughton almost wet his pants.

"Well, what have we here?" slipping off his coat, laying a pistol down and removing his tricorner hat, the man looked the boy full in the face, recognizing him. "You didn't get hurt here, did you, Anna?" He turned to his wife, who smiled and kissed him.

"Not at all. This young man had meant to carry out an ill-advised plan, and I've been discussing that with him. His name is MacNaughton, which you'll recognize." Turning to the trussed boy, "This is Stephen Davis, and I'm Anna Davis. What's your first name?"

"C...Carver, ma'am." He was almost too paralyzed to speak, but then the words tumbled out. "An' I'm thet sorry I busted in here. I know I shouldna, knowed better, but I wuz...daid set on...wal, after m'brothers'n me, we run into you an' t'others thet time on th' road, we...I mean, I..." He was at the verge of tears, which he tried mightily to control.

"Carver MacNaughton, looks like you've what, run off from home? And you've found me, and you wanted to get back at me for that time. But I know you and your brothers were out to rob us, had stalked us, probably set an ambush. So you had nothing to avenge. Nothing but some twisted sense of hurt pride in the eyes of your kinfolks.

"Well, I can tell you, the whole clan of you is about to be rounded up and hanged, or run out of the country. The people at Saltville won't put up with your family any longer. I'd say you were smart to leave when you did, even if it was for the wrong reasons.

"Now, realizing you've probably tried to attack my wife, I'm justified in shooting you dead right now. But she can take care of herself, as you've found out. That doesn't mean I'll let it pass, though." He picked up his pistol. "The idea that you could find us, try to kill me, rob us, makes me very, very angry. Your cousins, I guess they were, tried the same thing here and they're dead. Decent people just won't allow that sort of thing to go on."

Carver was looking down the barrel of the pistol, and it seemed as big as a cannon. He was paralyzed with fear. The man continued.

"You're young, and I'd say you probably haven't done as much damage as others of your clan. But you've taken on the work of a man, and you'll have to face what you've brought on like a man. Tomorrow, we'll take you to the village, and put you on trial. Whatever the good folks there decide, that's what we'll do with you." He held up a hand. "No, I don't want to hear anything from you. No explanations, no lies, or you'll make me angrier, and that's not something you want to do. Ever.

"We're going to have to keep you tied, and one or the other of us will watch you all night. I warn you, if you make *any* move to escape, I'll kill you. Do you understand?"

"Y...Yessir, I do."

"Good. Now, Anna, can we give him something to eat?"

"I offered, but he said he'd already helped himself to our root cellar and smokehouse."

"I see. So you've already robbed us. I don't know what has made you people think you can just take what you want from others who've worked hard for it, but that kind of thing just won't stand any longer."

Anna didn't know just how hard Stephen was going to be on this boy, and the Christian side of her wanted to give him another chance. But she remembered again the cousins and knew that when a person had a snake pinned down, he didn't let it up again. Just how dangerous this misguided specimen was or would be again, she couldn't guess. She'd leave most of that up to Stephen. And yes, the whole settlement should hear this and pass judgement.

But the thought of hanging this boy repelled her, which she suspected would be more for what his relatives had done than his own transgressions. She would speak more of this to Stephen, who had spared his life before, and she knew wanted to again. She signaled her husband toward another room.

They left the boy tied and went into the other half the dogtrot house to talk. Stephen was preoccupied, trying to find some way to make this situation right. While it wouldn't do to let the boy go, with his evident attitude toward robbery and possibly worse, he didn't want to see him judged too harshly. After all, no real harm had been done here, though the thought of his ambushing Anna scorched him with an almost blinding anger.

"I think we're letting too much of what we know about this boy's family influence us here," Anna began. "Isn't there a way we can… help him, some way?"

"He has to take responsibility for what he's done, Anna. Stalking us, robbing us, holding you at gunpoint. I won't tolerate that, no matter the rest."

"I have to agree, but he's just a boy. I can't help but feel that if given the chance, he could still make something of himself. And I see a heavy punishment as just driving him further down the wrong road."

"Unless we hang him, and you already know I don't want that to happen."

She was thinking over the probable reaction in the village.

"Todd and Harvey both saw him with his brothers, that time on the road. He can't pretend to be a stranger here. But they didn't actually rob you, did they?"

"No, but it was only because we acted first. The boy was wild, going for his gun that way."

"I wonder how much of that was trying to prove to his people how tough he was?"

"Doesn't matter in the end. Todd and Harvey knew the situation, too. I had to do something. If the three of them had been faster, they could have killed us. The other wagons were in a line behind me, and if they'd gotten me, the others wouldn't have had much of a chance. Todd can do a lot with one arm, but we were all surprised, and bolder robbers would've seen that and taken that opening."

"Yes, and I know you did the right thing. The question now is, just supposing we did give the boy another chance, do you think he'd take it? Or do something violent the first chance he got? Or run away to whatever bloody life he could manage?"

"No answer to that. Unless we try it. I could talk to Todd and Harvey, who're the only ones who've seen him, and see what they think. But it'd be like having a snake in our midst, if we let him free here."

The snake thing, again. But was this actually that bad? This was, after all, a Christian settlement...almost the entire village came to church services, helped the missionaries, joined in their activities. Perhaps they were being given the opportunity to practice their faith here, instead of judging.

Let him who is without sin cast the first stone.

"And," Stephen went on, "the boy might not take to it. Having to live among us, knowing that at least some of us knew the truth, feeling constantly watched, doubted, our hands always close to our guns. I'm trying to see it from his side, I guess."

"Yes, I am, too. But if we're wrong, and he's beyond help, he'd be a danger to us all. And with all the children..." She let the thought trail off.

Stephen smiled at his wife. He'd known she would try to mitigate the MacNaughton boy's offense; there was absolutely no meanness in her.

Nerve, yes.

"And, if we *don't* give him a chance to turn himself around, you and I will always wish we had. Something like that won't ever leave us alone, will it?"

"No, I'm afraid it won't." She kissed him, clung to him a long moment. "Should we find out what Reverend McKnight thinks?"

"No, I believe we should pray about it, and find out what God thinks."

Back in the kitchen, the boy hadn't tried to move, just hanging his head in what appeared to be shame. Or was he pretending, waiting for a break? Against the present odds, that didn't seem likely.

Had they already jolted him enough to make him see he'd been on the way to self-destruction? Or would a short lifetime of the twisted values of his clan have shaped him beyond repair?

Questions.

They fed him again, and Stephen took him out to allow him to relieve himself. Then Anna went upstairs to bed, planning to take the second watch. With any luck, Stephen reasoned, the boy would be asleep by then, and even less dangerous.

Anna prayed long and fervently for guidance in this dilemma, trying to open her mind to whatever was God's will. No revelation came, and she eventually drifted off into a deep and dreamless sleep.

Stephen tended the fire, watching as the boy dozed off, to come erect again later, stare wildly about him in the half-light of the flames. Then he'd settle again, head drooping forward, to uneasy sleep. It couldn't have been comfortable being tied to a chair, but Stephen knew this was more of the need to get the boy's attention. *Let him feel more of what outlawry will get him.*

Two hours after midnight, Anna roused, dressed, and came downstairs quietly. Stephen watched her, feeling again how incredibly lucky he'd been to win this woman. How he'd almost lost her, how now life and a whole world of joy was before them. He rose, kissed her, handed her his pistol, slipped upstairs while the boy slept.

Fifteen

Reginald Cabot's party arrived at Ketchum's Mill at midmorning, a clearing day of mild wind. The smell of newly-turned earth was in the air, the regular rasp of the whipsaw set a cadence, and there was activity around the church. He stopped his lead wagon a bit aside so the others could have this first sight of the village. His was already a proprietary air...this was to be the center of his fiefdom. He'd be independent here, away from prying eyes, the constant knife-edge existence of his life outside the law.

The others took in the scene: the rushing whitewater of the creek, the smoke rising from the several chimneys in sight, the children playing around the church and the striking young woman among them. Smells of good cooking came from the new inn where Belle Ketchum and the two McKnight daughters could be seen coming and going.

The reactions of the travelers ranged from relief at having finally arrived, to disappointment at this tiny place, to a feeling of having come home.

Their appearance caused the expected stir, and it seemed most of the village was there to greet them. They were shown rooms in the inn, where Belle made them at home. Cabot bustled around, affable, very much in his element.

Stephen was not present to welcome them. He had ridden through the settlement before anyone was astir, with a newly-scrubbed Carver MacNaughton. They'd gone up to the men's cabin, where only Harvey Campbell and Todd Epsworth lived.

And talked the situation over the entire morning. The men recognized Carver instantly, and questioned Stephen about him. He told them the facts, leaving it for them to draw their own conclusions. Throughout the exchanges, the boy sat silent, unless asked a question. He seemed small and almost weak in the presence of these three ex-soldiers, who exuded a kind of hardness he could sense.

"So, I wanted to hear from you two, who're the only ones who know Carver by sight. Thought about putting him on trial before the whole settlement but Anna and I feel there might be another way. Now, we've all been in the war, and we know how to deal with the enemy and outlaws. But well, we're also all Christians, though I'm still trying to catch up to you on that, so let's see what we can work out here."

Todd got up to put more wood on the fire in the still-chilly room. He flipped a stick into the air, grabbed another, and caught the first in the crook of his one arm. Carver's eyes widened. He and his brothers had written off this one-armed man as no threat back at the planned ambush.

All three men were silent for several moments. Stephen and Harvey kept cold eyes on the boy. While he considered, Todd took his rifle down off its pegs above the mantel and began cleaning it, quickly and efficiently, gripping it between his knees. Then he re-charged it with powder, set a ball, primed the pan. All with such ease the others were impressed.

These ain't ordinary men, Carver realized. And Christian or not, he also knew they'd shoot him dead if he tried anything, now or later, if they let him live. He resolved in that moment to try and fit in here, settle, if they'd allow him. No need to travel west, penniless and obviously not the bold robber he'd envisioned himself to be.

"If we let you just join in with us here," Campbell began, as if reading his mind, "we'd keep a sharp eye on you. You so much as scratch yourself wrong, we'd be all over you. But we're Christian, like Stephen says, an' we believe in givin' a man a chance. I'd say, for my part, you could maybe move in here with us single men, work your way, and we'd see."

He looked to the other two. So did Carver, with hope in his eyes. Surprisingly, Todd shook his head.

"Th' Lord's seen fit for me t'lose one arm already. Makes it harder t'do jist about ever'thing. Now I gotta be on th' watch every minute, make sure this boy don't slip up on me? That'd be hard, men. Oh, you all know I c'd tear him to pieces, even one-armed, but even forgivin' him, takin' him in, I'm some worried."

Stephen summed it all up, putting the perspective of the whole settlement on it.

"You'd have to earn the right to live among us, Carver. That means watch yourself close, till none of us would mind leaving you with even the young children here. That's a long way to go from robbing and threatening with a gun. If we do this, we three men and my wife would be the only ones to know about what you've been. You'd start with a clean slate, and have to keep it clean. I don't want Todd here to have to keep looking over his shoulder at you to make sure he's safe. Or any others of us.

"And you'd have to go to school with the others. No shame there...we've got students older than you my wife's teaching. We'd want to see you make something of yourself. Think you could do that?"

The boy didn't hesitate. "Yessir. I already been thainkin' I might 'prentice m'self to a blacksmith. I'd take to that, I'm shore." But there was something else he wanted these men to know.

"'Nother thaing. I'se gittin' tired of doin' all th' work 'round home, an' th' way m'brothers 'n them wuz always layin' 'round, drinkin', doin' nuthin'. M'cousin Ansted, he tried t'teach me some, git me t'where I c'd make it out on my own, come time t'leave out.

"But thar wuz this other: I thought I hadda...mebbe prove myse'f, y'know? Show 'em I wuz as good as they wuz, b'fore I c'd go on, try t'make somethin' outta m'life. I dunno jist how t'say it in words, but I had this idee I hadda be mean an' tough if I wuz t'make it ennywhar.

"Now, I know I done wrong, comin' after you lak I done. An' shore wrong, bustin' in on yer wife thataway. She throwed me up 'ginst that wall lak a sack of taters, an' right then I knowed if a woman c'd do thet, I wuzn't near as hard as I thought. So whut I reckon I'm sayin' is, if y'all give me th' chancet, I'll work as hard as enny man here, an' yeah, I'll git all th' learnin' I can." He took a deep breath.

"An' if enny you see me gittin' outta line, I *want* you t'shoot me, er leastways knock some sense into me." He looked around after this speech. "An' I reckon thet 'bout sez it all."

There was silence as the three men looked from one to the other, the question in their eyes. Todd Epsworth was the first to speak.

"Well, if you're serious about that, then I wanta work with you, Carver. I'll take responsibility for you m'self. If it's all right with Harvey, you c'n come stay with us, an' I'll be th' one to see what we c'n make of your life. I'm thinkin' maybe God's brought you here, which I know you never thought of, jist so we c'd do what we're s'posed to, help one another." He thought a moment more.

"And shucks, you c'n be my other arm." He clapped his hand on the boy's shoulder, and all four of them grinned.

And it was Todd who introduced the boy to Anna and the others at the school.

"This's Carver MacNaughton, Miss Anna, a friend of mine come to stay with Harvey an' me. He wants to learn all he can, here at your school."

"Glad to have you, Carver," Anna greeted, as if she'd never seen him before. "As you can see, we have all ages here," indicating Alice McKnight, who'd come from the inn, Sam Leslie, the three White children, and others of the village. "We'll stop now for dinner, then begin again."

"I'll jist take Carver on to th' mill then, ma'am. He wants t'talk t'Mr. Ketchum about smithin'." The boy gave Anna a look of gratitude as they left, with a generous dose of respect.

Killebrew Ketchum was at that moment adjusting the pitsaw, while the forge fire died down. He returned to it, pumped the bellows a few strokes, then put an iron chain hook back into the fire. Just then, the pitsaw hung, and he rushed back to it to disengage the drive belt from the water wheel pulley. Todd and Carver watched him, waited for his return to the forge.

"Dang thing. Man cain't be two places 't oncet. Whar'd Stephen go? Y'know?" he asked Todd.

"Down to talk with Mr. Cabot and the new people. But you go on, Killy. We'll watch this while you fix that."

"Obliged. I'll have it freed up in a minnit." Which he did, as Carver pulled the bellows handle, the smith shortening the travel of the pitsaw blade ratchet so it wouldn't bite as deeply. Then he re-engaged the belt and the mechanism stroked smoothly again, streaming sawdust as it cut through the log.

"All right, then. Who you got thar, now?" squinting at the boy.

"Friend of mine, come t'join up with us. Thinks he might jist like t'learn smithin'. Reckon you'd take on an apprentice?"

"Hmm. Dunno as I got that much work, till th' iron thing gits goin'." He shook his head.

"Well, Carver here, he'll be in school part of th' day. Maybe could help you some of th' time, jist when you need him."

"Might work, thet. Y'ever done enny forge work?" to the boy.

"Jist a little, fer th' smith at Saltville. But I c'n learn, I know I kin."

~ * ~

Anna Davis had her misgivings about the boy MacNaughton, but reasoned he had nothing to gain and everything to lose if he got out of line. She'd try her best to treat him well, and trust that he'd respond. If not, then as had often happened in outpost settlements, he'd be dealt with as he deserved.

Carver seemed sincere. He dug into the lessons at the school with energy, not being shy about asking for help from her or from the other older students. And not knowing his background, they were not averse to sharing what they were learning.

Anna had developed a teaching style that related directly to her students' lives, instead of using the unfamiliar classic texts and examples educators had published. Mathematics involved the numbers of chickens or pieces of firewood, or of monetary values when buying necessities. She taught that proper grammar would open doors for the students once they pursued their lives beyond the classroom. She was aided in this by Alice McKnight, Sybil and Sam Leslie, and Amelia White, all of whom were well-spoken. Without holding them up as examples, she saw to it that the others emulated them, a bit at a time.

Obviously, educating the backwoods children to the level of those from the cities would take time, but she resolved not to hold the leaders back to accommodate the followers. They'd catch up if possible, or they'd reach a point that would enable them to function in some way in their society, whatever that turned out to be. But she demanded a lot from them, knowing they could do more than even they knew.

And Carver MacNaughton earned a degree of respect among the others for his apprenticeship with the smith. Ketchum worked him hard, and he learned fast. Given the chore of making nails, that never-ending necessity, he made a game of seeing just how many he could turn out in a given time. And once he learned the secret of welding chain links, that too became a measure of his productivity. It would be long before he mastered working with steels, or the intricacies of lock work or gunsmithing, but he embraced his new trade with enthusiasm.

He and the two bachelor missionaries shared the work of their cabin equally, and the three became close, in time. There was still much Todd could not handle, and both the others helped when they could. The result was a trio of workers the settlement came to rely upon.

As for Reginald Cabot's enterprise, Stephen and George began work on the ironworking mill, using the plans the man had brought with him. The dam would wait for low water in the summer, along with the sluice to power the water wheel and machinery. Here several of the missionary men were also employed by Cabot, and the work proceeded steadily. Ketchum's mill was constantly busy, the pitsaw turning out siding and roofing boards in slow but dependable quantity.

This demand would constitute much of the output of both mill and smithy, and the need was already heavy. Stephen discussed the situation with Ketchum, and the two agreed that a second, or larger, shop could and should be built as the requirements grew.

"Cain't do it all, old's I'm gittin'," the miller-smith pointed out. "You're good at all this, Stephen, and I'd be obliged if you c'd spend as much time with me as you kin. I know Cabot's dependin' on you, but some of th' others c'n handle a lot of thet down thar. I'd say you oughta become sorta a ...speshulist."

"Hardly that. But yes, I enjoy the challenge of advanced ironwork. Maybe, as soon as we get the basic frame up, I can shift to here more." He was also thinking that he'd rather be in the village, closer to Anna, than down the creek doing mostly manual labor. "Oh, and George wants to learn smithing, too. I'd say we can manage, among us."

Everyone had expected news from Anna of an impending birth, but that hadn't happened yet. All the women in the setlement began to give her sly advice, but she just smiled and said nothing. Tildy Driscoll was particularly 'helpful', but Anna changed the subject when it came up.

~ * ~

Jedediah Mason was deeply concerned about his double Clem O'Malley's being shot. While grateful that he'd survived, and also glad that the ruse had worked, now the investigator knew the situation between him and the criminal element in the capital had escalated. There was no earthly way he could prove who'd tried to kill him, but he vowed to step up his efforts to eradicate what he saw as a tight robbery organization, run by someone who knew how to operate.

He'd narrowed his suspects to a few leading businessmen in the city who seemed to be more affluent than their trades would allow. Mason knew about profits and the costs of doing business, and some of these men just were spending more and living better than seemed possible.

So, with robberies taking money from many, and a few living lavishly, the simple conclusion was, to him, that some of those same Philadelphia social leaders must be getting that very money. Commerce and trade in the new nation were admittedly brisk, often hard-driving, and sometimes downright brutal, what with competition everywhere. And yes, of course some men just had a knack for making money.

But take that Codington fellow: his leatherworks employed fewer than a dozen craftsmen, and Mason knew to the square foot how much product he shipped. Yet the man rode in a new carriage, lived in an upscale neighborhood, wore finely-tailored clothes. His wife was among the elite of the city, and that, Mason knew from experience, cost a lot. So where was Codington getting his money?

Investigation had shown the man was from a poor background, his father having been a small farmer up the Susquehanna River. And further digging revealed that he had begun spending heavily even before opening this business. No proof yet, but Mason and his men were still digging.

And then there was Reginald Cabot, the flamboyant carriage-maker, the well-met Bostonian whose background in that city, he learned, had been less than savory. The man had been disowned by his wealthy relatives, supposedly pulling himself up by his own bootstraps here in the capital. Well, certainly the manufacture of high-grade carriages was a lucrative business, but again, the money just didn't add up. Another relatively small operation that somehow yielded a lot of profit, it seemed.

And there were others still under investigation. A lot of new money in the city, Mason acknowledged. His own fortunes had risen appreciably with his successes in the work he was doing, and he had to admit that other new enterprises were paying well. But in all those cases, the proprietors, the thinkers and innovators had to work long hours, weeks, years to flourish. And for most of those suspected men who didn't, the rate of success in their new businesses was well above the failures.

Mason's *modus operandi* had always been to look for the unlikely, the obvious always being shunned by his adversaries. So there wouldn't be some shady crime bosses in smoke-filled rooms directing the systematic robberies year after year. No, rather just those upstanding citizens who seemed too good to be true. Which, he'd learned, almost always meant they weren't true.

His crackdowns had netted minor figures involved in robbery, yes, but never anyone with real power. It was obvious to Mason that the money went higher up, with these street-level and even middlemen passing most of the take along.

The banking business was relatively new in this country, and as yet not strictly governed by rules and the discipline that would soon mark it. From his former profession as a merchant, Mason had working relationships with several bankers, and these he mined for information. The result was that most of the suspected merchants he was investigating did not have large accounts.

So, did that mean they were spending it as fast as they got it? Or investing the money somewhere legitimate? An astute man would choose the latter. A wise crook would gradually build legal enterprises, and a step at a time, distance himself from his unsavory connections. Not that there were that many wise crooks, but this operation suggested that someone, or a small group, was that sharp.

Mason had what he must admit was a grudge against Reginald Cabot. The man was just too arrogant, too smug, too sure of his abilities, to suit the investigator. Personable, yes, the man could charm his way among society, but his Boston accent had a touch of the streets in it, his methods a bit of the sinister. Or so Mason imagined.

He'd had the man followed for many months, switching off his best operatives to avoid suspicion. He knew Cabot's closest associates, which included the aforementioned Codington and a close circle of others like him. There was the gnomelike Ichabod Darby, the lawyer. And hawkish Isaiah Black, whose business was almost a caricature: funeral director. Mason had always wondered how an undertaker could be rich, but had supposed such a man didn't spend much.

That proved not to be the case. Black also had a number of acquired properties in the city, which brought in a steady stream of wealth. Nothing wrong in that, the investigator admitted, but how had he come to own so much?

It all added up to a secret organization of thieves, but there was absolutely no proof, no breakthroughs to lead to culpability, no place to crack open this nut. Suspicions were all well and good, sometimes leading to answers, but this tight-lipped group gave no hints.

The surveillance did yield visits to Mason's circle of suspects by less upstanding characters, some of them known criminals. These he'd left alone, hoping to be led to actual dealings. And he'd learned just enough to stoke the fires of suspicion, but no more.

Frustrating, all this. If it hadn't been for his successes with isolated robberies, Mason couldn't have continued his work. But as with the firearms manufacturer Coulter, there were enough businessmen who needed him to finance his organization and allow him to pursue what had apparently evolved into an almost-impervious crime circle.

"Cabot's still my main suspect," Mason told Leighton Chiles not long after the shooting of O'Malley. "He slipped back into town months ago and lay low all winter. So out of sight we only discovered he was here by luck. Now, an honest man has no need of such actions. Oh, we know he and his wife don't get along, and yes, he could have had a mistress hidden somewhere.

"But that's not like the fellow. He'd practically flaunt such behavior, being who he is. No, I suspect he's onto something big, and it involves hiding out. We do know he had one meeting with the dirty crowd we've suspected: Codington, Black, Darby and the rest. Oh, and another lawyer named Eddins, who hails from Virginia. Nothing illegal in that, I know, but it all adds a bit at a time to my suspicions.

"Now he's disappeared entirely. His wife's not seen him since last fall, she says, and is sure he's left her. No doubt has. She doesn't know any more than that.

"But here's the weird part: robberies have slacked off, as you've seen, just in the past few weeks. Oh, the odd theft, but not the bold, inside-contact hauls we've been trying to stop.

"Now, our chief suspect leaves town, and the robberies slack off. Coincidence? Those just don't happen in our business. Again, no proof, no place to start. What's your opinion?"

"Well, I wanted to call your attention to what our friends at the banks have reported, sir. Seems Cabot has withdrawn all his money from the banks we know of. Here are the amounts." And Chiles produced sheets of the blue rag paper. Mason scanned the figures.

"All right, then. Not that much in any one account, but he seems to have had several. Still not that much, total.

"But that's not all, sir. Charles Little at the Continental, Cabot's chief bank, told me he'd seen our Mr. Cabot leaving his bank one day, just as he was returning. Said he asked one of the tellers, a new fellow, what Cabot's business had been. The man didn't know any Cabot, he told Charles; he'd just handled a large withdrawal for a depositor named Cantwell. Charles was immediately suspicious and took a look at that account. Regular deposits over a long period, then that lump sum withdrawn.

"Charles first made certain Cantwell was indeed Cabot, then he contacted associates of his at some of the other banks. Seems the Cantwell alias had large sums in several places, and had just closed them all out. He was able to get some of the figures by trading favors with the other bankers, and look at this, sir." He laid more accounting sheets on the desk. Mason ran his eyes over them.

"Astounding! The man's richer than Croesus, Chiles. And he's taken it all out, it appears. Now what's this?"

"Seems to be an account set up solely for Mrs. Cabot. That tells us he has indeed left her, and surely plans to stay gone, him and the rest of his money."

"No doubt. So where has our bird flown, do you suppose?"

"Well, knowing him as we do, he won't be content to plant himself idly somewhere safe. He'll get into something exciting, as he always has, legal or not. The man's prideful, arrogant, as you know. Our problem is, he's got the entire country to disppear in, and a rising tide of industrialism to blend into. I'd have to say he's eluded us, sir." Chiles shook his head ruefully.

"Perhaps. But I still suspect him of hiring O'Malley's shooter, sure he was me. Do you think he believes I'm dead?"

"Probably, since he's fled. I got a look at his man, but haven't been able to learn anything about him. You've given Cabot a chase, even without proof, and he's the kind would hold a grudge. Also would want to protect his cronies here, I'd say."

"But the robberies have lessened. Good and bad, for our purposes. Less to go on. Which should please our clients, of course. But could we be working our way out of a job?" Mason smiled.

"No, there'll always be crooks, and where there's honey, there'll be flies in droves. And that brings up a thought, sir: Where would you say the new industrial centers will develop?"

"Good thought. I'd say in the South, with the cheap labor there. But what raw material is there? Cotton, but hand-processing it is slow. Sugar cane, but same problems. I *have* heard reports of prospecting for minerals. There's that natural salt deposit down at the end of Virginia, for instance. And the iron deposits on the Jackson River, up in the mountains. St. Louis is mostly fur trade, timber, and the lead mines southwest of there. Some gold here and there, but no heavy discoveries."

"You're agreeing that our Mr. Cabot might have found a new potential somewhere and has gone to capitalize on it, right?"

"That's my thought, yes, Chiles. Fits the man's character. Another thing's the lack of law and order out on the frontier, you know. That'd appeal to him, too. I'd say he won't try the established industries: fisheries, agriculture, that fur trade, timber. Man's got a huge ego, and would want to be at the center of something new, wherever he might find it."

"Well, you're probably right. But he's gone, and that lawyer Eddins with him, incidentally. Which fits with a new venture…the necessary legalities. Oh, I'll see if I can find out when Cabot left, and anyone else who might've left with him. Seems he'd need some expertise in whatever field he's getting into. I can't see him building carriages out on the frontier."

Sixteen

When the assassin Hiram Garst had stopped at his favorite tavern on the way out of Philadelphia, he'd heard from the barkeep some disturbing news.

"Word's out th' law's onto you, Hiram," the man warned him. "Some talk of you doin' in a feller was some important. Now, I ain't jedgin' you, nor what you been doin', but y'bin a good customer these years, an' I jist figger y'oughta know what's goin' round."

So, not a moment too soon. Garst thanked the man, gave him a generous tip, and left immediately. He'd ride straight through then, to put as much distance between him and this town as possible. And yes, he'd best try to follow Reginald Cabot, his only connection outside his old haunts.

All he'd been able to find out was that the man had left right after paying to have Mason killed. So, had he slipped away intentionally or had a message failed to reach him? He suspected the former. A man in his profession couldn't trust anyone, and he knew Cabot would want to distance himself from the deed itself. But why leave town? Seemed like, once the investigator had been eliminated, he'd be free to pursue whatever it was he did. Which was clearly illegal, Garst knew. Honest men didn't pay to have others killed.

Well, if he could find Cabot, he'd insert himself into his benefactor's operation again, whatever that proved to be. If not, he'd at least be in new territory where no one knew him. With a remnant of his fee still intact, he knew he could survive for a short time in a degree of style. Longer, if he watched his spending. That was surely enough time for him to find some other use for his talents.

That would mean locating in another large city, though, where the pickings would be good for those who controlled things. Baltimore, maybe. Or Alexandria, which served a large area. Or maybe way down in Richmond, rebuilding after the British invasion. Charleston, maybe? Or surely, if he could get there, New Orleans, which he'd heard was full of intrigue.

But for now, he'd just ride south and west, get away from whoever had found him out. And he couldn't help wondering just who that could be. The city was full of informants, connections, both above and beneath the law. He guessed it'd just been a matter of time till he'd have to run, and yes, now he was doing it.

~ * ~

Stephen Davis had never known such well-being. After the winter he and Anna had spent largely and blissfully at home finishing the house's interior, making furniture, building fences, everything was going ahead beautifully. The school had resumed with the end of the coldest weather but was now recessed while the children helped their families clear, plant and build. The inn was finished, with the McKnights, Cabot and his iron-venture people in residence. Belle Ketchum was delighted with her new job, and Killebrew's mill ran tirelessly, cutting lumber as fast as the pitsaw allowed.

Most of the men in the village, while not farming, were engaged in beginning the new mill for the iron processing downcreek, cutting timber, leveling land, hewing beams. Stephen divided his time between that site and the mill and smithy, helping forge the necessary ironwork and with Ketchum, keeping the mill running.

Stephen looked forward to the prospect of fatherhood, but that would come when it was supposed to. Meanwhile, it seemed Anna was always smiling, these days of spring, and everyone just enjoyed being around her. Whenever possible, Stephen arranged to meet her at noonday for the meal together at the inn. They were so obviously deeply in love that the older residents just smiled and shook their heads, perhaps remembering.

So far, Carver MacNaughton had kept his word, studying hard, working hard, doing his share at the bachelor cabin. What had begun as fear of the settlers, especially of Stephen and his wife, gradually changed to respect and admiration. It seemed the entire settlement looked up to the tall craftsman, both for his skill and for a certain air of leadership about him. Carver had learned some of Stephen's background: sharpshooter in the Continental Army, and bits let fall about his cleaning out a bunch of outlaws up in Virginia. Some of this was gossip, surely, but the boy never doubted a word of it.

He took pride in his achievements, a feeling he'd never known among his kin. With each new discovery at school and each new level of skill at the forge, he felt the distance grow between himself and the cousins and brothers back at Saltville. He often wondered about his family, but resolved to make his own way here, and sever all bonds to them. Wouldn't do to mess up his chances, now he'd been given them.

Not that he was totally converted. He still caught himself dreaming of quick money, traveling without restraint across the broad land, beholden to no one. But he also knew he had it better here than he could hope for anywhere and forced such fantasies out of his mind.

~ * ~

Reginald Cabot was everywhere, it seemed, whether conferring with Stephen or Archie Nolan about his ironworkers or in the midst of every phase of construction. He could and did delegate, but was so keenly involved in it all, he could always be found nearby. He made almost instant decisions as the need arose, but respected his men's expertise. He'd chosen well, and knew enough to leave most of the details to them.

His engineer, one Thaddeus Stillwell, arrived in May, when the masonry smelter construction was well on its way and the mill was largely framed up. Cabot showed him the proposed cutoff road route, and the man unpacked his transit and began to shoot some preliminary levels.

"Be a huge job, sir," was his initial assessment. The engineer was short and slight, but with a businesslike mein that told the others he knew his trade. They'd borrowed young Abe Holloway, Cabot's wagon driver, from the construction crew, to set the sight pole and help handle the surveying chain. The revealed levels were startling to Cabot.

"Doesn't look as bad as your instrument's telling us," he marveled.

"No, you get used to seeing slopes, and don't realize how everything's tipped up. Take the mill that fellow's building. No one else would have thought he'd have to have that high a foundation on the downcreek side, though I'm certain he did. Seems to know his work."

"Yes, we're fortunate in having Stephen. Man's a wizard at woodwork, and smithing, too. I'm happy with the crew we're assembling here, Mr. Stillwell. But to the work at hand: do you think my plan's feasible, given what you've seen so far?"

"Feasible's a relative term, sir. Possible, yes, with enough blasting, filling, cutting. But the cost will be high, as I'm sure you already know. We'll have to see what's beyond that ridge to get us back to the existing Saltville road. I can tell you that we'll have to head up into draws a lot to keep any sort of grade, which will make the road a lot longer. It will, of course, be proportionately later before the cost is absorbed, but it could be well worth it, assuming the efficiency of your operation."

"So, if there's enough iron here, and we do it right, the road cost won't kill us, long-term."

"Exactly. But I can see from here it'll take many kegs of powder to get through that ridge ahead. The stone from that cut will fill the ravine between us, there, and that's the way we'll do it all. To get the grade you want, instead of just that we'd need for a wagon road, we'll be spending a lot more money. You might want to consider a cheaper, steeper road at first, till your foundry operation can produce the rails you talked about, then take on a second phase of lessening the grade."

The two talked on, and Cabot began to realize just how complicated this part of his plan would be. He'd continue to need sobering advice like this, all right. But Nolan couldn't tell him how much ore could be extracted from this region, and neither could anybody else.

Well, that was the kind of gamble any innovator faced. The trick would be to keep his investment within reason, so if the venture dried up, he wouldn't be caught out. So yes, the wagon road idea was probably the better option. At least for now.

~ * ~

Lester Cummings thought occasionally about the smooth man from Boston who'd stopped by, prying into his iron business. Man was deluded, thinking he could make money out in those other, distant mountains, with no way to market. He'd obviously wanted to work some kind of deal here, buy his way in. But Cummings had built this operation from scratch, owned it outright, ran it in every detail, and wasn't about to give up even a part of it.

Just another monied dabbler, he'd dismissed Cabot. There'd be a lot of them, he was sure, moving into new territory now after the war. There was no doubt that iron and steel would be the backbone of the new country's industry, but you couldn't hide yourself out on the frontier that far and expect it to work.

Here he had a relatively short journey down the Jackson to the James River, which was navigable by bateaux in all but dry summer, and he could always ship small loads by wagon to the Valley shops between orders from Richmond. Cabot's scheme would cost him dearly, and probably not make him a shilling.

He wondered how a man so out of touch with reality could have made his money, and concluded that it might well have been in something illegal. Maybe stock swindling, and now he wanted far away from the cities where too many knew him. Or he just might have inherited it all: he *was* a Boston Cabot. *Yes, the easy way to wealth.*

Not his concern, Cummings told himself again. *He'll be just one more ruined speculator if he follows through on his pipe dream.* Oh, there was iron in those mountains, Archie Nolan had told him, but it'd be for a future generation to mine and process, after a closer market grew with new settlements. Cabot might just be a few years ahead of his time, then.

But enough about him. There were orders to fill, details by the hundreds waiting, no time to waste on a dreamer. God knew, this place was isolated enough.

~ * ~

Hiram Garst rode into Baltimore asking about for traces of Reginald Cabot. It'd been weeks, though, and nobody remembered him. A lot of traffic south these days, a tavern keeper told him, and the travelers all got to looking the same, it seemed.

Garst was enjoying a cool ale at one of the smaller tables, resting from his journey, when a red-faced man he'd seen somewhere entered. He couldn't place the fellow, but tensed, knowing he'd be either friend or, more likely, foe. He touched the pistol butt inside his coat, trying to place the man. *Could he have followed me?* he wondered.

But the new arrival paid him no mind, settling himself at the scarred bar and ordering a pint. Garst considered slipping out, but his curiosity was aroused. He wanted to know what he was facing here, with this man out of his past in this city.

Not one of Mason's men, he knew. Not one of Cabot's shadowy associates. Who, then? Just a traveler who looked like someone else? No, he was sure he recognized the man.

"I know you, friend," he said, walking up to him. "Just can't remember from where." Garst now had his hand firmly around the pistol.

"Why yes, sir, you may indeed," the other replied. "I was Mr. Reginald Cabot's driver, back in the capital. Seems I may've seen you several times too, times I'd take him in the carriage."

"Ah, then. Yes, now I remember. So what brings you to Baltimore?"

"Lookin' for work, I am. The boss sold out, left out for parts unknown, and offered to keep me on, but I had to tell him I'm not for the wilderness. Nossir, I'm a city boy. But couldn't find another place around home, so here I be...new town, hopin' for a new job." He sipped his ale.

"Well, you should find work here, all right, a lot of shipping and such. But tell me, where did Mr. Cabot go? He left without telling me."

"Some Godforsaken place clear down across Virginia and into Kentucky Territory, he said. Going to start a new business there. Hired some people in iron founderin', he did, and the lot of them just struck out, some weeks back."

"I was away on...business for a while and guess I must have missed him. He'd promised me more work, so I was some disappointed to learn he'd left."

"Sudden-like, it 'peared to be. One day he was meetin' with those merchant fellows of his, an' the next, he's up and gone. The man's got a flair for making money, he has, and I'm guessin' he got wind of somethin' big off out there. Swooped down onto it, for sure, the way he does things. Either lucky, or smarter'n most, he is."

Garst bought his informant another drink, stayed a while, then left, considering his options. Seeing the driver here, he knew he might also run into others who'd know him if he stayed around; the main roads led everyone to the same places eventually.

So: Kentucky. He'd only a vague idea where that was, but knew it was a long way off. No towns near, for certain. And probably no big men needing competition eliminated, either. Or protection.

But Cabot had gone out there. The iron business...well, there was surely a lot of money to be made in that, with everybody needing the stuff. So maybe Cabot would set himself up well. And for sure he'd make enemies; hard-driving businessmen always did. Or just needed that protection from others of his stripe.

Well, he could just keep on riding that way, and see what developed, he guessed. No other plan just now. Might run onto something else too, if he kept his eyes open.

~ * ~

Jedediah Mason was growing angrier at his double's having been shot. He was almost certain that Reginald Cabot was behind it, but with the man gone weeks before he had absolutely no proof. And it didn't make sense: try to kill the man who was after him, but not until ready to leave town. Of course it could have been a simple grudge thing. He toyed with that idea for a moment. No, Cabot wouldn't focus on revenge; he was all business, the business of making money illegally. And if he were indeed gone permanently from the capital, he'd be far away, well beyond our reach.

All right then, what should our next step be? Just let the bird fly, with no effort to catch him? Given the lack of hard evidence, that seemed prudent. But Mason knew his suspicions of the man would gnaw at him forever.

He and his men could maintain a tight watch on Cabot's known associates, of course. One of them might let something slip, given time. Or perhaps even one of them might have ordered the shooting. Which would mean he—they—would continue with operations, without Cabot.

That thought intrigued Mason, and he set men to dog Codington, Black and Darby, wherever they went. He cautioned them to be discreet; it wouldn't do for the quarry to suspect. He was gambling that these men, or more likely one of their shady contacts, would stumble, eventually. If not, he might nail one of the contacts and see if he could be made to disclose what he knew.

Mason was keenly aware that the news had surely gotten about that he hadn't been killed, and if not Cabot, the man responsible would try again. Understandably, O'Malley declined to assume his former role as double, so that option was out.

Perhaps it was time for Mason himself to leave town for a while, too. He didn't like that idea, having no lead on Cabot's whereabouts, but perhaps he just hadn't tried hard enough in that direction.

Someone would know where he'd gone, and perhaps even why. Cabot's wife insisted she didn't know, his associates wouldn't tell, so who did that leave?

An employee of the carriage shop, most likely. Cabot had sold the business, but Mason would wager the new owner had kept most of the help on, just good management. Or perhaps the new owner himself might have heard. Worth a try.

But the owner had no idea of Cabot's plans, just that he'd said he was starting a new enterprise. Mason asked to speak to the shop superintendent, who'd been kept in that position. The man greeted him and Chiles and seemed inclined to talk.

"Well sir, Mr. Cabot, he always left most of the runnin' of th' place up to me, bein's I been at it so long. Didn't interfere, an' that's what I liked about him. Best to leave a man knows what he's about 'thout too much pesterin', an' that's what he done.

"Come as a surprise, him sellin' out thataway. I know he had other businesses here'n there, spendin' no more time here than he done. I did ask him once about that, but he said, no, he was sellin' them out, too. Now, I was took back b'that, I was, knowin' he was so well set up here in th' city an' all. 'Goin' t'new territory?'" I asked him, "natural curiosity, y'know.

"'Oh yes,' he told me. 'Goin' to try an' do somethin' 'bout th' high price of all this iron we been havin' t'buy from Fort Pitt,' he says. I knew how that'd always bothered him, kept us f'm makin' th' profits we coulda got. Y'know, from th' sale of th' carriages an' all.

"'Fort Pitt's got a stranglehold on iron, all right,' I told him. 'Reckon you're gonna buy somebody out, then.'

"'No,' he said, 'I'm off to th' frontier, give 'em some real competition.' That's all he'd say, though I wondered. Then he just handed this place over, an' was gone that quick."

Mason thanked the man for this bit of information, not that it was that helpful. He did learn that Cabot had ordered several new wagons made prior to his departure, obviously for the trip.

The frontier, then. But which part? Everywhere west fit that description...But iron? Where were iron mines? Chiles didn't know either, but they soon were able to find out. Seemed there were some activities in Virginia, shipping to Harper's Ferry and Richmond. Other explorations being conducted by the major firms in Fort Pitt, looking ahead to a time those deposits would play out. Northern Ohio apparently had iron, but it had hostile Indians, too. He doubted Cabot would risk that area.

So, Virginia then. Some activity apparently along the Shenandoah River as it wound north toward its confluence with the Potomac. More on down on tributaries of the James, too.

But, he asked himself yet again, did he really want to go off on a wild goose chase after a man he couldn't arrest? All Cabot's enterprises had seemed legitimate, although taken all together, they couldn't account for the man's evident wealth. Perhaps he'd best forget him, write him off, now that he was gone.

But there was this other thing: he, the hunter, might well still be a target. Didn't like that, much. And Leighton Chiles, the best man he knew, hadn't been able to protect O'Malley well enough. A determined foe could and might well succeed next time. The thought raised the hair on the back of Mason's neck.

Considering the thing more closely, he tried to find any clue he might have overlooked that would unravel the knot he found himself in. And eventually he remembered the lawyer, Eddins, who'd also left town.

"What do we know about this Eddins, Chiles?"

"Not much. Came up from Virginia late last summer, the way I hear it, and started doing legal work for Cabot. Seems to have been in on some of the meetings with the other suspects, too."

"Virginia, again. And wasn't that other fellow, that Hayes who was here a few times, from Virginia?"

"Believe so, yes. Nobody's seen him for a year or two, though. You're thinking Cabot may have had connections down there?"

"Just a thought. But say he did, or still does, that's where there's some iron. I'm thinking it just might be prudent for me to take some time away, Chiles. You advised that, and it's probably safer for me, at least for a while. And what would you say to going along with me?"

"Well sir, I've always wanted to see some of that new country. Got no family here either, to miss me. I'd say, if you go, I'd be glad to go, too."

"Done. We'll leave the business in O'Malley's hands, now that he's up and about again, and just take ourselves a trip. Even if we don't find out anything, it should frustrate our enemies a bit. I'll just tell Letitia it'll be for a month or two, so she won't worry overly. I daresay she'll be somewhat relieved that I'll not be attracting enemies for a while, too. She worries too much."

Seventeen

It was early summer and the gardens and fields of the settlement at Ketchum's Mill on Troublesome Creek were green and growing. The new ground, rich and black, sent the seeds up as if propelled, and the grass grew thick, promising cuttings of hay from the sloping fields.

School was out until after harvest, the children being needed at each farm. Anna spent most of her days at home up the hollow, content to garden, spin, weave, and look after her man. He was deep into the construction of the mill, the ironwork, even some of the new road work. Stephen was busy and happy and rode home each day full of news of the overall progress.

And on Sundays they attended the church, where Anna taught the young people Bible study. She'd encouraged Carver MacNaughton to join them, although he'd never so much as entered a church. Didn't matter, she told him, there was a lot more to this existence than just staying alive: God had a purpose for all of us, and see, Carver was living out his. Not an accident, she insisted, that he'd been guided there.

Carver wasn't so sure about all that, but if it was part of what he had to do, he'd do it. He'd developed a profound respect for his teacher, whom he credited with his not having swung by the neck from a tree limb those months back. He did enjoy being with the other children, especially the older girls. Gradually any shyness he'd had wore away, and he was coming to feel almost equal to any of them.

Sissy Blair was pregnant with their first child. Anna spent time with the young woman, indeed with all the missionaries' and settlers' wives. She'd become such a part of the community, people worried if they didn't see her a week at a time.

So she had visitors, too, being just a mile from the mill. The women would walk, carrying baskets of food to share or quilting or sewing, every time they could get away from the work on their homesteads. Their visits never failed to reinforce Anna's sense of belonging to this mountain hollow and its people.

That feeling had communicated itself to Stephen also, and Anna noted that his bad dreams from the war came seldom. She didn't push him about religion, trusting he'd see God's plans working themselves out, and come to the faith in his own time. She had no doubt whatsoever that they'd both been directed there, the way things had worked out, and knew he was seeing more of that, too.

She did worry about his deep immersion in Cabot's venture. Everyone seemed to depend on Stephen's presence, his judgment, his skill. She saw that even the engineer consulted with him often, as did the others heading aspects of the project. She couldn't define exactly why this bothered her, but soon realized it had to do with Cabot himself. It was as if he were *using* Stephen too much.

The man was just too smooth, too jolly, too willing to spend his considerable money for her to think of him as quite real. The old adage of being too good to be true came to mind, and perhaps he was that. He had assumed a sort of leadership role in the village, which she supposed was only natural. Where Stephen was looked up to as the master craftsman, Cabot filled the role of benevolent ruler, really. Everyone deferred to him, it seemed, and perhaps she considered that a bit too forward of him.

No matter, though; his motives were undoubtedly good, and he'd certainly sparked the tiny settlement into life. More people trickled in, the men to be put to work at the mine or the smelter or the new mill or the roadway, and everyone had something gainful to do.

If Anna were to admit it, she was apprehensive; when life was this good, she'd often noticed it could change for the worse. She didn't want that to happen.

~ * ~

Kentucky. Hiram Garst knew enough geography to realize this territory was the very outpost of civilization, unless one traveled clear to St. Louis. Yes, Kentucky was part of Virginia, represented at Richmond back during the war by the explorer Daniel Boone, who'd helped open the land up to the new settlers. Big place, though, he understood, and he'd no knowledge of any cities there, except for some mention of a settlement called Louisville at the falls of the Ohio River.

But what better place to become invisible from people who might know him? The chance meeting with Cabot's driver had told him the main roads all led to the same towns, and that sooner or later he'd run into...well, on the positive side, more of his specialty work, or on the other hand, maybe a waiting noose somewhere. Definitely negative, that.

Better new territory, then? Even if he had no idea what he'd do there? He wasn't about to become a farmer. Merchant, maybe? Like the men he'd killed for? Or just let things play out the way they would and go along, see what developed.

Yes.

It was weeks later he heard of the iron mining west of the village of Lexington in Virginia. That way led to Kentucky, all right; might as well ride out and see what was there. Maybe Cabot, or surely someone else in the iron business, was generating money. He knew to follow the money first, whatever else later...no point in trying to deal with poor folks.

So Hiram Garst came to the Jackson River ironworks owned and operated by one Lester Cummings, a hard-eyed New Englander who seemed to run everything himself. There wasn't much else around but a store, workshops, a tavern, activities generated by the iron business itself. Well, he'd ask, anyway.

He inquired about, and eventually was able to meet the man Cummings himself.

"Cabot? Why yes, he was here some months ago, sniffing about my operation. Friend of yours, sir?"

"Business associate. Lost contact with him in Philadelphia, and heard he was planning to get into ironworking. This being the center of it hereabouts, I know, I expected to find him here."

"No, he's off down toward Tennessee, then west, he told me. Don't know just where, but up in the godforsaken mountains of Kentucky Territory. Not a chance of succeeding there; too far to any market. Man's a bit of a dreamer, I'd say. Strike you that way?"

"He's always been one for taking the long chance, yes. But it's always seemed to work out for him."

"Hmmph. Won't this time, there at the end of the world. Well, good day, sir, and I hope you locate him, whatever your reasons are." Cummings terminated the visit, hustled off on some errand.

Well, I didn't like you, either, Garst said to himself as he pondered his next move. Pretty obvious there was nothing much between here and the Bluegrass region of Kentucky but mountains. So he guessed he'd go on back down the Valley, see what was there.

But his money was running desperately low, and he had to think about survival. The thought of manual labor didn't appeal to him, so he considered a little highway robbery. If he could do it clean, and be far away quickly, that might work.

Hiram Garst had never been picky about how he'd acquired money. He'd taken it from women who'd been attracted to him. Taken it from foolish men who liked to gamble but didn't know how. Never much at a time, till he'd found his current trade. And if he could just do a job once or twice a year and live well on that money, that was what he wanted.

But that'd have to wait. He needed to find a place and an employer first, and to do that he'd have to get by in the meantime. So he began to watch for a lone, affluent-looking traveler on a deserted stretch of road.

Unfortunately, those were rare. Men with money traveled by coach, or in a party of others for mutual safety. And no one went unarmed in the newly settled country, for just the reasons he sought to exploit. He'd need to gain his victim's confidence, catch him off-guard. Or just shoot him first, and chance that he carried money.

No need to draw undue attention to himself, however. *So, just get on back to the main Valley turnpike and head south again, see what develops.* He'd give himself three days at most. After that, he'd be destitute, and have to sell either one of his guns or his horse.

Not a good prospect.

~ * ~

Stephen Davis often reflected on the almost-perfect way his life had turned out. He'd won the woman he loved, and if they weren't expecting their first child yet, that was no disappointment. He had challenging work he was good at. Add to that the apparent success in rescuing Carver MacNaughton from a wasted life, and his own coming around to more of the faith Anna had, and he was content.

Each day saw major progress in the completion of the iron mill and the foundry, as well as the road work. The missionary men and the others from the settlement, along with some of the newcomers, made a workforce that just needed supervision which he, Leslie, Stillwell and White were able to provide. All under the watchful eye of Reginald Cabot, who fairly rubbed his hands at the progress.

The inn was full, with its inhabitants only gradually claiming land out beyond the village and beginning to build dwellings. Belle Killebrew bustled about, employing two more of the local girls to help. Stephen's own small fields were fenced, with a stand of corn, potatoes, and a vegetable garden Anna tended with a sure hand. He could foresee a future for them here at the edge of the wilderness for many years to come, even if the iron venture did not succeed.

And that concerned him not a little. The road work was tedious, being done all by hand with picks and shovels, mules, scoops, stoneboats to cut down the high places and fill the low ones. Culverts had to be built of continuous arch stones across where water ran in order to keep the grade at its desired manageable level. And considerable blasting into the solid rock of the ridges had been necessary.

That meant sending often back to the Valley for supplies, the list of which grew as construction progressed. Cabot didn't seem to mind, saying he'd allowed for this expense. He did urge the men to as much speed as possible, pointing out that no money would come in until iron went out.

But Stephen wasn't sure it would all add up to profit with the distance, the labor, the obvious competition from the Jackson River works and the distant Richmond and Fort Pitt industries. It wasn't his worry, he knew, but he felt Cabot was taking a longer chance than would pay off, at least until the demand increased greatly from closer by.

There was just something not quite right about the man, he thought for the hundredth time. He and Anna had talked it over, and both agreed that money poured into this project might not ever come back. Which led to the question of just why he was doing it.

Part of the answer seemed to be that he was setting himself up to be the ruler of this, his private fiefdom, where his word was, in effect, law. But since he didn't push any unreasonable demands on the people, they supposed they could live with that well enough. What would happen when and if the venture failed would be another matter. This place would never be self-sustaining from farming. And timber production faced the same transportation problems as the iron.

That meant the jobs would dry up, and a lot of the people would have to leave. As far as the two of them were concerned, that wouldn't matter much...they could survive nicely on their mountainside meadow with simple needs and the thrift they practiced. Stephen had also told his wife of the money he'd brought from Virginia, which would support them for many years to come.

At first she'd been taken aback that this was originally stolen money but agreed there'd been no way to find out where it belonged. And both agreed that Stephen's turning in the other chest of gold to the court in Charlottesville had been the right thing to do, and she no longer worried about the other share Tom Logan had given him, which he'd kept.

Inevitably, there was speculation about building another road over the mountain west, to link the settlement with that territory beyond. That would be a huge job, and there'd be no profit in it for anyone till well into the future. So the place would likely remain the end of civilization for their lifetimes.

Which wasn't all bad. The place was beautiful with its clear-rushing creek, the dense-forested mountains, the abundant game. The village was sheltered in winter, high enough in elevation for coolness in summer. The people were compatible, the church was growing in membership, and some culture was arriving, a little at a time. Stephen and Anna foresaw the place growing into a pleasant community, then probably leveling off naturally, at least as long as the iron work went forward.

It surely beat hell out of dodging outlaws, Stephen often reflected. His three years on the creek in Virginia had been a continuous battle, first to get established, then to survive the systematic attacks of that sophisticated robbery ring. He couldn't envision anything like that happening here on Troublesome Creek.

So it was with a jolt one day that he saw the lawyer Samuel Eddins conferring with Reginald Cabot at the inn when he rode into the village one summer morning. And yes, there was no doubt this was the same man.

"Stephen," Cabot called, "come meet our legal arm, Mr. Eddins."

Eddins started at sight of Stephen, whom he'd last seen being acquitted of charges he himself had brought against him in Charlottesville. The man's eyes grew big, and he stammered and pointed.

"That's…that's Stephen Davis," he managed to Cabot, the accusing finger shaking.

"It certainly is. Do you know him?" Cabot was puzzled that his lawyer should react this way to his master craftsman, literally the man making most of it happen here. Then the light began to dawn, as Stephen rode closer.

My God, it must be the same man, then! The man who wiped out our operation in Virginia, whom Eddins prosecuted in court. Cabot didn't know how to handle this development, but Stephen defused the situation by dismounting, greeting Eddins affably.

"Good morning, Mr. Cabot. And hello, Mr. Eddins. Glad to see you under these more favorable circumstances." He bowed.

"Uh, well yes, Mr. Davis. Uh, Mr. Cabot tells me you've done quite a lot in our interests here…"

"And I'm glad for the opportunity to use whatever talents I may have to move things along. I was told a lawyer was working on behalf of the venture but had no idea it was one I knew. Welcome to our little settlement, sir."

Cabot was so taken aback by this development, he was uncharacteristically speechless. But it wouldn't do here in front of everyone to let any animosity show. He conferred with Stephen as if nothing had changed, then saw him on his way to the construction sites downcreek.

"Well, this is a shock," Eddins said. "The very man who wrecked our entire Virginia activities, here working for you."

"And doing the hell of a job for us, too. So, this'll take some thought, Eddins. Part of me wants to wipe him off the face of the earth for what he did to us, and another wants to keep him building, making everything work."

"I say we can't afford to have him among us."

"Well, he doesn't suspect a thing, or didn't till you showed up. And besides, he's the most popular man in the settlement, and rightly so. Can't kill him off and expect to survive ourselves."

"Unless it's an accident." The lawyer plainly felt Davis would destroy what they were doing, again.

"That'd set me back a long way, though. No, if he doesn't know of your part in our operations back there, I see no need to eliminate him. If he *does,* however, he'll smell a rat, certainly."

"That Virginia judge, Amos Edgerton, was convinced I was part of something big and illegal. Kept me locked up till he ran out of suspected connections. I don't see how Davis could be ignorant of the facts, Cabot."

"Hmm. Well, there's absolutely nothing illegal about what we're doing here, so what could he do, really? I know he doesn't link me with the Virginia operation, and can only suspect you. But, if we keep ourselves honest here, he'll be no threat."

You're being naïve. And you haven't been locked up like some common criminal, either. Which is really what you and I have been, I suppose. But Eddins said nothing more, seeming to agree with Cabot.

He did not agree, not in the least. Having Davis among them was like a bomb with a lit fuse, he believed, and the man would cut them down again, he was sure. He had that maddening righteousness about him, like a dog digging for a hidden bone. No, if Cabot wouldn't act then he must, to ensure staying out of jail. Hell, Cabot could find another builder; they were plentiful in this postwar time. He'd just gone soft, apparently.

Where was the implacable leader who'd ordered the assassin Justin Ames to avenge the Virginia debacle? And later who'd sent Hiram Garst to kill their nemesis Jedediah Mason? Davis was a gnat, a dangerous irritation to be dealt with before he could cause more damage.

For his part, Stephen had masked his concern at seeing the lawyer there. One of the dying outlaws back on the creek those months ago had identified Eddins as one of the circle and here he was again, out of jail and into Cabot's good graces, it seemed. Now, did that implicate Cabot? Or had Eddins lucked into the relationship, a bad man seeking whatever he could get out of an honest one?

As he rode the distance downcreek to the building site, Stephen turned over the possibilities in his mind. He didn't believe in coincidences, and the nagging suspicions about Cabot had just been reinforced.

And that wasn't all...Eddins almost certainly was aware that Stephen knew of his complicity in the Virginia operation, and the man wouldn't take the chance he'd just let it slide. Stephen's instinct for survival told him he must not let his guard down with that man involved. There'd be others, too, he was sure, in whatever scheme Eddins was a part of. In a worst-case situation, Cabot and even these men he'd brought here: White, Leslie, the engineer Stilwell, could all be part of another ring of illegal thievery of some sort.

That would explain Cabot's wealth. Or just he and Eddins might be the bad apples in the barrel...the specialists could be, and probably were, just what they seemed to be. They were certainly, like Stephen, dedicated to making this operation succeed. If there were some ulterior design at work on their parts, it wasn't obvious.

Oh, hell: here it goes again. Even here at the end of nowhere I'm—we're—not safe from conniving and unscrupulous men. And maybe that's just why they're here; beyond law, hidden from justice.

He'd certainly talk this over with Anna tonight. His bride had a clear head he was learning to appreciate more, and an insight he admired. And with her and their future at stake, he couldn't take any chances they could come to harm.

~ * ~

Lester Cummings received another visitor late one summer day, not long after Hiram Garst's inquiry. This Jedediah Mason was a crisp, business-like man who knew what he was after, and the transplanted New Englander liked him immediately.

"I won't beat about the bush, Mr. Cummings," Mason said. "I'm on the trail of one Reginald Cabot, whom I suspect of outright banditry. Now, I've learned he's interested in iron production, and it's well known you're the man in this region to see about that. I doubt you've had any dealings with Cabot, but I'd like to know if he's been in contact with you, and if you'd possibly know where I can locate him."

"All right, you're evidently a man who knows what he wants and doesn't waste others' time getting to it. He did come through here some months ago, angling for either a part of my business, or just picking my brain. Went on back and down the Valley, then west into Kentucky Territory unless he lied to me. Told him he could never make a shilling, far as that country is from markets, but he struck me as the kind of man who never listens to good counsel. I'd say go down to one of the settlements and ask around, and you'll likely find him."

"I thank you, sir. So there is iron ore out there?"

"Oh, yes. Man by the name of Archie Nolan prospected all through there, told me what he'd found. In fact, if this Cabot is keen to produce iron, he's almost certainly contacted Nolan. If you can find him, I'd say you'll find Cabot close by."

"So he'll be in competition with you, assuming he follows through."

"Not in the least. Man's apparently got his head full of notions of making a fortune where there's none to be made. No, he'll never be able to compete with me; just too many things standing in his way."

"Well, I thank you again. I won't trouble you further..."

"Oh, do stay, Mr. Mason. We're just closing up here for the day. Do accompany me to the tavern, yonder. It's seldom I meet a man of clear purpose out here."

"Then I will, yes. You've an impressive operation here, sir, and I hear you've built it all from nothing. I admire that."

"Thank you. Took years, and some shrewdness, if I do say so. But tell me, if you will, just what is your occupation, in relation to the likes of Mr. Cabot?" Cummings' eyes narrowed; he wanted to know more.

"I was in commerce for many years, and discovered a great deal of organized theft, of my operation and others I knew of. I was fortunate to root it out, then others around Philadelphia learned of my work, and employed me in the same capacity. Now I have a staff, and we work with the local police, exposing illegal looters."

"I doubt your success was all just good fortune. So this Cabot is suspect of that sort of thing?"

"The man has had his fingers in many pies, so to speak, none of which could produce the kind of wealth he's amassed. Comes from a prominent Boston family, but they threw him out years ago. He's sold out everything recently and fled just ahead of us. I'll say this: he's clever. Wherever he goes, he'll talk others into investing, or giving him the chance to get his hands on their money, one way or another."

"Then I'm glad I sent him on his way. Man seemed a little too slick for my tastes." They had joined Leighton Chiles, whom Mason introduced. The three reached the tavern and went inside. It was on the shady side of a sheer cliff and was pleasantly cool in this late afternoon. The conversation continued over springhouse-cooled ale. Mason was at a loss to divine just what Cabot might have in mind, out in the wilderness. He spoke his thoughts.

"So, if Cabot does get into the iron business, you're certain he'll lose money?"

"Without a doubt. I knew of those ore deposits from Archie Nolan but dismissed any notion of expanding there."

"Then what would the man want in such a place?"

"Hard to imagine. Unless he can make some sort of start, then convince others it's a veritable gold mine, get them to invest as you suggested. But even a blind fool would know he's too far from markets." The bodyguard Chiles had said nothing, but nodded in agreement. *Sounds like our man, all right.*

"Well, I intend to track him down if I can, and see for myself what he's about. But I do have to admit I don't have the kind of hard evidence against him I really need."

"Then you're far from home on what may be a hopeless quest, I'd fear."

"Perhaps. But there's this: the man apparently ordered me killed, which was attempted some days after he left the capital, no doubt to divert suspicion from himself. He thinks I'm dead, which is an advantage I have. And that attempt proves to me, at least, that he's crooked. An honest man wouldn't have sent an assassin."

"Fortunately, one who was evidently a poor marksman."

"Yes and no. He shot the wrong man, but only wounded him. I've tried to discover the shooter, who should also lead me to Cabot, if he's close to him. Oh, and another gunman was sent by him last fall to Virginia, I've learned, to avenge the destruction of a group of his associates who were receiving stolen money. Don't know the particulars of all that, but that man was himself killed."

"Bloody business. So this Cabot apparently enforces his operations with an iron hand, if you'll pardon the reference." That got an almost-smile from the taciturn Leighton Chiles.

"Exactly. Which makes the mystery of his going out to the frontier more inscrutable. Unless he simply wanted to disappear. It was difficult, finding out as much as I have. The man's secretive, works beneath the surface of things, but seems to succeed. Or has thus far."

"Perhaps I should fear he'll try to eliminate me as competition, then, be on my guard? That's not something I've thought seriously about, until now."

"Oh, surely not. No, if he'd had his sights on your operation, I could see that, perhaps. But surely he'd have made some sort of move against you by now. No again, if what we've learned is true, the man is uncharacteristically headed for ruin in a place where he's cut off from any kind of comeback. Unless, of course, he has a deeper motive, and this is just a diversion. As I said, mystifying."

"Well, Mr. Mason, all this is quite intriguing...we've devils among us. And I shall be on the lookout for any overt action from our Mr. Cabot. Let me know what I may do to help, in any way I can. Now, will you travel on? Or stay with us a few days?" He included Chiles in what was essentially an invitation.

"We would like to learn more of the overall iron production operation, sir, if that's all right. It'll help to understand what Cabot's up to, whether his venture is real or perhaps masks something more sinister."

"Just so you don't plan to become my competition, too." All three of them laughed.

Eighteen

The coming of summer had seen heavier travel along the main turnpike south from the Shenandoah Valley toward Saltville and on south and west. The MacNaughton clan had ambushed travelers more boldly even with their numbers decreased. The brothers Paul and Silas often worked as a team, preying on lone riders, robbing anyone they felt they could overpower.

The Saltville constable, Taylor Bridges, under increased pressure from the citizens and travelers alike, finally decided on an ambush of his own. He quietly recruited several hard-eyed deputies from among the settlers, then let it be known one day around town that a shipment of supplies was due in from north the next day.

"Lot of gold comin' down," he told several of the villagers, taking care that the lounging Silas would hear. "Payroll fer that iron outfit on out to Ketchum's Mill. Lotta supplies, too, I hear."

"Reckon they'll be heavy guarded, then," one of his deputies remarked.

The constable didn't want the fictitious shipment to sound too big to rob, so he downplayed it.

"Naw, they think roads'er some safer now down t'here, so they'll mebbe hire a couple guards here 'mongst us t'see 'em on out there, rest of th' way."

"When they due in?" another asked.

"Man rode in ahead of 'em said 'fore midday t'morrow. Reckon they'll stay over, rest th' teams an' all." The men drifted off, still speculating.

The seed thus planted, the group waited till dark, loaded hay onto several wagons, and covered it with canvas. Then, toward daylight, they drove out of the village north a few miles and waited, heavily armed.

Silas MacNaughton had rushed home to report this news.

"Thar's t'be gold, an' all kindsa supplies," he told old Abner, the clan chief. "Reckon if thar wuz 'nuff of us, we c'd git ourselfs set up right fer a haul lak thet?"

The men talked it over, and it was decided that a robbery of that size would indeed be worth it.

"But we gotta be keerful, somethin' this big," the old man cautioned. "Git thar wagons an' teams clear up in thet far holler off'en th' pike, whar nobody'll ever find 'em. Sorta braing some out as we need 'em, y'know. Be clean here, if thet const'ble Bridges gits nosin' 'round."

"Aw, he's too dumb t'do ennythaing." One of the cousins spat a brown stream of tobacco.

"Now, thet's jist whar y'git in trouble," the patriarch warned. "Don't never thaink th' man yer comin' up 'ginst is dumber'n you." A stern look at the assembled kin. "Even if he prob'ly is." Laughter all around.

The plan was to utilize the narrow gorge track the late cousin Ansted had favored, where the men could ride quickly out, surround the wagons, and head them away before anyone might come along. By covering their faces with cloth to mask them, they'd be unidentifiable. They'd kill any troublesome drivers, send the rest off on foot, and be much the richer for this easy picking. But then no, they agreed it'd be better to kill them all, leave no witnesses.

And if somehow something went wrong, or the wagons didn't come, why there'd be enough of the MacNaughtons just to take whatever else came along, including a guarded stage, if necessary. Or again, they might be able to trail that shipment toward Ketchum's Mill and rob them on the way there. The whole adventure raised everyone's hopes, and there was a deal of whiskey-drinking and plans to spend the money they'd surely get.

The constable and his determined men were on the highroad back toward the village by ten o'clock that morning, driving the teams, each man with pistols and rifles within easy reach.

"Now, if them boys comes after us, don't give 'em a chance," the leader advised. "Ennybody goes for a gun, shoot 'im. If they give up, we'll jist run 'em outta th' country, but it'd let 'em know we're serious if we kill one er two of 'em off."

To a man, the deputies had had enough of the MacNaughtons and their lawlessness, and they aimed to rid the territory of them all, one way or another. So it was that they had their guns in hand as they approached each blind turning of the road or opening up some hollow.

When the ten raiders charged out of the side track, they split, half of them racing to head off the wagons while the others rode to the rear, waving their rifles and shotguns. What they met was a barrage of fire, and four of them fell in that charge. The deputies then grabbed more guns, dropped behind their wagons, and opened fire again.

Paul MacNaughton was among the first to die, followed by the patriarch Abner, and in the second fusillade, more of the clan. Silas wheeled his horse and spurred him back the way they'd come, keeping low, certain of a killing ball in his back. Powder smoke hung in a pall behind him, and the shooting raged. Then it stopped suddenly, but the man did not look back, or slacken his pace. He raced off the woods road into thick trees, up a steep ravine that led into rocks near the top of a ridge where he hoped he could lose any pursuers.

He cursed the lawmen, cursed having been taken in by their plot, ranted at the obvious loss of most of the able-bodied of his kin. Resolved, if he escaped, to avenge himself on constable Bridges and all his ilk.

The horse labored up the steep incline, over bare stone, across a trickle of water, between tall trees and through dense brush. Horse and man were scratched, torn, heaving when they reached the top. Then Silas dismounted, pistol out, and led his trembling mount along a non-trail.

He dared not return to the clan's holdings. The lawmen already knew who the raiders were, even if they'd killed all the others. They'd be at the homeplace any minute now, he knew, and the few women, children, ailing men would be shown no mercy.

"So, guess I gotta git m'self on outta th' country," he decided. It wouldn't be long till Bridges and his men would find out he'd escaped and start the hunt for him. No time for revenge against such odds. He'd have to leave there completely, go where they'd never find him. Like Caleb and Shelby had. And yeah, even little Carver.

But where?

Kentucky, that's where. He'd ride toward that Ketchum's Mill, then on over the mountains west. With nothing on him but his guns, he'd have to use them to get supplies, and that was just the way it'd have to be. Mad as he was, he'd rob the first man he met. And for sure those missionaries, if he got half the chance.

~ * ~

Stephen had told Anna his suspicions regarding the lawyer Eddins. She remembered him from the trial in Charlottesville, and was inclined to believe everything evil about him. But like her husband, she couldn't quite justify Reginald Cabot's being of the same extreme stripe. Developing this piece of wilderness, donating to the church, financing the inn, giving the local people employment, just didn't fit with her idea of a robber baron.

"Unless he's trying to become a philanthropist for his own devious ends, whatever they may be. He *is* just a bit too smooth."

"My feeling exactly. But I can't for the life of me figure out what his goal could be. He's spending money like water, and we're all the beneficiaries, it seems. So either he's honest or, as you say, there's a motive so deep we can't find it. But I want to watch this Eddins closely. Apparently he was cleared of complicity before, but he was in it all, deeply, and people don't change that much." He remembered the dying outlaw naming Eddins as among the circle of criminals, as his last words.

"Well, I hear he's been filing claims on the land all around the works, representing Cabot," Anna mused, stoking the cookfire under a kettle. "And while we've filed and proven up on our claim, I doubt that others in the village have. I hope the man isn't claiming the whole place and will turn all the others out."

"I think getting them to file legally would be a good first move then, if he hasn't already done something like that. But again, what good would that do him, here where it's so steep you can fall out of your corn patch?" Stephen turned his palms up. "Archie Nolan says there's no ore this far up the creek. And incidentally, he also told me he's filed on some more of the land himself, on down. Says there's coal under a lot of it but he hasn't let Cabot know; apparently smells a rat, too. That's in confidence, of course, but you're the last person who'd mention it." He gave his wife an affectionate hug, and they stood, listening to the pleasant bubble of the kettle a moment, there in their hidden sanctuary.

"I'd say, then," Anna picked up the thread of their discussion, "that we watch, as you said, for anything out of line, but be ready to get the settlers to act if it looks as if we're to be the subjects of some kind of plot."

"Sort of feel the others out quietly then, get their views ahead of time. Yes, I like that. But I keep coming back to the fact that, with all Cabot's investment, getting the iron down out of this place will sink the whole venture. Maybe I'm missing something."

~ * ~

Discreet questioning hadn't turned up anything against the Davis man, Samuel Eddins had found. Seemed to be just what he appeared, a craftsman everyone depended upon. So, was he that clever? The lawyer didn't think so; ex-soldier, good with his hands but uneducated, even if he, as did his wife, spoke well. But that didn't explain what had happened back in Virginia.

But about that...the man certainly wasn't spending money lavishly. He'd surely taken the Weston group's money, but where was it? And yes, he might have come here to hide, but what, then? Didn't make sense.

The obvious thing to do here was to arrange for Davis' elimination, quietly, as in an accident. But the kind of men they'd utilized before for such work weren't to be found here, apparently. Oh, there were those robbery suspects back around Saltville he'd heard about, but such bumbling louts couldn't be depended on for assassinations without leaving a trace.

Eddins chafed under the man's presence, the fact that he was so highly thought of, the certainty that he would somehow undermine what he and Cabot were doing with their admittedly ill-gotten money. Davis had to go but the time, place and method were still to be discovered.

Meantime, he'd continue with the legal aspects of the operation, the securing of land and rights-of-way, the mineral rights to land beyond their ability to claim. Cabot didn't seem overly concerned, but he'd keep after the man, build his distrust of Davis, until he'd agree to a plan.

~ * ~

Hiram Garst had sold his rifle and was painfully stretching the money he got for it. He was no stranger to camping but the food he could afford was too much like that back in the Continental Army. He wanted a clean bed, decent meals, and could sorely use some new clothes. So far he hadn't robbed anyone, the other travelers on the turnpike south usually being in groups or appearing too poor to have anything he needed.

But he'd had enough of that. South of the New River crossing, he began to search for a camp of prosperous travelers. He could handle a small number, he felt sure, with his two pistols and knife. But it wouldn't come to that, he wagered; he could threaten his victims, relieve them of their money, stampede their horses, and be away without a shot fired. He just needed to find the right camp.

So he rode late each night, following the smell of woodsmoke, to spy out one knot of men after another. The third night, he saw three well-dressed men, their good horses tied close by, packs opened and settled in for the night. He left his own horse tied back off the road and approached in the half-moon's light, noting that none of the men seemed to have a gun on him. He paused, letting his nerves settle.

Then, stepping into the circle of firelight, pistols leveled, he confronted the men.

"Just stay where you are, gentlemen," he commanded pleasantly, "and no one gets killed. I'm in need of finances, and I ask you to empty your pockets, all in a pile, please."

The men were dumbfounded, evidently not having had to deal with a situation like this before. They looked toward each other, then at him, no doubt weighing their chances of taking him, three on one.

"And don't make that mistake. Two of you will die instantly, and I'll be all over the third with a very sharp knife. I suggest you do as I say, and quickly, before my good nature wears thin. *Now!*"

The men complied, eyes on the yawning barrels of Garst's pistols. Their money made a small pile.

"Now, open those saddlebags, and very carefully. I'm certain there's more there, and you'll hasten your deliverance by complying. Or, as I said, I can kill all of you and take it all. You choose."

One of the men, a round, red-faced fellow who looked like a storekeeper, had gone as nearly white as possible. He reached slowly for a nearby saddlebag, opened it carefully and emptied its contents. Coins spilled out. Garst kept his eyes on the others, alert for any sudden movement. But they were as if frozen, their astonishment not yet turned to outrage.

"Now, back away, all of you. I'll just trouble you for that saddlebag, after you've returned the money to it," he instructed the portly one. The man complied clumsily, hastily stuffing the coins back. He held the bag out, at the same time scrambling back.

Garst took it, pointed his pistols at each man in turn, without a suggestion of a tremor. The menace was like another presence in the air.

"Wise actions, gentlemen. Now, I can untie your horses, send them off into the woods to delay you. But I've the feeling you won't be coming after me, because I'll have set an ambush farther on. Which way? I'll leave that for you to ponder." And he backed slowly away, mindful of any reaching for a weapon. None occurred.

Retrieving his horse, Garst walked him quietly on down the pike, mounted and, out of hearing, was away at a brisk canter. He expected the men to report the robbery at the next village, but that should take time, and he'd be out of the country by then, in which direction they would not know.

But he was smart enough to know also not to stop at an inn or tavern anywhere near, so rode on, eventually dropping to a walk, to put steady miles between him and his unwilling benefactors. He reasoned they'd had more money with them anyway, and while angry at the robbery, wouldn't risk much to find him.

"Well now, we'll just go on with the plan. Become a sure enough pioneer, if nothing better. And if our friend Cabot has nothing for us, wherever he is, we'll simply go on to greener pastures. Anonymity has its benefits, and in this godawful outback, there's plenty of that." His horse flicked his ears and continued the nighttime pace.

~ * ~

Life wasn't all that easy for Carver MacNaughton. Sometimes Killebrew Ketchum yelled at him for a mistake at the forge or grumbled that he wasn't fast enough at some chore. And the lessons at the school weren't simple, either...that Mrs. Davis expected a fellow to do his best, and then some. More than once the boy had considered slipping off over the mountain west to go on with the original plan to seek his fortune elsewhere.

But the thought quickly passed. He often reminded himself that he'd never find a better situation, a young stranger on his own. Here he had the growing friendship of the bachelors Todd and Harvey, and strangely, the respect of the Davises. And there were the other young people. Alice McKnight was a pretty girl his own age, if somewhat in the shadow of her older sister Marina. Sybil Leslie was a year older, but a pleasant girl who seemed to like him, along with everyone else she met.

And there were the village children, some of whom also were teenage. And with the influx of more workingmen to the iron operation, their offspring added to the circle of young people. There were square dances, parties, pie suppers, along with the church activities.

Carver didn't know how he felt about the religion thing. Anna Davis and the other missionaries made it the center of their lives, but it was still a foreign concept to him. He guessed a man had to get better set with the folks around him, surer of his livelihood, before he could concentrate on things beyond survival.

But meantime he'd work, study, and try hard to get along with everybody. He was encouraged by people like Belle Ketchum, who assured him that Killy's bark was just that, and that the smith really liked him. And Mrs. Davis never let on that he was less than any of the others. His awe of that woman and her husband, grew daily, and any thoughts of betraying them made him ashamed.

So Carver MacNaughton seemed to have found his place in Ketchum's Mill. He could foresee growing a couple more years, then maybe even courting one of the girls, plan on getting himself a piece of ground and sure enough settling down. He specially liked pretty Alice McKnight, easy to talk to, the right age, and had been friendly toward him.

It all seemed more than he could have hoped for, just those months ago, back raiding with his raffish kin.

~ * ~

Silas MacNaughton was astonished when he saw his brother, from the very vantage point Carver himself had used months before. He knew that remembered hard-eyed fellow and the missionaries would recognize him, so he spied out the village all that day, noting the bustling inn, the church, the mill, and a number of men coming and going downcreek to what he supposed was that iron-mining business he'd heard about.

Silas hadn't expected to see his little brother there and working. He looked for sign of his cousins Caleb and Shelby but didn't see them. Could be down at the mine, or maybe had indeed gone on over west, back when they disappeared.

He pondered his next move. He'd managed to rob a lone traveler a day out of Saltville, but the man hadn't had much. Going on west from here was a chance...he'd heard there was nothing for many, many miles that way. He guessed he'd have to get his hands on money and supplies here if anywhere, enough to keep him until he found whatever was beyond the mountains.

The inn would have money, from all those people obviously staying there. So maybe would the mill, which seemed to double as a kind of store. But be hard for a man alone to rob such places...

But wait! Right there was his brother, working the bellows at the smithy. If he could just get with him, the two of them could find a way to take what they needed, then ride on west together, find whatever adventure lay ahead of them. The boy must have some way convinced the people here he was just needing an honest job, and he'd sure be able to get inside, slip away with what they'd need. And now he had to be about the only family Silas had left.

He watched as the day ended, the smith handing Carver over to two men who'd come upcreek. He knew those men: the one-armed one and the other had been the ones they'd tried to ambush that time. Now, what in hell was his brother doing with them?

Was he their prisoner? Could be, since they'd have known who he was. And just where was that tall fellow was so quick with his gun? Just what kind of place was this, anyway?

About then, Stephen Davis rode up to the church with some other men, some on foot, obviously also from the mine area. Davis dismounted, went inside the building. In a moment he and a very tall woman emerged. She untied a second horse, the two mounted and rode on through the village, speaking to others as they passed.

Silas couldn't figure it out. But he knew he must reach his brother, so he noted the direction he and the two men had taken, up a narrow hollow that seemed to go nowhere but up to the wall of the mountain. He noted the long slant of the sun, calculating the time till dark.

But he'd have to think this out better: If he could get Carver free tonight, they'd have to rob the inn and be off before daylight or they'd get caught. And ride hard to outdistance pursuers on the dim and steep trail west. Not easy, he could tell, in the dark that way.

So, wait till daylight, then? No, too easy for the villagers to catch them. Unless he could create a diversion that'd let them just ride away undetected. Yes, maybe that'd work: set fire to something, rob the inn in the confusion, then race away. So the first thing was to set his brother free, and for that he'd have to get a good look at how those men held him.

After the village had settled down in the summer darkness, Silas tied his horse, crept down, keeping quiet, moving around so the slight breeze was toward him to foil dogs. Then along the roadway past the mill, the inn, the church, and up the hollow he'd noted earlier. Before long it branched, and he took the right fork at a guess. There was a cabin up ahead, lighted with candles. Smoke drifted from a small cookfire in the fireplace, coloring the interior light with its flame.

He slipped closer, peering inside the open shutter. A young man and hugely pregnant woman were there. *Wrong cabin, then.*

Silas retraced his steps, then turned up the other fork. Up a distance was another lone cabin, and this must be the one. He stepped silently, avoiding the worn path with its gravel, staying in the grass alongside. There in candlelight he saw the two missionaries, and with them was his brother Carver. They were talking easily, and the boy didn't appear to be tied or anything. *Good. Make it easier to git him away.*

But how? Silas sat back against a tree and thought it over. He could shoot both the men with his two pistols, take whatever was in the cabin, and slip back to his horse with the boy and steal another. But somebody would surely hear the shots, and the alarm would spread. No chance then to rob the inn, and they'd have to ride for their lives with nothing.

No, have to do this on the quiet, but *how*, again?

A diversion, yeah that was it...make some kind of commotion that'd draw the men outside. Then he could get close to Carver and the two could slip away.

Not a fire; that'd bring help. Just some noise...

A pigpen caught his eye in the dim moonlight. He could maybe stir up the pigs, get them squealing. He crept that way, past the cabin. Sure to be wolves and panthers hereabouts, so that's what the men would think was near. No dog to warn them, either. He reflected that he'd eluded every dog in the entire village. Strange, that, the way backwoods folks always had packs of dogs. Lucky, that's what he'd always been, and dog smart.

He picked up a long, sharp stick and prodded one of the sleeping pigs. It squealed, jumped away. He poked another, harder. Another squeal, and a general shuffling. Then another, and the noise level rose. He backed away into shadows, watching the house.

A man came out, armed with a rifle and a candle lantern. It was the older missionary. Silas gripped one of his pistols by the barrel, waiting while the man cautiously approached the pigpen, searching about in the weak light.

The animals crowded the far side of the pen, so the man approached this side, looking for the intrusion. His back was to Silas as he bent to inspect the wall of the pen.

Silas took two quick steps and brought the gun butt down hard on the man's head. He grunted, then collapsed, the lantern going out. Silas grabbed the rifle, then retreated again. He knew the other man would come out to see what had happened, and he'd just have to wait.

It didn't take long for the rear door to open again, and a form emerged. Only it wasn't the one-armed man, it was Carver MacNaughton, coming right to him! He couldn't believe his luck. They'd be able to leave, with this rifle, then go start that fire.

Carver saw the form of Harvey Campbell lying against the pen wall, and came quickly to him, bent over.

"Carver," Silas whispered hoarsely, "over here."

The boy turned, searching the shadows. He'd noted that Campbell's rifle was gone, and the hair on his neck stood up. He made an instant decision, then lunged away down toward the cabin at full speed. Who had called him by name? He knew that voice, but...He didn't wait to find out.

Silas was shocked that his brother had run back to the house. Now the other man would come, armed, and he'd have to shoot him for sure. The boy had been scared, he guessed, not knowing who was here to rescue him. Silas cursed himself for not letting Carver know who he was.

But the door to the cabin didn't open, and no one came out. That didn't figure, unless the man was too afraid. Have to go down there, then, shoot him through the open shutter. Silas began to creep down toward the house.

Todd Eppsworth and Carver had slipped out the front door opposite and, both armed, had split up to encircle the pigpen in the shadows of the trees. They both saw Silas approaching the cabin, Harvey's rifle extended ahead. Both closed on him.

"Drop the rifle!" Todd called from ten yards away.

Silas whirled at the voice but had caught sight of the second dim figure on the other side. He knew he was a dead man if he gave up.

He leaped aside, hitting the ground running, the rifle falling to the ground. He was between the other two, and wasn't sure who they were, being sure the one-armed man and Carver were still inside. He dodged, feinted, lunged ahead, aiming to cut the corner of the cabin, get downhill fast, and away. Escape was the only thing on his mind, and expecting gunfire any second, he kept zigzagging, sprinting for safety.

He passed the cabin with long, frenzied strides, hurling himself down the path. No shots came. Had he escaped? He had. He reached the fork in the trail, then came within sight of the village. All quiet. He slowed to a cautious walk, breath heaving.

Why hadn't the boy come to him? Oh, he must've known of those other men out there, the ones who'd discovered him. Damn, how many were there?

Well, he'd not get another chance to free his brother. Have to get his hands on whatever he could, then just leave this place, fast as he could. Those men would spread the word, and he had little time.

Emboldened by his need for haste, and counting on surprise, Silas opened a pasture gate and caught a horse, led it out by a rope he'd found, and tied it near the inn. Then he drew both pistols and marched right up to the inn door. Light was inside and voices came through. He opened the door and stepped in, startling the four people seated around a table. An older man had been reading from a large Bible while a woman and two teenage girls listened.

"Don'tcha move, er I'll shoot," Silas warned. "Now, I'm needin' all th' money y'got. Jist pile it on thet table, an' hold real still."

He knew any money the inn had would be locked up somewhere, and he'd observed the woman from the mill going in and out of here all day...probably kept the cash at the mill. The man at the table spoke in a deep voice.

"We haven't money, my man. There's nothing to buy in this village. I am the minister of the church, and it is a poor church. I will let you have what's on me, but it isn't much." And he slowly withdrew several coins from a pocket. "Now, I'd put those pistols away and leave quietly, before you're apprehended." The minister seemed unafraid, even if his wife and daughters were petrified. Silas knew the man was probably right. So what now? He'd acted rashly, he guessed, coming into a place where there wasn't much to steal. Then, his eyes on the daughters, he had an idea. He holstered one of his guns.

"All right, I will leave. But I'm takin' this'n with me," and he grabbed fifteen-year-old Alice McKnight by the arm and hauled her toward the door. She screamed, which unnerved him, but he pointed the other pistol at the girl's head. "Quiet, gal! An' y'all make jist enny move, an' I'm gonna shoot this'n."

The reverend McKnight had half-risen, but realized this man was serious. He sat back, casting about for any way to distract him, get help. It happened the other residents of the inn were working by lantern light down at the ironworks, stoking the furnace, waiting for the molten iron to run out of the smelter openings. The lawyer Eddins had gone back to Saltville some time before. There was no one else there.

Silas backed away, holding the girl with one arm, and his hand over her mouth. Someone might've heard that scream, and he wasn't about to let her cry out again. The others remained frozen at the table.

"Enny of you come after me, this gal gits herse'f kilt," he gritted. "Now, you'ns jist wait right chere an' nuthin's gonna happen." He dragged the girl with him out and across to the mill. She tried to fight him, but she was small, and deathly afraid.

"Jist you hush up, now," he tried to calm her. "Won't nuthin' happen, lak I said. I jist gotta git me a way outta here."

He pounded on the mill door with the butt of his pistol, noting that the miller's house was built onto it. Sounds came from within, and he called out, "I got th' preacher's daughter here, 'th a gun on her. Now you jist open up, an' she'll be all right. You don't, an' I'll hafta shoot her."

In a moment the door cracked open, and Killebrew Ketchum eyed the man over the muzzle of a cocked shotgun. Silas had expected that and had the girl in front of him as a shield.

"Jist you put thet gun down, now," he ordered, pushing the girl in ahead of him as the miller retreated. Then the man laid the shotgun down and raised his hands.

"I won't do nuthin," he said. "Just take whutever you want, but you leave Alice alone."

"Whut I want is all th' cash y'got, ole man. Now, an' be quick about it!" A woman had come into the room and stood, wide-eyed at the scene.

The miller turned slowly, keeping his eye on the gun in this man's hand. Alice had gone still, but her eyes sought help. Ketchum knew he couldn't make a move to free her with that cocked pistol at her head.

"All right, now. Here's all we got," and he piled coins on the counter.

"Put it inna sack. Tie it up tight. *Now.*" The miller moved carefully to do so. Silas caught a movement from the woman, and turned, holding the girl before him.

"Wouldn't try nuthin', lady, er this gal's gonna die," he warned her. The woman stopped reaching behind sacks of grain. The money was tied, and Ketchum held it out.

Now Silas had the problem of too much to hold at once.

"Jist you keep quiet now, gal," he told the girl, "an' I'm 'bout t'let y'go." She nodded through tears, and he removed his hand, but kept the pistol at her head. With his other hand he grabbed the sack of money, tucked it under his arm, and grasped the girl's waistband, pulling her toward the door, still using her as a shield.

"Let her go, now," Ketchum warned him, "or th' whole damn place'll be onto you like stink on cowshit."

"I don't thaink so. Not yit, leastways. But you reach fer thet gun, an' this gal's brains gonna be all over, an' it'll be yore fault." He was out the door.

Nothing moved in the village, although Silas knew it would be only moments before the men from the distant cabin, perhaps the minister, and certainly the miller, were upon him. He could hear a commotion in both the inn and the mill. He pushed the girl ahead of him to the tied horse, freed it, managed to climb onto it while holding her tightly by one hand, then hauled her up with him. As people charged out the doors of both buildings, he struck his heels into the horse's flanks, guiding it in the darkness with his knees toward the creek ford and the place well beyond where he'd left his own mount.

They'd reached the other side of the shallow water before anyone could find a horse, although Ketchum was yelling for help, waving the shotgun. Lights came on dimly at Daughtry's cabin as big George thundered out, rifle in hand. The minister appeared, grasping an ancient pistol.

"He's taken my daughter," he gasped.

"I know. Now Rev'rend, you jist stay quiet," the miller assured him. "We'll git yer girl back, quick's we kin git th' men t'gether." He'd seen a group of them coming from downcreek, their work obviously finished for the night. And that was Todd Eppsworth, with Carver, running down the far draw, a torch held high.

Ketchum quickly told the men the situation, among whom were Cabot, Nolan, Leslie, White and the engineer Stillwell. Nolan took a torch and ran toward the creek ford to look for tracks. The others armed themselves from the inn and the mill, saddled horses, and followed in moments.

Silas held the girl in one arm again, beyond the sound of the voices, and again had clamped his hand over her mouth. Wouldn't do to have her give them away, now they were clear.

"Now, y'gotta keep quiet, er I'll shorely kill you," he shoved the pistol against her forehead as he removed his other hand. She merely whimpered a little.

He hauled the roped horse sideways into the trees where his own horse was tied, dismounted, still holding Alice in place as he took rope from a saddlebag. He forced her to lie crossways, face down across the unsaddled horse's back, and tied her hands and feet with the rope across underneath. Then he freed his mount, leaped into the saddle, and led the way through the trees in a wide arc. Earlier he'd found the very route Carver had taken to reach the western trail by rounding the hill, and was able to follow it, picking his way cautiously in the dim moonlight to what he was sure was complete freedom.

Nineteen

Nolan and the others found the place where torchlight showed Silas' wet horse tracks leading away from the road beyond the creek, and after a quick consultation, Ketchum led half the men that way, while the others, with George Wellerby in the lead, rode for Stephen Davis' cabin. They too, knew how the back trail led the long way to the route west up the mountain. Todd Eppsworth was with them.

They backtracked, turned up the creek trail, pushed hard, and were nearing the way up to Stephen's place when Silas burst out of the woods, fording the low creek, just ahead of them. He turned, pointed the pistol at Alice, and warned her again not to cry out, both of them having seen the approaching torches in the distance. She was crying silently, hanging there, face and arms scratched by the brush they'd come through.

Damn, lost m'headstart. Gotta move fast, now, an' not 'nuff light.

Moments later, George pounded on Stephen's door, shouting his name. Stephen opened it sleepily, but with a pistol in his hand. Seeing it was indeed George, he stepped back.

"Some feller's got th' preacher's daughter, Stephen," George managed, catching his breath from the steep ride. "Headed up round th' hill offa th' road, an' tracks show he's ahead of us this side th' creek, goin' west. Got 'nuther hoss, an' took all th' money Killy had. Y'gotta help us git him."

Stephen nodded, grabbed clothes and boots, snatched his rifle, powder and shot, and a second pistol. Anna appeared, and George told her in a few words what had happened.

"You've got to reach him, Stephen," she urged, "before..."

"Yes, I know. And we will. Now, you stay inside and bolt the doors. We hope it's just the one man, but..." and he was gone, leaping astride his horse that Todd had saddled and brought around. Stephen was amazed anew at how well the man worked with his one arm. He reflected briefly on how often he'd seen Todd grip straps in his teeth.

As this group of men rode out of sight up the trail, the others splashed across the creek as Silas had, and saw the distant torches, noted the myriad tracks. They followed, knowing that Stephen, the best shot among them, was surely with the others.

Carver MacNaughton was with the men with Ketchum, riding old Daughtry's horse. He'd been trying to place the voice back at the cabin, and now was certain it had been his brother Silas. He'd joined the others before he'd realized this, but his anger at Alice's abduction overruled any feelings he might have for his depraved brother.

Jist like Caleb an' Shelby, he's gone after a girl. An' it's not jist enny girl, it's Alice. Rage built inside him as he pictured his brother's hands on the minister's daughter. Just then, he knew he could shoot Silas himself, or at least help with the rope when they hanged him.

~ * ~

Seeing the torches in the distance behind them fade as the men turned up Stephen's trail, Alice felt the hope in her heart fade. This insane man wasn't going to let her go; he needed her to keep the others at bay. And tied this way, she couldn't possibly get control of the horse and turn him, ride back to safety.

If only they come in time, she prayed. She'd been taught that God would protect her in any situation, but at fifteen, she'd already seen enough times when that apparently hadn't happened. Good men had come back from the war, maimed and sick, and a lot of them hadn't come back at all. And babies died, and saintly old people, so where was He then? She tried to believe, tried to have the faith her father had, but found herself wondering just how he felt now, seeing her taken from before his eyes.

But maybe God had sent those other men, and they were really just behind. Maybe they'd put the torches out, so they could slip up on them, free her. Hope swelled again inside her, but couldn't extinguish the worry and fear.

She knew what this man would do to her the minute he felt he'd lost their pursuers. He'd turn off the trail, find a place her screams couldn't be heard, and beat her, rape her, kill her. He could ride farther, faster without her once he was sure he'd escaped.

She tried to think of some way, any way, she could get away. All right...he'd have to stop the tiring horses, laboring as they were up this steep trail. But he'd reach that hiding place first. What could she do if the chance did present itself?

He had a knife in his belt. If he gave her an instant, she might grab it, conceal it until he forced her to the ground, then shove it through him as he mounted her. Alice was a sensitive girl, but she knew the mating rituals of farm animals, and had heard all the whispered tales among the other girls, of what men did to women. Her mother had told her little of this, but she knew the basics.

Women weren't supposed to have to defend themselves, she thought, their men were there to do that for them. But men were like animals too, barely holding their lust in check, putting on manners, playing the game until they could have their way. And the girls played the game, too, flirting, pretending, until it was their turn to ensnare their chosen ones.

All that didn't apply here, though. This filthy fellow with the foul breath wasn't even a decent animal. What he'd done, and what he planned to do to her was inhuman, outside all the rules of civilization. He was a brute, and she was to be his victim. The realization made her faint, jolting along, tied like a deer carcass, helpless.

~ * ~

Stephen realized his man could see his pursuers' torches long before they could reach him, so had ordered the others to douse them and follow him as well and as quietly as they could. He knew the man would have to rest soon: the steep trail would exhaust any horse in minutes. He stopped the men, listened.

Far up the trail he heard faintly the clatter of stones knocked loose from under a horse's hoof.

"I'm going ahead," he told the others and dismounted, handed his reins to Todd. "Leave the horses here."

He strode rapidly up the twisting trail he knew well, keeping as quiet as he could, but trusting to the sound of the hooves ahead and the horses' labored breathing to mask any sound he made. He heard those hooves moments later and judged that he was within only a few yards of his quarry. But in the dim light he knew he couldn't get off a good shot. He thought he'd just have to trail the man until he sought a hiding place to rest before he could slip up on him.

Then the horses crested a rise, and Stephen could see the outline of the man against the slightly lighter sky. The second horse was still in the dark below, just a darker lump. He knew he had just a momentary chance.

He dropped to one knee, instantly but smoothly training his rifle on the distant shape, and fired.

Silas MacNaughten felt the blow of the ball jolt him forward before he realized he'd been hit. He tried to spur his horse, but his legs didn't seem to want to move. There was suddenly no feeling in them, and he was aware that he was no longer upright, the ground rushing up to smash him in the face.

Stephen shouted to the men to light the torches again, bring the horses, and hurry along. He knew his shot had pierced the man's heart as surely as he'd known the men he'd killed in the war were dead as soon as he'd pulled the trigger. He ran to reach Alice, grabbed her horse's rope. She was sobbing.

"It's all right, Alice," he soothed her. "We're here for you. That man won't harm you now." He untied her as the other men rushed up, Carver wide-eyed in the lead. The boy put his arms around the girl and together he and Stephen eased her from the horse.

"It's me, Alice. Carver. We got you. You're all right now. Ain't nuthin' gonna hurt you enny more." She sobbed against his chest, heaving for air. He held her close to stop her trembling, and Stephen watched them a moment.

"Let's get her home, men," he instructed. "Here, Alice, you can ride with me." She could see them now, in the flaring torchlight, and she climbed up, helped by Carver. She gave the boy a brief smile through her tears. Stephen cradled the small form in his arms. The fallen Silas was mercifully out of her sight as Stephen turned the horse, indicating with his head that the men should do what was necessary.

Carver MacNaughton got a good look at the dead man in the light of the torches. Yes, that was his brother. A tide of emotions ran through the boy as he remembered wanting so to be like him, to grow up to be his equal. He turned away, wondering why Silas had come here alone, glad the others couldn't see his face as tears began. He stifled them with an angry swipe of his sleeve, realizing how close his brother had come to violating Alice McKnight. But he couldn't quite make himself hate him either, seeing his dead face this way.

~ * ~

Anna was waiting at the cabin trail, just out of sight with a pistol in her hand. Seeing Stephen with Alice, she rode out.

"I'll take her now," she told him, and he handed the girl over. Anna began to talk soothingly to her, holding her in her strong arms, letting her horse find its way down the mile-long trail to the village. The others trailed behind, their talk muffled as Stephen held back to give his wife and the girl some privacy.

At the inn, Anna handed Alice down to her father, and she burst into tears again.

"She's not hurt, Reverend, only scratches. Stephen and the others reached her in time." Dismounting, she went inside with the others and helped Ella McKnight and Marina bathe the girl, tend to her bleeding arms and face, speaking calmly to her. Finally, in a clean nightgown and in her own bed with her mother beside her, Alice was able to drift off to sleep.

"I can't thank you enough, Stephen." Armistead McKnight put a hand on his friend's shoulder. "You brought my little girl home." There were actually tears in the man's eyes, and the erect carriage he affected, slumped.

"All of us helped, sir. She's our girl, as well as yours, you know."

"And God's."

"Yes, and God's."

~ * ~

Next day, Hiram Garst rode into Ketchum's Mill, eyeing the scant village in the midmorning sun. *Some place*, he mused. What could Cabot want here? Well, the ironworks were obviously on down the well-worn road alongside the creek, and he guessed that was where things were happening. Whatever could happen in this godforsaken wilderness. He noted chickens pecking around the mill, and heard penned pigs grunting nearby.

He tied his horse at the smithy, where an older man was working. He tipped his tricorner hat to him.

"Morning, sir," he greeted. The smithy seemed to be a part of the mill. "Is Mr. Ketchum in?"

"I'm Killy Ketchum," the smith replied, laying his hammer aside and banking the coals. "What c'n we do fer you, sir?"

"I'm an associate of Mr. Reginald Cabot, and I was told he'd relocated here to run an iron operation."

"Oh, that he did, an' he's done a sight of good t'this place, he has," the miller-smith assured the man. "C'mon into th' inn, Mr..."

"Garst. Hiram Garst. Yes, I would welcome a cool drink, if I may. Where would I find Mr. Cabot at this time of day, sir?"

"Oh, he's down to th' smelter an' foundry. Goes ever' day t'oversee things. Got a reg'lar beehive of stuff goin' on, mile or so downcreek. Reckon you c'n most hear th' mill thumpin' away, if y'listen close."

Garst followed his host into the inn and was pleasantly surprised to find it new and clean. The woman at the counter introduced herself as Ketchum's wife and served him ale cool from the springhouse. He thanked her and inquired about business here as the smith returned to his forge.

"Oh, it's good now. Bit lean at first, but Mr. Cabot's brought in th' iron fellers, an' we got th' preacher an' his fam'ly here, an' th' prospector, Mr. Nolan. Others too comin', an' they ain't all honest." She looked him directly in the eye. *Now, what's this...?*

"Don't s'pose you c'd of heard, but we had us some 'citement here last night," she went on. "Some feller robbed us, took th' preacher's daughter, an' most got away, but our boys, they tracked him, got her back." She looked upstairs. "Girl's all right, but her mama's up with her, gittin' her over it all. Don't seem like we kin git far 'nuff away from such doin's, even here."

"What happened to the man?"

"Oh, young feller done a lot of th' buildin' here wuz a sharpshooter in th' army...he took care of 'im, all right. An' last fall, 'nuther two men come in, tried t'git to th' missionary wimmen, but our Stephen agin, he'n m'man Killy kep' that from happenin'. No law hereabouts yet, so we gotta take keer of things ourselves."

"Sounds like you've been able to."

"So far, all right. Well, reckon you aimin' t'stay with us?"

"That'll depend on my friend Cabot. He may have work for me, but I'll just have to see. We were associated up in Philadelphia." Garst began to envision this remote settlement as a tight-knit community. Maybe that was what Cabot wanted: anonymity, and maybe the chance to run everything himself, little as that would be. If what the Ketchums said was true, he'd assumed a leadership role.

After engaging a room, Garst took his leave, riding down the road alongside the creek. He saw the new church and heard lessons from within. There were cabins up the hollows, and newly-cleared fields on the slopes, the mountain soil held in place with rough walls of stone picked from the fields. Everything had a newness, a lack of decay so common in rural settlements. Cabot's money was evidently at work.

Well, if the man didn't need his skills, he could probably obtain a little money from him, sort of for past favors, and ride on west, his alternate plan. But he could appreciate the remoteness of a place like this, and if a man like himself could make a decent living, he could perhaps see settling.

Of course, that wasn't his first, or even his second or third choice. He was good at one thing: killing men. Any other trade involved too much work.

Garst rode into the mining and smelting operation a few minutes later, noting the new foundry operation just further along. Another creek joined this one to fill a large forebay that powered a mill wheel. Even at low water, he could see that a significant drawdown would enable machinery to be run for hours at a time. Whoever had built this knew milling, it appeared, although that wasn't something Garst understood well.

He learned that Reginald Cabot was involved in directing a crew of men working on a deep fill in a new road across a ravine in the distance. He crossed a new bridge, following the surprisingly level roadway. And saw Cabot, in the thick of things, waving his arms, next to a small man with a surveying instrument.

"Mr. Cabot, hello," he called as he rode up. The man turned, squinted in the summer sun.

"Why, Garst, it's you," he exclaimed. "However did you find us here?" Momentary confusion, but quickly replaced by Cabot's famous affability. "Do join us...we're constructing our roadway down out of these mountains." *Now what the devil does this man want, here? I thought I'd left him behind. Oh, probably things got too hot for him in the capital, but how did he manage to locate me?*

"Certainly, sir. I heard from acquaintances of yours where you'd headed and decided we could continue to work together. Long way, but here I am, at your service, as always." Garst eyed the other man meaningfully.

"Well, yes, of course. And we'll have to talk about that. Oh, this is our engineer, Thaddeus Stillwell. Hiram Garst and I worked together in Philadelphia." Garst bowed to the man. "Yes, let's go talk about your place with us here, Hiram." And Cabot led the assassin aside out of hearing.

~ * ~

Stephen had recognized Silas MacNaughton, and had spent some time with young Carver, Eppsworth, and Campbell, who was still sporting a large knot on his head. Stephen had also heard, second-hand from Hiram Garst's report of the wholesale eradication of the rest of the MacNaughton clan outside Saltville. It was apparent that Carver had no family left.

"I know this is hard on you, Carver," he sympathized, "and it'll take some getting over. But it's really just another example of where that road would have led you if you'd followed it. Sounds like Silas was trying to get you to join him, too. Now, I don't mean to sound harsh, but carrying off a young girl like that is about the lowest thing a man could do."

"Oh, I know that, sir. An' Silas, he had it comin'. I'd of shot him m'self, I reckon, if I'da had th' chancet. But bein' m'brother an' all..."

"And I'm sorry it was your brother. And about the rest of your kin. But if he'd managed to get away from us, you can imagine what he'd have done to Alice. We have to protect the innocent whenever we can."

Carver remembered the sobbing girl who'd clung tightly to him that night, and what he felt for her crowded out his grieving for his late brother. Losing all the others would take some getting used to, he knew, but he'd really started that process when he'd ridden away, months before. Hard, yes, but he reckoned it was all part of becoming a man.

"And I see no need to let the others know who he was," Stephen concluded. The other two men agreed.

"Reckon that's best, yes," Carver reflected. He thought a moment more.

"An' well, I guess I c'n live with it."

~ * ~

Jedediah Mason wasn't far behind Hiram Garst, even after his pleasant stop at the Jackson River ironworks. He'd stopped briefly in Roanoke, then other villages as he came to them, but no one knew of any ironworks in that region. So, staying over in Saltville to rest the horses and ask around, he was astounded to see Samuel Eddins from a distance, emerging from his law office.

"Chiles, that's the lawyer who was part of Cabot's circle in Philadelphia, isn't it?"

"Sure looks like him. So maybe we're close to our man. Did he see you?"

"No, went right on down the street. I'd say he's here doing deeds, property work for Cabot, so the operation must be out of here, most likely west."

"So, I've not asked you, sir, since I knew you'd have to work one up, but just what's your plan to be now?"

"Honestly, I haven't gotten any farther than hoping to catch the man in something illegal. That'll mean watching him closely, and that won't be easy. He knows me, even though I'm quite certain he thinks me dead. And he's seen you, too. So has Eddins, so we're not free to snoop the way I'd like. For now I want to find out just where Cabot is, find a way to spy on him there, and pick up any information we can that we might use to skewer him."

"Then I'd say, first off, we get ourselves new names, wouldn't you?"

"Yes, and alter our appearances also. Neither Cabot nor Eddins has seen us close up, and if they assume I'm dead, it'll be easier to pose as someone else."

"That should work at a distance, but we won't get close, I'm afraid. I'd suggest an accomplice, but we know absolutely no one here."

"Then we'll spend a few days as two different men, and scout out this town as well as get a bearing on Cabot's operation. It's just possible we can recruit someone we can use without telling him too much. Really, all we need is an honest man, as did Diogenes with his lantern."

"Don't know that one, sir, but I agree. And since we're recognizable as city dwellers, why don't we become frontiersmen? Seems a lot of gentlemen have come west since the war to find opportunity, and we could be just two more."

"Buckskins, rifles, broad-brimmed hats, store the carriage for the present. Yes, I suppose we could handle that."

So the two men who emerged from the inn the next day and went horse-hunting were nothing in appearance like the two who'd come into town. Mason had given out the story that they were employees of a well-to-do merchant who'd be coming along shortly with his family to claim his carriage, with an eye to starting a business there. The two had dressed down before engaging a room at the inn and hoped their ruse would be successful. Mason had foregone his wig, and his close-cropped head was now perpetually hidden under his hat. Chiles already looked like a dangerous man, and in his new outfit, exactly resembled a hardened frontiersman, the kind one did not trifle with.

They eventually procured two good horses, tack and basic camping gear. Then they began asking cautiously about what kinds of industrial activity might be in the region, and immediately heard of the Ketchum's Mill ironworks on a distant creek improbably called Troublesome. And yes, the fellow heading it all was one Reginald Cabot, a likable fellow who apparently had no end of money.

"Allus sendin' men in to buy supplies," a storekeeper confided. "Got a young feller name of Holloway from around here hired don't do much else, way I hear it, but run an' fetch. Been a lotta folks headed thataway, ever since them missionary folks settled thar last year. Warn't nothin' but old man Ketchum's mill thar b'fore that, but I hear buildin's been goin' on ever since."

Mason learned that people in the region were quite high on Cabot, even this soon after his arrival. *Spend enough money, and the public thinks you're God.* But none of this got him any closer to whatever it was the man was planning. So far it seemed he was legitimately building up the Ketchum's Mill community, establishing a needed industry, and gaining the support of its citizens.

Could Cabot be changing his stripes, like those jungle cats? Mason didn't think so. In his experience, men who'd profited greatly, above or beneath the law, wanted more than anything else to reach farther, get richer, have more influence, power. And he couldn't see how this man could attain much of that here at the end of the civilized world and beyond.

The talk around Saltville was still of the constable and his deputies' having wiped out a clan of robbers that had been preying on the travelers through there for years. So maybe some order was being imposed on the region, Mason conceded. And, if Cabot's ironworks did happen to succeed in the face of huge odds, he supposed the man would be in a position to take some sort of leadership role. He recalled having read somewhere that it was considered by some a greater achievement to be the master of one's own fiefdom, however small, than a senator in Rome. Or words to that effect.

But with the very real presence of the canny Cummings' already-established works on the Jackson River, Cabot could never hope to compete. No, the physical obstacles of the very mountains that held the precious ore would see to that.

Unless, and the thought intruded again, Cabot planned to eliminate that competition. Now *that* would be more in keeping with the man's ego: monopolize the iron and steel market in this entire remote but still needy region. If he could do away with Cummings, even destroy his works, it would be years before another hard-driving manager could rebuild, and by then Cabot would have seized the market.

Mason talked this over with Leighton Chiles, always receptive to his associate's ideas.

"He's the kind would do something like that, all right," Chiles mused. "Then he could charge as high a price as he wanted. All this new ground, just the need for plows, harrows, axes, chain, horseshoes would support the business. And with new gristmills going in, wagon works, the shipping down the rivers, I'd say the man could be a lot richer very soon.

"And he wouldn't hesitate to take out Cummings if that's what stood in his way. Seems like your friend should definitely be on his guard, all right."

Mason was doubly grateful for his man's insights. It paid to have a suspicious nature. He resolved to send a letter to Cummings warning him specifically of the perceived danger.

But for now, they'd have to depend on their disguises to spy on Cabot without his knowing it. If he had indeed been the man who'd ordered Mason killed, he'd do it again. And, of course, that should work with Eddins too, so they both must be able to move more or less freely while gathering whatever they could against their targets.

"I guess we could just show up at this Ketchum's Mill, looking for business opportunities," Mason mused. "Of course, Cabot won't want competition, so we'll have to come up with some other venture. In that landlocked location, nothing seems natural, though."

"Well, he's going to need to sell his iron, so why don't we pose as buyers?" Say we've developed a new approach to flour milling, maybe, and plan to sell our system all over. We'd need a steady supply of iron, and what better place to get it?"

"Maybe. But what'd be our new idea, there?"

"Oh, I don't know. Milling: far's I know, you dump grain in a hopper, the stones grind it, you sift it, then grind again. Seems pretty simple." Everyone had seen this much-needed operation at one time or another, which had continued unchanged since Roman times.

"All right. Where in that operation could a machine do the work a man normally does, then?" Mason asked.

Chiles went over the steps again in his head. A man had to climb a short ladder to get to the hopper, and gravity feed the grain down to the stones. Then the collected meal of flour was bagged, and carried to storage, or delivered to the customer. He ticked off each phase again on his fingers. How could some mechanical device speed up the process?

"The ladder," he concluded. "Man has to climb a ladder with a sack of grain. Heavy, slow. Why couldn't we invent some way to get the grain up there?"

"Like a big wheel, maybe with buckets on it, like a waterwheel?" Mason was thinking also.

"Have to contrive a way to dump it at the top. Well, why can't we keep our secret device a secret so nobody can steal it, just say we've perfected it and need a lot of iron to manufacture it? No details."

"Chiles, you should be a snake oil salesman. Yes, that's who we'll be—inventors, with a revolutionary idea, in need of Cabot's product. That way we'll get an inside look at all he's doing, talk to his people, find wherever he's weak, locate a special angle to work from. Eddins is here in Saltville, and we can pick him up as soon as we can uncover their operation, get evidence against him, so let's go on out to Ketchum's and see what we can find."

Mason posted his letter to Cummings, warning the man to be on the lookout for anyone Cabot might hire to eliminate him. He genuinely liked the man and admired his Yankee tenacity in establishing a flourishing business so far from his markets. Then the two prepared to ride west.

Twenty

Reginald Cabot was having mixed feelings toward the young builder Stephen Davis. Now that he knew or suspected the man's role in destroying the late Dr. Weston's operation in Virginia, he wanted to even that score: kill him. But he was so useful here, that didn't make sense. He knew Eddins was set on eliminating Davis and supposed eventually that would be their course. Davis could find out more in time and become dangerous to them, though that seemed unlikely here on the frontier.

And there was the fact that he was so well thought of among the settlers, the missionaries. One didn't just remove a popular figure and hope to get the deed past his supporters. Eddins was undoubtedly working on some scheme, and he'd just let the lawyer worry about that for the time being. He'd warned the man not to interfere...things were going too well here and Davis was vital in the work. *So, just let it ride for now.*

That work, with the exception of the roadway, *was* moving ahead rapidly. The road was inching along, costing a great deal as the men assaulted the mountains with their puny picks, shovels, mule-operated scoops. They'd connected with the main route to Saltville, via the new bridge, but that old road was full of loops, steep grades, and unstable rockslides. Every trip to the town had necessitated working the wagons over fresh mud or places the soil had eroded to bare uneven stone. The engineer Thaddeus Stillwell assured Cabot that the road could be built, but again warned of the high price.

So it was decided the close grading that would allow the eventual use of the rails would indeed have to be abandoned for the present. Cabot directed Stillwell and his crews to repair the Saltville road as best they could for wagon traffic, leaving the grander scheme till later, as advised.

But the smelting operation was producing a growing supply of pig iron, and the foundry operation was handling the next stage as fast as the drawdown on the forebay allowed. At this summer season, both creeks were low, and the overnight filling only provided for a four-hour run before closing the sluice gates to refill. Then a short run before dark added its production.

It was barely enough to be efficient, and Cabot looked forward to fall rains when the creeks would rise and they could run the machinery continually. He aimed to have a good supply of iron on hand as soon as the road could carry it.

And now it was time to decide what to do about marketing the iron. Saltville was the logical depot for further distribution, and Samuel Eddins oversaw construction of a warehouse there, a simple barnlike structure for storage. He was also to engage men with wagons to haul iron stock to the various villages, smithies and large farms in the region. They would be paid a percentage of their sales, to encourage them to try harder. Eddins would head the office located in the warehouse, keeping track of inventory and sales.

It should work out well, except for one major obstacle: Lester Cummings' having already supplied the region. And that definitely meant removing him as competition.

Hiram Garst had become a sort of assistant to Cabot, seeing that his orders were carried out around the operation, while the owner concentrated on shipping and the aforementioned details of marketing. Now Cabot gave him orders to eliminate Cummings.

"The community there is high on the man," he warned, "as you might have seen when you were there. You'll have to make it look like an accident, because I'm the only man who'll profit by his death. Can't just shoot him. So plan it carefully, see what he does that's dangerous, then make it happen."

Garst was grateful to escape the humdrum errand-running around the ironworks, and rode out of the village armed with a new rifle, his pistols and knife. He also had a sizeable advance, so wouldn't have to camp this time, once past Saltville. He looked forward eagerly to staying at the best inns and taverns, to return perhaps before fall.

He encountered two men riding in the direction of Ketchum's Mill, who hailed him. One of them was an evil-looking specimen, and Garst felt he should know him from somewhere. But he was obviously an anonymous frontiersman in buckskins, no doubt illiterate, abstractedly chewing tobacco and saying nothing. The other man, who was older, also resembled someone he should know, but again, that was close to impossible, here at the end of the world.

"We hear there's an ironworks on up the road," the older man said. "Now, we've the need for a good supply for our venture in milling. Can you tell us anything about the place?" Altogether a pleasant-seeming man, in contrast to the other, who seemed perhaps not quite right in the head, that vague expression on his ugly face.

"Well sir, my employer does have a good stock on hand, yes. He's just beginning to set up marketing, so you're in good time. More so if you can arrange your own transportation. This road, as you can see, needs help before there can be much heavy traffic."

"Indeed. And what might your employer's name be? By the way, I'm Archibald Carson, and this is my associate, Martin Bone."

"And I am Hiram Garst, sir, working as representative for Reginald Cabot, a most far-sighted entrepreneur. He's worked wonders at Ketchum's Mill, which wasn't much until he arrived. Regular beehive now. I'm sure he'll be able to supply you well." Garst was keeping an eye on this Bone, whose eyes wandered off, adding to the vacant look of him. Some of the tobacco juice had dribbled onto his scraggly beard. He wondered just what job this specimen held with the affable miller.

They parted, Garst checking over his shoulder as he rode on. Something wasn't right about that pair, but he couldn't put his finger on it. Well, Cabot would deal with them. And this could be a good sign, consumers seeking him out this way.

"That's your failed assassin, Mr. Mason, I'm certain of it," Chiles told him excitedly, as soon as Garst was out of sight. "I didn't get that good a look at him that time, but I'm convinced he's the man."

"Really? Well, he didn't seem to recognize either of us. Pleasant enough, but that's been the odd thing about those fellows, now I think about it. Makes them harder to spot. Well, should we shoot him, trail him, or arrest him? I doubt we'd have much of a legal case for any of that."

"It's him, I'd swear it. But you're right...no evidence." Chiles had to suppress the anger inside him: the picture of the man's shooting O'Malley. "So then, what's he doing here? More dirty work for Cabot? And where's he heading, do you suppose?"

"Saltville, certainly. Yes, let's trail him back there, see if he contacts Eddins, then maybe we can find out more..."

"I know where he's headed," Chiles interrupted, snapping his fingers. "If Cabot has that iron on hand, he'll not be able to sell it with Cummings already supplying everyone. I'd wager he's sent Garst to kill off his competition, just as you feared."

The two turned their horses and followed the assassin. Again, they had only their suspicions, but these would surely be reinforced if there were indeed a meeting with Eddins, and if the man then headed up toward the Shenandoah Valley. They did not intend to let him get far.

~ * ~

Stephen Davis was relieved to see Garst ride out of the village. The man had a hardness about him that belied his unfailing courtesy. He'd seen that too often: the cold eyes above the smiling mouth. And when Cabot had taken him on, with no apparent need for him, that fueled the suspicion that had grown inside him. He and Anna had reached the conclusion there was more to Cabot than was healthy, and this Garst's appearance added to that.

"All I can say about the man is, whatever work he did for Cabot in Philadelphia surely wasn't legal," he told his wife. "I've noticed the way his hand goes often to his gun, sort of a caress…he knows how to use it. And now he's off on some mysterious errand, and I fear it's to be a bloody one."

"But what could that be? You think he was—is—some kind of bodyguard for Cabot? Could he be in some sort of danger?"

"Maybe. Obviously Garst's ex-army, with that discipline he has. People even still see it in me, I'm told. Killing men seems to have that effect."

"But you're not a killer, man of mine. Protecting against snakes is different from seeking them out to destroy them." She gave him a kiss. "You're an honest builder, craftsman, rescuer of innocent maidens, among whom I am a grateful one."

"I just wish evil would let us alone. I've the feeling this whole Cabot thing is going to erupt somehow and hurt us all. If I could just figure out what's amiss in it all, I might be able to head it off."

"That's not really your responsibility, Stephen. Why can't we just live our lives and stay out of it? We have our hands full keeping this place up. Let others take over."

"I suppose you're right. But I do enjoy the challenges of this venture. I get to use my skills, we get paid, the settlement benefits. I guess I've sort of taken on a role I don't need. I'm not the center of things around here after all and have no desire to be."

"Well, you've taught the men to build, Carver is learning blacksmithing, Cabot's men seem to have the work well in hand. The road's being built. I'd say you've helped immensely in getting it all this far along, so why not back off a little, just enjoy this place and our life together?" She put her strong arms around him, hugged him tightly to her.

"You make a persuasive case, all right. I guess I've just developed an eye for trouble, with all that's happened, and I don't want to see more of it."

"Oh, about that—I'd forgotten this, but I heard a rumor from Belle Ketchum. Seems she overheard just a bit of Cabot's talking with Garst at the inn just before he left. He was supposedly offering the man the job of constable when he returns. Now, despite your suspicions, that would at least put the responsibility of peacekeeping on him. What do you think? If that's even true?"

"That would trouble me even more, to tell you the truth. Cabot, despite his generosity, seems to want to be a sort of king of the mountain here, and with Garst enforcing whatever law he might dictate, that's scary."

"He hasn't shown any ulterior motives, though."

"Not yet, no. But something's not right, and with Eddins and now Garst involved, it's moving toward a situation I just don't like."

"Belle also said the people here would want you to take the job as constable. But I wouldn't want you to do that, with our recent history of outlaws. Besides, we have enough to do."

"Me as a lawman? No, I wouldn't want that, either. It's one thing to join our neighbors in protecting ourselves, but put myself in the position of having to arbitrate every squabble, investigate every lost cow? No, thank you, ma'am. I will indeed immerse myself in this life we're building for ourselves here."

~ * ~

Samuel Eddins knew Cabot had ordered Jedediah Mason killed those months before. But he hadn't known Hiram Garst back in Philadelphia. So when the man stopped by the warehouse construction site with letters from his employer, he'd no idea who this was.

"Mr. Eddins, sir, I'm Hiram Garst. I've done work for Reginald Cabot back in the capital, and he's engaged me again here. I'm aware of your part in the operation, and just thought I'd stop by, deliver these letters, and meet another of the organization."

"Well, Mr. Garst, I wasn't aware of your existence, but welcome. You can see we're coming along nicely with our warehouse here, and my office as head of sales and shipping will be part of this. What exactly does Mr. Cabot have you doing for us?"

"You could say I'll be part of the...sales effort also, sir. Right now, I'm off to visit the ironworks on the Jackson River to learn how their network is run. I'm sure there are valuable lessons to be learned from so successful an operation."

Eddins found it extremely odd that Cabot hadn't mentioned this man. His suspicions were immediately aroused, and he wondered if this was part of a scheme to cut him out. Garst didn't look like a salesman: pleasantly spoken, yes, but with a hard-eyed look and a habit of fingering his pistol that would put off potential buyers.

Then it hit the lawyer: this must be another of Cabot's assassins, like the Dinkins couple back in Virginia and that fellow Ames, who'd been sent to avenge Davis' destruction of that operation. And yes, his orders were no doubt to eliminate Lester Cummings' competition for the iron market.

So the boss hasn't lost his taste for removing his rivals: good. And this Garst could take Davis too, after he returned. Altogether a shrewd move by Cabot, who obviously was still on top of the game.

"Well sir, I wish you luck in your quest. I suppose we'll be working together then, and I look forward to that. But I have a question for you: what do you think of Mr. Cabot's employee, Stephen Davis, if I may ask?"

"Oh, Davis seems quite the craftsman. Certainly knows his building and machinery. Why do you ask?"

Eddins decided to give up a little information here...this man could certainly be useful.

"Well sir, this very man destroyed a lucrative business arrangement we had operating in Virginia. Complicated, but the end result was that we lost a great deal of money and several of our staff. Frankly, I find it quite dangerous for Cabot to keep the man around."

"Really? He didn't say a word about that to me. Keeps a lot to himself, doesn't he? Well, that'll require some thinking about, won't it?" Garst could see another fee in his future.

"That's in confidence, you understand. I just don't want to see this Davis try to do the same thing to us again. He knows nothing of

Mr. Cabot's role in that other operation; it was run by an associate. Now deceased, of course."

"Interesting. Davis doesn't look that dangerous, though there is a certain...hardness about him, I suppose you'd say."

"He was a sharpshooter in the war, I understand. I actually prosecuted him in court on several criminal charges, but unfortunately, we lost to a sympathetic judge. Now I'm telling you this because I feel Mr. Cabot may need the perspective of some of us who...shall I say, see the picture more clearly."

"Oh, I'd say we can help look out for our employer's best interests, Mr. Eddins. Yes, I appreciate this information, and we'll certainly monitor developments. Thank you."

"Of course. And let me know if I can be of help, anytime."

Garst bowed, mounted and departed. Eddins' mind was working, speculating how this new turn of events would affect him. So Cabot had probably invented some legitimate role for the assassin, and he'd be handy to act whenever a complication like Davis arose to threaten their operation. He wasn't thrilled that Cabot hadn't let him in on this man's hiring, but then he'd always played his cards close to his chest.

Well, back to business. the plan for sales here had been to offer the iron at a lower price than that of the Jackson River product, even if it meant losing money. At first. So now, Eddins realized, with that threat soon to be eliminated, they could raise their prices to whatever level the traffic would bear, and yes, profit immensely.

Of course, someone else could take over Cummings' operation but it was, he'd heard, a one-man operation, and it'd take time for the pieces to be reassembled. And where the New Englander had made it all work, a less forceful man shouldn't be able to for years to come. Eddins' appreciation for his employer rose. If one were to ally himself to a criminal, it was wise to choose a successful one.

~ * ~

Mason and Chiles observed the meeting between Eddins and Garst from a distant hilltop through a spyglass. They'd expected it, and it really didn't change the equation, but neither did it weaken their conviction regarding Cabot's guilt.

So now they had a decision to make: should they follow Garst back all the way to Jackson River to find out what he was up to? Or just take matters into their own hands and shoot him from cover? Confront him? They talked it over.

"I'm that positive that he's the man who tried to kill you, sir. And that's good enough for me. I'm for ridding the world of the snake."

"Ah, but we've hewed to the letter of the law up till now, Chiles, and never crossed it." He'd obviously had misgivings, following the man. "Let's look at our other options here: the first, killing him, is all but out of the question. Wouldn't be difficult, but where would it lead us, anyway? The second, to capture him, try to get facts incriminating Cabot out of him, might be better. Only again, even that would leave us with little we could actually use in court.

"No, I'm afraid this man won't do us much good in our quest. Now, I hate to leave him to his devices, which are no doubt evil, but we've bigger fish to fry. I've no doubt Cabot would send him to kill Cummings, but we've warned him, and we can hope that canny man will take care of himself. I can see Garst actually riding right into a trap."

"Perhaps you're right, sir, but it galls me no end to let him go, after he's tried once to kill you, and cerainly on Cabot's orders." The bodyguard's hands worked, and he looked as if he would crush Garst's life out of him, if he could only reach him.

"And another thing: I suspect that Garst will return, unless Cummings' men kill him, and we may get another chance to even that score, along with nailing Cabot, if we're still here."

Mason was able to mollify his associate, and the two reluctantly rode west again, discussing their next move. Since Ketchum obviously had a mill going there, Mason knew he couldn't hope to get too technical regarding his supposed invention. But suppose the miller wanted to buy one of the devices, which of course didn't, and never would, exist?

"We'll have to spend some time there," the investigator said, "and I'm afraid our little story is a bit thin."

"Why don't we just say we've several inventions in the works, then," his companion suggested, "and we're not that far along with any of them. I'd think we could get away with that, for a while."

"We'll soon see, then. I don't know how long we can keep my identity a secret from Cabot, either. With Garst gone, it'll be easier, because I don't think the man's ever had a close look at me. But that's tricky, too. If he suspects, he almost certainly will try again."

"Unless we take the bull by the horns, as you've said often, and eliminate him first." Chiles was obviously in favor of direct action.

"Again, we've not enough evidence. But with law enforcement nonexistent out here, you're probably right; if and when we have our case, the only logical course is to administer justice ourselves. I don't like that much, but our hand may be forced." He thought that over for several minutes.

"And maybe that will be best, especially if we find we have to defend ourselves."

~ * ~

Reginald Cabot hadn't come this far without covering his bases. He knew the righteous Stephen Davis and the others here, especially the missionaries, would rise up against him at the slightest sign of any illegalities. Cummings' murder should never come back on him, unless some nosy person made the connection between Garst's leaving and the deed. The distance to that operation was great enough that even that news shouldn't reach this remote place for months.

And he'd eventually have to deal with Davis himself, but not soon, he was sure. The man was also too important to his designs just now, and as long as he presented no immediate threat to the operations, he could live. After Garst got back, the two of them could discuss how and when the craftsman would be eliminated; but again, that would depend on what danger he posed.

Although the thought of what Davis had done to the Virginia operation still rankled. Well, Cabot would just let some time go by before making a move in that direction. Right now, he had to concentrate on getting some iron to market and recouping some of the money he'd so freely spent here. He did reflect that some of that money was going to the very man who'd wrecked the Weston activities the year before, and that didn't sit too well, either.

But to business. Road crews had been dispatched to try to make the Saltville route usable, the men camping on the way for a week at a time. Cabot had shipped his first iron to the Saltville warehouse for sale already and hoped to send much more before fall. He also planned to have a sizeable supply at stores in the various villages along the closest main roads in Virgina before winter. That should bring in some cash over the cold months and allow the works to produce a surplus, ready for next spring shipment.

He expected Cummings' distributors to be out of their product within weeks. That should give Eddins, selling at his reduced rate at first, a chance to have the market in hand even before the Jackson River iron ran out. Then when that happened, their own prices would go up greatly, and the money would roll in.

Cabot conferred with Archie Nolan about what he'd learned about how much ore was available. Disappointingly, the man had intimated that his original estimates might not have proven to be accurate, now the operation was up and running.

"Well sir, it's like any raw material. This we're mining close is the easiest to get to, but it'll run out eventually, and we'll see a decrease, maybe as early as next spring. We'll have to do what everyone does then: go farther for more, at increased costs. I'd say, if you can increase efficiency in the operation here, that should balance out the higher cost of mining and hauling to the smelter and foundry.

"Or, for the long term, I'd suggest that Stephen Davis and I scout out another location for a second smelter, and eventually another foundry, wherever there's power to be had. Right now I don't know of such a site, but there'll be one somewhere. Iron ore doesn't just occur in isolated deposits. And moving the finished iron is, of course, cheaper than moving the bulky ore."

"You're saying we'll have to extend by spring? I'd hoped there was more here than that."

"Oh, there is, but the cost of going deeper for it will be more than a newer operation very soon. They used to pick it up off the ground at Saugus and Fort Pitt, but that was decades ago. Same thing will happen here. I know you and I discussed this at the beginning."

"Well, yes, we did. And I knew all along this whole thing would be a gamble, just like any business venture. I guess I just hoped for a better, closer supply to get us up and going."

"We've had that, sir. And overall, it looks like you're all set now, actually. If your salespeople will do their jobs, you'll be strong competition for that fellow Cummings up on Jackson River."

There it was again: the New Englander. But he wouldn't be competition for long. In fact, Garst had probably had enough time to take care of him by now, if the opportunity had presented itself. He could expect that word in as soon as the end of the current month, and that buoyed his spirits.

And that about Davis: yes, he'd need the man's expertise in locating and developing water power for another branch when the time came. *Well, nobody ever said this business would be easy. Have to make sure that man doesn't become suspicious of anything, that's all.* He'd extracted every ounce of power out of this location, and had given the foundry mill the maximum running time each day. With the fall rains due in just a few days now, that would improve.

Yes, couldn't do without Davis, yet. If he just hadn't meddled in other people's affairs back in Virginia, he could let the man live out his life. As it was, Anna Davis was destined to become a widow.

Cabot had been drawn to the craftsman's tall wife from the start. Educated, capable, attractive. And not burdened with children. He'd been without a woman for too long already, and he began to speculate on a future situation. If Davis *were* to die accidentally, he could offer the young woman a comfortable life. She was as well thought of as her husband in this settlement, and yes, she could just become the perfect wife for him.

When the time came.

After all, he mused, *Shakeskpeare's Richard Third managed to kill off an enemy and seduce his bride in very short order. Of course, that was fiction, but that could be a worthwhile challenge.*

The others at the foundry wondered what their employer was smiling about.

Twenty-one

Lester Cummings had received Mason's note by post just days before Hiram Garst reappeared at the ironworks. He'd liked the investigator and took his warning seriously, though at first he didn't think the information, and even the connection with this associate of Cabot's, posed a threat.

The assassin had taken a room at the tavern, and was apparently just looking around again, as he had earlier. Cummings was in his office above the foundry late one day when he got the report of his presence from one of his men, who remembered Garst from before. *All right, then, I'll have to look into this in view of what Mason's written me. Now, just what do I know?*

First of all, there was the confirmed connection with the dreamer Cabot. Who, if he *were* actually to succeed in producing a trace of iron, would have to market it. And he, Cummings, already had the region covered. The man wouldn't be serious competition, with his high production and shipping costs, so he was no real threat. But this Garst, now. Gone after Cabot, and supposedly found him...

Ahh, that would be it, then...either he's sent this man to spy out our sales and distribution operation, or...

He didn't like the next thought that occurred to him. *What if Cabot does actually intend to eliminate me as* his *competition?* No, he didn't like that thought at all. So much so that he reached into his desk drawer for the pistol he sometimes carried on his rounds of the plant. He hadn't fired it in weeks, and reflected that he should draw the charge, reload and re-prime at once, then keep it with him at all times.

He was going about that chore when the office door opened and Hiram Garst entered, his own cocked pistol trained on Cumming's heart. He'd waited till the last of the man's employees had left, then simply climbed the steps to the office and walked in.

"I'd suggest that you put that gun away, Mr. Cummings," Garst said pleasantly.

"The devil you would. And *I'm* suggesting that you leave this instant, whoever you really are. If you plan to rob me, you won't get far before my men will have you and hang you." The words belied the realization that this man was actually an assassin, sent by that same Cabot, who no doubt did his evil business this way.

"Oh, they've all gone, as I'm sure you know. Now, I want you to precede me out this door. You have quite the view of your entire operation from up here, I see."

"And if I don't?" Cummings eyed his pistol, still with its old charge. *It might just still fire.*

"Then I'll kill you in cold blood, be on my horse in moments, and outride any men who figure out what's happened. *Up!*" He waved the gun.

Cummings thought fleetingly of all he'd built up here over the years, the huge part of his life he'd devoted to developing this industry, the livelihoods of many men—families—that depended on him. This outlaw was *not* going to take that from him.

"Then I appear to have no choice," he agreed, rising, leaning, reaching for his hat. As he'd hoped, Garst's eyes followed his hand, making sure he wasn't reaching for another weapon.

And he snatched his pistol, cocked it in a millisecond, and pulled the trigger.

The gun misfired.

"Pity," Hiram Garst said. "Now, as I said, you'll go ahead of me out to that platform at the head of the stairs."

Cummings knew he was a dead man. His chances of grappling with the assassin at his age were almost nonexistent, but he wasn't ready to give up yet. As he passed him, head bowed in defeat, he lunged sideways, grabbing for Garst's gun hand.

Only the hand wasn't there. The pistol crashed down on his head, and pain exploded in his skull as he stumbled. He was dimly aware of the man's dragging him out the door toward the light wooden railing of the platform, fifty feet above the rocky slope below.

Cummings couldn't get his arms to work as Garst kicked at the rail, splintering it. Then he felt hands on him again, and was suddenly in space, unable even to cry out.

Hiram Garst turned, re-entered the office and took a sack of gold coins from a desk drawer. Then he walked quickly out, down the many steps to his horse. Before leaving, he poured oil on several darkening buildings and struck flames to them. Then he mounted and rode away into the late summer night.

Reginald Cabot's Troublesome Creek ironworks should be safe from competition for the near future.

~ * ~

Jedediah Mason and Leighton Chiles neared Ketchum's Mill looking nothing like two Philadelphia natives. With what appeared to be his perpetual scowl, Mason reflected that his associate looked at first glance more like an outlaw. Well, that couldn't be helped... as soon as folks knew him, they'd realize he was a polite member of society.

What concerned him most was that Cabot might recognize him, or both of them. The man had obviously had his spies in Philadelphia, and unlikely as it was that the investigator would turn up here on the frontier, he might make the connection.

"Then there'll have to be a confrontation," was all he could tell Chiles. "I don't want to have to shoot our way out of here unless there's no other way."

"Tell you what, sir. Why don't you hang back a day, let me go in first, and we'll stay apart to begin with. That will lessen the chances he'll recall us as a pair. He might have somebody here from Philadelphia, too, who might've seen us together."

"Good idea. You look more like a man who's a product of this kind of country—no offense—and you can scout things out with less likelihood that he'll suspect."

"Done. I'll camp, instead of staying at the inn we heard about, and we can meet later."

That being the plan, Mason followed a side stream up into a hidden hollow where he could spend the rest of that day and night more or less comfortably. He could get a proper bath and a good bed the next day.

Alone, he reflected that they'd gone to entirely too much trouble to hunt Cabot down. If the man had just dropped out of circulation, he supposed perhaps he should have just let him go, get on with business.

But then he remembered the circle of supposedly honest tradesmen in the capital who were almost certainly in some sort of robbery ring, probably still being run by Cabot, even from this far away. There were just too many unsolved mercantile thefts to ignore, and if he could manage to eliminate the leader, he could close down the operation.

It's what I do.

Meanwhile, Leighton Chiles rode on into the village, noting the busy smithy, the lazily turning mill wheel, school activity at the church beyond. The inn was new and spacious, somewhat of a surprise this far from civilization. Probably Cabot's influence...he'd want a nicely appointed place to stay.

He dismounted at the smithy, where a teenage apprentice was forging chain.

"Hello. The smith around?"

"He is. There at th' mill. Mr. Ketchum runs both this'n that, an' his wife runs th' inn. G'on inside, store's in thar, too." The boy hadn't stopped working the bellows, bringing the iron loop to heat for the welding. Chiles watched him hammer the link together, sparks flying. Then he entered the mill, to find the owner adjusting the millstones.

"Mr. Ketchum? I'm Martin Bone. I was told there was an iron operation hereabouts. Could you direct me to it, sir?" Chiles' rough appearance was, he hoped, offset by his politeness.

"Why yes, Mr. Bone. It's downcreek a mile or so. You looking for work?"

"I am that, sir. I don't know much about the process, but I'm hoping there'll be a place for me."

"Well, Mr. Cabot—that's the feller owns it—he's got all sorts at work down thar. Buildin' goin' on, smeltin', foundry work. Oh, an' 'bout t'finish a new road outta here, round behind thet hill yonder. Big job, that. You hungry? Wife'll still have somethin' left f'm dinner, over to th' inn."

"Yes, thank you. I'll stop over there, then. And I'm obliged, sir. By the way, your apprentice seems quite dedicated." Indicating Carver MacNaughton, industriously hammering a new link of chain.

"Good lad. Goes to th' school in th' mornin's, then comes t'help me here. Well, good luck at th' diggin's, then."

Chiles entered the inn, which was pleasantly clean and tidy. Belle Ketchum greeted him, asked what he'd have.

"I spoke with your husband at the mill, ma'am. He said you'd have a bit of dinner left. Anything you have would suffice."

"Well, sir, I've stew, yes, and biscuits aplenty. Supper'll be some later'n usual, since th' men, they got to come up from th' ironworks yonder. You travelin' far?"

"I am, yes. Heard of the operation here along my way, and came looking for a position. I've been sort of...well, trying to find my place, I guess you'd say, since the war."

"Oh, a lotta men thataway, I reckon. Why, one of our leadin' men here, he was s'posed t've had them 'war nerves' they say, couldn't settle down. But he come here, he'ped near ever'body build their cabins, th' church, this inn. *An'* he headed up gittin' rid of some outlaws got in here. Why, one of 'em even took th' preacher's daughter, till Stephen follered him, shot him dead."

"Sounds like quite a man. What's his name?"

"Stephen Davis. Was a sharpshooter in th' army, they say. Don't talk much 'bout hisself, though. Married a sweet young woman here, one of th' missionaries, an' I 'spect they'll start a fam'ly 'fore long. Oh, an' he's in charge of jist about all th' buildin' down at th' ironworks. So whatever got to him in thet war, he's shore got over it."

"I see. I'd like to meet this fellow. Is he working for Mr. Cabot, who I understand owns the ironworks?"

"Is. Mr. Cabot, he come in here, had this inn built, give money to th' church, got this place up an' goin'. Wa'n't fer him, Killy an' me, we'd be 'bout th' only ones doin' much. You c'n see it's sorta at th' end of things, I reckon." She bustled off to the kitchen.

So, we have ourselves a team here, do we? Cabot and this Davis? I'd like to know more, and this Mrs. Ketchum is an information goldmine, if even part of it's true.

"Well, thank you, ma'am," Chiles retrieved his hat, paid for his meal. "You seem pretty high on this Mr. Cabot, and I suppose the entire village is also?"

"Wal, not ever'body, t'put it plain. There's some thinks he ain't all he seems, but I ain't namin' no names. Why, even m'man Killy, an' yes, Stephen Davis, has their doubts 'bout him, truth be knowed. But we're all workin' with him, best we kin. Give a man th' benefit of th' doubt, I always say." She added the coins to her cash box, reflecting.

"But if y'want t'know more, I'd say g'on down to th' ironworks, talk to Stephen. He'll likely have you a job of work, an' y'll git th' truth outta that'n, shore."

"I shall. And I look forward to seeing you and Mr. Ketchum again." Chiles took his leave.

He noted that the church was well-built, as was the inn. He supposed, if Cabot's money held out, that this outpost might become a prosperous village. The stories about Davis intrigued him, especially the part about ridding the community of outlaws. That didn't fit with his work with Cabot, however, perhaps the king of outlaws according to Mason's information of several years. And there was that about having his doubts about Cabot.

Intriguing.

The ironworks was a buzz of activity, with the smelter going, the foundry pounding out shaped iron, and new buildings going up in several places. He sought out the man in charge of construction. Davis was consulting with a huge workman about a complicated multiple mortise, and the man was nodding. As the builder turned away, Chiles hailed him.

"Mr. Davis? I'm Martin Bone, late of Philadelphia. I was told you were in charge of construction here. Could I have a few minutes of your time, sir?"

"Certainly, Mr. Bone. What can I do for you?"

"Well, I've come looking for employment, but I'm no craftsman, so perhaps I'm in the wrong part of the operation. But the smith and innkeeper spoke so highly of you and your work here, I felt I should meet you first."

"I'm not in charge of anything but the building, although I do work with the machinery, too. Are you by chance a mechanic?"

"I'm afraid not. Since the war, I've done a bit of law enforcement, and also aiding a businessman in the capital. He's due here soon and may have dealings with Mr. Cabot. I was hoping there might be some place for me, however, whether I continue with Mr. Carson or not."

"Then you'd want to meet with Mr. Cabot himself. He has several operations going on here and might have a place for you. There's a sort of aide to him who's off somewhere just now also, who handles employment." Stephen eyed this man closely. His instincts told him this was perhaps a marksman like himself, or one who'd had command of some sort in the military. Well-spoken, he seemed more than an ordinary individual seeking a job.

"Where did you serve, sir, if I may ask?"

"Oh, around New York, mostly. My unit did not go with General Washington to Yorktown. We were assigned to cover their move and keep an eye on the British there. Saratoga, before that, and yes, Valley Forge, till I was wounded. And you? I heard you served also."

"In the south mostly, but Valley Forge at the end of that winter. Then later Yorktown, of course. Under generals Morgan and Greene, mostly. What was your rank, sir?"

"I attained the level of lieutenant through field promotions. You?"

"I, also. Well sir, we should spend time comparing notes, as they say, if we get the opportunity. Now, you'll find Mr. Cabot somewhere along that new road over there. He's concentrating on improving the track toward Saltville, as you probably saw coming in, but is intent on a future plan to grade the entire route."

"A daunting task, from the looks of the land."

Stephen couldn't explain why, but he found himself liking this homely man. Perhaps it was the war service, or the mention of law enforcement. He didn't like the prospect of being called upon again to go out after outlaws like the MacNaughtons. Maybe the community could support this man in that capacity? He'd like to know more about him.

For Chiles' part, he'd decided on first impression that this man wasn't one of Cabot's thugs...far from it. Just what his relationship was, it might not be more than as an employee. He'd disclosed that about law enforcement deliberately, hoping for a negative reaction, which hadn't come.

Chiles was a bit nervous about confronting Cabot face to face. While he'd seen the man often, he'd have to rely on his disguise, and hope he wasn't recognized. He'd take a different tack with him, since it'd be easy for the man to dismiss him without a hearing, since he apparently wasn't qualified for work here. He found him at a stone culvert under construction, conferring with an engineer. He waited for an opening. It came.

"Mr. Cabot, sir, I'm Martin Bone. I'm here ahead of my employer, Mr. Archibald Carson, to enquire about a source for iron for his enterprises." He watched for any sign of recognition. None appeared.

"Well, Mr. Bone, that's good news," offering his hand. "And what might your employer require?"

"He's developed some innovative machinery for use in milling, sir. His plan is to begin marketing it away from the population centers and perfect it completely before taking on the industrial complexes."

"Hmm. Shrewd. When do you expect Mr. Carson?"

"Soon. We were obliged to part at Saltville, but my curiosity prompted me to come ahead. You've quite the operation here, I see." *Touch the man's vanity; maybe he'll let something slip.*

"Why, yes, I'm quite proud of it. I've gathered fine craftsmen, mechanics, engineers here, despite the area's remoteness. Like your Mr. Carson, I see the advantage of smoothing the operation before invading, shall we say, the more lucrative markets." The man's smile was smug, as if sharing a clever move no one else would have thought of.

"My concern, and I know Mr. Carson will agree, is transport. I see you're improving the road to Saltville, but the distance still seems daunting."

"Well, that's a question your employer and I shall discuss. If perhaps he has the means of transport, we could arrive at a very satisfactory pricing, you see. If not, perhaps there's another way." A man approached them with a surveying instrument.

"I see you're quite busy, sir, so I'll take my leave. Thanks for your time. I'm quite certain Mr. Carson will be able to work with you." He bowed and left. *Well, the notorious Cabot didn't recognize me, and let's hope he also doesn't identify Mr. Mason.* He resolved to walk about the ironworks further, since the people who mattered knew he supposedly had a legitimate interest, and learn what he could.

Of particular concern was learning more about Stephen Davis and his opinion of Cabot. Not even the smoothest deceiver could hoodwink a perceptive man forever, and perhaps Davis actually knew something that could help him and Mason. He approached the giant who'd been working with him before.

"I see you're adept at woodworking, sir. Did Mr. Davis teach you?"

"He did that. I heered your name, Mr. Bone. I'm George Wellerby, as helped Stephen build his house, I did, an' though I'm still larnin', he's taught me heaps." The big man extended a paw that reminded Chiles of that of a bear.

"Well, I don't want to interfere with your work now, but I've heard a lot about Mr. Davis, and it's all been good. I hope I can somehow work with him, if I could find a way to fit in here. Perhaps I can get him aside after work for a visit."

"He's that busy, sir, what with this buildin' an' all. An's got his own place up from th' village to tend."

At that moment Stephen himself joined them.

"Ah, Mr. Bone. How did your interview with Mr. Cabot go? Well, I hope."

"We didn't get to talk much, I'm afraid. I think I'll wait till my associate Mr. Carson arrives, and let him present him with his ideas and needs. I was hoping, sir, that you and I might have a bit of time to talk further. You seem to be the man who knows what everything's about around here."

"Hardly. I'm hired help, like all of us here. But yes, let's find time, shall we? If for no other reason than to relive old campaigns."

"I'll be about the inn later then, if you're not in too much of hurry to get home. I hear your place is new, and must require a lot of work."

"Not as much now. Oh, if you will then, stop by the school and tell my wife Anna we plan to be a little late, would you? She'd appreciate that."

"Glad to. I also hear much about her. Seems you two are at the center of the activity here." He bowed to Stephen and George and took his leave. Stephen watched him go.

"George, I've a feeling about that man. What'd you think of him?"

"Oh, just a feller lookin' fer work, I'd say. Well spoke, he is, an' a sharp eye on him. But now you ask, he ain't got thet shifty look 'bout him th' feller Garst has. Don't like Garst none."

"Neither do I, you know. Well, I'll see what he's about, perhaps. Good job on that joining, George, that was complicated." He slapped the big man on the back, eliciting a beaming response.

"Warn't nuthin' to it, after you 'splained it to me."

Chiles was impressed with the tall young woman at the school, which she was, at the moment he rode up, dismissing for the day. He introduced himself, telling her of his and Stephen's plans. He noted that her somewhat preoccupied countenance had softened into a radiant smile as she sent the last child homeward.

"Well, Mr. Bone, I've grown accustomed to the schedule my husband must keep. I won't pretend to understand all the ins and outs of the operation he's become a part of, but he does enjoy the work."

"A remarkable man, I've both heard and observed. He and I talked briefly about our war experiences."

"Ah, yes. I've observed a comradeship among veterans that is quite binding." She looked more closely at this man, so frankly homely, but with a certain polish about him. "Shall we walk to the inn? I've no need to hurry home and can catch up on events from Mrs. Ketchum."

"Thank you for the privilege, ma'am. Yes, a fountain of information, that lady, I've already learned. It would seem she and her husband, and you and yours, have been key to the growth of this outpost."

"Our intention, the other missionaries and I, was to bring the Word of God to the wilderness. We never expected things to come alive so quickly. But it's been gratifying, the response we've had."

"Indeed. And I suppose the generosity of Mr. Cabot, whom I just met, has fueled that growth." He watched for a response at mention of the man's name. It produced a hesitancy on her part.

"Oh, yes. Although his...methods, I suppose you'd say, have been somewhat swift and...unusual." She didn't want to cast Cabot in a negative light to this stranger. Still...

"Oh? I'm hearing nothing but praise for the man. My employer, who will join me soon, has hopes of doing considerable business with him."

"I'm certain that can be profitable, Mr. Bone. I've no head for business, however. But I've a curious nature. Tell me, if you will, what your own impressions of our benefactor are."

Ah, this lady knows something, or suspects it. Not your average retiring housewife, this. I can pursue this just a little.

"Let's just say I shall advise Mr. Carson, my employer, to be... on his guard, shall we say? Nothing definite, but since you ask, I detect a certain...flamboyance, perhaps, in his manner. Rather like he enjoys being the center of things, which can't be all bad. But frankly, I've observed that men in trade with that attitude seldom succeed, and Mr. Cabot seems to have done so quite well. It does make one wonder. But I exceed the bounds of good manners, I fear. I've nothing to base such feelings on. I apologize."

"Don't, sir. You must know, both my husband and I have detected the same trait in the man, though I admit it's an entirely subjective appraisal. Perhaps *I* should apologize." They had reached the inn.

"No, not at all. You see, when one can have advance knowledge, even of minor details about one's prospective business associates, that knowledge is invaluable. I shall, of course, respect your candor ma'am, and I thank you for it. I look forward to spending as much time with your husband as he can spare, also." He bowed, handed her up the steps to the inn. "Perhaps we shall meet again."

"Yes, certainly. Thank you, Mr. Bone."

After he'd ridden away, Anna reflected on their conversation. The man had admitted a lot, for a stranger, and to a woman. Not your average insensitive businessman. She had the feeling he was probing for information, which he'd admitted, but there was something else. If he were to become part of Cabot's strangely profitable ventures, she and Stephen should beware.

But the man didn't raise any alarms in her, as Cabot had. And certainly not as that slippery Hiram Garst had, even at first acquaintance. No, a far different man, this. She'd be quite interested to hear what Stephen had to say about him.

For his part, Chiles was satisfied enough at his foray into the workings of this place. Nothing concrete, but he could report to Mason that their cover seemed secure, and they could go ahead with their plans. So instead of spending further time there, he rode back to their place of parting.

He found his employer later that afternoon, seated comfortably before a campfire deep in the forest, and reported his findings.

"Cabot's spread his money around and bought himself a position at the center of things, sir, but he has apparently aroused at least some questions among some of the more insightful among the villagers." He told of the woman innkeeper's reservations, and those of Anna Davis, and by implication, that her husband too, had his… well, suspicions.

"Well then. We must find a way to talk with these people. If you're to meet with this Davis, you'd best be on your way again. I'll ride into the village tomorrow morning…you can meet me at the inn and tell me on the way to the ironworks what you've found out, then we'll go see Cabot. We'll take that bull by the horns, all right, but not before we've armed ourselves with whatever those others can tell us. Be better prepared."

After Chiles had left, Mason considered carefully this head-on meeting with the man he'd hunted for so long. If he were recognized and Cabot made a move against him, Chiles would have to kill him outright. That would ensure a wholesale fight, before he could expose the criminal's past. If not, he'd go ahead with the story about needing the iron, ingratiate himself there, and build his case against the man.

Whatever that could be. From what they'd learned, Cabot had bought his way into this remote place without bloodshed and without creating enemies, or so it appeared. It was just possible he'd changed his rapacious ways, but Mason doubted it very much. There *was* the mysterious errand by the man Garst to consider, and Chiles was surely right: he'd gone to kill Cummings, eliminate Cabot's competition completely, create a monopoly.

He recalled that Chiles had suggested simply shooting Cabot from cover and escaping. That didn't appeal to Mason's sense of honor, but it had its merits. Be better to do what they had to do lawfully, of course. But perhaps, if all else failed, they'd talk more about that. *Proof, though. I need proof.*

Twenty-two

"Not to put too blunt a point on it, Mr. Bone," Stephen Davis told him, "but I get the impression you're here for more than employment. You said you have an associate coming." The two had met and were watching Killebrew Ketchum's pitsaw work its way through a log.

"In fact, I do. I'll admit to using the need of employment as an opener, to use a term."

"I've had a short conversation with my wife, who also wonders at your purpose. Now don't get us wrong...we're not accusing you of anything. On the contrary, you may well be able to clear up some things that have been nagging at some of us here. Ah, here comes Mr. Ketchum. Why don't we join Anna and Belle inside, and discuss this further?"

"As you wish, sir. And no offense taken. And I would have to say you are an insightful man." Chiles smiled, which had the effect of erasing his severe expression. They went inside the dimly-lighted mill for some privacy from the group at the inn. Anna was waiting for them, as was Belle Ketchum.

"We don't want you to think we're putting you in front of an interrogation squad, Mr. Bone," Stephen began, "but you might say we four have been sort of the core of things here since before Mr. Cabot stormed in. We'd like to know more about him, as you seemed to, and thought we might pool what we know."

"Stormed in…I like that. Sounds just like the man's tactics, from what I know of him."

"Which is?" Stephen was insistent.

Chiles looked from one face to another. He saw no evidence of ill will here but was loath to disclose too much. He wanted Mason present, but that would have to wait.

"Let me be frank. I did use the story of seeking a job as cover for my—our— purpose in finding out more about Cabot. My employer, Mr. Archibald Carson, sent me on ahead to see what the situation was here. I've already reported what little I found to him, at our camp back up off the Saltville road. He'll be here tomorrow morning, and he can answer much better than I, our concerns. Not to be evasive, but I shouldn't speak for Mr. Carson, who has been my employer since the war.

"I had hoped to pick up more from you, Mr. Davis, in conversation, and I sense there are some…doubts about your benefactor here among all of you. I will go this far…we are not allied in any way with Mr. Cabot. And with that I must beg of you your forbearance until Mr. Carson can better explain. I hope that is acceptable."

"You tantalize us, sir. But I believe we can respect your wishes. I will enlighten you a bit about our initial concerns, however. I discern that you are a man who is adept at using that pistol when necessary. It's in your manner, which I've been told is a trait I share.

"Now, Mr. Cabot has employed, with no particular duties, a man of similar mein, albeit of a certain…shall we say *darker* aspect? You display no such demeanor, sir, but you can appreciate our concern: are we presented with another of Cabot's mysterious associates? Evidently not, but you understand, surely." Stephen spread his hands. "Oh, and I will add also that his sales director in Saltville is a lawyer I've had negative dealings with back in Virginia. It seemed to be adding up."

"I *said* you were an insightful man, Mr. Davis. And I would still value comparing notes as it were, with you, regarding not only our wartime experiences, but our activities since. I think we have much in common, and I mean that as positive."

Anna had taken this in thoughtfully. Like Stephen, she'd liked this man somehow, even on first impression. But what could his connection with Cabot be? Law enforcement, he'd told Stephen. That could mean a lot. Well, perhaps this Archibald Carson could shed light on the matter.

"I can't speak for the Ketchums, Mr. Bone," she told him, "but I must say I'm very glad to have met you. Please feel welcome, as far as Stephen and I are concerned."

"Thank you, Mrs. Davis. Having learned what you all have accomplished here, that is indeed heartening." He rose, preparing to depart.

"An' that goes fer us, too," Killy Ketchum assured him, grasping the newcomer's hand. "We've had a sight of folks come in here recent, an' we ain't judgin', but y'seem th' sort we c'n tie to."

"Thank you, too, sir." He bowed to the group, stepped out into the night and mounted his horse. "We'll stop in tomorrow, but go on soon to talk with Mr. Cabot at the ironworks. Goodnight." The sound of his horse's hooves faded.

"Well, do we have ourselves a mystery here?" Stephen asked the others.

"Seems so, don't it," Belle Ketchum replied. "That's 'bout th' homliest man I ever seen, but he comes acrost kinda...honest, I guess y'd say, don't he, Killy?"

"I reckon. Wal, it's gittin' late. Shut th' mill down, an' we'll jist see whut's whut in th' mornin'. Y'all want to light a torch, Stephen?"

"No, the horses know the trail. Goodnight, then." He handed Anna up onto her mount, joined her on his, and the two rode off into the fall night, lighted by glittering stars above the mountains.

~ * ~

Hiram Garst was pleased with himself. Not only had he carried out Cabot's orders to the letter, destroying part of the ironworks and eliminating Cummings, but he had the pouch of coins to spend as he saw fit. Which he would proceed to do, on his leisurely way back toward Troublesome Creek.

There were always pleasures to be had for a man with money, and he soon discovered them. Fearing pursuit, he'd ridden on past a camp that had sprung up downriver from the Cummings complex, complete with makeshift tavern and camp-following women. But when he reached the settlement at Lexington, he resolved to stay over for several days there and enjoy himself.

He put up his horse, took the inn's best room, ordered its best meal, and partook liberally of its whiskey, before and after dinner. Then he asked the innkeeper if he could find some female company for him. The man seemed at first somewhat put off by the request, but upon receipt of several coins, directed Garst to a tavern a short distance beyond the village, on the Maury River.

There, the assassin sampled that establishment's whiskey, and arranged for a woman. The next three days passed in a blur of drink, debauchery, and diminishing money. At the end of that time, on a cool fall morning, he found himself outside the tavern on the ground, penniless, cold, and very hung over. He managed to stagger back into the village, collect his horse, and ride unsteadily south.

Normally, Hiram Garst planned further ahead than this. Last time, he'd finished the trip by resorting to robbing travelers. This time, discovering that he no longer had either rifle or pistol, even that prospect seemed dim.

"Must've had a good time, but I don't remember much of it," he mumbled to his horse. "And now I'm dirty, hungry, a long way from any sort of home, and I'm out of ideas what to do about it." The horse flicked his ears, plodding on down the Valley pike.

For perhaps the hundredth time, the man rued the way his life had gone. But his aversion to productive labor reasserted itself as his head cleared, and despite the ache in it, he began to consider his options. Such as they appeared to be.

So, he couldn't rob anyone. Maybe steal food from some root cellar, if he could slip up on one that was unlocked. He really should clean up a bit, and that he soon accomplished at the next secluded stream crossing, though the water was icy. The sun eventually dried his clothes enough to put them back on, and though still shivering, he felt a fraction better for it.

All right, he'd try to steal something he could sell, get a little cash. He knew he'd have to get his hands on a firearm of some sort soon, or his attempts to feed himself could well get him killed. He could let the horse graze along the road or in any fallow field he passed, so that'd have to do for him.

He resolved to hunt for a farm off the main road, one with the promise of something saleable, and if possible, food. He'd hide till dark, letting his horse graze out of sight, then make his way toward whatever reward he could manage. Dogs would be present, of course, but he could perhaps get them to go after some strange sound he could make before circling them to the buildings. Dogs had a way of barking at perceived danger, then sustaining their noise well beyond any reason.

It was admittedly an audacious plan, and one that could easily backfire. But the growling of his empty stomach goaded him on, and he scouted two places before deciding on a third one. At this farm, two old people seemed to be loading produce onto a wagon, no doubt to head to market, although this was late in the day for anyone to make such a trip. Perhaps they'd stay over; he had no idea what day this was.

He saw live chickens going into crates, potatoes and carrots in baskets. From this distance, he couldn't make out more, but this should be his opportunity. And perhaps if he could get the horses to bolt, he might pick up some spilled produce along the rough road. He mounted, waited in heavy timber just off the lane that led to the pike.

The wagon approached, driven by an elderly man, with what must have been his wife beside him. *Wait, now… if nobody's home, I'll just go there instead.* Reasoning that he could always catch the wagon if he ran into resistance at the house, he held back, letting it pass beyond sight and hearing. Then he rode boldly up to the farmhouse, dismounted and called out.

"Hello! Anybody home?" As expected, dogs had come out barking, but they soon quieted, nosing around him. No sound came from the house.

Garst went directly to the kitchen garden, where some vegetables had been dug, and proceeded to pull carrots, dig potatoes with a mattock the people had left on the porch. He filled his saddlebags, then went to a smokehouse to see what he could find. It was locked, but the crude lock and chain didn't look substantial. He smashed it with the mattock, opened the door, saw a single ham, and took it with him.

Next, he searched in sheds and the barn for anything he could use for a weapon. Nothing seemed suitable. He considered forcing the door to the house, but was reluctant to do that. *Could be someone in there, maybe another old person, perhaps with a loaded gun.*

But he couldn't travel with just his bare hands, and so he overcame his concerns and smashed the wooden latch to the back door with the mattock. There was no sound from anywhere, so he proceeded to search. He took a butcher knife, a small metal cooking pot and a blanket, but could find no firearm. He supposed the old people had taken their shotgun or whatever they might've had, with them. And nothing else here caught his eye, so he left, propped the door shut, and mounted his horse.

Back on the turnpike, Garst put several miles between him and the farm, then turned off into woods to camp along a small stream. Striking a fire, he scrubbed the vegetables, cut ham into pieces, propped the pot over the fire. This was going to have to be his mode of survival, he supposed, and it could be a lot worse.

~ * ~

"Well," Jedediah Mason observed next morning as he and Chiles met with Stephen, Anna and the Ketchums at the mill, "first of all, I'm pleased to meet all of you. And I realize now my intended plan to pose as a mill specialist in need of iron from our Mr. Cabot's operation just won't wash, from what I've learned about you. You gentlemen," addressing Stephen and Killy Ketchum, "would see through that in an instant. So I think it's best I lay all my cards on the table, as it were, and although I do not know what your reaction will be, I shall do that."

"Please do," Stephen told him. It was early, and Anna's students had not yet arrived at the church for school. Men were departing the inn for the ironworks, but the mill interior was quiet and private.

"Let me say outright then, that we are here under disguise, however effective that might prove, and our names are not Bone and Carson. I am Jedediah Mason, and this is Leighton Chiles. We are from Philadelphia, where we have what is a rather new profession, that of investigating commercial and industrial thefts. We work closely with the police to apprehend thieves, to put it bluntly.

"Now this is the delicate part, because we know what Mr. Cabot has done here for this community. But at the risk of getting ourselves tarred and feathered or worse, I can tell you that Cabot is suspected of having created a ring of operatives who regularly steal from a wide area, along with some supposedly prominent citizens who in reality are part of the same organization. These men divide the spoils, invest, and fund seemingly legitimate businesses although they are in reality common thieves, themselves."

At this, Stephen reacted visibly. The information had a familiar aspect to it. Mason registered his expression but continued.

"As I said, with your not knowing any of this, we're prepared to hear protests from you, but I assure you, after years of work, we are certain Cabot is the leader of this operation." Mason sat back, his hands spread. Chiles watched the group warily for their reaction to what both men knew would be this startling revelation.

Instead, Stephen Davis and his wife exchanged a long, knowing look that combined a bit of wonder with something akin to relief. The Ketchums registered only surprise. Stephen turned back to Mason.

"We appreciate your candor, Mr. Mason. And now I must tell you of events back in Virginia last year that may relate to your work, and to Mr. Cabot." And he told the investigator of the group headed by the late Dr. Weston, and that it had received gold from somewhere at regular intervals, and that the similarities seemed more than coincidence.

Mason listened attentively, facts fitting together in his mind. He'd known of Weston, the short-tempered Jacob Hayes, and had suspected further involvement somewhere out of his territory.

"What exactly happened to Dr. Weston, sir, and the rest of that group?"

"They met with unfortunate ends, Mr. Mason. They thought I had one of their shipments of gold and came after me. With help from friends, we were able to defend ourselves against them, and as far as we knew, all of them died."

"I see. Is the name Jacob Hayes familiar to you?"

"Hayes? Certainly. He came into my furniture shop waving a gun, threatened me and my partner, and died in the attempt. He'd been carrying a shipment of the gold, which we later found and turned over to the court in Charlottesville."

"All right, then." Mason was growing excited. "And Samuel Eddins, was he involved?"

"Eddins was the prosecutor who tried to convict me of the killing of Hayes, unsuccessfully. And you may or may not know, he's now in Saltville, allied with Cabot."

"I do know that. He was one of the suspected ring in the capital, as was Hayes. It seems, Mr. Davis, that we are discovering details of the very same operation, with Reginald Cabot at its head."

"Thet's hard t'believe, sir," Killebrew Ketchum interposed. "He is sorta sudden, some ways, but whut yer sayin' is he's jist a common crook?"

"A very crafty one, yes. And very good at giving the impression he has everyone's welfare at heart."

"Well, don't thet beat all," Belle said. "Seems y'cain't trust nobody these days."

"No ma'am, you can't," Mason replied. "But there's something else you probably don't know, Mr. Davis. An assassin was sent from Philadelphia to your part of Virginia some time ago to avenge the ring against whoever had wiped out that operation. That would have been you."

"Really? Oh yes, my friend Ned Drake mentioned a bit of that in a letter. Must have been after I left, in late summer."

"It was. A man named Justin Ames, employed by, I'm quite certain, our Mr. Cabot. But the man ran into a planter in Caroline County, and was killed."

Stephen exchanged a look of realization with Anna, who nodded.

"That would certainly be Ned, who helped destroy that bunch. So Cabot, or whoever was—is—at the center of things there, has killers to enforce his operation. Oh, one of the ring in Virginia apparently had the same duties, fellow named Dinkins."

"Yes, we've heard of him, too. But there's more. Shortly after Cabot left Philadelphia, someone tried to kill me, but mistook an employee of mine for me, and only wounded our man. Mr. Chiles suspects that this man is also in Cabot's circle here. We met him on the Saltville road, and established that he and Eddins have some relationship."

"Hiram Garst. Yes, he left here some days ago, on some errand for Cabot."

"And Mr. Chiles and I have guessed what that errand may well be. We met with a Mr. Lester Cummings on Jackson River, who runs the ironworks there. We suspect Garst has been sent to kill Cummings and remove Cabot's competition."

"That's a serious conclusion, but Garst is—how shall I put it—a somewhat sinister individual. I remarked on that to Mr. Chiles last night."

The morning had advanced with those revelations. Anna excused herself to the school, having contributed nothing verbally, but absorbing all the details. She felt a foreboding, the real sense that their life here wasn't as secluded, safe, as she'd hoped. But perhaps whatever evil was afoot could be forestalled. She'd just have to trust that this would be so.

Killebrew Ketchum also left the conference to start the grain mill, harvest having begun to come in. Belle, although fascinated by all this, hurried to her duties, after being warned to keep any and all those disclosures to herself. Stephen and the other two men continued comparing notes, experiences, getting a clearer picture of the Cabot operation.

"Unfortunately, we have no solid proof that Cabot is at the center of all this, but we do know that he and his ring of associates in Philadelphia have amassed very large fortunes from relatively unproductive business operations. All our evidence points to Cabot, but we're at a loss as to how to bring him down. Our plan was to come here, which incidentally seemed prudent also, with someone out hunting me in the capital, to try to find out more, and eventually get proof."

"You've certainly come a long way, sir."

"Well, one thing sort of led to another. We learned of his interest in iron, and the known ore deposits led us to Jackson River, where Cummings was able to tell us of Cabot's intended general destination. And I'll admit to what is practically an obsession with tripping this man up...he's been too successful in his chicanery, and it has its dark side."

"Indeed, if he's the one who tried to kill you, and who sent someone after me. Well, I'm overdue at the ironworks, Mr. Mason. May I ask what is your next move?"

"You may. As I said, I'd intended to pose as an inventor of mill equipment for handling the grain more efficiently, an enterprise that required a source of iron. That would get us next to Cabot, where we'd hoped to learn more. Also, we could see if our new personae succeeded. I don't know if Cabot knows me by sight, but suspect he does. He did not, apparently, recognize Mr. Chiles yesterday, who was, so to speak, scouting for me.

"So we need an excuse to be here. Leighton is quite valuable as my protector, but just so we two aren't recognized together, we'll keep a certain distance. He seldom left my side in Philadelphia."

"Yes. Well, I don't see why you can't go ahead with your plan. Killy and I can back up your idea for the mill equipment, whatever that is. You've learned of my milling background, I'm sure."

"I have, and that and the rest are most impressive. What you've accomplished here is amazing, Mr. Davis. You and your wife have certainly contributed greatly in building up this village, as Leighton observed."

"Thanks. Now, why don't we go to the works together? I can say we've talked about your inventions and recommend you to Cabot. What, incidentally, are they?"

"In my general ignorance of the workings, I'd just imagined a continuous leather belt with cups attached, to elevate the grain, dump it somehow at the top, where it would slide down chutes to the millstones. Sounds too simple, though. Except that, drawing it out yesterday, I couldn't figure out how to dump it without getting it all over everything. Does the basic idea sound reasonable, or would it to Cabot?"

"Hmm. Intriguing concept, but yes, it'd take some refining. Why not tell Cabot as little as possible, keeping the details to yourself? After all, you don't want just anyone stealing your ideas."

It was decided that Chiles would hang back, near enough to be of service if the need arose, but not close to Mason. If trouble broke out, he'd protect his employer, even from a distance. He had his rifle with him.

Mason still felt some trepidation at approaching his quarry directly, but took heart at Chiles' staying within range, if ostensibly still just observing activities at the works. And he was with Stephen, who he realized was as good an ally as he could have found. Stephen always carried a loaded pistol on him.

"This is Archibald Carson, Mr. Reginald Cabot," Stephen introduced them. "He and I have been discussing his concept for improved milling techniques, which I find quite insightful. He'll need a steady supply of iron, so it would seem the two of you have a common interest." He watched for a sign of recognition from Cabot, which did not come.

Mason too, scrutinized the man's face, but detected no hint that he'd been discovered. After all, Cabot surely thought him dead.

"Yes indeed, Stephen, and I thank you for your spending time with Mr. Carson, and your discernment. Mr. Davis is quite knowledgeable regarding milling, as I'm sure you've perceived, Mr. Carson. I value his judgement."

"So, apparently, do others, sir. Well, I see you've quite the operation here. I'd expected a deal less, this far from population centers."

"My approach, exactly. Here I can provide employment for the settlers, perfect my operation without the pressures of direct competition and higher production costs, then move into the market at my own pace."

"But the transportation costs. Surely they'll undercut your profits."

"Not with my eventual plan, sir. For a while, yes, we'll have to ship by wagon over that wretched Saltville road. But as I can, I'll perfect the ideal mode of transport, and be able to provide iron cheaply to the entire region. But speaking of that, do you perhaps have access to your own transport? That would allow a most attractive pricing for you."

"It's possible. I've been in touch with drayage operations in the region, and with the general lack of employment opportunities hereabouts, several of these men are open to an arrangement."

"Ah, you've done your advance work, I see. I shall enjoy doing business with you, Mr. Carson. Now, as you can see, I've much to do here. Why don't we meet tonight at the inn to discuss your needs further? I'm certain we can begin arrangements."

"Thank you, sir. Might I look over the operation here? I've picked up a bit so far, but I'm quite impressed with what you've accomplished."

"Certainly. Stephen, could you spare time from construction to show Mr. Carson around? And perhaps learn more of his requirements? It'd save us all time."

"I will, yes sir. Come along, Mr. Carson. And I believe I see Mr. Bone yonder. We'll tour the plant together." Stephen led the investigator away.

"Well, I don't believe the old fox recognized me, Stephen, or if he did, he's an accomplished actor."

"I'd say your identity is safe, sir. But I'm at a loss to see how you'll uncover anything against him you can use."

"All in good time. If I can manage to stay on here without actually having to consummate a deal with Cabot, anything I learn could be useful."

For his part, Reginald Cabot had harbored a tiny suspicion of the man Carson. A customer this far from his market just dropping out of the sky was unlikely. And while he'd come in Stephen Davis' company, a knowledgeable miller, that didn't preclude some sort of trouble. *After all, Davis and our Virginia operation...*

He'd see if Carson turned out to be a genuine sales prospect. There was something not quite right about the man, and Cabot had built his fortune partly on judging men. Yes, he'd tread carefully around this one and yes, that ugly Bone fellow, too.

Leighton Chiles, aka Martin Bone, had been watching this meeting carefully, standing beside his horse with his hand on his sheathed rifle. He'd been prepared to drop Reginald Cabot with a well-placed shot if the man had made an overt move against his employer. Now he relaxed, and joined Stephen and Mason for their tour of the operation. His whole assessment of Cabot had led him to believe in the necessity of shooting the man outright, further evidence or no. But forced to go along with his boss' careful methods, he'd reined himself in. At least they seemed to have allies in this end-of-the-world place their quarry had hidden himself in. But how the community at large would react to their benefactor's demise was another question.

He felt he and Stephen Davis could, between them, find a way to do what was necessary, but he sensed rightly that the marksman wouldn't agree to an outright killing. The man had his place here, which he'd forfeit with that kind of action. *The problem is, these people don't realize they've got a snake in their midst. Hope they don't find it out too late.*

~ * ~

Anna let her mind wander while the children practiced their handwriting. This whole series of events foretold an eventual crisis. There was Cabot, now clearly exposed to the inner circle of them, as the villain. There was his no-doubt assassin Garst out there somewhere. There was the lawyer Eddins, clearly an opponent. There was the murky but sinister-seeming purpose Cabot had for all of this philanthropy and development. It must surely come together in violence, one way or another.

She felt that Mason and Chiles could be relied upon and was glad for their presence. A slick operator like Cabot would be hard for Stephen to handle alone unless he simply shot the man, as he'd been forced to do his attackers back in Virginia. But her man would not act without proof or an imminent threat.

It all had the effect of unsettling her, of casting a cloud over their lives. Why did trouble always seem to find Stephen? Was that his destiny to be the righter of wrongs among the victims of the world? She thought of young Alice McKnight, now with head bent industriously over her slate, and of her ordeal. And of course, the rescue at the women's cabin the year before. *Thank You, God, for Stephen, but please protect him.*

She remembered so clearly the warmth of his lean body next to hers in their bed at home, the comfort of having the man she loved with her every day. Their little intimacies, the affectionate touches as they passed, the quiet words of their shared love. Stephen was her world here in this wilderness, and would be anywhere. But their private circle of light and warmth could easily be shattered, with evil men working their will around them. And as Stephen had done in the past, now they must both work to keep that threat from their door.

Twenty-three

On his ride back down the Shenandoah Valley, Hiram Garst had time to do a lot of thinking. And one thing that had been nagging at his mind was that chance encounter with the two men on the road to Saltville. There was something familiar about the ugly one, something that should trigger alarm, but he couldn't put his finger on it. And the other man, too, it seemed, he should know from somewhere. Perhaps it was only that the two of them together resembled two others from his past.

He'd put this out of his mind repeatedly, concentrating on survival, but it kept coming back. The vacant stare of the obviously weak-minded one made him doubt whether he'd seen the man before. There were many retarded individuals managing somehow to stay alive, usually by attaching themselves to successful people who needed simple chores done.

Had to've been in Philadelphia...that's where I've been since the war. But these men were both from the country. Miller and his helper. Got those all over...

But it just wouldn't fall into place in his mind. He continued south, stopping to let his horse graze along the way, stretching his meager supply of food. He resolved to lay the question of the men's identity before Reginald Cabot when he reached Ketchum's Mill. Surely the man would recognize someone from his past.

Garst began replaying the events that had led to his being so far from home. Eventually he reached the memory of that job Cabot had ordered just before he'd left, that Mason assassination. He'd done it right, following the man and his bodyguard on that lonely road...

That's it! The bodyguard. Ugly man I'd seen with Mason. His adrenaline surged with the realization.

But all the way down to Kentucky? Surely not. Maybe just somebody who looked like the man. And Mason wouldn't have hired a simpleton to guard him. But Mason himself, now. He'd had a brief look at the man on several occasions in the capital, and he also looked a little like the man on the Saltville road.

Impossible though, since he'd killed Mason. No, it just didn't add up right: a miller and a retarded backwoodsman at the end of the world and a now-dead investigator with a fearsome bodyguard in Philadelphia? Just too unlikely.

But Hiram Garst had lived by his wits too long to dismiss this possibility completely, however far-fetched. He'd just broach this to Cabot, yes. The man needed all the information he could get, even conjecture, to stay on top of his game. So did he, Garst, for that matter. *Never let your enemies get the edge on you.*

But that'd be weeks away, and he had to find more to live on in the meantime. If he could just steal a gun of some sort, he could rob someone. Or break into another farmhouse. But he'd been lucky that one time, with the people gone, and it likely wouldn't happen again.

He thought of just stopping at a tavern, ordering a meal, then leaving without paying for it, but that would bring on a fight, surely, and he didn't want that. He could handle a lone tavernkeeper, but not if the man had help.

He could look for work since this was harvest time. Get fed that way, at least for a few days, maybe. The thought didn't appeal to him, but it might be the only way. And once accepted onto a place, he could surely steal at least food, and less likely, a gun.

He eventually caught up to a mule-drawn wagon at the side of the road loaded, with walnut logs, with its off rear wheel leaning against a tree. The wagon driver was winding grass stems around the spindle, a last-resort attempt at a bit of lubrication when a wheel bearing had gone dry. It wouldn't last long, though.

"Dry bearing, looks like," he remarked to the driver, who'd raised the wagon up with a wooden wagon jack. "Got far to go?"

"Too far, I'm 'fraid. Hopin' somebody'd come along with some grease, but ain't nobody."

"Well, I've the last of a ham rind, little fat still on it. Let's rub the spindle with that."

"Why, thankee, sir. Yeah, that'll do nice. Kinda ruin it fer soup, though."

"Doesn't matter, if it'll get you on your way. I've been in need of help many a time myself."

"Wal, thet hired man I got, he greased up th' wheels, and plumb fergot this'n. Man cain't count, I reckon. Thar, thet should do it. You travelin' fur?"

"All the way to Kentucky, yes. Had a bit of bad luck at Lexington, though. Got robbed of everything I had, but they didn't find my horse. Hadn't of been for some work I did for a fellow, I wouldn't have had that ham."

"Don't say? Robbers bad, man by hisself. I gen'rally have th' hired hand with me, but couldn't spare him outta the fields. Tryin' hard t'git finished with th' harvest, but th feller at th' sawmill's been pushin' me t'git these here logs to him. Reckon you'd help fer a couple days?"

"Be glad to. Not afraid of hard work, never have been. You taking these to a mill close by?"

"Yeah, old man Manes, off th' pike a mile, he's got 'n old pitsaw goin', wanted some walnut fer a feller makes furniture. Had these loaded, an' now I need m'wagon bad back at th' place. I c'd put you up, few days, pay you a little, feed you."

"I'm your man, then. We should be able to reach the mill on

that ham fat, and the miller will have grease. I'd say we ought to check all the bearings before we go back."

"Fer shore. Man I got works hard, but he ain't right bright. Shoulda done this m'self, but I wuz thet busy, y'know? Wal, jist you foller us on then, an' we'll git these off an' back home. Got taters t'dig, hay t'git in, an' 'bout a hunderd other thaings waitin'."

So Garst had stumbled onto another potential bit of luck, it seemed. And he guessed a few days of labor wouldn't kill him. Certainly too, there'd be the chance to steal something and sneak away.

At the mill, they rolled the logs off; the farmer dickered with the miller for a several minutes. Garst hoped the man would pay the farmer in cash, so he could then rob him, but that didn't happen... some sort of trade, he guessed. Then they were on their way back to the pike and back north a short distance. The track to the farm wound up between hills, following a small branch, then the land spread out into fields, with a cabin and outbuildings beyond. Smoke rose from a stone chimney on the house, cows grazed a rail-fenced pasture, and a bent man was at work with a scythe among tall grass outside the fence.

"Y'enny good with a scythe?" the farmer asked.

"Not the best. But I can dig potatoes, let you do the mowing."

"Good 'nuff. We'll load 'em right into th' wagon then, an' I'll he'p git y'started. Turn y'hoss in with th' cows. Oh, y'et t'day?"

"A little. I'll be all right till sundown." He rode his horse to a gate, dismounted, removed the saddle and bridle and turned him loose inside. The farmer returned with a worn mattock and shovel, and the two began to unearth the potatoes.

Garst's hands weren't hardened to such work, and he knew he'd have blisters soon, but no help for it. And he was hungry...the thought of a good meal soon made him determined to do this work, whatever the cost in pain.

And pain it was, with his back beginning to ache within an hour from the constant stooping, scraping away the soil, freeing the potatoes from the earth. He was on his own now, with the farmer scything alongside the hired hand in the distance. Doing work he hated. But looking at the pile growing in the wagon box, he took a certain perverse pride in even this humble accomplishment. *Man's gotta do what he's gotta do, I guess. And t'won't be for long.*

He planned ahead, to the time he'd no doubt join these people at the house for supper. He could see what he might get his hands on then, and go from there. Ideally, he could take what he needed and be gone tonight, but he doubted, as a new employee, that the farmer would leave anything out that he might lose. No, probably have to stay at it for a few days. Maybe do something else tomorrow, not so hard on his back.

It took forever, but the sun finally touched the season-turning leaves of trees to the west, and the farmer came over. The wagon was heaped with potatoes, and the man nodded approvingly.

"Y'done good. By th' way, whut's yer name? Mine's Chester Abbott." He offered a hard hand. Garst winced at the grip on his own blistered one.

"Hiram Garst. I've business with the new iron foundry west of Saltville when I can get there. This is a fine place you have here, Mr. Abbott," straightening his back, surveying the hillsides in the golden sunlight.

"It'll do. Hard time clearin' it, on back, but it's turned out good. C'mon, now. This's Rufus Stevens, m'hired hand."

Stevens had a permanent stoop, and the mark of age about him. Easily sixty, but Garst had seen him swing the scythe hours on end steadily. It was this kind of necessary labor that allowed a farmer to survive, and the whole scheme had no appeal for him at all.

At the cabin, a pack of hounds sniffed the newcomer. Abbott's wife Samantha filled a washbowl with hot water, gave them lye soap and a worn towel. She was round and red-faced, and smiled often.

"This here's th' new hand I tole y'about, S'manthy. He done good on th' taters, but he'll need some a thet salve y'got fer his hands. Been a while since y'done diggin', I reckon?"

"Has. But your crop is as fine as I've seen. That field should keep you all winter, for sure."

"Oh, yeah. Taters does good, here. Cain't keep th' deer outta th' corn, though. I've took t'tyin' a couple of th' dawgs out in th' field, an thet works all right. Rufus here, he's a good shot too, so they eat m'corn, we eat them." He chuckled at his joke.

"Sounds fair. Miz Abbot, whatever you're working on smells better than anything I remember. I can tell you're a fine cook."

The woman blushed a deeper red, smiled widely.

"Wal, since th' chillun's all gone off, ain't but th' two of us an' Rufus, so not much call fer fancies. Hope y'like biscuits an' stew."

"My favorite. Never learned to cook for myself, though I've been on my own all my life. And I'll take a home-cooked meal over tavern fare any day."

They sat while the farmer muttered a short grace, then ate hungrily. Garst let his eyes travel around the lean-to kitchen, but it was just that: a kitchen, with nothing he needed out in sight. There'd be the main room, and a sleeping loft here, with probably the hired man out in the barn or in one of the sheds nearby. He'd surely be expected to share space with him, which would make any theft harder.

Samantha Abbott applied a liberal coating of a pungent salve to Garst's blistered hands, which at least had the effect of giving him hope for them. He knew tomorrow's work would be painful, but there'd be no help for it. *Have to stick this out, keep my eye out for my chance.*

He was indeed to bed down in the barn loft, in a partitioned-off space that was at least tight against the rising autumn wind outside.

"Rain comin'," the monosyllabic Rufus observed. "Won't be no way t'git out in th' fields. Reckon we'll patch an' fix, then." He rolled away on his straw pallet and was soon snoring.

Garst reflected that with rain, he might be spared the hardest labor. And yes, see more of this place and what it might hold for him. He was certain he could find a way to get out of sight for a few minutes, even in daylight, to get away with enough to see him far down the road.

He lay awake thinking, listening to the other man's snoring, aware of the sour smell of his sweat. *Let's see: Abbott said Rufus was a good shot. So where's his rifle? Could it be here, somewhere? Or would the farmer keep it in the house?* If he could just find a gun, he could be off, to rob another traveler.

No, he'd have to stay longer, watch for his chance. Maybe, working inside tomorrow, he'd see what he needed. He drifted off to sleep, adding the sound of his own raspy breathing to that of the hired man.

~ * ~

The news of Lester Cummings' death reached Ketchum's Mill well ahead of Garst's return. One of his iron salesmen in Lexington relayed the fact, along with that of the destruction of several of the buildings at the ironworks. From there, a fast stage carried the word to Saltville, where young Abe Holloway, the odd-jobs millworker there for supplies, heard it. He'd been urged by Reginald Cabot to return as quickly as possible with any mail, so rode on ahead of the men driving the wagons.

So it was that Stephen Davis, Killebrew Ketchum, Jedediah Mason, Leighton Chiles and Archie Nolan, who had happened to be at the inn that evening, all got the news together. Cabot was still at the ironworks. The men heard what Holloway had to say, which was bare-bones, since he'd heard no details. Mason waited until the young man had left to report to Cabot, then turned to Stephen.

"This is no accident," he declared. "It's Cabot's usual method of eliminating competition, and there's no doubt in my mind that Garst's the assassin. I sent a warning, but apparently it wasn't enough."

"How long would you estimate it'll take to rebuild, and find someone else to take over there?" Stephen asked.

"Years. Cummings had done it all himself. And even if someone else got investors to take over, rebuild, get the works going again, Cabot will have moved in solidly. And he'll continue to sabotage any intrusion from Jackson River or anywhere else. We'll see hijacked wagons, disappearing loads of iron, even more killings. The man's ruthless."

"And he must be stopped," added Leighton Chiles. This would surely nudge these more cautious men to action, he hoped.

"But folks hereabouts is so dead set on him as th' provider," Ketchum pointed out, "thet y'cain't jist outright gun th' feller down. 'Sides, y'ain't got proof." He led the men over to the mill, seeing others returning from the ironworks.

"That's unfortunately true," Mason agreed. "But this news is one more nail in his coffin. We were on the point of leaving, having learned nothing solid, but Cummings' death fits too well with the overall picture. Now I want to stay, get more details, wait for Garst's return. Again, we've no proof against him either, but some spying is in order. He'll report to Cabot, and we need someone to hear what's said at that meeting. Please be thinking about all this, gentlemen, and let's come up with a plan."

Anna joined the group, and Stephen soon left with her, the two talking on the way upcreek.

"Mason says Lester Cummings was a decent, hard-working man, with the interests of his employees at heart," he told her. "If Cabot's had him killed, he must be dealt with. He won't stop there."

"No. I'm afraid this is turning out to be more of what you had to deal with in Virginia. Only now it's all undercover, with no outright threat yet, and again, no obvious villains."

"Well, we've a choice here: either you and I ignore these evil doings, as I'd about decided to do, or we help dig out the facts, the guilty, and deal with them before anyone else gets hurt."

"I'm certain Cabot has already found out from Eddins that it was you who destroyed that part of his operation in Virginia. So yes, we are the likeliest to get hurt next. He's used you, but now he's almost all set up, and you're expendable."

"I've had that on my mind, and have been watching my back, believe me. The man's so slick, it's hard to believe what kind he really is, what he's capable of. But yes, I'd say he'll make a move as soon as Garst's back. I don't see Cabot himself taking me on."

"Maybe, if he's that clever, that's exactly what he'll do...what you least expect. I'm worried, Stephen. There are snakes among us, and we should kill them before they strike."

~ * ~

As soon as Reginald Cabot heard the news of Cummings' death, he decided to put the next step in his plan in motion. He'd held off dealing with Stephen Davis because he'd needed the man's skills, but now the way was clear. His operation was up and running, the competition was eliminated, and he must protect himself against enemies. And he couldn't be certain this news of his competitor's death wouldn't spur Davis into action, so the man had to go.

Garst will be back soon surely, and we can devise a plan that won't implicate me. Davis must pay for what he did in Virginia...no one crosses Reginald Cabot even once, and here's the threat of his doing it again.

He also knew the man might well suspect that there was more to the lawyer Eddins' connection, here. As part of the former Weston operation, even though that hadn't been proven, the lawyer's being involved had surely put Davis on the alert.

He mustn't underestimate this man, although on the surface he was nothing more than an ex-soldier and frontiersman. He tried to imagine what Davis thought of him and his work here. Had he succeeded in winning him, and everyone, over? Couldn't take that for granted. No, the man might well just be doing his work, taking his money, biding his time until he learned something solid, then he'd act.

I'll have to act first. He might even suspect Garst; the man doesn't inspire confidence. So yes, I'll take him out now, not wait for him, just as soon as I put together the plan.

And the plan proved to be quite simple. Cabot arranged for Archie Nolan, the engineer Thad Stillwell, and Davis to accompany him on an exploration ride further into the mountains to see what the prospector had found. It should be easy to separate Davis from the others, then the two of them could conceivably be attacked by Indians or something, with Davis getting killed. Here in Kentucky, the red men had by no means been driven out, and this was still their hunting ground.

Or, failing to get Davis alone, Cabot could kill all three of them. Either way, he'd return, the survivor of the attack, help fortify the settlement against further violence. He'd be rid of a threat and have evened the score against the man. And he was sure he wouldn't have to lose the other two...he was resourceful after all, to have succeeded so often.

And he could also then pursue the desirable Anna Davis, who'd need consoling, sympathy, and security. It might take a while, but he was certain he could win the grieving lady.

Yes, it was definitely time for some latter-day Boston back-street justice, the kind he was good at.

Accordingly, on a fine October morning with the sky a deep blue and the maple leaves the color of blood and flame, the four men set off. Cabot knew he'd have to watch Davis closely, and not assume he was ignorant of danger. All of them were heavily armed, with rifles, pistols and knives. And Davis had that reputation, one he'd earned. Well, so had Cabot, although no one here was supposed to know that.

He'd also suspected the man Carson and his assistant, since he hadn't actually purchased any of his iron. In fact, his plans for milling equipment seemed mostly thin air. *An inventor, a dreamer, not to be taken seriously.* He'd surely move on soon.

Or if he proved to be a problem, why Garst could take care of that easily. These wilderness outposts were full of accidents, what with hunters out, that possibility of Indian raids, the sheer hardships of living out here.

So, focus on the immediate problem: removing Stephen Davis, the sharpshooter, the frontier dealer in justice, the fly in Cabot's ointment.

He'd never liked flies anyway.

~ * ~

Anna had confided her fears at hearing that Cabot wanted Stephen to go with him and the others. Once she'd accepted the fact that the man was indeed the enemy, she suspected his every move.

"Stephen, I've the feeling Cabot may be up to something, asking you to go along on this prospecting trip. Why does he need you? He's got Nolan, who knows the territory better than anyone. And he has Stillwell, to plan his access roads."

"Well, he'll need to know which streams can be used for power, and how to set up the extended construction. I'd say I'm the logical choice. And surely with the others along, he won't try anything. I don't know much about Stillwell, but Archie's certainly loyal to me."

"As he should be. But I've been thinking Cabot probably has more men here who're part of his schemes than just Eddins and Garst, who could stalk you. I suspect the worst, now that we know what kind of man he is."

"I'll watch my back, you can be certain. And we should be back in three days at most." He'd kissed his bride then, mounted with a reluctance to leave her, and ridden away.

He made it a rule to be the last in the group of riders, letting Nolan lead, alongside the eager Cabot, with Stillwell after them. He'd keep his eye out, and his hand close to his pistol.

~ * ~

Hiram Garst rued the way he'd so casually lost that pouch of gold he'd taken from the Jackson River ironworks. Now, laboring alongside the hired man Rufus, he was losing heart. The rain day, they'd worked inside the toolshed, sharpening axes, mattock, hoes. Abbott had a small forge there and they made bolts, wagon braces, horseshoes and nails. It was little easier work than the digging had been.

Now they were in the fields again, and Garst's raw hands hadn't hardened to the work yet. The blisters had responded somewhat to Samantha Abbott's salve, but were still painful.

Worse, he hadn't found a firearm of any kind he could steal. His only time in the farmhouse was for meals in the kitchen, and he caught no glimpse of rifle or shotgun. He supposed he'd have to make off with just what food he could lay his hands on, and hope for better luck further down the Valley pike.

Accordingly, he dug a hole just at the fence around the potato field while alone, and put several of them in it, covering them lightly. He'd seen inside the smokehouse, but Abbott kept it locked. Potatoes alone wouldn't do, however; he needed meat, at least.

That morning, Rufus had seen the ravages of deer in the not-yet-harvested corn, despite the nearby dogs. He vowed to shoot them, even if it meant staying out in the field all night. Abbott agreed, and at the end of the day gave his man an ancient shotgun, powder and shot.

"Moon t'night: y'd oughta be able t'git us one, y'stay downwind. I'd go too, but my eyes ain't whut they usta be."

Now, if I can just get that gun away from Rufus, I can be out of here tonight. Get some corn for the horse, too. Garst's mind was feverish with ideas for siezing the gun, but he knew he must act quickly and silently. He'd have one chance only.

He and Rufus went first to the barn to wait for full darkness. There, Garst weighed his options. He could knife the hired hand, clamping his hand over his mouth to keep his dying quiet. Or he could hit him over the head hard enough to kill him or knock him unconscious. Either way, he'd have time to saddle his horse, retrieve the potatoes and some corn, and ride away with the shotgun.

He looked about for a weapon. A pair of singletrees hung from a beam by their chain hooks. Of stout hickory, one of those would make a good club. He'd follow the man down the ladder on some pretext, grab the weapon and hit him hard.

Rufus carefully loaded the shotgun, pouring the coarse black powder down the barrel, pushing wadding in, then the buckshot, then more wadding. He primed the pan, then set the gun aside, glancing out the open shutter at the rapidly-darkening sky.

"Few minutes, I'll git on. Deer won't come early, 'count of th' dawgs, but they's had a taste now, an' they'll be back." He hung the powder horn and shot pouch from his belt.

"So we'll have venison by morning, will we?"

"Shore will. Y'hear me shoot, come on an' help drag it in. Reckon Chester'n them be asleep down t'th' house."

"I'll do that, then. Cool enough, we field-dress it here?"

"Yeah, an' skin it out, cut it up in th' mornin'. You enny good at butcherin'?"

"Done it some, but not that good. I'd say you'd have it done before I got good started."

"Wal, we'll see, then." He looked out again, grunted, picked up the shotgun, started for the steep steps down.

"I'll come too, get a torch ready," Garst told his retreating back. Rufus only grunted again.

Once on the dirt floor of the barn, with the hired man only a step ahead, Garst reached up, took one of the singletrees off its nail, gripped it in both hands, and swung it mightily down toward the man's head.

The free hook at the end of the singletree made a slight noise, and Rufus turned partially as the stout club landed, glancing as it hit. He uttered a grunt, trying to bring the gun around, but Garst hit him again, this time solidly, and the man slumped to the ground. Then, shotgun, powder and shot in hand, he went to the stable, led his horse out. Saddling him quickly, he mounted, seeing the hired man still unmoving on the ground.

He grabbed several ears of corn, put them in a coarse sack he'd brought from the barn, rode to the potato field fence and unearthed the potatoes.

The moon was just rising as he rode away from the farm. He'd put a lot of distance between himself and this place before stopping. He could camp in deep forest before dawn and travel at night for a few days to avoid pursuit. Abbott knew he was headed much farther south, something he shouldn't have told him.

Well, I'm much better off now, anyway. Stay hidden and I can be clear out of the country in three days.

He spared not a thought for the deer-ravaged corn, the farmer Abbott and his wife, or their hired man quite possibly dead on the dirt of the barn floor.

Twenty-four

The prospecting team had followed up a side creek that Archie Nolan was familiar with toward a dig he'd begun several months before. As they rode, the engineer Stillwell made notes of the approximate grade, the feasibility of cutting a road up the slope. Stephen saw him alternately shake his head at a rock outcropping, then almost smile at a near-level meadow before the next rise.

He knew, and perhaps everyone here did, that extending the operation further from the present site would greatly increase the costs, and Stephen also knew Cabot must have another reason for this trip. Even with exorbitant pricing of the iron, he couldn't expect to profit greatly from the Ketchum's Mill works. That left two possibilities: either the man was hopelessly naïve financially, or there was indeed a darker purpose at work.

It was about three miles to the test pits Nolan had dug, and they stopped there. They'd try to estimate the extent of this ore-bearing soil, then plan whether to go further, or perhaps even decide that this was as far as Cabot was willing to extend the operation.

Subsequently, they fanned out, each man taking samples of the soil to a depth beneath the organic overburden. They then gathered well before noon for Nolan to evaluate their finds. He rejected some, smiled over others, setting them out in a miniaturized array that told of their locations.

"Well, Archie, what's your conclusion?" Cabot asked him when he'd placed the last sample pouch of soil.

"Looks good as far as quality goes, and that's the best part. The worst is that this just isn't a big enough deposit to be worthwhile, sir. If it follows the site we're at now, we can expect only about six months' supply."

"Ah. I'd hoped for much more than that. You're including tunneling into the slope, of course."

"Yes, based on what we've found down on the main creek. Now Thad can tell us more about the cost of putting in a road, but I'm thinking it might not work." He shrugged. He hadn't been able to get this much sampling done on his own before, and the efforts of the four of them had greatly cleared the picture for him.

"Well then, I say we go a maximum of a mile farther, to that ridge you told me about, instead of making camp here, since there's little to keep us. You said there were two locations about that far, didn't you?"

"I did. And they're close together, so combined with this on the way it might be worth the effort. Yes, let's move on."

They repacked and rode on up onto the high ridge overlooking two deep draws far below that spread out along two small brooks. Nolan led the way atop a sheer drop down the ridge toward a lower gap that might accommodate a road.

"See here, Stephen," Cabot called back to him, "come up and give me an estimate of power here." He gestured down toward the two small streams. Stephen noted the other two men riding on ahead, but focused on the waterways, coming into view between trees below. They were spring-fed and perhaps, if their flow could be combined... He rode his horse closer to the edge, peering down for a better look.

He did not register that Cabot had eased his horse alongside him until he actually felt the heat of the other horse and man. He turned his head, the hair rising on the back of his neck, and his hand went for his pistol.

Just as Reginald Cabot slammed his boot into Stephen's horse's side, causing him to bolt. Crowding him in that same instant, Cabot shoved man and horse over the edge of the cliff toward its rocky bottom easily two hundred feet below.

Stephen was taken completely off-guard, and was thrown from the falling horse into nothing but air. Strangely, he had no sense of falling, but felt the impact of a stone ledge as he slammed partially into it. Instinctively, he grabbed for a twisted cedar bush, but missed it. Then he was dimly aware of being hit as if by sledgehammers from all sides, the pain surely of death.

Although he was quickly knocked unconscious and didn't know it, his body caught on a four-inch tree growing from a crack in the stone and ripped it out of its mooring. That slowed him considerably and he tumbled at last onto another, wider ledge below, followed instantly by a shower of small stones that all but covered him.

Cabot yelled for the other men, who turned and raced back along the ridge.

"It's Stephen! His horse bolted, and went over! Oh, my God, men, he's gone!" Cabot dismounted, crouched, peered over. Dust hung far down the cliff, and the uprooted tree still bounced and tumbled out of sight into denser growth at the bottom. As the air cleared, they could see the horse, or part of him, strung out over a series of narrow ledges, crumpled, dismembered and unmoving.

"He was checking out the streams down there," Cabot barely got the words out, pointing. "And then he was...just *gone!*" The shock was plain on his face.

The others looked too, then drew back.

"He's dead, no doubt of it," Thad Stillwell pronounced, shaking his head.

"Oh, God, what'll we tell Anna?" was all Archie Nolan could manage.

"That's right, his wife. Oh, that poor woman," Cabot lamented. "Oh, this is horrible. Forget the project, men, we need to go back…"

"And leave him?" Nolan was incredulous.

"No use from up here," the engineer observed. "But let's ride on down, see if he's all the way where we can reach what's left of him. God, what a fall."

So the three of them rode down to the gap, on among the trees and back under the rising cliff to where they thought they were beneath the spot.

"There's that tree," Stillwell pointed up. They dismounted, started to climb the talus slope. Soon they reached the remains of the horse, but just up from there was sheer stone face for many vertical yards.

There was no way up.

"He'll be in pieces up there," Cabot speculated. "And nothing but the birds can reach him. Oh, God, the buzzards…" He turned away in anguish, hiding his face and the crafty glint in his eyes.

"Nothing for it but to ride back, then," Stillwell agreed. "We could come back with a long rope, maybe let somebody down, but I'm afraid all we'd find is pieces."

Archie Nolan's mind was working. *This was no accident. Stephen would never be that careless.* He looked long at Cabot's back, but said nothing. Then he looked at the angle of the sun.

"All right, let's ride hard back to the village, let the folks know. Miss Anna will have to decide whether to try to get what's left of him or not. Might be kinder just to leave him."

They rode hurriedly in silence back along the base of the cliff, reached the flattening-out place that led up to the gap. Up and over it, then down the other stream, moving as fast as Archie's horse could navigate the stony way.

~ * ~

Stephen had fallen about eighty feet, tumbling partway, momentarily caught then released by the uprooted tree. He gradually regained consciousness, finding himself on his stomach, stones piled on top of him. His mouth was full of rocks and broken teeth, and the world was a red haze of pain. The worst seemed to be his back, but a hip throbbed, an arm burned, and his face bled.

He tried to move, but succeeded in shifting only his head, to see down over the ledge to sheer drop. He dislodged stones, and was aware that he had only a little room to move. Finally, he freed the arm that hurt the least, and carefully pushed stones off him. They free-fell, then clattered far below on the talus slope.

His vision cleared, but the pain was overwhelming. He began to shudder, feeling cold. Then all went black again.

When again he swam back up out of a vortex of pain, he had no idea how much time had passed. The sun was still well up, though; he could see through the sweat in his eyes. *Strange, being cold and sweating.*

Stephen had seen soldiers in shock before and guessed that was what was happening to him as the convulsions began again. *Yes, and Abby that time.* He willed his body still, but the blackness returned. His last thought this time was that he must not roll off that ledge.

Again he revived, to a blinding thirst. But his mind was clearing, and he replayed the last moments before his fall.

Cabot. Cabot had deliberately shoved him. Cabot, the arch-center of the crime ring Weston and the others had been only a part of. Cabot, the smooth-talking, evil manipulator, the criminal, thief.

Murderer.

The others couldn't have seen. He heard nothing, and even though he'd spat out the stones, he wouldn't call out. Cabot could shoot the three of them. Perhaps he'd already killed the others.

Why did I wait? Eddins, Garst, all that Mason told us. Why didn't I agree with Anna: strike first...?

But recriminations could also wait. He didn't know if he'd live or die now, but wagered on living. Just how he'd get off this ledge was another matter. If either of the others could get back to the village for help...but Cabot would foresee that, and surely would forestall any attempt to rescue him.

He peered over the edge again, saw his mangled horse far below. Speculated. Surely Archie Nolan would have insisted they go down and try to find a way to recover his body. But that sheer drop...no, they'd surely believe he was dead, in pieces down the face of the cliff. Maybe that would keep Cabot from killing them.

He felt the shuddering coming on again, and relaxed his body, letting the darkness envelop him like a black cloud.

~ * ~

Archie Nolan dropped back on the ride to Ketchum's Mill. He didn't trust Reginald Cabot now, and resolved to get away from him at the first chance.

"Let me ride over this way, men. I know a closer way to Stephen's place, and I can let Miss Anna know first. She'll be home by then. You just follow this branch on down, then up the main one. I'll see you in the village." Without waiting for a reply, he turned his horse up another rise, glancing back to be sure Cabot wasn't trying anything. In a moment he was lost among trees.

He pushed his horse hard up and over a hill, one he knew would lead to another small branch, then eventually up another to above the draw where Stephen had built his house. It was getting late, but he figured there might be time. Anna wouldn't want to wait till the next day, and the two of them could... What *could* they do? *Well, cross that bridge later*. Right now, he wanted to reach her before she could learn anything from the others.

So he rode down into the clearing just as she came up the trail from the creek on her horse. He hailed her, trotting hastily around the barn, the house.

"Miss Anna! I'm afraid there's been trouble. Bad trouble..." He didn't know how to continue.

"It's Stephen, isn't it?" she cried out. "What's happened, Archie?" She was off her horse, clutching him fiercely, almost pulling him from the saddle.

"It was...no, it wasn't an accident, Miss Anna. But Stephen...he's had a bad fall. Cliff. Horse bolted, Cabot said, but I...well, that can wait. We need a long rope if you've got one, a heavy one. The others have gone to the village the long way, and you and I need to ride hard back before dark, try to lower one of us down, see what...well, what we can find..."

She was suddenly calm, the wide eyes now hard glints. *No time for suspicions. No time for anything but action. Rope, yes...*

She led her horse quickly to the barn, Nolan following. She willed every thought away but the need to act. She found two long ropes, all they had that were thick and strong.

"Will this be enough?"

"Maybe. But let's take these chains, too. Now let's get a torch, in case we're too late. I mean..."

"This will do. And we might need whiskey. Let me get bandages, a knife." She ran to the house, was back in an instant. Mounting on the fly, she followed the hastening Nolan up the slope, noting the westering sun.

~ * ~

Sometime later, Cabot and Stillwell reached the ironworks, where they told the dispersing crews what had happened. Then they rode on up to the village in the waning sunlight. Cabot went first to Killebrew Ketchum at the mill and told his version of the "accident." Stillwell informed the minister and others at the inn of the tragedy.

"I think we should go first thing in the morning and try to recover the body," he declared. "Though there might not be much left. It was a long fall, and the horse was torn to pieces."

The universal reaction was one of shock, but Jedediah Mason heard the news with a grim countenance, and Leighton Chiles' hands worked as if he were seeking something to strangle. Reginald Cabot was all remorse, lamenting the loss of his "best craftsman, the man who'd made his success here possible."

Reverend Armistead McKnight's first reaction was to take others to aid and comfort Anna Davis.

"Archie Nolan's gone cross-country to tell her," Cabot assured him. "I'd say tomorrow would be soon enough. She'll need time to get over the initial shock." Eventually the minister and those of the missionaries present agreed. Soon people sought out those who had not yet heard and passed on the bad news.

"This was no accident," Mason told his assistant. "Cabot knew of Stephen's role in the Virginia affair, through Eddins. He'd have worried that his whole scheme here, whatever it is, was threatened. He needed Davis at first, but he'd become expendable."

"I'm still for eliminating the man, clear evidence or no." Chiles' face, already formidable, turned darker.

"As I've surely said before, that would put us on his level... common killers. No, this is a major setback, and it's adding to the weight of our suspicions, but we can't become the man's executioners." He reflected a moment, thinking of Anna Davis, the settlers here, Stephen's role among these frontiersmen.

"Although I may well change my mind on that."

~ * ~

Nolan urged the horses on with a speed bordering on recklessness as they crested the hills and eventually struck the party's trail up to the first prospecting site. He cast anxious looks at the sinking sun and urged his blowing horse on. Anna followed, her face set, envisioning what they might find of her husband.

Tragically, that morning she had confirmed that she was finally pregnant and had looked forward to telling Stephen he was to be a father. Now she put that thought out of her mind, steeled it to the purpose of rescuing her man if that was God's will, or at least recovering his body for burial. The thought of wild animals tearing him apart made her shudder, and she banned that picture, too.

Up on the ridge at last, they dismounted. Nolan tethered the horses, tied the two long ropes together. He peered over the cliff alongside Anna, and estimated how far the ropes would reach.

Not far enough, he feared. He linked the two chains together also, hooked them around the nearest stout tree, then looked at Anna.

"I'll go, Archie. Take a turn around that smaller tree and let me have slack slowly." She ignored his protests as she knotted the rope securely around her waist. Then she tied a canteen of water also, and stuffed a clean cloth into her waistband.

Then Anna Compton Davis stepped off the edge of the world, clamping her hands around the rough rope, scrabbling with her toes at the stone of the cliff face. She did not look down, but concentrated fiercely on the descent, keeping off the surface, controlling her stance as Nolan paid out the rope. He'd found a spot where the stone lip rounded, avoiding any sharp edge.

Down and down she inched. Saw where loose stones had been knocked from a narrow ledge. Saw where broken roots showed a tree had been torn loose. There was only one direction for her, and she stilled any other thoughts but that of reaching Stephen.

Above, Archie Nolan paid out more rope, anxiously watching the dwindling coil of it next to the anchor tree. He prayed there would be enough. Somehow, he hadn't accepted that the man who'd saved his life those many months before was in reality dead. He knew that Anna too, refused to believe it, that the force that drove them both was hope.

Surely, he reasoned, a benign God wouldn't let a man like Stephen die, and at the hand of a man whom he now believed had deliberately pushed the craftsman over. *Stephen wouldn't have ridden to the edge like that. Cabot's got something going on we don't know about, as I've always suspected. And now this...*

Anna's feet touched loose stone. She looked down to discover she'd reached a ledge piled with fallen rocks from above. A wider ledge.

And then she saw part of Stephen's head, and one arm.

"Stop, Archie!" she called, amid a tumult of fear and relief. The rope tightened as she knelt, placing her feet away from the body.

At her cry, Stephen opened his eyes, staring through a red haze, trying to focus on the sound. Then her hair fell about his face, her lips were on him, tears flooded his bruised cheeks. A deep peace settled over him, and he was certain he was dying, here in his wife's awkward but tender embrace.

Anna snatched stones off him, uncovering him in moments, mindful of their precarious position but determined. Then she turned him carefully, lifted his head, gave him small sips of water. She noted his shallow breath, saw the blood from his wounds. *Maybe, praise God, he hasn't lost too much.* She brought him gently up to a sitting position.

"Can you stay this way?" The words floated softly in the air above him, sinking into his consciousness.

"I think so, yes. How did...?"

"Not now. I'm going to tie this rope around you under your arms. I'll climb up, and Archie and I can pull you up. It'll hurt like hell, Stephen, but it's the only way." She untied the rope from herself, gave him more water, trussed him securely.

"How can you get back up?" His head was clearing. Right then, dying wasn't a part of the plan, he could see. He drew strength from this incredible woman, as he'd drawn it since first meeting her. But he also craned to look up at the sheer height above them.

"I'll do it. Try to stay calm. You'll bump the cliff, but push off if you can so you don't hang up." She was dabbing the wet cloth at his seeping cuts, again noting deep bruises through his torn clothes, but not huge amounts of lost blood.

Then she called up to Nolan, who was peering over the lip far above her.

"Hold fast, Archie; I'm climbing up." She took a deep breath, said a quick prayer, gripped the rough rope and lifted herself off the ledge. She willed herself to climb methodically, each move measured, but also as fast as she could, fearing fatigue.

Very soon pain began in her shoulders and arms. She tried to find breaks in the stone face to help push herself up, but they were few. She dared not stop, knowing her muscles would freeze and fail to respond again afterwards.

Anna Davis was a strong woman. She had worked her father's farm since childhood, equalling any man at the intense labor, always doing more than her share. Here in Kentucky she'd worked alongside the men hewing cabin logs, raising beams, clearing the land, plowing, harvesting. She'd helped Stephen and big George Wellerby put up their house, and in her husband's absence never slacked in her work at their homestead.

Now that strength was being put to the ultimate test. That she might not make the climb was a spectre she would not let into her mind. She *would* succeed. The seeming miles of rope above her would shorten, she would feel Nolan's strong grip very soon. She must simply keep on, using the will and the strength God had given her to preserve precious life: hers, Stephen's, and yes, the tiny life within her.

Instead of despairing, Anna began to thank that same God for His blessings, and a renewed strength and power filled her. Hand over hand she rose, sure now as never before that she would reach safety and bring Stephen back to their gift of life.

A hand reached, gripped her wrist. Nolan had looped the tight chain—yes it *was* the chain—around his other hand and now pulled, solid as stone, to bring her up and over the lip of the cliff. She collapsed, breath heaving, at his feet.

"Is he...how is he?" The man's face under the wisps of white hair was furrowed with worry.

"He's...he's alive, Archie. We can pull him...up, now." She started to rise.

"Not just yet, Miss Anna. Get your breath first. Oh, your hands. Should've brought gloves." She looked at her raw and bleeding hands but felt nothing. Those hands still had much to do.

They stood solidly near the edge, and took the slack out of the rope, the chain behind them clinking softly in the deepening darkness. Then they pulled, gently at first, then with a concerted rhythm, the heavy weight of Stephen's body a huge effort.

After perhaps thirty feet, Nolan stepped back, keeping the rope tight, to go around the snubbing tree. Anna took the section he offered her, and the two of them rested a moment. She could imagine Stephen, halted in midair below them, but secure now, while they gulped air.

Then they repeated the maneuver, hauling up, snubbing, resting a few precious moments before doing it all again. It seemed that hours passed, and every muscle in Anna's body screamed for release.

She knew white-haired Archie Nolan must be in pain, too. She hoped his heart was sound.

And then their burden stopped, against the cliff edge. Nolan snubbed the rope, tied it off, and he and Anna reached down, each gripping an arm under Stephen's shoulders. One gigantic heave brought most of him up and over, and she scrambled to grab his legs, swing them up to safety. He was limp, unconscious. Both his rescuers lay back, panting, sweat pouring off them.

With the crushing tightness of the rope gone from his chest, Stephen gradually came around, feeling the blood flowing again through him. The pain was there again, but there was nothing to do but bear it. He'd known pain often, but never to this degree. His body was on the verge of shutting down again but he fought it, focusing in the darkness on the shapes next to him, scenting Anna's body, feeling her hand on his brow.

He was alive. Incredibly, he was *alive!* And his mind began to work.

They must not stay here. Any moment Cabot could come back to make sure he was dead, to put on a show of trying to rescue him, with the villagers in a torchlit circle, perhaps repeating the very work Anna and yes, Archie Nolan, his friend, had just done.

"We need to leave, Anna." His voice was strangely calm, or so he imagined it. Logical, reasoned. "Before Cabot comes back."

"Cabot?" She turned to Nolan. "Was that what you meant when you said it wasn't an accident? *Cabot?*" Her voice cut like an axe striking the block.

"I didn't see it, really, Miss Anna, but…"

"Yes, it was Cabot," Stephen supplied. "He shoved my horse so it bolted, and we went over. Now we must get home, Anna, and say nothing of this. Let him think I'm dead, which is a…possibility…I…" The darkness was coming again, but at least the convulsions had stopped. He drifted away from them.

They lifted him gently, laid him across Anna's horse, tied him securely. They retrieved the rope, the chains, just as the first moonlight began to flood the ridge. Nolan struck a light to the torch and led the way on foot, back down the slope toward the test site. The moonlight brightened, as the just-past-full shape cleared the trees in the east.

"Can you find the way without the torch?" Anna asked him. She was walking beside Stephen, holding him, feeling his pulse periodically, hearing his quiet breathing.

"I think so. Yes, best not to let them see. Be hard to find the cutoff to your place, but it won't be far, now. Downhill most of the way, with just the two long hills to get over."

She envisioned this area as a sort of quadrant...the ironworks, the mill on the outer curve of the creek, and knew they were cutting straight across, a much shorter distance. She prayed. *Dear God, help us here to reach home, and please, please keep this child of Yours alive.*

They stepped carefully over stones, fallen logs, threaded their way among trees. Patches of white moonlight showed them the way their horses had come earlier, and they worked their uneven way homeward.

At last they came to the head of the draw that led down to the house. Anna felt she'd been walking a thousand miles, and she knew aging Archie Nolan must feel the same. They reached home, untied Stephen, brought him gently down, carried him into the house.

"Someone will come. We'll put him up in the loft. No one must know he's alive, Archie." She lighted candles and they carried the still-limp form up the stairs, then on into the tiny attic space. There she prepared a pad for him, sent Nolan to heat water at the fireplace, set about cutting the last of his torn clothing from him. The bruises covered his body, and scrapes and gashes oozed red.

She washed him carefully, applied a little whiskey to the wounds, grateful that he could not feel the sting. Then she used some salve Belle Ketchum had given her, plus some powdered herbs her mother and their native ancestors had taught her to prepare. Last, she bound him almost head to foot with clean cloths, smooth and tight. He seemed to be resting easily. And miraculously, nothing seemed broken. Perhaps some ribs, but no obvious limbs. She thanked God again, and left him briefly.

Downstairs, she warmed food and insisted that Nolan eat. She had no appetite herself, but took care of this friend, eliciting from him the details of the tragedy.

"We'd gone ahead, Thad and I, to find the gap down to this draw I knew had ore in it. I heard Cabot call to Stephen to look down at the two branches below, see if he thought they could work for power. The next thing I heard was Cabot shouting for us, said Stephen's horse had bolted and he'd gone over the edge with it. We could see part of the horse, and that tree that'd come uprooted, still tumbling down. Couldn't see Stephen at all, just like you and I couldn't.

"We rode around and down, but couldn't get up—cliff goes up straight near the bottom. So we headed on back, but I knew you'd want to hear first, and the farther I came, the more I knew we had to go back."

"Thank God you did, Archie. He'd have died before morning. Now, we know Cabot did it. And he'll have told his version to everybody. It's best, as Stephen said, to let him and everyone believe he's dead. When he recovers, we'll deal with our Mr. Cabot."

She didn't say this to Nolan, but a resolve, hard as stone, began to form inside her. She felt, despite her faith, that she was chosen to be the instrument of God's will that would destroy Reginald Cabot. Just how, she didn't know yet, but the conviction grew, as surely as the new life inside her was growing, biding its time, inexorable in its purpose. She knew she must pray to banish this evil from her consciousness.

But her prayer was tinged with blood.

Twenty-five

The next morning a somber group of villagers, led by an aching Archie Nolan, followed the trail of the prospectors, carrying long, thick ropes. Cabot had declined to accompany them, claiming that he must prepare to leave on a business trip north. He expressed his deep regret for the loss of Stephen Davis, and wished the others whatever success lay ahead at the accident site.

Nolan headed the expedition, going over the location on the clifftop in his mind. Something nagged at him about that. He replayed his and Anna's efforts, every step of the operation. He was tender and yes, sore in the arms and shoulders, but otherwise sound. He guessed his life of prospecting, climbing, digging in rugged settings had kept him strong, and he was thankful.

It finally came to him as they were nearing the ridge top: the snubbing tree would have rope burns on it, and the others would wonder at that. So within several yards of the cliff, he told the others to dismount, tie the horses while he went ahead to find the exact spot.

He took a hatchet from his saddlebags, walked quickly to the tree, and blazed it, shearing off the rope burns.

"This's it," he called to the others, peering over the edge. They gathered around, looking over, each holding onto the person next to him, marveling at the seeming sheer drop to the forest below.

"I'll go," Nolan volunteered, again taking charge before anyone else could offer. "Tie the rope off to that tree yonder, and snub around this one. Help me make a harness, here." He and Harvey Campbell accomplished that, creating a sling that required only his holding on. "Let me down slow, men."

He stepped to the edge, saw that the men had the snubbed rope tight, then slid over the lip, being careful to go where the stone was rounded. He faced the wall as Anna had done, keeping off it with his toes.

He passed the narrow ledge, then later the torn roots of the tree. Looking down, he saw the wider ledge nearing. As he reached it, he saw pieces of Stephen's torn clothing among the stones there. He reached, pulled one loose as he pushed out over this edge, put it in his pocket. There was no other place a body could be, so he let them lower him further, over the ledge, swinging free outside an overhang with dark recesses. He peered into them, seeing evidence of some sort of den. Bones lay scattered about, leaves had blown in.

"Stop!" he roared up to those above. He hung there, wondering how an animal could ever get to this place. Maybe an eagle's nest. There was another, very narrow ledge leading away, and he speculated that bobcats or even panthers could possibly have reached there also. He formulated his report.

"Bring me up!" He felt the instant tug, and guided himself past the overhang. Up again, with the steady pull of the men at the top, he recreated Stephen's fall. The tree had saved him, plainly, although there was no telling how much damage it'd done to him. But he was alive and under Anna's care and, with God's blessing, his friend and lifesaver would survive.

He was grim-faced when the hands pulled him up over the edge. He stood, started to untie the ropes. The others crowded around.

"Hate to tell you this," he began. "But there's an overhang down there where some critters have denned up. Stephen must'e lodged there, probably in pieces already. Anyway, there's bones there, and I fear what's left of our man's been dragged back in there." He produced the torn and bloody piece of Stephen's clothing, and shook his head sorrowfully. "Best to leave it as it is, I'd say."

Todd Epsworth, Harvey Campbell and young Carver MacNaughton fashioned a crude cross lashed together with rawhide and set it with stones at the site. Todd said a short prayer of commital for his friend among the bowed heads. No one spoke then, as they coiled the rope, moved to their horses. It was an even more subdued group that threaded its way back toward the village.

~ * ~

Samuel Eddins welcomed Hiram Garst back from his trip north. The man had made it a priority to call on the lawyer, for obvious reasons.

"Got myself robbed in Lexington," he explained. "Had to work my way back here, a few days wherever I could find someone who'd pay me."

Eddins doubted that this man, who he now was certain was Cabot's assassin, had done much honest work to finance his way south. He was threadbare, thin, and carried an ancient shotgun he'd probably used to get food and money.

"Well, it's good you got back. Things have been happening in your absence." The lawyer sat back in his chair, motioning his visitor to another one.

"Oh, anything of significance?" Garst sat, casually leaning the gun against a wall.

"Well, I've suspected that fellow Stephen Davis at Ketchum's Mill of planning to sabotage Mr. Cabot's operation all along. He did something similar back in Virginia, as I told you. I'd urged our employer to take some action, but he seemed to value the fellow's skills in getting the ironworks set up and running. And he *did* seem to know what he was doing, the way he got things built." He paused.

"You're going to tell me something's happened to the man." Not a question.

"You are an insightful man, Mr. Garst. Yes, it seems Davis got too close to a cliff while prospecting with Mr. Cabot and others on up from the operation, with an eye to expansion, you know. And our ex-soldier, sharpshooter, is no more." Eddins watched for a reaction from the other man.

"So, then. No, I didn't know of Davis' past, any more than the local gossip. Seems to have done a lot for the community there, but did Mr. Cabot consider him a problem?"

"Sort of brushed off the possibility, but I've known the man for a long time. He never forgets a slight or an enemy. There was that group of businessmen in Virginia that Davis got into trouble with over a runaway slave, and in the end all the group died. Except for me, and the local judge there was convinced I was guilty of something, kept me under lock and key for weeks with no evidence. So Davis was not one of my favorite people."

"I see. But surely losing one builder hasn't crippled the operation?"

"Not at all. We heard of Mr. Lester Cummings' death on Jackson River, and the loss of part of his ironworks. So our competition has vanished, and our prices are rising to cover the cost of shipping, and to ensure a profit. That was something Mr. Cabot thought would have to wait while we operated at a loss at first." Again, Eddins watched Garst's face for some sign. As a lawyer, he prided himself on his ability to read people, but the assassin's eyes showed nothing.

"Really? I met with Mr. Cummings, as I told you I would. Accident must've happened just after I left. Pity. Self-made man who ran a tight organization. How did he die?"

"Apparently fell from an office atop one of his buildings. Railing seems to have given way. Nobody knows how the fires started that gutted his buildings."

"So. Our boss has hit a streak of luck. I must get on back to report my own efforts to him, but I'm somewhat seedy. Do you suppose you could advance me a bit of company money to outfit myself better?" It was not an idle request, Eddins reflected, seeing again the shotgun close. This was not a man to hinder.

"Certainly, sir. Whatever your...work has been, I'm certain Mr. Cabot will be happy you've accomplished it, and yes, we'll set you up properly. Here are some coins for clothing, and get yourself a good room at an inn, and some solid food. Looks like you've had a hard trip."

"In some ways, yes. Be glad to get back to the village. Mr. Cabot indicated he will have a substantial position for me, now that things are, shall we say, *stable?*" Garst smiled. He suspected this man knew of his real work, and keeping the truth just below the surface was fine with him. Never antagonize a man who could be of further use was an axiom of his, and here he was at least to return to Ketchum's Mill in proper form.

He could work with this lawyer.

~ * ~

Stephen healed gradually, under the constant ministrations of his wife. She brewed willow bark tea and made him drink quantities of it to numb the pain. She'd also sent word that in her grief she would not continue teaching and asked that the missionaries find a replacement. She also asked that no one call on her for a while, till she could get her life back together.

Thus no solicitous neighbors barged in on them, and she was able to harvest the last of the garden, care for the place, and nurse Stephen devotedly. She marveled that no bones except two ribs seemed broken, but his still-painful hip continued to plague him.

"That must've been where I snagged that tree on the way down," he theorized. "Maybe dislocated it, and it popped back in?"

"I suspect just a deep bruise. But that tree was Providential, love. It surely slowed you down enough for you to come to rest on that ledge. Without it, you'd have smashed yourself into a smear. I'm grateful for whatever saved you."

"So am I, yes. And that was you, mostly. How you ever climbed that cliff is a mystery. Women aren't supposed to have that much upper-body strength."

"God was with me, my dear. Couldn't have asked for better support."

"You've convinced me. Along with the fact that I'm alive at all. But now I'm troubled about just how to set things straight with my would-be assassin."

"Please don't trouble yourself about him right now. From what Archie's told me, he's gone off on some business. With Lester Cummings' ironworks shut down, he's raised his prices a lot, and the foremen are shipping metal regularly. He shouldn't be a problem for the time being."

"But he must be dealt with. I expect more evildoing when his man Garst gets back. It was an oversight for me to think I'd not be a target till that man returned. Cabot is obviously quite able to do his own dirty work."

"Certainly a master at manipulation. Oh, Archie also told me that Mr. Mason has barely been able to restrain his man Chiles. Left up to him, Cabot would be a dead man by now."

"I like that man. Straightforward, sees a situation for what it really is. But of course, Mason must watch the legal aspects of his actions, I suppose. What's their excuse for staying on?"

"Apparently Mr. Mason is redrawing his diagrams of the milling inventions, supposedly with the aim of refining his exact needs in iron. I suspect Cabot has seen more to him than the inventor image, though. I fear for the man as perhaps the next target."

"With Chiles around, that'll be difficult. But again, when Garst gets back, he'll probably take charge in Cabot's absence. He could probably engineer some disaster. You're right...with his nature, he'll suspect Mason and Chiles."

"He surely has, and has just been keeping it to himself. From what Mason's told us, he's been on Cabot's trail for years. Hard to imagine he could still be anonymous."

"Well, as soon as I'm mobile again, we need to coordinate some strategy with those two and, of course, Killy Ketchum. We can't have snakes among us."

"There's another aspect to this, dear. I can't stay secluded forever, or the good villagers will think I've become unhinged in my grief. Very soon, the ladies will come calling to assuage my sorrows.

You'll have to stay up here under the roof and be very quiet, I'm afraid."

"I can do that. Especially since we still have that store of books we never had time to read. I hate the inactivity, but I know it's necessary."

"You've been the ideal patient. I hope that willow-bark tea has helped with the pain."

"Yes, but I fear this hip may ache for a long time. I can't put weight on it."

"You've been trying to stand? I take back what I said about being an ideal patient." She shook a finger at him.

"Well, how will I know what I can do if I don't try? Oh, all right… I'll be good, at least for now. But watch out for me when I'm able to move…you won't be safe from me." He gave her hand a squeeze, mischief in his eyes.

"I can't wait. And by the way, man of mine, I've been keeping a secret from you." Her dark eyes sparkled, and she took his face in her hands.

"I'm afraid to ask."

"We're going to be parents, Papa." She kissed him.

"We…we *are?* Why, that's…that's wonderful! When?"

"Late spring, early summer sometime. I didn't want to dump that news on you till I thought you could handle it. So, I don't want you planning to put your life in danger taking care of our evil Mr. Cabot. *We* need you." Patting her still-flat abdomen.

"Well, that certainly puts things in a different light. No, there's no criminal who needs dealing with worth…you said spring? That's such good news!"

~ * ~

Reginald Cabot's plans were coming along nicely. Competition was gone, the crusader Davis was gone, Eddins was selling his iron; it was going out, albeit over that wretched road. Soon he would begin consoling the desirable widow Davis. There remained but one other major undertaking ahead.

He'd provisioned himself for the road, armed himself, and bade farewell to the villagers without waiting for the report of the search for Davis' remains.

"Business calls, I'm afraid. I should return before any serious snowfall. Mr. Garst should be back soon, and I may well meet him on the way. Either way, he'll take over the operation, deferring of course to the foremen in charge of the various workings. May God be with you all, and give my sincerest condolences to Mrs. Davis when you see her." He'd ridden away, smiling to himself.

His destination was the Jackson River ironworks, now reduced to a chaos of burned buildings, with no leadership. Some relative of Cummings' would no doubt have reached the works and should be thoroughly befuddled at the wreckage. That's when he, Cabot, would appear, a knowledgeable colleague, ready with an offer for it all that couldn't be refused.

It was just too perfect.

He met Hiram Garst very soon on the road, and the two led their horses off into the woods for a conference.

"As you've heard, Jackson River's works are virtually destroyed, sir," Garst reported, unable to conceal a smile of satisfaction. "And Eddins tells me sales have become brisk at that news."

"Yes, you've done well, Garst. And I'm on my way to buy out what's left. I'll control all the iron and steel in the entire region, and we'll all grow rich. Eddins probably told you that our suspected enemy Stephen Davis was killed."

"He did. So what's to be my job while you're gone?"

"I want you to take care of overall supervision. Stillwell, Leslie, White and the other foremen are capable of running things, but there will be questions of priorities, shipping schedules, that sort of thing you'll have to manage. Does that suit you?"

"Perfectly. I'll warrant you'll find the operation running smoothly when you return. Oh, did that miller fellow and his ugly assistant get to the village? I've been thinking something about them."

"Ah, so you met them. And what was your assessment?"

"At first, I was glad for a potential customer for us, but on reflection, there was something false about them both. And I felt I should know them from somewhere, unlikely as that was."

"And?"

"And, the ugly one bears an uncanny resemblance to the late Jedediah Mason's bodyguard back in Philadelphia. Could be a look-alike, since this man here seems a bit vacant, though."

"Vacant? I didn't sense that. Seemed fairly intelligent, well-spoken."

"Now that's strange. When we met on this road, he was dribbling tobacco juice down his beard, acting imbecilic."

"Hmm. What did you think of Carson himself?"

"He seemed what he said he was: a mill specialist with ideas and a need for iron. But he also seemed somewhat familiar."

"Well, the two of them have been snooping around the ironworks, drawing up plans and redrawing them, not buying anything, for too long. And they've had what I'd have to term clandestine meetings with Davis and the miller Ketchum. Of course, milling's something they're both adept at. But something's going on with those two, although with Davis gone, they're probably harmless."

"Nobody's harmless who's been working with Davis, from what Eddins tells me."

"Yes, Eddins almost got wiped out in that operation in Virginia at Davis' hand. Why don't you find out what you can about those two then, who have no reason to stay on, with my absence? And I'd say, if you find they're a threat, go ahead and take care of that. Discreetly, of course."

With that, Cabot passed a pouch of gold coins to Garst, who thanked him. The two then rode on in opposite directions.

~ * ~

Stephen wanted to bring Mason and Chiles into his confidence, to begin planning their next move. He was afraid the two men would leave, now that Cabot had gone, and he'd have to deal with the man, and probably Garst too, on his own. He asked Archie Nolan to bring them after dark, on a day he'd visited.

"You're sure?"

"It's a chance I'll have to take. They've been after Cabot for years, which is why they're here, Archie. Up till now, they haven't had anything solid to charge him with, but his attempt on my life can get him hanged, and the rest he's probably guilty of will add weight to his sins."

Accordingly, a somewhat stunned Jedediah Mason and Leighton Chiles came later to Stephen's bedside, hats in hand. Nolan hadn't told them what to expect, and they'd been somewhat nervous at calling on Anna this way.

"My God, man, you've cheated the Grim Reaper!" Mason exulted. Chiles' dark face lighted in a wide grin. Both men took Stephen's hand, pressed it gently. He felt a warmth, an alliance solidifying among them. Anna brought hot cider from a wagonload of Shenandoah Valley apples, and the investigators and Nolan settled themselves around the attic bed with her.

"Yes, God apparently has more for me to do in this life, gentlemen. And through the superhuman efforts of Anna and Archie, He's undone my demise." He gave his wife's hand an affectionate squeeze.

"Now, with Cabot gone and Garst in charge, as Archie tells me, things should go along uneventfully for a few weeks. My guess is that Cabot's left to try to buy what's left of Cummings' ironworks, giving him a monopoly. That's the only end I've been able to conjecture for his whole presence here. The real profits will come from there, and he'll probably let this place die when the close deposits play out.

"The man's ego is boundless, and there's nothing he won't do, no morals, no ethics to bind him from coercion, intimidation, murder, to achieve his ends. He's got to be stopped here, along with Garst, who's undoubtedly his assassin. I'd like to hear what we can all come up with to protect ourselves and wipe this evil blot out of our lives."

Stephen lay back, visibly exhausted, but his eyes keen. These were his confidants, indeed the men who could take the burden from him, of righting the wrongs Cabot had committed. Leighton Chiles glanced at his employer before speaking.

"You all probably know I'm for eliminating the man at first opportunity, and Garst along with him. We've seen what can happen when we wait for a better time. We came close to losing you, Stephen, and I cannot let that sort of thing happen again. I feel Cabot's suspicious of Mr. Mason and me, and wouldn't doubt but he's already given Garst orders to kill us."

"That would be blatant, Leighton," Mason objected. "And too obvious. I agree we're possibly his next targets, but he'd be subtle, I'm sure."

"Not to contradict you, sir, but remember, he hired Garst to shoot you in the back in Philadelphia. That he had the wrong man, and only wounded him, doesn't change the intent. If and when he makes the connection, that you're who you really are, he'll spare nothing to destroy you."

"Well, I'll concede that is the man's nature...doesn't ever forget a perceived wrong. What do you think, Mr. Nolan, Mrs. Davis?"

Anna deferred to Archie, but he waved a hand.

"This is difficult," she began. "Being a practicing Christian, I must decry outright killing unless it's in self-defense. One might argue, as you have, Mr. Chiles, that here we have only a matter of timing. Must we wait to stop the killers until they act? And haven't they already? I'm afraid I've lived close enough to nature to have learned that one doesn't give the snake the chance to strike before dispatching it."

"Well said, ma'am," Chiles agreed.

"As a man who's been the target of greed already," Archie said, "I see little difference here between a complicated version of it layered in 'business' and the outright robbery and murder my late partner Jamie and I suffered. We live in a rough part of the world, but there's a close parallel to life in the cities: Wrongs are punished, but too often after the fact. We need an eye to the future to forestall disasters, and I believe here we have those wrongs."

Eyes turned to Stephen, who'd taken this in thoughtfully. Mason was the only one to hesitate, and that was clearly because of his law-abiding background. In the late war, there was no time to weigh one's actions: it was kill or be killed. And as Anna had said, here it was perhaps just a timing issue.

But could they be wrong? No, not in Cabot's case; he'd tried his best to kill the man who'd brought down part of his operation—all that part in Virginia—and wouldn't hesitate to complete the job the moment he learned of his failure. Mason and Chiles might or might not be next; there was no way to tell.

Perhaps those two should leave, find safety. Then he could deal with Cabot himself as soon as he was healed. But no, that'd defeat their purpose in coming all this distance. Mason's work was to be lauded, his motives good. They should act together, certainly.

"When had you planned to go back north, Mr. Mason?" he asked.

"That's a good question, Stephen. Cabot said he'd be back before serious cold weather, which this high in the mountains is probably in less than a month. If we're to deal with him decisively, we should stay on some pretense, or perhaps relocate to Saltville, keep an eye on Eddins, who'll surely be in contact on the man's return. Then we could come back, carry out our plan, whatever that turns out to be."

"Of course, you have your operation in the capital. Or you might trail him to Jackson River on your way and, if you agree with Mr. Chiles, just eliminate him there before he can consolidate his monopoly. And before he can do more harm among us here."

"Now that's the best idea yet," Chiles interposed. "And I'm the man for that job, which I believe is long overdue."

"Perhaps," Mason mused. "But I'm afraid I haven't come around to that stance just yet."

"No offense, sir," his assistant began, "but could that be because you weren't the one pushed over the cliff? I'm afraid I'm long past observing the niceties of the law here, given what this man has done."

"I deserved that, surely. Leighton has always cut to the chase, and I suppose I need that. But I've the feeling there's a line to be crossed here, or not, and I don't want our actions to descend to those of the level of the criminals we're after. Do the rest of you understand that?"

"Certainly," Stephen replied. "I've fought with that demon many times. And it's seldom a clear choice...each situation has its own complications. I wouldn't want to make a damning mistake, take out the wrong man, for instance. But Cabot's not the wrong man."

"No, and neither is Garst," Chiles said. I saw him try to commit cold-blooded murder in Philadelphia. The man's a hired assassin, and none of us doubts he killed Mr. Cummings."

Anna had heard these arguments, had added her own, conflicted as she was with her beliefs at stake, against her resolve to avenge the blatant attempt on her husband's life. She proposed a partial solution.

"Why don't we wait till Stephen's back on his feet, gentlemen? By the time Cabot returns, he may well be strong enough to defend us here, at least. Meanwhile, for your safety, Mr. Mason and Mr. Chiles, why don't you return to Saltville or somewhere else away from Garst until then? I don't foresee any reason for violence before that time, and much as I dislike the uncertainty, we may also see or learn something else to add to our ultimate decision."

"A wise suggestion, Mrs. Davis," Mason declared. "I, for one think that's the course to take. The end result may well be the same, but it'll be after more consideration, after we're in better shape"—he indicated Stephen—"to act."

"Guess you're right," Archie Nolan agreed, "but I'll go around imagining a target on my back. Cabot doesn't really need me anymore either."

"That's true of all of us. We're no longer necessary, as he proved with me," Stephen agreed. "I made the mistake of thinking he needed me for future work... I was wrong."

"Well," Anna mused, "we can always modify our course quickly, if events make that necessary." She reflected for a moment. "However, I think you all should know, my position here is that Cabot tried to kill my husband, and ultimately, if necessary, I will kill that man myself."

This was delivered in a quiet, controlled tone, but no one present doubted her in the least.

Twenty-six

Reginald Cabot conjectured again that by the time he reached the Jackson River ironworks, some relative of the late Lester Cummings would be in residence, no doubt trying to decide how to deal with the disaster. He'd present himself as the savior of the sad situation, the fellow-entrepreneur in the industry who could take the entire worrisome problem off the new owner's hands. For, of course, a fraction of its worth.

The season was advancing, and frost rimed the roads he traveled each morning. He stayed at the best taverns and inns on the pike, but often these were less than satisfactory. Accommodations in this part of the country still fell far below his desired level of comfort.

Still, a little irritation could be borne, since he was so close to realizing his goal of mastery of the entire iron and steel industry in the region. And with his penchant for choosing the right subordinates, he could build himself an estate anywhere he chose and run his empire from there. Damn the distances...he could have whatever he wanted brought to him.

Most likely, the Ketchum's Mill site would continue to be too isolated for his tastes, despite its value as a remote hiding place from the law. No, he'd search out the ideal location, somewhere with at least a little culture, and establish himself there.

Which brought to mind again the winsome Anna Davis, the mourning widow of his late enemy. He could offer her everything and take her away from that frontier hole. Together they could build a life that would be the envy of all. Yes, he'd initiate his suit just as soon as he returned and have all winter to pursue it.

Reginald Cabot savored the thought of this courtship. He might not be a young man now, but he was far from decrepit. He'd never had trouble winning any woman he wanted, and he was sure Anna would be at worst a challenge, the acquisition all the sweeter for it.

After long days of travel, but with the reality of winter still some time off, he arrived at the devastated ironworks. Inquiry revealed that a Mr. Elijah Wadsworth, a cousin of the late proprietor, had recently arrived to sort out the business. He called on the new owner.

Cabot was taken aback at the appearance of the man, who rose from behind his desk, on which lay a loaded pistol. Wadsworth wore a grim countenance that projected a don't-waste-my-time message. *Altogether too much like his late predecessor.* He bowed curtly to his visitor, then asked his business. Cabot felt a chill.

"Well, sir, I visited with Mr. Cummings some months back, relative to my plans for establishing a similar operation in Kentucky. He was most helpful, but predicted that the distance to markets involved would be ruinous. That has not proven to be the case, and to speak right to the point, I'm interested in acquiring this works, if it should please you to offer it for sale."

"I see. Yes, my late cousin Lester wrote me that a man with an impractical plan had come around. He himself had looked briefly at the reports of one Archie Nolan's prospecting in that area and decided not to pursue expansion.

"But since you've been blunt, I shall be also: this works is not for sale. Lester and I both came up through the operation at Saugus, and I am well-versed in all aspects of this one. Added to the already-established markets, I expect to be fully functioning by spring. I wish you well in your efforts, but suggest you concentrate on markets further south and west."

"Well then, it appears circumstances have decreed that we shall be competitors, sir. I'd hoped to avoid that."

"Competition has never concerned me, Mr. Cabot. An efficient operation will survive nicely, as I'm sure you're finding out. I do find it...unusual that you could be turning a profit so far from customers."

"I've developed a highly efficient transportation system, Mr. Wadsworth, which will remain my secret for as long as possible. Expensive to install, but worth it." He rose. "So we cannot do business: I regret that. And I've been remiss in expressing my condolences concerning your late cousin. A remarkable, forceful man. Just seeing all he accomplished here inspired me, I don't mind telling you."

"Yes, well. And I'll tell you, sir, the circumstances surrounding his death I find quite troubling. I do not believe for an instant that it was accidental." Wadsworth rose also, his hand very near the pistol.

"Why, that's terrible! Whoever could have purposely...Do you suspect robbery?"

"Not really, since only a small amount is missing. No, the destruction of facilities here suggests a grudge, perhaps by a former employee. I'm afraid Lester was, as you probably observed, of short temper, and he did create enemies."

"No, I didn't get that impression. Well, let us hope for justice in that matter, above all. And yes, I'll confine my marketing efforts to the newly opening-up territories. As you know, the mill and smithy are always the first industries in new settlements, and they're proliferating."

The hard-eyed Mr. Wadsworth did not like this smooth-talking man, and was not a little suspicious of him. But there was a huge amount of work to be done, and he wanted to be about it.

"Good day, Mr. Cabot. Thank you for your offer, and for your condolences regarding my cousin." He saw his visitor out, again registering the long drop from the railed walkway. He closed the door behind Cabot.

Damn the man, Cabot thought, *he's flintier than Cummings was. Well, I don't take kindly to opposition, and we'll just have to devise another plan to acquire this operation. I've come all this way for nothing? Never.*

One simply did not stand in Reginald Cabot's way when he set his mind to a course of action. Lester Cummings' demise had been simple; this Wadsworth would be harder to dislodge. He glanced below at the beehive of activity as men rebuilt, repaired, salvaged. *Witnesses.*

But remove this man Cabot would, and in a manner above suspicion. Just how to effect that remained to be seen, but he had no doubt whatsoever it could be done.

He rode away inwardly fuming, revising his plans, but also focusing on the method he'd use to eliminate this competition forever.

~ * ~

Hiram Garst didn't like running the ironworks. Too much work, seeing to shipments, scheduling labor, answering the endless questions put to him by the foremen and the workers themselves, who he was sure wouldn't have troubled Cabot with their trifles. They seemed to regard him as just what he was: a substitute not to be taken seriously, and certainly not above them in his position.

He was gratified but also a bit rueful at the departure of the nosy Archibald Carson and his ugly assistant Martin Bone. He'd become almost certain Bone had somehow been transported from Philadelphia to this end of the world, but the recurring vacant stare the man had resumed belied that. And again, the dribbling of tobacco juice into his beard, his obvious fumblings, just wouldn't fit with the image of the investigator's fearsome bodyguard in the capital. He wondered again at Cabot's description of him as normal.

Still, he'd come within inches of simply shooting the man with a rifle from cover, now that hunting season was in full swing. Hunters *did* get themselves shot, out in the woods that way.

But now they were both gone, and all right...he could concentrate on running this troublesome business. He reflected that it was a good thing Cabot was to acquire the Jackson River works, because it was becoming evident to all that the supply of ore here was thinning. And Archie Nolan's reports of the additional deposits farther away weren't that promising.

He looked forward to Cabot's logical relocating back closer to civilization. Probably not on the Jackson Rver itself, another outback, but at least at Lexington, which could well become a pleasant town, situated as it was near the southern end of the Shenandoah Valley. That thriving breadbasket of the region could do nothing but grow, with its direct route to the northern Virginia, Maryland and Pennsylvania centers.

Garst knew he was not popular with the villagers. He didn't particularly care but knew he mustn't antagonize them. Any hostile action, or any decisions he might make that would be harsh, might incite these frontiersmen to a tar-and-feather rage. He'd been able to flee dangerous situations several times in the past and felt sure he could read these bumpkins well enough to stay ahead of them, but he knew enough to realize he'd best be cautious.

Consequently, he treated everyone with deference, and was polite as pie to them all, despite his inner aversions. With the exception of the minister, the former schoolteacher, some of the foremen and missionaries, these were a collection of crude, unlettered, backwards people, and the sooner he could be rid of them, the better.

The only man he would have feared was Stephen Davis, and he was conveniently dead. That meant he could relax his constant habit of suspecting enemies behind every tree and do this odious job until Cabot returned. He'd learned enough from Eddins, and certain things Cabot had let drop, how Davis had destroyed a profitable setup in Virginia and had sensed there'd been a deal more to the man than had appeared.

Garst did miss the company of women. The few single female settlers consisted of under-age daughters, and the odd work-weary widow. Most of those older ones were missing teeth and were bowed with the burdens of survival. Hardly human. Certainly not what he'd call attractive.

Well, there *was* the late Stephen Davis' young widow who, while quite tall, was easily the prettiest woman in the village. Garst had no idea his employer Cabot coveted this woman and began to think about ingratiating himself with her. Life on her own must certainly be difficult, what with winter coming on. Perhaps he'd shoot a deer or a brace of turkeys and make her a gift of them.

But the man was also aware that one didn't, in polite society, just go calling on a recent widow alone, without observing the formalities. So he'd enlist one or more of the women, perhaps the talkative Belle Ketchum and yes, the minister's wife, Ella McKnight, on a mercy visit. He'd made it a point to attend the church while here, to try to establish himself as a solid citizen. And these two women were pillars of the community.

Yes, Hiram Garst, man of the world would see if he could relieve the loneliness of the settlement's most recently available woman. The thought excited him; she was part Indian and he'd heard the red women were wildly sexual, and really slavish toward their men. He began to envision a pleasant winter hiatus as the man in Anna Davis' life.

~ * ~

The supposedly late Stephen Davis continued to mend on into the late fall season. On his prospecting expeditions, Archie Nolan also hunted and regularly brought deer, turkeys and small game to the secluded cabin where his friend slowly gained back his strength. With Mason and Chiles gone back to Saltville, supposedly to perfect their milling inventions out of sight, the secret of Stephen's existence was safe.

When delegations of villagers came to bring food and other condolences and company, they found the young widow coping well with the situation and apparently handling the place efficiently. In her quiet way, Anna presented a picture of acceptance none of the other women could be sure they could manage given the loss of a husband. These visits weren't unwelcome, but she did not encourage them, and gradually they lessened. So sad, the visitors said, losing her man so young, and now she had nothing.

Anna had not told anyone else of her pregnancy, and it did not show yet, unless one knew. She and Stephen spent many hours contemplating the new life that lay ahead of them as parents, and it was a time of quiet joy. He chafed at being hidden away, and spent the hours when visitors were below, up in the attic reading until they left.

Now he could hobble downstairs, depending heavily on his hands on the railings, and was beginning limited exercises to loosen stiff muscles. He could and did help inside the house, but Anna wouldn't let him go out. No telling when another well-meaning visitor might round the last bend in the trail and be confronted with what must surely be his ghost.

The plan was still to await Reginald Cabot's return, for which Mason and Chiles would watch in Saltville. They'd follow then, with the idea of someone's being able to find out what he reported to his man Garst. Just how this was to be done hadn't been worked out yet, but Stephen was sure that in the inn there would be a way. Or perhaps down at the ironworks, even if the two moved aside, at least a watcher could report what he could see, if not hear.

Stephen wondered somewhat at his not planning simply to eliminate both men as evil forces loose in the midst of the missionaries and settlers, but attributed that hesitancy to the fact that he was now a family man. In the past he'd seen little difference between defending himself against British soldiers bent on destroying him during the war and the same action against the violent men who'd sworn to kill him back in Virginia.

But in light of the plans he and Anna were making, the life they were living, he just didn't fit the role of the hardened veteran, now seeing evil versus good as not nearly so black and white as before. He'd like nothing better than for Mason and Chiles to find sufficient cause to wipe out Cabot and his hired assassin, and was sure the homely bodyguard could do it quickly and efficiently.

But he also knew that law and a sense of order must prevail here if this settlement were to continue as a civilized place to raise a family. No, they must not descend to the level of the evil men themselves, as Mason had insisted, even in their need to protect their homes and lives.

Stephen knew that as soon as the investigator and his assistant showed themselves, Cabot would almost certainly order their killing. He also suspected that Chiles would take the entire matter into his own hands, despite his employer's concerns when that situation became evident.

But would it? How much did Cabot know or suspect of Mason's true identity and work, his hunting the man for so long? But that probably wouldn't matter. He imagined Cabot would act even on a suspicion at the first sign of danger, or even before that.

Yes, and Chiles might well need help in cleansing this place of those two. Archie Nolan wasn't a killer. But Killebrew Ketchum had proven a courageous man when necessary, and certainly George Weller, Harvey Campbell and Todd Epsworth. The ex-soldiers could be counted on to help dispense justice.

Some of the others might resent any move against their supposed benefactor, but with time's passage, Stephen felt the eventual collapse of the iron venture would show them that Cabot hadn't been their savior after all.

Even if he weren't eliminated, it hardly seemed natural for the man to stay there after he'd consolidated his iron production with the Jackson River works. He'd probably set up nearer civilization. Unless he wanted to stay hidden from enemies in Philadelphia and elsewhere.

Stephen couldn't manage to second-guess Cabot, or to put himself into the man's shoes. He just didn't think like someone who was always out for an advantage, no matter anyone he harmed. Trying to figure him also gave the recovering craftsman a headache.

~ * ~

The lawyer-sales manager Samuel Eddins knew of the return of the miller and his vague assistant to Saltville but was not overly concerned. He hadn't heard anything solidly negative about the pair and assumed they might be just who they said they were: prospective customers for iron. Indeed, Archibald Carson had actually paid

Eddins a visit to discuss an elaborate plan he'd worked out before with Stephen Davis' help, ostensibly to see if the materials were currently available.

Eddins had no conception of the squiggles on the blue rag paper Carson showed him, but nodded sagely and assured the man that Cabot's iron could satisfy his every need. For a price, of course...the difficulties in transport had indeed made it necessary to raise said prices significantly. Surely Carson could appreciate that, given his recent visit to the ironworks and the deplorable state of the long road from there.

Then the pair had disappeared, and Eddins assumed they had gone elsewhere on some scheme or other. He had concluded they were an odd team, anyway.

Now, alone with Chiles, Mason asked his assistant his assessment of the lawyer.

"Well sir, I'm of the opinion, from what we know of him before, that he's in this up to his neck. It's like Cabot to surround himself with people of his stripe, and Eddins is certainly that. I think we should include him on our list of boils to be removed. He's escaped once, up in Albemarle County, and he has it coming."

"No doubt you're right, but again, he was released from jail there, and we haven't compiled much solid against him, either here or in the capital. I'm afraid we're still floundering here as we were in Philadelphia, without a clear course of action before us."

"Clear enough for me," was all Chiles would comment on that.

Mason also chafed at being away from home this long, on what had so far turned out to be a fruitless quest. But the decision by Stephen Davis and the others to wait for Reginald Cabot's return still seemed the best course. Mason felt the whole affair would come to a head at that time, for better or worse. If the man made a move against him and Chiles, they'd defend themselves, and it would all be over.

He continued a train of thought he'd been exploring for some time: force Cabot into some action that would bring about the elusive confrontation they needed. For that they'd need a clear-cut, powerful accusation the man couldn't brush aside. He discussed this with Chiles.

"Well, sir, my recommendation is to capture the assassin Garst, and make him admit that Cabot hired him to kill first you, then Lester Cummings. I'm quite sure I can devise a way to get the information out of him. And with that evidence in our arsenal, we'd have the right to hang Cabot ourselves. I'm sure the good people of Ketchum's Mill, once they knew the facts, would support us."

"That wouldn't be quite legal, though, in accordance with the law."

"The villagers have already protected themselves against outlaws twice, by the direct action of shooting them dead. How is this different?"

Mason considered this for a few moments. Chiles was certainly right. Both Davis and Ketchum had killed the marauders who'd attacked their people. And there had been that ambush of the MacNaughton clan the sheriff here in Saltville had headed. Clearly, frontier justice was—had to be—direct, as Chiles had said.

But then, with that reasoning, why not just go ahead and kill Garst and Cabot, and yes, Eddins too, outright. Certainly the evidence they'd compiled against them should justify that. But Mason knew they couldn't depart that far from the legal and moral course the new country espoused.

The end result of their lengthy discussion of the matter was that Mason agreed they should indeed pressure Hiram Garst to reveal Cabot's crimes, then act accordingly, along with the settlers. Communities of isolated people had always been compelled to protect themselves forcefully, and that would be the case there.

~ * ~

Reginald Cabot's personal anger at being thwarted by the man Wadsworth had cooled as he returned south. In its place was forming a more business-like plan to carry out his original purpose: remove the competition. If he didn't do that, he couldn't possibly sell his iron at the prices he'd have to get.

But common sense told him he couldn't repeat Garst's actions this soon. Too many people would see through that, and he could envision the countryside rising up against him. This sparsely-settled region wasn't likely to produce a mob, but then it didn't take many of those hard-eyed frontiersmen to band together to avenge a wrong. Another strike at the Jackson River works and its new owner would be seen as a major blow to the livelihoods of a lot of men. And it wouldn't take a genius to figure who'd profit from such an action.

So his method would be simple robbery. He'd gather some desperate men of his own and they would lie in wait for Jackson River iron shipments south toward Saltville. That way he'd get the product free, resell it at his inflated prices, and while not a perfect solution, it would do till he could work out something better. He would not let those other New Englanders best him in this.

Of course, he'd have to pay those highwaymen, but hell, a man had to pay for everything. The kind of men he'd need were those who didn't plan beyond the next day's whiskey, ready women, and the fun of taking what didn't belong to them. He could put Garst in charge of that part of the operation.

Of course, too obvious an undertaking of that sort would soon attract attention, and sooner or later that busybody sheriff at Saltville might mount something like that ambush of the MacNaughton clan. But if the shipments were robbed over a long stretch of the pike, the system should work for the near future. The important thing was to stop any other source of iron getting to the southwest Virginia/ Kentucky territory long enough for him to make this iron venture pay.

And in time, another accident could be arranged for the flinty Elijah Wadsworth, late of Massachusetts. *Damn New Englanders, anyway.* Well, he was from there, too, and he certainly knew how to play their game.

A more dangerous, deadly game.

~ * ~

Carver MacNaughton had, since his arrival at Ketchum's Mill that spring, become a completely different young man. He'd accepted the hard work as the only way out for him after his botched plans for a career as a dashing robber. Now, with his increasing proficiency as a blacksmith, he could justifiably take pride in his accomplishments. He was encouraged by everyone and had drawn quite close to the two former soldiers, Campbell and Epsworth.

He'd always had an eye for Alice McKnight, the minister's younger daughter, especially so after her abduction by his outlaw brother and her subsequent rescue. Her clinging to him out on that mountain trail was for him a life-changing experience, one he wouldn't forget, ever. He always sat close to her in the schoolroom and stole glances at her whenever she passed the smithy. She always had a smile for him.

Carver was acutely aware of the differences between them: her educated family primarily, as opposed to his barely-literate state. But folks here seemed not to hold that against him, so perhaps with time, he might prove he was worthy of her. He figured a couple more years of hard work and study would show everyone who mattered that he was a solid young man with future prospects.

He had been devastated at the news of Stephen Davis' death. He'd wanted to be the one to go down that rope to find the body, but Archie Nolan had insisted. Now he was getting used to Stephen's being gone, but not Anna's absence. The teacher had inspired him to work and study hard, but her replacement, Tildy Driscoll, didn't have that kind of charisma. This teacher ran a tight ship, tolerated no nonsense, and drove the students to the limits of their abilities.

"Best to set a high bar for 'em," was her explanation to a concerned parent of a struggling child. "Grade it down for th' slow ones, and you punish th' sharp ones. Better to bring 'em all along, aim high. If some of 'em don't get it, that's just the way it'll have to be."

Carver told himself repeatedly that it didn't matter; learning was the important thing. But he'd really liked the tall woman who'd slammed him against that wall and jolted some sense into him. Liked her still, but the picture of her, clad in black, alone up in that hollow, was the saddest thing he could imagine.

And Carver MacNaughton didn't believe for an instant that Stephen had stumbled over that cliff. He'd pegged Reginald Cabot for a pompous, overbearing and maybe even dangerous man from the first time he'd seen him. He resented the man, to put it simply. Oh, he'd provided work for them all, spread his money around like butter, but also made it clear, at least to Carver, that he was 'way up on a pedestal of some kind, above the plain folk here.

He talked cautiously about this feeling with his housemates, Todd and Harvey, one Sunday afternoon.

"He's like a high-up officer in th' army, Carver," Todd made the comparison. "Maybe stuck-up, hard t'like, even mean. But, end of th' day, he's th' one in charge, and th' troops don't have to like him."

"But I get th' feelin' he thainks he's...bought us all. Don't y'all s'spect that?"

"Maybe a little," Harvey put in, tapping out his pipe. "When you look at it, any man's built himself a business can hire other folks to work for him, he's got 'em a lot like slaves. Free t'go an' come, but dependin' so much on that pay, they won't leave, unless he's so bad they can't stand it."

"Well, 'nother thaing...I won't b'lieve all he's said 'bout Stephen Davis fallin' offa that cliff, don't care whut ennybody else thainks."

"Now, what makes you say that, Carver?" Todd asked, his keen eyes on the boy. These two were closer than anyone else in the village, outside families.

"Th' way Archie Nolan told it, that's whut. Said he'n Stillwell was on down th' ridge, an' nobody but Cabot an' Stephen up at th' edge. Now, Stephen wuz as good on a hoss as ennybody I ever seen. So, sayin' he *didn't* stumble, whut's thet leave you?"

"Now that's right close to accusin' Cabot of murder, boy," Harvey Campbell pointed out, catching Epsworth's eye.

"Don't keer whut it is...I'm sayin' th' man pushed him. Spooked his hoss. Oh, mebbe I'm jist some s'picious, been around too many bad'uns, but that's th' way I see it." He looked from one to the other with a spark of defiance. "An' I'd like t'know jist whut you'n's thaink."

Todd looked out the window of the cabin at the browning, drifting leaves, noting the chill in the fall air. Then he turned to Harvey with a question on his face. Harvey cleared his throat.

"Gotta remember, Carver, we're all Christians here. Not s'posed to condemn a man, or point fingers at others, 'cause we all got our faults. But now you bring it up, neither one of us believes that'uz an accident, either. We don't know what kinda grudge Cabot coulda had against Stephen, but we've heard enough about his bustin' up a gang of thieves back in Virginia t'know there's prob'ly people were out to git him.

"Now, I can't imagine Cabot'd be one of them, but take that feller Garst, him so close to th' boss an' all, an' now in charge…I c'd see him as th' type. An' some way, yes, they could both be in somethin' bad." He refilled his pipe reflectively.

"All of us got our doubts 'bout Mr. Cabot, Carver," Todd picked it up, "comin' in here, spendin' money like water, maybe tryin', like you said, t'buy his way. An' now Archie tells us th' iron ore will play out here next year, so that's kinda a mystery. Just what is th' man doin' here? We don't know, and so far, we been all right with just waitin' around to see.

"But it don't take a smart man t'figger that with that ironworks up on Jackson River goin' down, an' Cabot's hustlin' off up there, he's gonna try to take that over. Now, t'me it seems some odd that his man Garst went off on some piece of business, then right soon we get word the owner up there, Cummings, has died in'n accident and th' operation's burned out. Now that's just gotta look just too convenient t'me." He looked at Harvey.

"And I reckon there *could* be some connection with Stephen, but we don't know what that c'd be," his friend continued. "So all we got is suspicions. But for me, ennything Garst's connected with has a dark side to it, don't y'all think?"

"Oh, he's a sly one," Carver agreed. "Wouldn't trust thet snake fur's I c'd th'ow him."

"So maybe he'd told Cabot somethin' about Stephen, happened back in Virginia. And some way, they thought he'd maybe find out too much down here. Long shot, but it fits, if Cabot *did* have somethin' t'do with Stephen dyin'."

Just then someone hailed them from down the track. Archie Nolan rode into view, dismounted, tied his horse. The three opened their door to him.

"Good t'see you, Archie," Harvey welcomed him. As the oldest of the trio, he'd assumed a sort of senior brother relationship to Todd and Carver. "C'mon in an' set a spell."

Nolan nodded to the others, removed his hat, and took the proffered chair before the slow fire. He hadn't been a frequent visitor lately, explaining that he wanted to get in as much prospecting as possible before winter. In truth, he'd spent a lot of time at the Davis cabin, helping wherever he could.

"Enny news?" Todd asked the white-haired prospector.

"Not a bunch. Been goin' way out, lookin' for iron ore's 'bout all. Stoppin' by t'help Miss Anna a little now'n then. But she's managing, doin' well's could be expected."

"Poor woman," Todd commiserated. "We all miss Stephen, but it's gotta be so much harder on her, losin' him so soon. Less'n a year they had." He shook his head sadly.

"Bad, all right. So what you men know? Anything new while I been out in th' woods?"

"Naw, we's just hashin' over stuff," Harvey replied. Then he fixed the man with a penetrating look. "We *was* talkin' over th' way Stephen had that accident. Know you've told us all there is t'tell, but th' three of us, we still got a doubt or two."

"Or three," Carver put in.

"Well, like I said," and Nolan stretched his feet toward the fire, "Stilwell and I were on down the ridge towards where we could get down into that draw. Heard Cabot call Stephen up where he was, right at the edge." He glanced from one to the other of the listening men, all of whom had leaned forward eagerly.

"Now I remember it, Stephen had held back some all the way up there. Guess that was from him bein' in the army and all...always liked to keep things and people out in front where he could see them.

Anyway, we didn't see him ride up, just heard Cabot yell that he'd gone over." He spread his hands.

"How long, would y'say?" Campbell asked, his eyes keen. He was envisioning the scene.

"Oh, just real quick. Wouldn't've had time t'see whatever it was Cabot wanted him for. Almost like he rode right over the edge, no longer'n that."

"All right. Now I'm gonna ask you, Archie, an' I want you to tell me true, whether you think t'was really an accident or not?"

Nolan looked from one concerned face to another. He had to decide whether or not to trust these men. Certainly, Stephen wanted his recovery kept quiet, but they could use help. He decided to go halfway.

"No, I don't, Harvey. I think our benevolent Mr. Cabot shoved Stephen over, or at least spooked his horse. Why, I don't know, but I do know there's a lot more behind the man than what he shows us. Now, where we're supposed to go with this will be up to you all and the rest of the settlement." He waited for a response.

"Oughta hang th' man," Carver blurted. He'd been so torn up over Stephen's supposed death that having someone to blame was like a dam bursting.

"Now, we ain't got proof," Todd cautioned them. "Can't go accusin' th' man of somethin' that serious without proof. B'sides, half th' folks here would come down on us hard, way he's set ever'body up."

"But let's look at that a minute," Nolan proposed. "Not enough ore close to keep the operation going past spring, and too expensive to expand. Now, I couldn't know that ahead of time, and warned him of it, but he wanted to go ahead. So what does that say about what he'll do, then? Have to shut down, that's what. And this place'll dry up, no more than the folks can grow crops to feed themselves. I don't know why he came here in the first place, but he'll lose everything in the iron business, and the people who depend on it, too."

"Wondered about that, when y'first said there was only so much here," Harvey mused. "World's fulla speculators tryin' to get rich, make th' wrong choices, an' that may be all this is. But with what we s'spect about Stephen, and th' man Garst bein' here, it's all got a bad smell to it."

"Now, I think we've all got to th' place where we agree Garst's an evil man," Todd agreed. "Tries to hide it, comin' to church and all, but it shows, 'least to me, he's always lookin' for a way to do some meanness. So, by him bein' that close t'Cabot, that adds some to what we're talkin' about."

The men were silent a while, staring distractedly into the fire. Finally, Carver MacNaughton had a new thought.

"Y'don't s'pose Cabot's blamin' you fer th' ore runnin' out, do you, Mr. Nolan? I mean, like he thainks you mebbe got him in here, caused him t'spend all thet money, then tole him wasn't 'nough here? Reckon he'd go after you, er send Garst t'do it?"

"Well, I hadn't thought of that, but it's possible. I didn't lead him on one bit, expecting him to put just a small operation in here to supply a few settlements. But the man doesn't do anything in a small way, and I'd say he got greedy, took what I told him the way he wanted it to be."

"All right, I been thinkin' too," Harvey said. "How d'you figger this feller Carson an' his man Bone into it?"

"Nobody seems to know what they're up to," Nolan replied. "They haven't bought any iron, as far as anybody knows, and have hung around a long time. Gone now, but you have to wonder why they'd come all the way out here with that idea of mill machinery, with a better market back east."

"Thet feller Bone scares me," Carver shuddered. "I git th' notion th' man'd soon shootcha as look at you, you crossed him."

"But he don't seem to be looking for trouble, like Garst," Todd countered. "I like Bone, f'r some reason. Seems t'me like more of a...bodyguard t'Carson than a businessman, though. An' remember, he's old army, like us, and that c'n leave a man sorta hard."

Nolan ached to let these good men in on the truth, but that ultimate disclosure would, of course, be up to Stephen, when he reported their feelings to him later. And he wanted to find out more, get an idea just how far their suspicions reached. Maybe it'd be an indication of how more of the settlers viewed all this.

"Been thinking, men...just suppose we *did* uncover something, like being able to prove Cabot killed Stephen, or that he's a wanted man—something like that. What'd be your thinking, then?"

Harvey Campbell eyed him keenly. That old soldier was a sharp one, Nolan realized. He hoped he wasn't letting too much out, but he did want to hear what they thought.

"You know somethin' we don't, I'll wager, Archie. Or strong s'spect somethin'. But yeah, then we'd hafta have us a hangin', I reckon. Folks here thought too much of Stephen to stand for anybody killin' him, no matter th' reason."

"Not to pass judgment," Todd agreed, "but I'll hafta go with Harvey on that'n. Stephen was th' best man I ever met, and Miss Anna, she's 'bout as close to an angel as we'll see this side of Jordan. I'd say God would s'pect us t'handle that, sorta be His hands, here."

"Amen," from Carver.

Twenty-seven

Reginald Cabot had reached a decision regarding the recalcitrant New Englander Wadsworth. After the several-day ride back to Saltville, he went straight to Samuel Eddins' office in the new warehouse.

"Well sir, how'd it go on the Jackson?" the lawyer asked him, offering a half tumbler of whiskey and pouring himself one.

"Didn't go well at all, I'm afraid. Cousin's taken over and doing the helluva job getting the operation up again. Wouldn't even talk about a sale. Damned discouraging at first, until I thought it out on the way back." He took a deep swallow.

"Ah, another plan, then. I knew you weren't the man to let a setback like that stop you."

"No, not at all. Here's what we'll do, Eddins: let him get set up again, but before he can ship much at all, which will be spring, he'll meet with another accident. Have to be well-thought out, but we'll work on that. The point is, you'll prepare papers showing the sale of the entire operation to me, dated just before his death. Then, despite whatever his men might protest, that should hold up in court, shouldn't it?"

"Well, done right, it certainly will. The trick will be to avoid any taint of complicity in his...passing. I don't see how we can use Garst again, for instance."

"No, we'll have to be more subtle than that. But we'll have the winter to plan it. And in the meantime, I want you to set up a system of confiscating any and all Jackson River iron shipped to this region." And Cabot gave his lawyer the details of the planned hijackings of Wadsworth's shipments. Eddins fairly beamed at this assignment, envisioning an endless supply of iron to be resold, at almost one hundred percent profit.

"Oh, I suppose you've heard the ore supply is petering out at Ketchum's?" Cabot went on.

"I did hear, and I feel that man Nolan misled you with his projections."

"Maybe a little. I'll confess to just hoping for more, though. Doesn't matter in the long run...we'll not miss a delivery, with the Jackson River works coming into my hands before the Kentucky operation slows. I *had* planned to stay in Ketchum's Mill, it being virtually beyond prying eyes, but I believe now I can establish myself somewhere closer to civilization and still prosper."

"In Ketchum's, and even here in Saltville, there's little to offer in refinement, I'll agree. Of course, all that'll change, once we have control of the market in the whole region. Our trade will be good for everybody. Prosperity will follow."

Cabot had noticed before how the lawyer always referred to the enterprise as belonging to "us" instead of to him, the real owner. Obviously, the man fancied himself a sort of partner, and that was all right, for the present. But lawyers could be bought anywhere, and if Eddins were to become too brash, Cabot could certainly replace him.

"Like a horseshoe," he mumbled.

"What's that, sir?"

"Oh, nothing. Have to get my horse shod, is all. Well, you be working on the details of what we've discussed. You'll need a land description of the works up there on the Jackson, and I'll authorize you to send someone for that. I'll go on back to Ketchum's, get set up for winter work."

"Certainly. But I fear there won't be much to occupy you there till spring."

"Oh, I've a pursuit in mind that'll fit in quite well with the weather." He was thinking of the attractive Anna Davis. Then, as he stood to retrieve his hat, another thought came.

"By the bye, have you heard from that fellow Carson? Has he actually bought any iron yet?"

"No, he hasn't. He came by here with some more sketches, then disappeared. I think he and that Bone fellow have left the region for parts unknown. I'd say we're rid of him, whatever his business really was. Strange people."

"Yes, had his head in the clouds about those inventions of his, although Davis and Ketchum said they were sound. Well, as you said, strange, both of them." He took his leave, envisioning the coming months, snug in the inn, or calling on the young widow up at her cabin.

That thought made him smile.

~ * ~

Keeping well out of sight, Jedediah Mason and Leighton Chiles nevertheless also kept a keen eye on the warehouse and office of Samuel Eddins. So they observed, from a distance through a spyglass, the arrival and departure of their quarry. Cabot mounted and rode off, still early in the day, toward Ketchum's Mill.

"Well, we don't know whether or not he was able to buy the Jackson River works," Mason mused, "but he's headed back for the village, it seems. So as we agreed, we'll follow, and one way or the other, force things to a head once we're all back there."

"Can't be soon enough for me, sir," Chiles responded. He'd had quite enough of playing cat and mouse with the elusive Cabot, even before they'd left Philadelphia. Now he just wanted an end to it, one that would remove this smooth villain and his assassin from the face of the earth. He'd been patient with his employer's hesitation, but now vowed to himself to take the situation into his own hands at first opportunity. Caution was all right in the capital, where law and a sense of order prevailed, but this was the frontier, where a man had to dispense justice to protect himself and others. And do it decisively.

Chiles also thought of Stephen Davis, crippled by Cabot, no doubt in revenge for the destruction of the criminal operation back upstate. And while he remembered that Davis had agreed to wait, he felt the man would approve direct action: blowing Cabot into pieces. That this craftsman and his young wife should suffer at the criminal's hand was intolerable to Chiles...decent people should not suffer from the greed and avarice of others.

So if it were meant that he, Leighton Chiles, would be the instrument of Cabot's elimination, so be it. He was ready, and quite capable of the task.

As the two men followed Cabot along the road to Ketchum's Mill, Chiles devised plans to carry out his mission. He'd like to be able to keep on his employer's good side, of course, which would mean waiting for more evidence, or having to defend themselves against an attack. That didn't seem like a good idea, given the nature of the men they were up against. Chiles had learned that gun battles often were complicated, messy, and prone to get out of hand.

He didn't like the prospect of shooting men from cover, either. Perhaps they'd need help then, to confront their quarry directly, with backup to ensure the right outcome.

Chiles would continue to plan his own course, while Mason was also trying to devise a strategy that would achieve the same end.

~ * ~

Carver MacNaughton was more convinced than ever that Reginald Cabot had deliberately killed Stephen Davis. The youth had grown up with meanness, seen greed, cowardice, scheming, violence all his life. The peaceful village had become a haven for him, and being around decent people had opened a door for him he hadn't imagined existed.

Now, for the man who'd given him his chance for a good life to have been ruthlessly murdered kindled in him a fierce thirst for justice. He began to plot to avenge Stephen's death. Surrounded by the missionaries, who were committed to forgiveness and tolerance, Carver nevertheless saw in his friends Harvey and Todd a steely backbone of perhaps military principle, the need to right wrongs. Just how that fit with the Biblical teachings they studied, he didn't quite know.

But there had to be justification for making things right, he was sure. It seemed to have something to do with becoming God's instrument of righteousness, the way he understood it from Reverend McKnight's preaching. The minister had cautioned that people must not assume they were those instruments, just because they felt the need. No, he'd emphasized, justice and revenge were the Lord's, not to be taken into folks' own hands.

But he'd also acknowledged that people had to protect themselves from evil, and that's where it got sticky for Carver. What was the difference, he wondered, between defending yourself from somebody who was out to kill you during the attack, or before it could happen? Jesus had said turn the other cheek, but Carver knew from experience that'd get you stomped bad. And it wasn't in his nature to let somebody meaner than him get him like that.

Of course, Cabot wasn't after Carver MacNaughton himself. But he'd killed a good man, and probably a lot of others, kind of man he was. It was all very confusing, and neither Harvey nor Todd could shed much light on the proper course. All three of them shared the belief that Cabot was guilty, but the situation was too complicated for them to tackle outright.

"I know I oughtn't say it," Carver ventured, "but I thaink it'd be best fer us all if somebody jist laid fer th' man an' done 'im in, like he done Stephen."

"We feel th' same way," Harvey agreed, "but as Christians, we must wait t'learn God's will in this. Th' Bible says he who lives by th' sword dies by it, an' that's what'll catch up with Cabot, sooner er later."

"Besides," Todd reflected, "we still don't know all th' facts. Could be we're seein' just what we want to, here. No, best wait an' see what's s'posed to happen, even if it means it galls us."

Well it surely did gall Carver, and he wasn't about to let this go just yet.

~ * ~

Stephen Davis saw the changing season with impatience. He'd recovered during those weeks of Cabot's absence, to the extent that he felt he could aid Mason and Chiles in dealing with the man and his assassin. And the conviction that they should act quickly grew in him. It just wasn't wise to let that snake—two snakes—live among them any longer. Archie Nolan would stand by him when he told of Cabot's cowardly attempted murder, and that should be enough in itself to justify the settlers' executing the man. And then there were Mason and Chiles, who could and were eager to add their findings to the charges.

But Anna, while she agreed that Cabot must go, and soon, would not consider Stephen's confronting him. Or lying in wait to shoot him. Or taking any part in dispensing this justice now, while he was still weak and a long way from complete recovery. She would not allow him to engage in an action that might get out of control. Having almost lost her husband, she was determined to keep him safe.

And if that meant she herself must destroy Cabot, then she'd have to make her peace with God about that. The man would try again, just as soon as he learned he'd failed the first time. And there was that evil Hiram Garst to deal with also...

No, there was no room here for hesitancy.

Accordingly, Anna spent time well away in the woods ostensibly hunting, but also honing her shooting skill. She fancied she could keep cool under fire, and drilled herself to make sure her first shot would always drop an enemy before he could drop her. The advantage lay in the fact that men just didn't expect women to be armed, or to be able to hit what they aimed at if they were.

Surprise, Mr. Reginald Cabot: this woman won't give you another chance at her man.

~ * ~

Killebrew Ketchum had fumed ever since the news of Stephen's death. Since first learning of the craftsman's skill at milling and smithing, a bond had grown between them. And that bond had strengthened when the two of them had killed the MacNaughton cousins in their attempt to attack the missionary women. And later too, Ketchum had been in the forefront of the settlers tracking the abductor of the minister's daughter.

Killy Ketchum was not a complicated man. His life had been one of clearcut purpose, be it establishing a mill or dealing with injustice. And while reluctant to believe that Reginald Cabot would deliberately shove Stephen off that cliff, he couldn't accept the fact that it'd been an accident. It was just too complicated, that situation, but he'd lived long enough to know that evil men often were the smooth operators like Cabot, masking their misdeeds in generosity and good works.

The village he and Belle had established here at the end of the world had grown prosperous, thanks to the man's investments, but for the miller it all had a taint of corruption. And now, with the death of his closest friend, he couldn't just sit still and let things go on without some action.

He met again with Archie Nolan, the man who knew the most about the prospecting expedition. Not that anything had been left out of his report, but in an effort to determine a course of action. Ketchum wanted to know whether he should begin forming a sort of citizen's group to take whatever action against Cabot the settlers could agree on.

"Problem is, too many folks depend on th' ironworks now," he observed as he and the prospector settled before the fireplace in the quarters attached to the mill. "'Fraid they'd ride me outta town on a rail if I spoke out er done ennything 'gainst th' man."

"Maybe not," his friend began. "I know for a fact that some of us don't believe Cabot's all he says he is. And you might be surprised at how much support you'd have if you put together such a movement." He was thinking of Stephen's working with Mason and Chiles. Of course, he understood the fewer who knew of the craftsman's existence the better, but he'd wondered why Stephen hadn't confided in Ketchum. Or for that matter, the quartet of Carver MacNaughton, Harvey Campbell, Todd Epsworth and the rock-solid

George Wellerby. Put together, that core of responsible men would be a formidable force.

And at that moment, Nolan decided he'd encourage Ketchum in his idea. Wouldn't hurt to have the villagers on their side when they acted against Cabot, which would be as soon as the man returned from his trip north. Yes, and it was also time to elect someone to enforce law around there, instead of letting Cabot run things as he had.

"Been thinking, Killy…who'd you say would be the best man to take on the job of constable here? We're big enough now to need one, and there's been too much meanness already."

"That'd been Stephen, fer shore, an' that burns me moren' ever," the miller responded. "But now? Hafta be somebody th' folks'd respect." He reflected for a moment. "Not one of th' missionaries, though Harvey er Todd'd be good. Naw, need a tough man, but one could do th' job with th' people behind him." He thought some more, gazing into the flames, going over the men who'd come to constitute this outpost.

"Would you take the job?" Nolan asked him. He too, had been considering prospects in his mind. Now he hastened to shore up a case before the astonished miller could object. "You know how Cabot's tried to take over the place, like it was his little kingdom. You and Belle built what was here when I first came, and you should rightfully keep control of at least that aspect of it. I don't want Cabot dictating to us, and I surely don't want him appointing Hiram Garst to the job."

"I'd heard he was mebbe plannin' t'do just that, all right. But me? I've got th' mill an' th' smithy t'run, an' Belle, she's got th' inn an' all. How 'bout George? Good man, an' no nonsense 'bout him."

"Yes, but I don't think George would be…well, hard enough, if you know what I mean. This job would take judgment, and a willingness to take whatever action necessary, with no holding back. Yes, Stephen would have been ideal, but he and I had spoken of it, and he was set on just being a family man. He'd had more than his share of keeping the peace, you know."

"Well, yeah, that's true. Makes me madder ever' time I think 'bout him dyin' thataway."

"I even seem to remember he mentioned you'd be the man for the job," Nolan went on, pressing his point. "You know everybody here, the good and the bad, and we all know you'd be fair, no matter what the situation. Or *who*," he added significantly, knowing Ketchum wasn't really intimidated by Reginald Cabot and all his money.

"Um. Well, I'd hafta study on that some, I reckon, Archie. Talk with Belle on that 'un, all right. Hadn't thought none 'bout such as that."

"Well, you just think about it, Killy. I know we'd all be behind you all the way, if you'd take the job. And of course, we'd come up with a salary of some kind, since any time you'd spend away from the mill and smithy would cost you."

"'Preciate that. An' I will think on it, now it's come up."

~ * ~

With the return of Reginald Cabot imminent, Stephen decided he needed to consolidate the forces against the man. He wanted to include Killebrew Ketchum, Harvey Campbell, Todd Epsworth, and George Weller in the core group who'd know he was still alive. He'd have to caution Killy against telling his wife; Belle could easily let something slip. That'd be six men, and he'd be the seventh. When they acted, which they would, Cabot and Garst wouldn't stand a chance against them.

"But you won't be the seventh man," his wife told him firmly. "If I have to tie you up, you're not going out against those two in the shape you're in." The look she gave him said there was no negotiating this stand.

"I'm getting stronger every day."

"Nobody ever comes all the way back from what you've been through. God gave you back to me, and I won't lose you, Stephen. Six good men can take care of two outlaws, if we do it right. Be content with helping plan it. Please." She didn't add that she could well be the seventh dispenser of justice, if it somehow came to that.

"I guess you're right, and I shouldn't think I'm that necessary. We've a family to put ahead of everything, I know. It just rankles that I must let someone else do the job I'm meant for."

"That's what loyal friends are for. Thank heaven you've many of them."

So it was that Stephen requested that Archie Nolan arrange another meeting immediately, ahead of Cabot's expected return. That would be before Mason and Chiles could join them, but the plan would be to have everything they could in place. If they waited, Cabot or Garst might see or hear something that would make them suspect. One man could later bring the investigator and his assistant up to date on the plan, avoiding any sort of additional group council.

It was imperative that Garst not suspect any activity against him or Cabot. He was running the ironworks as smoothly as could be expected, and Stephen wanted him to think all was normal. He'd no doubt the man would act boldly at the first sign of trouble, whether Cabot were present or not.

The meeting took place after dark, with the men riding singly and quietly out of the village. Campbell and Epsworth told Carver MacNaughton they were going to a gathering of the core missionary group. Campbell rode ahead while his friend waited near the church, then followed.

Nolan had told each man only that Anna Davis had asked that he come to her house with him.

"There's something important she has to tell us," was all he'd say, other than she wanted it kept strictly quiet from everyone else. That request raised some eyebrows, but since these men all were suspicious of Cabot to some degree, they complied.

Killebrew Ketchum told Belle he'd promised to go to the Campbell/Epsworth cabin to hear some of their war stories. George Weller, who routinely visited practically everyone in the village, simply walked off as he usually did from Daughtry's house, telling him he'd be back sometime later.

Archie Nolan waited till the last man had slipped off up the creek trail, watching to see if anyone had taken notice. Garst was inside the inn, along with several of the ironworkers and the engineer Thad Stillwell. Belle and her helpers were serving supper to the gathering at the long tables.

The prospector followed the others, and once past hearing, increased his horse's pace to catch up. He'd told them to wait at the entrance path up to the Davis cabin, in part because he didn't want to miss the expressions on their faces when they saw Stephen.

So it was that Anna welcomed them with a radiant smile instead of the grieving countenance they'd come to associate with new widows. She seated them and brought mugs of hot cider from the kettle at the fireplace. Apples had always been among the priorities of the settlers when ordering supplies from Saltville.

"Now, gentlemen, with the exception of Mr. Nolan, you will receive a surprise," and she opened the door to the other half of the cabin. Stephen, still on his crutches, swung in, his own face wearing a wide grin.

"Oh, my Gawd!" Killebrew Ketchum burst out, bolting upright. The others echoed his astonishment.

"Yes, it's God's work," Harvey and Todd said almost simultaneously. George stepped forward, speechless, to give his best friend a hand, and his face was beaming.

"I'd have to say, the word of my passing has been a little premature," Stephen stated. "I'm a bit short of healed, but that won't take long, thanks to Anna and Archie. Now, please sit down, all of you, and let's talk about some serious things." He set the crutches aside as he sank into a padded chair.

"How did this happen?" a chorus of voices asked Archie, whose expression was one of mischievous glee. "You've gotta tell us all about this, first off."

"Well," Stephen responded, "it seems that our Mr. Cabot, instead of being the settlement's benefactor, is actually a notorious thief and outlaw back in the civilized world. Came here, I suspect, to hide from the law, and perhaps also from enemies he's made. He's the one shoved me over the cliff, as I'm told by Archie that you men have suspected. Must have found out I helped wipe out a profitable but illegal scheme of his and some others' up in Albemarle County. No doubt lawyer Eddins told him, since he was part of that ring. The only one who survived, I might add."

"I knowed it." Killy Ketchum struck his fist into his palm. "Y'couldna fell offa thet cliff 'less you wuz pushed."

"No, like a fool I rode close to see what Cabot was pointing out down below, and when he kicked my horse, it lost its footing. Archie can tell you I caught on a stout tree on the way down, tore it out of the ground, but it slowed me and I landed on a ledge in a shower of rocks. You all know my horse wasn't as fortunate."

"Stephen," big George Wellerby swore, "Cabot's a dead man, soon's he gits back here. No 'restin' him, no trial, no jedge ner nothin'. We gotta look after our own, an' 'tempted murder gits you strung up rat quick." He looked to the others for support.

Killy Ketchum just nodded, and looked at the two missionaries. Harvey, the hardened veteran, nodded, and Todd had his eyes focused on something far away.

"Vengeance is mine, sayeth the Lord," he quoted, but his hands were clenching and loosening, as if he wanted to rip Reginald Cabot to shreds. "What do you think, Miss Anna?"

"I've struggled with this, Todd, and what I should do as a Christian. But I've come to the conclusion that anything less than destroying Cabot is the wrong thing to do. Not just for what he did to Stephen, but what he's surely done to many others, including Lester Cummings, who had the ironworks on Jackson River. And to let him live to kill others is surely not God's will."

Then all eyes turned to Stephen, who'd listened carefully.

"It was easier in the war," he began. "Enemy was sighting on you, and you had to defend yourself. I'm afraid I see little or no difference here. Archibald Carson and Martin Bone-—and those aren't their real names—have been after Cabot for years, back in the capital. Carson wants clear proof, but Bone is ready to act, and I'd say he will, whether his boss says so or not. He's a man who sees situations like this in clear black and white. Now, they'll be back here shortly to help. I'm almost certain Cabot suspects these men and will order Garst to kill them or do it himself.

"So, not as vengeance for his attempt on me, but to protect us all here, I'm for eliminating the threat, as Anna says. I'd like it to be done with some sense of legal order, if no more than explaining to the villagers what he's done and getting their approval." He scanned the faces around him for their reaction.

"Might be hard t'get that," Harvey mused. "Lotta folks makes their livin' from th' works."

"I thaink, when th' rest've 'em sees Stephen alive, an' hears whut Cabot done, they'll git behind us," George offered.

"I think you're right," Todd agreed, his late hesitancy apparently set aside. "But what about Garst? We ain't got anything clearcut we c'n point to on him."

"Mason—that's his real name—believes Cabot tried to kill him too," Stephen supplied. "He had Bone—Chiles is his name—protecting the man Garst was apparently sent to kill, thinking he was Mason. Chiles got a look at the attacker, and swears it was Garst. I'd say Cabot sent Garst to kill Lester Cummings too, so he could take over his ironworks.

"You all know there's not enough ore here to justify the size operation he's set up. I think he means to grab all the foundry operations in the whole region, so he can set his own prices. And he's counting on the fact that we *don't* have effective law enforcement out here to stop him."

"Whut we do have ourselves is frontier justice," Ketchum put in grimly. "We gotta take keer of our own here, an' we done it b'fore, thanks t'you, Stephen. I'd say we should set up a welcomin' bunch th' minnit th' man rides in, an' waste no time stretchin' his neck. Garst, too."

"Well, I like the idea of the leaders among us taking on this thing," Stephen agreed, "instead of somebody just shooting those two from cover. Killy, I know Archie's approached you about taking on law enforcement, here. Would you take the job if we elected you properly?"

"I reckon so, Stephen, if you won't do it. You're a sight better at such as thet than me."

"This is your village, all of us feel. If you'll take on the task of defending it, I'm certain we'll all support you, and I know I'd be most grateful. Anna doesn't want me getting shot, what with our family on the way." He cast a fond look at his wife.

That took a moment to sink in, but then Archie Nolan's face opened in a grin.

"Well, that's fine news, Stephen, Miss Anna. Boys, you heard him...there's going to be a little Davis coming along. When, Miss Anna?"

"Early summertime. We didn't want to tell anyone before we'd settled the Cabot business, and let it be known the father is still among us." She squeezed Stephen's hand, and her smile lighted the room.

"Wal, I'll jist be switched!" Big George let out, and he started to slap Stephen on the back. Anna stopped him in time. "Oh, yeah, you're some tender, ain'tcha? Wal, I'm jist thet happy fer th' botha you." He bowed to Anna, then did a little jig that shook the house. The others crowded around, congratulating the couple.

The meeting ended with the agreement that the villagers would be informed of Ketchum's nomination as constable, to be voted on immediately. They agreed also on compensation, since the miller would necessarily be away from his livliehood on occasion. Archie Nolan would spread the news on the morrow.

Each man swore to keep the secret of Stephen's survival, and each focused on the goal of ridding the settlement of Cabot and Garst as soon as the two could be arrested. Yes, they'd tell everyone what kind of men these were, and hope that enough of the villagers would support their execution. None of the others had any doubt that after hearing Stephen's account of the alleged accident, everyone would agree to the hanging.

Twenty-eight

Reginald Cabot rode into Ketchum's Mill late at night, after all but the innkeeper were abed. Belle had not been included in the plans to arrest the man, and she welcomed him, fed him, and saw him to his customary room. Killebrew was snoring peacefully when she entered their bedroom, and she saw no reason to wake him.

So not another soul knew of Cabot's return. Even Hiram Garst had gone to sleep in his own room after a genial game of chance among the ironworkers and the engineer Stillwell. He was to sleep late, then nurse a hangover when he did get moving next morning.

Cabot awoke in high spirits after his short sleep, full of plans to harass the Jackson River iron shipments and push his workers for more output before serious snow time. That was almost upon them, he knew, but he'd do it anyway.

And he'd decided this was the day he'd go call on the widow Davis. He'd be full of contrition at not having expressed his grief before, but well, business had demanded. Surely the lady would understand that he put the welfare of the village ahead of anything else, especially with winter coming on and the future uncertain.

Altogether, he felt his usual confidence in his ability to shower the object of his desire with whatever blandishments, gifts, promises were necessary to win her. It should be a pleasant task.

He'd meant to report to Hiram Garst first thing, but visions of the young widow had filled his head on this last leg of his journey, and he asked himself, why not? No time like the present, he reasoned. Time for catching up on business later.

But he thought it best to keep his courtship quiet for the present. The good people of the settlement might take it amiss if he proceeded too soon. Just a heartfelt visit, express his condolences, offer to help in any way, certainly financially, for her loss.

Yes, he thought, washing up before the inn was properly awake, he'd just slip off and let the landlady tell the folks he was back. Nobody's business where he was going, after all. And looking ahead, he was sure Anna would want to go with him to some place nearer civilization, once he had the iron-producing region under his control. Let her pick the spot, he would. *Well, as long as it's reasonable, anyway.*

So Reginald Cabot saddled his horse when the late fall mist was still thick, although a hint of sun glow should dispell it shortly. He rode upcreek, aware of the first stirrings of the awakening village, but saw no one. He'd originally thought of taking along one of the settlement's upstanding women, perhaps that Tildy Driscoll, or even the minister's wife, Ella. And he'd do that probably, next time. But he wanted to see first what the lady's attitude was, then chart his course.

Oh, Reginald Cabot would launch a proper courtship. He'd be so attentive, so concerned for her welfare, that none of the soon-to-be-clacking tongues of the women here could find fault. He began to whistle a merry tune on the short ride to the Davis cabin.

~ * ~

"Cabot's back," Belle told her husband first thing. She was up and dressed, preparing to go over to the inn ahead of the lodgers to get breakfast going. She'd insisted her girls be early, so they'd no doubt already built the fire up in the big cooking fireplace and had water on.

"Say so?" Killebrew sat upright in bed, wide awake. "When'd he git in?" He swung his legs out, reached for his clothes.

"Late, jist as I wuz closin' up fer th' night. Didn't see no need t'wake you. Prob'ly some of th' folks up already. He'll prob'ly sleep late." She bustled about, not noting the stern look on her husband's face.

"Wal, I'll be over shortly, then, fer breakfus'." He wanted to find Archie Nolan first, then send for Campbell, Epsworth and Weller just as soon as he could. He splashed water on his face, pulled his boots and coat on. Belle went out.

Archie was emerging from his room at the inn just as Killebrew reached his door. He motioned for the prospector to follow him outside. From the look on the miller's face, Nolan knew what this was about.

The villagers had approved Ketchum's election as constable almost one hundred percent just the day before. Hiram Garst had been against it, hoping for that job himself. But without Cabot's support, he knew he'd have to keep quiet for the present. The two of them would work something else out later, he was sure. Now the new lawman told Nolan that Cabot had returned late the night before.

"And he's here in the inn?"

"Shorely is. Belle said he come in, she fed him, an' he went t'bed. Now I want Harvey an' Todd an' George here, soon's you c'n fetch 'em. Garst wuz up late drinkin' with th' boys, an' he'll be some hung over. I say we grab 'em both right now, an' haul 'em up 'fore th' settlement, sorta a speeded-up trial."

"Hold on a minute, Killy. We'll need Stephen's testimony before we can hope to get the people behind us on this. He's not fit to ride yet, and Anna's not going to let us carry him down here. I'm suggesting we wait a bit and do it right, with Stephen actually here to tell the facts. Anything less, and we'll be going against the whole place."

"Wal, mebbe you're right, but it galls me no end to think that snake's right 'mongst us, goin' 'bout his crooked bizness, him an' Garst, an' we gotta jis' let 'em alone."

"We'll keep an eye on them, one of us at a time. That way they won't suspect anything. Also, Mason and Chiles should be right behind him, I'd say coming in today. They were to watch at Saltville, you know, trail Cabot."

"If th' man's got it in fer th' two of them, he'll git right onto it, I'm 'fraid."

"Mason said they'll slip into town, maybe go to Stephen's place first. Listen, Killy, I don't want you to think I'm trying to do your job for you, but we need to have everything going for us we can, against those two. And while we're at it, we should figure how to eliminate that lawyer Eddins, too. Stephen said he was in the thick of that bunch back in Virginia."

"Oh, yeah. Wonder could we git him up here someway? Mebbe send somebody fer him, lak it wuz from Cabot? I mean, after Stephen's on his feet better? Whut about that, you reckon?"

"Great idea. You're starting to think like a lawman, Killy. Why don't one of us go up to Stephen's place, tell him Cabot's back, and get his ideas on just what and when we move on this? That make sense to you?"

"Does. Okay, if you'd do that, I c'd be runnin' th' mill here an' nobody's th' wiser. Give us a chancet t'try an' hear jist whut Cabot an' Garst's up to next, too, if ennybody kin git close 'nuff to 'em."

"Been thinking on that, too. I'd say young Carver MacNaughton's the one. They won't take him seriously, and with his smithing, he can be around close to everything they've got going on, doing his work. He's keen on nailing Cabot too, but Stephen didn't want him in danger when the fight starts."

"Reckon it'd be all right t'tell him 'bout Stephen, then?"

"Now that's a question, all right. I think the boy's loyal, but we'd have to respect Stephen's judgment on that. I'll ask him when I get there this morning. Yes, the boy should know what's happened." He thought a moment more. "But let's get him on spying on the two of them right away. He doesn't need to know about Stephen yet. And we need any and all the evidence we can get against Cabot before we confront him."

"Thet confrontin's gonna be pretty damn sudden, when it comes, too." The miller was anxious to bring this simmering situation to a head.

"I'll ask Stephen when he thinks we should act. He'll probably come just as soon as he's able, before Cabot does anything else rash." Nolan prepared to leave for the Davis homestead, taking along a ham biscuit from Belle in the inn kitchen.

~ * ~

Reginald Cabot turned his horse up the path to the widow Davis' cabin, his mind full of the strategy he'd use to lay the groundwork for his suit. Just a quick visit, this, to gauge the widow's frame of mind, then later he'd come again, with gifts. Yes, this would be pleasant.

Anna saw Cabot riding up the path from her kitchen window and the jolt she experienced sent her for Stephen's rifle. The guns were close, since they almost always came and went through the kitchen door.

"What is it?" he asked, rising painfully from the table.

"Cabot, if you can believe that. He's alone, and what he could want here, I can't imagine. Should I shoot him off his horse?" She was serious, checking the prime on her weapon.

He replied as he reached his pistol.

"Let's see what he's up to. I'll be right here, but keep him in the front room. If he makes a move against you, I'll kill him, never fear."

She gave him a searching look. *He doesn't want me to kill the man outright.* Then she nodded, put the rifle back, stepped through to the main room, closed but didn't latch the door. Stephen silently moved a chair close to the crack, sat, pistol primed and cocked.

Cabot dismounted, tied his horse at the front porch rail, climbed the steps. He knocked, called out.

"Mrs. Davis, it's Reginald Cabot. May I come in?"

Anna forced herself to open the door. She was dressed in black, never knowing when someone from the village might come. Every instinct screamed at her to destroy this smooth, evil would-be-murderer, but she willed herself to welcome him inside her house.

"So you've returned, sir." She took his coat and hat, indicated a seat before the fire.

"Yes, the most pressing of business demands. I apologize for racing off as I did without properly expressing my condolences at the terrible loss of your husband. I felt I must act quickly, however, as the welfare of my entire operation was in jeopardy. Allow me to extend my heartfelt sympathies now, if you will." He bowed, then took the proffered seat.

This is the devil incarnate. No ordinary man could brazenly come to the house of the woman whose husband he was sure he'd murdered.

"Accepted, Mr. Cabot. And I do understand your putting your business, and the subsequent welfare of the settlement, first." She moved to the ever-present kettle of cider hanging from the fireplace crane, poured two mugs, and set one before him. It was the very last gesture she wanted to make, but she managed it, before seating herself, some distance away from the man.

Stephen could see just a sliver of Cabot's form through the crack. He'd rehearsed a quick shove with his good foot to burst the door open, and he'd have a point-blank shot. And the desire to do just that boiled up inside him. *This man, this brazen impostor! To come here, to lie, so without remorse.* His hand tightened on the pistol. But he was also consumed with curiosity...why was the man here? What possible purpose could he have, calling on the widow of the man he'd killed? He held Cabot's life in his hand, and even if his pistol should misfire, his rifle was within reach. But he'd see first where this was headed.

Cabot noted that the young widow didn't seem haggard or distraught over her loss. *Good, she'll be more open to my courtship. She's smart; knows a profitable alliance could only be for the better. But not to push it...*

"I'm on my way to meet Archie Nolan on past here for more prospecting, Mrs. Davis, but wanted very much to take this opportunity to call." He rose, retrieved his coat and hat. "And to ask your permission to come again, after a respectable interval."

"Why certainly, Mr. Cabot," Anna replied, the real purpose of his visit dawning on her. She kept her face neutral, stifling the disgust that threatened to spill out of her. She'd always been able to present an impassive face to the world, and did so now, despite the urge to rip this man's throat out. "And I thank you for calling." She opened the door for him, knowing she could put a rifle or pistol ball into his retreating back, a little dizzy at the prospect.

He took his leave, and she closed the door gently. She felt she needed a bath after enduring the man's presence. She watched him mount, tip his hat to the house, ride away. A feeling of lost opportunity possessed her.

"Well, are you thinking what I'm thinking?" Stephen asked from behind her.

"I'm thinking that repulsive toad actually plans to come courting. But mark this, Stephen: next time I lay eyes on him, I'll kill him without a moment's hesitation. The gall! The brazen, evil *presumption!* Stephen, I wanted to dig his eyes out, to tear him to shreds with my bare hands!"

"And I came within a hair's width of pushing that door open and splattering his brains all over our house, believe it. And yes, I'm slower than you, my dear: I didn't see what he was after until right at the last. I guess the sheer incredulity of it kept me from killing him. Maybe that, and a bit of the Christian charity you've managed to instill in me.

"We'll go ahead with a proper arrest and trial." He was leaning against the doorway for support, but reached, enfolded her in his arms, kissed her long and deep. He would never let this woman out of his arms, his life. She was so much a part of him. He held her so tightly she began to squirm.

Then she laughed. Held him away and let the absurdity of it all spill out of her in peals of laughter. He too, threw back his head and joined in. The cabin shook with their relieved, shared hilarity.

Reginald Cabot reached the main trail smug in his belief of his own invincibility. He rode toward the village and breakfast, humming a merry tune to himself.

~ * ~

Archie Nolan nearly fell off his horse when he met Cabot on the trail. The man must've slipped away early, but what for? Nobody out here but the Davises. *Oh, my God! He's been to Stephen's place.* His hand moved to his pistol, but he noted the man's smiling expression. He turned his horse, hiding his gun hand, and waited.

"Well, Archie. Out early, I see. Prospecting?"

"I was...actually going up to see if Mrs. Davis needed anything. George Weller and I have been helping out there, with firewood and such, and it's my turn. But yes, I want to go further along the trail and see what I can find. I still hope we can discover a rich deposit of ore somewhere near here." He hoped he seemed calm, but his eye was on Cabot. *If he's done the slightest harm to Stephen and Anna, I will kill this man...*

"Well, I've just come from there. Feeling ashamed I ran out so soon after the accident, and it's been weighing on me. Wanted to express my condolences first thing. Business seemed the most important demand at the time, but I came to realize that I'd neglected my duty to call on Mrs. Davis. She seems to be coping as well as could be expected."

If you only knew, you slimy bastard. "Yes, well, the entire village has been trying to help, but she's quite the self-sufficient lady. George shot and field-dressed a deer for her quite late yesterday, and I'm to skin it out and help butcher it. Cold as it is, it'll keep nicely."

"She'll appreciate that, I'm sure." Cabot eyed Nolan. The man was white-haired, certainly no competition for the young widow's favor. And yes, she was highly thought of in the settlement...folks would be anxious for her welfare. He'd have to be sure to manage thoughtful services like this, himself.

"Well, I'm off to inspect the works," he said. "I wasn't able to conclude my business as well as I'd hoped, but I can assure you and the good people at the village that the operations will continue, whatever we have to do to ensure that. I'll join you on the next prospecting trip." He eased past the prospector and rode on down the trail.

Nolan rode out of sight, then nudged his horse into a trot, fearful of what might actually have happened at the Davis place. He couldn't trust a word Cabot said, and he wanted to assure himself. No doubt Stephen could and had protected them, and surely he'd stayed out of sight, but...

He was fairly lunging his horse around the last bend in the path to the cabin when Anna saw him. She stepped to the front door and called.

"It's all right, Archie. Everything's under control. Come in for breakfast."

"Oh, I met Cabot, and was afraid..." He was out of breath.

"No problems," Stephen assured him, bracing himself against the doorway. "I stayed hidden, wanted to hear what the man had in mind, and just was able to keep myself from shooting him."

Anna ushered both men into the kitchen and set plates before them. Nolan was so relieved he was shaking.

"I came as soon as I heard he was back. Thought he was still at the inn, but he'd slipped out early. Couldn't imagine what he was up to. And I'm no killer, but I came close to shooting him myself." He accepted hot tea, his hands steadying.

"Well, it seems the man has an eye for my wife," Stephen said frankly, and then had to reach to steady Nolan's hand on his drink. The astonishment on his face was complete.

"You don't mean... No, nobody's that insane. Half the village thinks he killed you, Stephen, and for him...that's just too unbelievable." Nolan was shaking his head.

"Can't figure it any other way, Archie. For a bit I thought he might suspect I'm still alive, and came to find out, but that didn't seem to be the case. But the man's capable of any atrocity, and we mustn't underestimate him."

"No, we mustn't. Killy wanted to grab him and Garst first thing, but I pointed out we needed you there to make the case against him. And that should be as soon as you can travel."

"Which won't be soon," Anna put in, before her husband could volunteer. "Which I know gives Cabot time for more of his machinations."

"We don't know what he'll do next," Stephen mused, "but I'm sure he's seen through Mason and Chiles by now, who should be back any time. I wonder how his dealings with the Cummings heirs went."

"He said something about things not working out as he'd hoped," Nolan remembered. "Could be they wouldn't sell."

"In which case, he'll have some other nefarious scheme planned. I just don't see him, knowing the ore is playing out here, just accepting his losses. No, he's working on something else."

"And we mustn't let him do more harm. When do you think you'll be able to come to the village?" Nolan looked at both of them.

"I'd say tomorrow, but my keeper here won't hear of it. Maybe next week?" He looked at his wife.

"Maybe…Oh, look, here come Mason and Chiles, just at the right time." She went to welcome the investigator and his assistant as they rode up to the porch. They'd taken the circular route around the prominent hill for concealment, and struck the trail, missing Cabot.

"Let's hope they've learned more than we have," Stephen said, rising from the table with some difficulty. Nolan took his arm, supported him. *No, he's not fit to ride. Let's hope Mason can come up with some other way to move ahead on this without involving Stephen at all.*

But the two arrivals had nothing to add to the plan, acknowledging that Stephen's presence would be critical to the case against Cabot.

"But I maintain that his attempted murder of Stephen is grounds enough for hanging," Leighton Chiles declared. "And my identification of Garst as the shooter back in Philadelphia should be enough against him." Clearly, the matter should be dealt with now, he insisted, before more harm could be done. He reminded his employer that between Cabot and Garst, with the time they'd had to study it, one or both might well have realized by now who they actually were.

"We're in danger the minute they find out we're back here," he concluded. Stephen agreed with him, and so did Anna and Nolan.

"I see I'm outnumbered here," Mason conceded. "And I suppose it matters not which of his atrocities consigns him to execution. Certainly you're right…whatever else we can't prove, his pushing Stephen off that cliff earns him the hangman's rope. I *would* very much like to uncover his whole operation, to get at others who're involved. But I suppose that won't happen." He turned his hands up in resignation.

"Unless we can get him to reveal it all," Stephen speculated.

At first Anna thought her husband was considering torturing the man, so uncharacteristic of him. Then she realized the direction he was heading.

"You mean make some sort of deal with him?" She was aghast.

"At least make him think he can wriggle out of a hanging. That Virginia business proved that leaving loose ends like those in Philadelphia just breeds more trouble. Speaking of which, I wish we could get Eddins while we're at it. He's capable of picking up where Cabot leaves off."

"Killy and I talked about that," Nolan told them. "He figured we could send for Eddins, as if Cabot needed him for something, then have the three of them here together."

"Well, Eddins got off back in Virginia, despite the local judge's suspicions," Stephen told them. "And we don't have a clear-cut crime to charge him with here. I'm certain he deserves hanging too, but we don't know exactly for what offense."

"And if we eliminate Cabot and Garst, he'll hear of it, and probably run on back to Philadelphia, then take over Cabot's operation there," Mason predicted gloomily.

Leighton Chiles listened to these comments with a growing impatience. He wanted to wipe the three criminals off the face of the earth and go back home. He could appreciate Stephen's wanting to establish a civilized legal system here, but that might well mean their quarry could somehow get away. *Never underestimate your enemy.* That was the thing they had to keep in mind with a man like Cabot. He decided to push his employer.

"Whatever we decide, our business in the capital is being neglected, sir. We must get back before the snow comes, which is really now, and I vote for immediate action, whatever that requires."

Anna had been quiet during the last few exchanges. Now an idea had come to her.

"Invite them here." It was such a simple solution, she felt it needed no elaboration.

"Cabot and Garst? On what pretense?" Mason asked her.

"Cabot doesn't need urging," Stephen answered, realizing what his wife meant. "And Garst'll come along. Or just have Killy arrest them. Bring them both here, along with an appointed jury, and Leighton and I'll testify. Have our own legal trial."

Mason thought this over for a space, then frowned.

"The villagers won't accept that, I'm afraid. Too many of them depend on Cabot's wages."

"Ask them all to come, then," Anna suggested. "Hear the evidence, learn the truth. Since Stephen can't go to the settlement, the settlement can come here."

Archie Nolan had been considering this tack and raised another objection.

"The Reverend McKnight and probably the other missionaries won't go along with a rump trial, I'm afraid. No judge, no lawyers, it'll be too much like an execution. Which I'm not that much against, understand," he hastened to add.

"Not everyone has to agree," Chiles pointed out. "If there's a representative jury, it might offend some, but justice will be done, as well as we can manage it here." *Or just let me ambush them on the trail, and this can all be over. And Eddins can meet with an accident as we travel through Saltville on the way home. After all, as soon as Cabot finds out who we are, if he hasn't already, we're in his gunsights.*

The frustration was mounting. With their enemies right under their noses again, nobody wanted to wait for an attack of any kind from them. But except for Chiles, all were hesitant to act. Then Stephen had an idea.

"Why don't we arrest both of them—no, all three of them—and keep them separated? That way we can tell each one that the others have sold him out, and see if he'll try to make a deal with us. I'll wager at least one of them will crack, and that can be enough for us."

"Cabot won't tell us a thing," Mason was sure.

"Then Garst, if we apply enough pressure."

"And then agree to let him go? I don't like that at all," Chiles demurred.

"If we can get Eddins to turn against him, we won't let him go." Stephen wanted a way for this to work.

Chiles felt it would be quicker and better all around if perhaps one or all the criminals could be shot while attempting to escape. They could arrange that easily.

The final agreement was to send for Samuel Eddins, with an urgent message ostensibly from Cabot requesting his immediate presence. Meantime Mason and Chiles would stay hidden for the necessary several days, and Ketchum would keep a close watch over the assassin Garst.

That left Cabot, the most dangerous of their enemies, free to do whatever evil he might have in mind. Nobody liked that, but both Mason and Stephen had argued for a convincing set of charges against the men to solidify village support for their execution.

Anna kept her counsel, though quietly siding with Leighton Chiles...dispense with the frills when dealing with killers. And if Cabot came calling again, which she was sure he would, she'd convince Stephen to act then and there. Or she would.

Decisively.

~ * ~

Carver MacNaughton was overjoyed when his mentor Killebrew Ketchum asked him to help find out more about Cabot and Garst.

"We dunno jist what they might be up to," the miller told his apprentice, "but some of us don't think Stephen had no accident. I want you t'keep yer ears open an' hear whutever y'kin, whenever y'kin. They might git 'spicious if Todd er Harvey er me wuz t'git close to em, but if you kin find ways t'be workin' on somethin' er just carryin' a piece of iron, like you wiz takin' it some'ers."

"You reckon they's gonna git after somebody else? I know in reason Cabot's th' one done Stephen in. Me'n Todd an' Harvey's talked about it."

"We dunno fer shore, but ennything you c'n find out's gonna help us. Jist don't git yerself caught. They say ennything to you, tell 'em I sent you. They's always scrap iron layin' 'round at th' ironworks, an' y'can be pickin' some of it up to bring here. Er takin' some bolts er somethin' down thar. I fixed it with George t'say he needs you t'take stuff thar, much as y'kin."

So the young man became the eyes and ears of the vigilante group bent on learning enough to hang Reginald Cabot and his associates. Carver spent time devising schemes to put himself close to their targets, always with a reasonable explanation for his presence. If Cabot and Garst were in conference inside the ironworks office, he'd slip up behind it to listen, holding a tool or part for some machine. If the two paused to talk on their way from one location at the works to another, he'd contrive to pass close by them, laden with some needed item. Yes, then maybe drop it, fumble for it, ears open.

Ketchum let it be known that his apprentice would be more often down at the works, since his own new duties as constable limited his time to see to the needs of the operation there. So nobody thought it odd that Carver seemed to be everywhere, on multiple errands, either legitimately with other workmen, or on contrived visits to big George Weller.

He still believed Stephen Davis was dead, and the idea of bringing his killer to justice appealed mightily to him. Cabot's flamboyance and imperious way among the settlers had put the boy off from the beginning; he'd seen slick operators among his own rustic kin. And knowing that others, including his housemates and his boss felt the same way, made him doubly determined to find out what they wanted to know.

Belle Ketchum too, was a valuable source of information, being in a position to overhear much of what was said in the inn. While not included in the inner circle of Stephen's allies, she nonetheless reported to her husband each juicy bit of news she picked up from everyone staying there, which of course included Cabot and Garst.

"Heered 'em talkin' 'bout that place up on Jackson River, Killy. Seems lak Cabot didn't git t'buy 'em out, after goin' up thar."

"He say ennything else? What you reckon he's gonna do when th' iron plays out here?"

"Wal, I didn't hear enny more, but he don't seem put off much. I'd say th' man, he's got hisself 'nother plan. His kind allus does."

Ketchum relayed this information to the rest of the circle, and the unamimous view was that the man would soon launch another effort of some kind to secure his ebbing fortunes. That made Stephen even more restless at the enforced wait their plan required.

"He'll sabotage the Jackson River works somehow," he predicted. "Maybe burn them out again or go after the new owner. The man won't take this blow to his ego without striking back."

"But with deep winter coming on, I'd warrant he'll wait till spring," Mason predicted. He and Chiles were temporarily camped in the barn at the Davis place, and both had taken on the chore of helping their hosts stock up for the coming snow time. That left Archie Nolan free to stay in the village and watch Cabot and Garst, another set of eyes and ears.

The immediate plan was for the investigator and his assistant to move into the cabin in foul weather, for the expected short time necessary to get their targets all in one place. Stephen and Anna welcomed them, as their presence provided further protection in case their enemies should somehow find out about Stephen and come after him again.

"I believe his failure to buy the Cummings operation will make him desperate," Anna feared. "His money has to be running out, and I don't think he'll be content just to wait out the season. He'll do something right away. I want Eddins back here, all of them arrested, and this whole nasty business cleared up."

Leighton Chiles was silent. He doubted that Cabot, or Garst for that matter, would go quietly. He envisioned a firefight when Ketchum and a support team tried to arrest them. He vowed to be among that group, and wouldn't hesitate to shoot at the slightest resistance. One simply shouldn't be constrained by the principles of law and order when the enemy wasn't playing by those rules.

Stephen would ordinarily have agreed. The simplest solution was the direct one, and that meant striking before Cabot got another chance to harm others, or himself, again. But he was, in a word, tired of violence, tired of killing. He found himself in the moderate camp more and more. The transition from sharpshooting soldier to upstanding citizen was in him now complete, with his coming role as family man.

Still, if it came to it, he wouldn't hesitate to pull the crucial trigger.

Twenty-nine

The entire question of how and when justice would be done was taken out of the hands of Stephen's circle of friends and supporters when Reginald Cabot decided to call on Anna again. The man was highly impatient and the thought of staying holed up in Ketchum's Mill all winter, even with his planned ambushing of his competitor's iron shipments, was intolerable.

It was a far more inviting prospect if he could win the young widow's favor now, or at least very soon. So that became his one immediate objective: court her, win her, bed her and let it snow all it would. In his mind this was already an accomplished quest.

He'd abandoned the idea of having one or more women from the village accompany him; proper as that would have been, it would clearly hamper his actions, and of course set their tongues clacking even more than a direct assault on the lady. He'd just call on her, press his suit beginning with that visit, and exert whatever charm and pressure necessary to make it happen. Reginald Cabot wasn't a man who dithered.

Accordingly, on a bright but chilling day, his resolve fortified by several drinks of the local whiskey, he set out upcreek, bearing two turkeys he'd bought from one of the settlement's hunters. He'd told no one his destination and, noting Archie Nolan's presence at the inn poring over maps, he knew he'd have Anna to himself. He hummed a tune as his horse followed the trail, flicking his ears at the sound.

So it was that Anna spied the man rounding the last turn in the trail, and alerted Stephen.

"It's Cabot, Stephen. I've just time to warn Mason and Chiles to stay hidden." She rushed out the back door, motioned to Chiles, who was stacking firewood in a shed. Mason was nowhere to be seen.

"Cabot's here. Stephen will be on guard, never fear." And she hurried back inside, grateful for this man's watchful presence as well as her husband's. Doubly so, since she had no time to find and conceal her customary pistol in the waistband at her back.

Cabot had dismounted, tied his horse and stepped to the porch, gifts in hand. Anna removed her apron, draping it over the back of a chair, and met him at the door with a smile she hoped wasn't too forced. Thanked him for the birds. She could smell the liquor on him.

"A small offering, dear lady, for one forced to survive on her own. I trust you are faring adequately?" He took the proffered chair near the fire, noting that Anna did not take the turkeys immediately into the kitchen. Because that was where Stephen watched, gun in hand.

"I am doing as well as could be expected, sir," she replied, offering Cabot a hot drink from the kettle at the fireplace. "It's good of you to call."

Cabot looked about the well-appointed room. He hadn't seen the rest of the place, but was struck by the fine joinery of the cabin. Davis had indeed been a gifted craftsman. And it occurred to him for the first time that he'd own this place when he took this lady to wife. Cozy place to spend the winter, too, if he could move that fast. Which he was certain he could.

"About that: I am naturally concerned for your welfare, Mrs. Davis—may I call you Anna?" His smile was ingratiating. "And please call me Reginald."

"I hardly think we are on such...personal terms, Mr. Cabot."

"Oh, but I have a proposal which might alter that, my dear. You see, I, among others, am quite concerned for your welfare, and I am in a position to offer you a situation far more fitting than being alone and snowbound in the coming season." He sat back, sipped his mug of tea.

"A...proposal, sir?" Anna was not only taken aback by the suddenness of the man's approach, she was sickened anew at his evil being itself. To think he could murder her husband, then brazenly launch a suit for her hand barely weeks after the fact? She knew she wouldn't be able to keep up this charade any longer.

"Yes. I propose that you move into the inn before the way here becomes impassable, and I shall ensure that you are well provided for. It is no less than my Christian duty." *He sounds so sincere, this snake, this Satan.*

"Oh, I couldn't possibly accept such a generous offer, sir. Why, that would be most unseemly, that...arrangement." She was actually scanning the room, searching for a weapon to smash this insolent toad.

"Not if you would accept my proposal of marriage," Cabot countered, setting the mug aside, rising and taking her hand. At that moment he felt completely that he was in total control...this prize was his.

Anna recoiled at the touch, the outrage of this monster's hand. And not only was he holding her, he was pulling her toward him, his intent clear on his smirking face.

"I suggest you remove your hand from my wife," Stephen Davis said calmly from the open door to the kitchen. He was standing, with the aid of his crutches, his pistol cocked and aimed at Cabot's heart.

The man reacted as if hit across the face with a club. His eyes widened; his mouth fell open. He was convinced he was seeing a ghost. Then, registering the crutches, he understood. In that instant of realization, he released Anna's arm and in a blur of motion reached for his own pistol, dodging partially behind her in the same movement. It was a reaction born of his survival on the streets.

Stephen had known it might come to this: all their planning, the need for legalities, their hesitancy, gone in an instant of needed action.

He pulled the trigger.

And in one of those rare instances in which his careful preparations of this kind had failed, his pistol misfired. The flash of the pan, smoke rolling, did not ignite the powder charge. Inferior powder, dampness, a tiny obstruction in the touch hole, any one of too many possibilities, the result was the same.

Cabot pushed Anna away, drew his own pistol, cocking it in one smooth motion. Whatever shock he'd experienced a fraction of a second before was gone: he was back in control. And he would kill this man this time.

But Anna had seized her apron, stepped behind him as she spun it into a rope, and looped it over his head as he brought the gun to bear. She jerked both hands in a grip so powerful it snapped Cabot's head back, and the gunshot went into the ceiling. He struggled, dropping the useless pistol and clawing at her hands. But Anna was taller, and her fury gave her the strength of a cornered bear. She fairly lifted Cabot off the floor, jerking the knotted cloth as if to cut the man's head off.

Stephen stepped back, grabbed his rifle, almost losing his balance. Seeing this with bulging eyes, Cabot knew he would die. Unless...

Forcing himself to ignore the pain, the fading vision, he plunged a hand for the knife he kept sheathed at his belt. He twisted sideways, reaching back with the keen blade for the woman's side, at the same time shielding himself with her body from her husband. Holding himself up, his rifle one-handed at his hip, Stephen had no clear shot.

Suddenly a thundering explosion filled the room, and Cabot felt a searing, shocking tearing at his vitals.

Leighton Chiles, his homely visage hardened into a mask of stony purpose, stood in the open back doorway, his smoking pistol rigid as Cabot convulsed, went slack in Anna's grip. Chiles stepped forward, catching the slumping man, and dragged him outside to bleed.

He re-entered the room with Jedediah Mason. Chiles gently led the trembling Anna to a chair, examining the scratches on her wrists and hands. Mason helped Stephen to her side, where he knelt against her for support, his arms around her. Long minutes passed.

"Well, I suppose this obviates the planned trial and execution of Reginald Cabot," Mason observed.

~ * ~

Hiram Garst sat in the ironworks office, going over the endless papers that recorded the activities of the operation. He hated this kind of work and was relieved that Cabot had returned, and he'd soon be outside again.

The two of them had discussed the formation of robber bands to ambush the Jackson River iron shipments, and he was anxious to be off to help Eddins start putting together those men. He'd figured four to a group, to easily overpower the likely two men on each wagon. Given the wide distribution area of that operation, he'd need men on all the major roads leading from the Jackson River site to all the settled regions. So, concentrating on the routes from Lexington, the men would lie in wait on remote stretches of these roads.

Garst wasn't worried about finding desperate men for this work and he'd just take over that chore from the lawyer. Enough ex-soldiers, disaffected younger sons, misfits, and those just too lazy for honest work, were available for quick money.

The assassin had guessed Cabot's infatuation with the Davis widow and accepted that. He understood why the man was leaving the running of the business up to him for longer than he wanted. But Garst didn't relish being stuck in Ketchum's Mill all winter, with more exciting places out there nearer civilization. He chafed this day at his employer's absence, wanting to be out of the village before serious snow came.

He'd paid no attention to the blacksmith's apprentice, always seemingly around on one errand or another. The boy worked hard, and apparently the men here needed him around to help with the myriad chores of the place. So it wasn't with any apprehension that Garst saw Carver MacNaughton carrying yet another odd piece of iron toward the part of the foundry that housed the office.

Only this time he was accompanied by Killebrew Ketchum, and there was big George Weller coming out to meet them. Garst's keen eyes caught the weapons all three carried, and that set off an alarm inside him.

But then the men drifted out of sight, and only the boy came on toward the office.

"Mr. Garst, sir, I've word from Mr. Cabot," Carver called. "He wants you at the inn soon's y'kin git thar."

"Oh, all right. He say what it's about?"

"Nossir, jist thet somethin' important's come up, all he'd say."

Something's come up? Now what could that be? Well, I'll soon know. He got his coat, automatically checking for his loaded pistol, secured it and his hat, and left the warmth of the office.

As soon as he stepped clear of the building, Garst saw he was facing Ketchum, Harvey Campbell and the boy, all suddenly with pistols drawn and pointed at him. *Now, what the hell's this?* In a flash of self-preservation, he calculated his chances. The boy wouldn't shoot. Neither would the missionary Campbell, he'd wager. So, take out Ketchum, duck back around the building, and he'd have a chance. *But what does this mean? What's happened to Cabot?* He hesitated.

"Garst, yer under arrest," Ketchum announced. "Git yer hands in th' air, an' don't make enny moves atall, or yer a dead man."

"Arrest? On what charge? This must be some mistake…" Garst understood that now was his only chance. Whatever had happened to Cabot, he'd go down with him. He tensed, ready to draw his pistol before Ketchum could react.

Then a strong arm pinned him from behind and George Weller lifted him off the ground in a crushing one-armed bearhug that took the air out of him. A big hand clamped his gun, then took his knife. Finally let go, Garst slumped to his knees, gulping air. Weller hauled him up again and marched him by the scruff of his coat collar to the others.

"W...What's this all about?" he managed.

"Wal, it seems yer boss has got hisself shot, Garst," Ketchum informed him. "But 'fore he died, he tole us you wuz his hired 'ssassin, had kilt a man named Mason fer him up in Philadelphia, an' thet you also kilt Lester Cummings, up on Jackson River. Now, we don't hold with no hired killers 'round here, so we jist figger t'have ourselves a hangin'."

Cabot dead? And he sold me out? Garst was aware that all the men from the ironworks had converged, forming a circle around him and his captors. But there had to be a way out of this; Hiram Garst wasn't going to be outdone by a bunch of backwoodsmen. His mind raced for something he could say or do, here in the center of this now-menacing mob.

Of course, Cabot hadn't told the men a thing, dying instantly from Leighton Chiles' gunshot. Stephen Davis had come up with the idea of pressuring Garst with the supposed last words of the dying man. And he'd instructed Ketchum to let the assassin speak, see if he could or would implicate the lawyer Eddins, on whom they had little evidence but ample suspicion.

And in the sudden silence that hung in the air like doom, Garst had that very thought: *Maybe I can trade them something... And just maybe Cabot's not dead at all...*

"Well, men, it seems you've made your minds up about this, although there isn't a word of truth in it. I don't know what Cabot might or might not have told you in some of his deal-making. But I do know a lot about his operations, here and back in the capital. I've got names the authorities will want to know, and I'm in a position to help wrap up his whole illegal shenanigans. That is, if we can discuss this." He looked around at the grim faces, hoping this offer could lead to his freedom.

But damn, these men don't care about Philadelphia...they want to get to us here. They won't listen to any deal off somewhere...

"Oh, and Cabot's lawyer Eddins, I can give you just how he's involved, how he and Cabot planned to take over the whole iron business all over. In fact, I've been working my way inside the organization just so I could help expose it. Sounds like now's the time." He had held onto his composure nicely, he thought. Now, if he could just get these men to take him to the village, where cooler heads like Archie Nolan and the preacher, and maybe the other missionaries were, maybe he could strike a deal with them all.

"Wal, thet don't seem likely atall," Ketchum spat on the ground. "But I guess we'll mebbe jist have ourselves a hearin' back up th' creek, an' decide whut's t'be done, 'mongst us all."

A great weight seemed to be lifted from Garst's shoulders as the men marched him the mile up to the village. The MacNaughton boy and others had gone ahead to gather the villagers for what was to pass as a trial, he assumed. And with each step, he felt more confident that he could fool these men with his version of the truth. His mind was busy with his defense, and pieces of it were falling into place. He suppressed a smile.

It hadn't been easy for Ketchum and the others to get the ironworkers to accept the fact that Cabot was in reality a criminal. Nobody had liked Garst though, and the men had agreed to hear more from him about their employer, plus what other information might be forthcoming back at the village. The fact that Cabot was dead had shocked them all, and they were keen to learn the circumstances of that death.

What this entourage found at Ketchum's Mill was a gathering of all the settlers, from old Daughtry to the youngest child. Garst scanned the faces as he was led among them, and was taken aback to see Carson and Bone, the latter looking more like the bodyguard from Philadelphia. And as he studied Mason's face, he realized he might actually be seeing the man he thought he'd killed back in the capital.

"This man Garst, he's done been 'cused of killin' a couple men on orders f'm th' late Reg'nald Cabot," Ketchum announced. "Now, we ain't got ourselves no judge here, but as th' elected lawman, I'm 'pointin' a jury, right now. You, Todd Epsworth, will you serve?"

"Yessir, I will," the one-armed veteran stepped forward.

"An' Harvey Campbell, you too?"

"Surely."

"Thad Stillwell?"

A jury of twelve men was thus selected to hear the evidence both for and against Hiram Garst, and the trial was set to commence. It was a dull day, with no wind and a leaden sky, but not cold. The villagers ranged themselves around the inn porch in a semicircle, anxious to hear not only what would be said about Garst, but to learn more of the sudden death of their sometime benefactor Cabot.

A commotion among those at the upcreek fringes of the assembly caused all to look in that direction. Anna Davis appeared, leading her horse slowly down the trail with a travois of two poles behind, on which lay her husband, cushioned on a padded deerskin fastened between them.

The crowd surged forward with an excited babble, although Ketchum, Weller and Nolan stayed behind to guard their prisoner. As soon as Anna halted the horse, Stephen sat up, seized his crutches and stood. He swung himself forward with an effort in the sudden hush that followed.

"Didn't want to miss anything," he explained, "and it's been too long since I've seen most of you. Reckon somebody could bring a chair so I can be a part of this?"

Those in his circle of confidants smiled, while the expressions of wonder, shock, amazement and joy shone from every other face. Anna helped her husband to an inn chair at the forefront of the crowd, and he sat, accepting a mug of hot tea from the bustling Belle Ketchum, only now convinced she wasn't seeing a ghost.

Hiram Garst felt his chances of surviving this trial fade with the forceful Davis somehow revived and present. He was certain the man had been the one who'd killed Cabot, whatever the circumstances. And with his reputation from back in Virginia, he'd probably wipe them all out.

But it'll be after the damn fight, he assured himself, summoning nerve to face the ordeal. He'd give them a lot and see if it worked. And yes, Davis, and if that were indeed Mason and Chiles, they'd want to know about the Philadelphia circle. His hopes rose a notch.

"Archie, would you be th' man in charge, here?" Ketchum asked. "Y'know, kinda keep thaings goin' th' way they oughta be?"

"Certainly." He turned to the villagers. "Mr. Hiram Garst is charged with one count of attempted murder and one count of actual first-degree murder, folks. We will hear evidence that the late Reginald Cabot ordered Garst to kill Jedediah Mason, whom we know as Mr. Carson here, back in Philadelphia."

The villagers reacted to this accusation of their supposedly beneficent leader, and also to the news that Carson was not who they'd supposed. Archie waited a moment for the murmer to die down.

"Now, Mr. Mason's real occupation is discovering outlaws engaged in robberies and thefts in that area, working with the local police. He will testify as to the activities of both Mr. Garst and Mr. Cabot.

"Further, we will hear testimony that Mr. Garst killed Mr. Lester Cummings, late proprietor of the Jackson River ironworks, on orders from Mr. Cabot, so that Cabot could take over that business. Let's see, now...oh, how do you plead, Mr. Garst?"

"Innocent. I was actually working against Cabot, to find out more..."

"You'll have a chance to defend yourself at the proper time. Miss Anna, would you please record these proceedings? I should have asked you sooner."

"Yes, sir. Belle, do you have paper and pen?" The innkeeper hurried off and returned quickly with the materials. Anna sat and wrote the essential information up to that time and read it back to Nolan.

"Does everybody agree this is what's been said so far?" he asked. The crowd affirmed the record, and Nolan continued. "We'll hear first from Mr. Mason, then. Mr. Mason, do you swear to tell the truth so help you God? Please raise your right hand, sir, and place your left on that Bible Reverend McKnight has provided."

"I do." Nolan nodded, stepped back, and Mason began.

"As background, I was formerly a merchant in Philadelphia, and I suffered several robberies. With help, I was able to track down the men responsible, and soon others who'd sustained similar losses hired me to do the same for them. Working with the police, I put together a team of investigators to detect and stop that sort of thing. Mr. Chiles here, whom you all know as Martin Bone, is my assistant. We used these false identities to track Reginald Cabot here, after suspecting him of directing numerous robberies in the Philadelphia area. We also suspected several others of his circle, but were certain he was the principal operator.

"Around the time he left the city, a man Mr. Chiles will identify as Hiram Garst, trailed and shot one of my employees who looks a lot like me. The man did not die, thanks to Mr. Chiles' aid. I will admit that much of the evidence we had on Cabot was circumstantial, but it was enough for us to follow him here and try to discover more of his activities.

"The death of Mr. Cummings, who was thrown from a high walkway at his ironworks, could only have benefitted Cabot, and we believe Garst was ordered to kill him and set his works afire. You all know he was gone from here at the time. That is all I can testify to, sir."

"I see. So, Mr. Garst, do you wish to contradict Mr. Mason's testimony?"

"I certainly do. None of it's true. I never saw Mason before in my life, and I certainly didn't try to kill him, or kill Mr. Cummings."

"Very well, then. Let's clear this up if we can. Mr. Chiles, would you take the oath and give us your version?"

Duly sworn in, Leighton Chiles made it clear that he'd identified Hiram Garst as the shooter of the man he'd obviously taken to be Mason.

"All right. Now sir, would you tell us the circumstances surrounding the death of Mr. Reginald Cabot?"

"Yes, sir. Mr. Mason and I, as he told you, were gathering evidence against Cabot. We left the village as you all know, shortly after him, with that goal. We had been told by you, Mr. Nolan, that Mr. Stephen Davis had not died in the fall from the cliff as everyone had supposed, and we'd met with him and conferred with him about our ongoing work."

"You men knew, all th' time?" someone called from the crowd.

"Not at first, but indeed we did. And we also knew Mr. Cabot had shoved Mr. Davis over the edge, but you can hear that for yourselves from him. Anyway, we decided to stay hidden when Cabot returned, as we felt he suspected who we really were. We were present when Mrs. Davis warned us he had come to the Davis home. I believe she can tell better what happened there."

"All right, then. Miss Anna, would you let someone else record this part, and tell us the details?"

Anna passed the papers, ink and quill pen to Tildy Driscoll, who seated herself and waited. Anna took the oath.

"As background, when Archie Nolan came to tell me of Stephen's supposed accident, he told me he strongly suspected Mr. Cabot. He and I took rope and rode as fast as we could back to the scene, and he lowered me down to a ledge where I found Stephen, covered in stones and debris from the fall, but thanks to God, alive. I fashioned a sling around him, and managed to climb back up, again with God's help. Then together, Archie and I pulled him up and got him back home. As you can see, he's still mending.

"Now, we knew beyond doubt that Cabot had tried to kill my husband, and that he surely knew the details of Stephen's destruction of a criminal element of several men back in Virginia. Also the recovery of stolen money, which he turned over to the court there. But you will recall that Cabot left the next morning after trying to kill Stephen, so we could take no action.

"The very next morning after his return, Cabot came to call on me, supposedly to offer his sympathies at my widowhood. We wanted to find out what his motives were, so, although Stephen, who remained hidden, would have been entirely justified in shooting the man dead then, we waited. Mr. Mason had said he wanted more information, more evidence, and we wanted to confer with him and others here we'd learned also suspected Cabot.

"The second time Mr. Cabot called, he'd been drinking. He brought two turkeys as gifts. I'd just had time to warn Mr. Chiles, who was out back, that he was coming, and again Stephen was hidden in the next room to listen. Mr. Cabot made...improper advances to me, and actually grabbed me. Stephen confronted him with a pistol, and Cabot reacted as if he'd indeed seen a ghost. But very quickly he recovered, dodged aside and drew his own gun, trying to use me as a shield.

"Stephen fired in self-defense, but his pistol misfired. I grappled with Cabot, and his shot went into the ceiling. He drew a knife and tried to stab me, but Mr. Chiles appeared in the back doorway and shot him. The bullet hole in our ceiling will corroborate what I've told, and both Mr. Chiles and Mr. Mason, and Stephen himself, can verify these facts."

The crowd had listened without a sound at this narration, and now drew a collective deep breath. That the man who'd done so much for the community had turned out to be not only a criminal, but he'd attacked one of their favorite people, had shocked them, and the angry voices swelled with the realization.

Tildy Driscoll was still writing furiously, and Nolan waited for her to finish. She had two questions about details, which Anna answered.

Nolan, Stephen and Mason noted as one, that any latent hostility regarding Cabot's killing was gone, and the three made eye contact. Stephen nodded.

"All right now, folks, have any others of you anything to add to this testimony, any part of it?" Nolan got everyone's attention, but no one had more to offer.

"Mr. Garst, you've heard what's been said. Now, we know you've pleaded innocent, and now it's time to hear what else you have to say." Nolan swore the man in, and he plunged ahead with his desperate plan.

"Like I was saying, I was not a part of Cabot's operation. I'd heard rumors in Philadelphia about a bunch of men robbing businesses of goods and cash, and I wanted to get inside it and find out what I could. I planned to go to the authorities as soon as I could find evidence.

"That's why I trailed Cabot here, and why I got a job with him. Seems like Mason and I were working on the same thing, without either of us knowing it. Now, you've all known me a while here, how I've taken over running the ironworks while Cabot was gone, and that I've treated everybody fair. There's just nothing to these charges that I was a hired killer for Cabot, and it should be obvious that there's no proof."

Garst was gambling on this lack of proof getting him acquitted, but he would fall back on disclosure of the others involved if necessary.

"Seems like Mr. Chiles' identifying you as the attempted murderer of his man in Philadelphia would contradict that," Nolan reminded him.

"Then Mr. Chiles is mistaken. He couldn't have seen me, because I wasn't there."

"So let's move on to the charge that you killed Lester Cummings. Everyone here knows you were absent when he was murdered. Can you account for where you were at that time?"

"I was doing work with Samuel Eddins, Mr. Cabot's lawyer, helping set up the sales distribution for the iron."

"And he can confirm that?"

"He certainly can." Garst sat back, feeling he'd succeeded. He wouldn't expose Eddins or the others unless it was to save his own neck.

"Is that all your testimony, then?"

"Yes, except that I had no idea Cabot had tried to kill Mr. Davis, or that he'd attacked his wife. I suspected the man was a criminal, but had no idea he'd stoop that low."

"Yes, we all seem to have misjudged him. Well, gentlemen of the jury, you've heard both sides now. If there's nothing else, then..."

"I'd like to say a few words," Stephen Davis interrupted him.

"Certainly, Stephen. Let's just swear you in."

After that was done, Stephen turned in his chair to the jury.

"Back in Virginia, one of that ring of criminals came into my woodworking shop with a story about my stealing a slave of his, waving a gun, obviously drunk. The man tried to shoot me, but I managed to defend myself with a hammer. Not long after, a doctor from Caroline County and another local planter brought charges against me for murder, and for stealing a large sum of money from the man I'd had to kill.

"I was tried and acquitted of all charges, but these men and others were convinced I'd taken their money. They began harassing me, searched my cabin, spied on me and my neighbor, another planter. One of the men even tried to abduct the planter's daughter, and two of them tried to ambush me, so I knew these men were not the good citizens they pretended to be.

"But others of them came after us and we had to deal with them. A friend and I found the chest of stolen money the man had hidden and turned it over to the court there. We'd learned the identities of all this circle in the region, but not where the money was coming from. We also learned that there were periodic gold shipments, some of which were going to establish plantations west of there.

"We suspected a more sophisticated group somewhere was actually behind what we'd discovered, but had no idea who or where they were. Then an assassin was sent to avenge the deaths of those in our area, but I'd already left, coming here. He was killed when he tried to shoot the friend I mentioned. And again, I have no proof, but I strongly suspect that Hiram Garst is the replacement assassin hired by Cabot.

"It's obvious to me that the men Mr. Mason was investigating in Philadelphia are the same ones who supported the criminal ring near my place, and that Cabot was the head of it all. The stolen money was clearly coming from there, and being used in part to fund the plantations, to make the enterprises look legal.

"Oh, and one of the ring in Virginia, identified by another of them just before he died, was Samuel Eddins, Cabot's lawyer. He was detained by the local judge while the case was investigated further, but nothing was proven against him."

Again, there was the murmur of the crowd as this bigger picture came into focus. Garst was amazed at Stephen's grasp of the whole operation, and he feared anew that these people would go ahead with his execution, proof or not.

"I see. That information tells us Cabot was a bigger and more skilled criminal than we could have imagined, although attempting to kill Stephen would have justified our hanging him. But we've been spared that duty, thanks to Mr. Chiles' quick thinking and accurate handling of the outrage he visited upon Mrs. Davis in her own home.

"So, after these revelations, does anybody else have anything to add?" Nolan asked. There was a deal of murmuring, but nobody did.

"Then it's up to you to decide, gentlemen. Why don't you go into the inn and confer, and we'll wait out here for your verdict." The men filed into the building, as Belle Ketchum and her helpers came from its doorway to join the animated conversations among the other villagers.

Leighton Chiles had heard from Killebrew Ketchum that Garst had offered to disclose more of Cabot's associates. But it was clear he wasn't about to do that unless he had to. That meant he was shielding them, and of course put him in the same flock of black sheep. Chiles mentioned this to Mason, and the two agreed to wait and see if the accused man would use this ploy if the verdict went against him.

Thirty

It did not take the jurors long to reach a verdict. They filed out of the inn a bare twenty minutes after going in and ranged alongside the spectators.

"Gentlemen, have you reached a unanimous verdict?" Nolan asked.

"We have," Todd Epsworth affirmed.

"And it is?"

"We th' jury, based on th' evidence we heard, find th' defendant guilty," he announced.

"And what is your recommended sentence?"

"Wal, we think he oughta hang."

Garst heard the pronouncement with a surge of fear. But no, this couldn't be allowed to happen. He had his fall-back proposition.

"Mr. Nolan, that being the verdict, I want to propose some information I've found out that could greatly aid Mr. Mason in his work for justice, and at the same time take care of the last of Cabot's men and his organization."

"A verdict has been reached and sentence has been passed, Mr. Garst. You should have volunteered this information when you had the chance." Nolan wasn't having any of this.

"I forgot. You'll agree that a man on trial for his life is bound to get nervous. But I ask this court to hear what else I have to say." He looked at the twelve men who'd just pronounced his fate. They looked from one to another and eventually nodded agreement. A hanging hadn't been welcome, especially among the missionary members.

"Very well, if the jury agrees, you may make an additional statement. Be reminded you are still under oath."

"Yes, sir. Well, with all the focus on Cabot, I apologize for not telling you all that I'd found out the names of the others in Philadelphia who were working with him. And I can also swear to Samuel Eddins' being right in the middle of them, back in Virginia, later in Philadelphia, and here in Kentucky."

"What are the other names, then?"

"First, I'd like to propose an arrangement. If I disclose these others, which I've gone to a great deal of time and effort to ferret out, I want a pardon from you people. Your case against me is weak despite your verdict, and I'm offering valuable information in the name of justice. I ask that you let me go, since my work is done anyway, in exchange for the identities of these criminals." *There: it's all out there now*. And Garst imagined a balance, a scale, with his life on one side and these names on the other. Would they deal? Or would they even believe him? The bit about Eddins was corroborated by Davis himself, so they had no reason to doubt him. Still...

Nolan and the jury drew aside out of hearing and considered this information. Then Nolan motioned for Mason and Chiles to join them.

"I'd like very much to learn these identities," Mason urged.

"Yes, but we've already found him guilty," the engineer Thad Stillwell pointed out.

"He's already confirmed what Stephen told us about Eddins," Nolan mused. "That makes me think his word's maybe good about the others. Of course, that could be part of a last-minute ploy."

Leighton Chiles heard this exchange with a grim foreboding. His boss might actually succeed in getting the assassin off, in exchange for the long-sought identities of the rest of the Philadelphia gang. *Well, he pays me, so I guess I can swallow whatever's decided, here. Up to me, we'd have the hanging right now.*

Stephen Davis had crutched his way to join the men and had a suggestion.

"Why don't we agree to let him go, then follow him when he leaves? We'll have Eddins, based on what we know now, so let's put the pressure on him to indict Garst."

"And then what, go back on our agreement?" from Nolan.

"No, but we can re-arrest him, based on what Eddins can tell us."

"I think that's what's called double jeopardy, Stephen," Nolan warned him.

"Well, I guess you're right. But the real problem is, even with Garst's word against Eddins, the man's already been acquitted back in Virginia, and we don't have any proof of serious wrongdoing, other than that he's part of the Philadelphia ring."

"We'll just get him here, then put him on trial, too. We've already sent Ab Holloway for him, remember."

"And without enough evidence, he may go free. I know you men weren't eager to hang Garst, but you've done your duty by all of us. I'd like to clean up the whole bunch, but maybe we can't."

"I know how you feel, Stephen," Mason told him. "And with the names Garst can give us, which I suspect we can match with our suspicions, we can close this whole thing out."

"Well, just suppose Garst's going to invent some identities, to get himself free. I'd say we have to keep him here over the winter till you can act on his information. No way can we trust this man's word." Stephen had his reservations, despite his suggestion.

"He's been sentenced t' hang," Harvey Campbell reminded them. "Now, as a Christian, I'm 'gainst killin', but we gotta pertect ourselves here, just as God's people've always had t' defend themselves 'gainst outlaws an' criminals. I don't think we oughta make any deals. An' sure not keep th' man here 'mongst us all winter."

With these differing opinions, Leighton Chiles sought to simplify things.

"Why don't we hear the names he has, and Mr. Mason and I can see if our suspicions match any of them. If they do, we can assume he's telling the truth. Then, if it's agreed to let him go, we do it. If not, he's probably lying, and we go ahead and hang him." Chiles actually had no intention whatsoever of letting Garst go, no matter what these men decided, but he kept that to himself. One way or the other, this assassin would get his reward.

"I can go with that," Stephen said. "Although it galls me to think he'll still be out there. I agree with Mr. Mason that getting the rest of this canker wiped out is important—more important than the fate of this hired hand. I'm very afraid that core group will just replace Cabot and keep on with their criminal pursuits. Which as we all know, reached even to here. And I for one owe Mr. Chiles, and by association, Mr. Mason."

Harvey Campbell, having expressed his belief, said nothing. Yes, it was a hard thing to reconcile his faith with a hanging, but the Bible had some different things to say about God's will, there. There were certainly situations in the Book that had called for extreme measures, and this seemed to be one of them. But he guessed he could go along with what good men like Mason and Davis thought. And there was the minister among the throng, who, though not on the jury, would surely oppose the hanging...

"I'll have t' agree with you, Stephen," Todd Epsworth volunteered. "If you'n Mr. Mason think it's best, I say make th' deal with him, an' see which way it goes. Long's we stay close to him an' can do whut's necessary if it comes up."

Nolan looked to each of the others. No one had anything to add. The men returned to the makeshift court area. The villagers became quiet.

"We'll hear what you have to say then, Mr. Garst, with this restriction: if none of the names you give us matches the ones Mr. Mason has already uncovered, you will be executed as ordered by the jury. If the information seems accurate according to him, you'll be set free. That's our insurance that you won't lie to us."

Garst closed his eyes in relief. He knew only three others besides Cabot and Eddins, but he could invent a couple more. He hoped Mason could corroborate at least one of the real ones. He summoned his nerve one last time.

"Well then, there's a man named Codington, has a leatherworks in the capital. Don't know his first name." He looked to Mason, but the man's face was a mask. "Then there's an undertaker, Isaiah Black." Again no sign of recognition. "And another one I know for sure besides Cabot and Eddins, and the late Doctor Horace Weston up in Caroline County, and the man Hayes, also dead, is Ichabod Darby, who's a lawyer. There's a dry goods merchant named Granger I hadn't been able to find out much about, and a livery stable owner, John Ellis, just out of town north. All of them have spent a lot of money that didn't come from their businesses, I've learned."

Garst breathed deep. He'd shot his wadding on this whole affair, including invented names, had nothing else to give. He hoped mentioning the names of Weston and Hayes, which he'd picked up from Cabot, would help convince these men.

"Mr. Mason, do any of these names coincide with your findings?" Nolan asked.

"Three do, besides Eddins and Hayes. We've suspected the man Codington from the first, as Cabot's second-in-command. And we've also known about Darby, and suspected Black. Garst seems to have these correct, so I'd say he's telling the truth. At least mostly."

"Then it's agreed we can release him, unless there's any other information that's pertinent." Nolan looked around at the intent crowd. No one spoke, although there were several frowns.

Anna was disappointed. She knew Chiles and Stephen felt Garst was an assassin, a smooth man of no morals who deserved to hang, but she did agree that this proceeding had shown at least an attempt to bow to a sense of order. So, the sooner the man was out of sight, the better. That would leave only Eddins to deal with, and she supposed there'd be another similar trial to deal with him.

"You may retrieve your belongings and your horse, Mr. Garst, and leave immediately, but we won't allow you to carry a firearm. And if you ever return here, you will be shot on sight. Do you understand this?" Nolan's voice was cold.

"Thank you, S-sir. And all of you. I am an innocent man, but you have heard me and decided, and I accept your judgment." He went ahead of Ketchum into the inn, returned in a few moments with one bag, which Nolan examined, and went for his horse. The crowd gradually dispersed. Ten minutes later, Hiram Garst rode out of Ketchum's Mill.

"Now, Stephen," Belle Ketchum insisted, "You have got to come inside fer dinner, an' not wear y'self out goin' back up th' creek. Anna, you sweet thing, you been through a bunch, an' we're jist so glad this's all over."

Before Stephen joined his well-wishers in the inn, he conferred with Killebrew Ketchum.

"Killy, I just remembered we sent that young fellow Holloway after Eddins. If Garst meets them on the road, I'm afraid there'll be trouble. So shouldn't we go ahead and have somebody follow him, catch up with him, make sure he doesn't warn the lawyer, or try to team up with him?"

"Yer right, Stephen. I'd say Harvey's right fer that." He called the veteran over, and they explained the situation.

"I'm your man, then," he agreed. "I'll take Todd with me, just in case. Don't trust th' lawyer none, neither." The two saddled their horses, provisioned and armed themselves, and rode out after Garst.

Stephen was worried about the people here who'd depended on the ironworks for their livelihood. He and Archie Nolan discussed this during the meal, between bouts of catching-up and celebration at his having survived.

"I guess I could run the place," Nolan mused. "But we'd have to ship some, get some money in before we could pay anybody. Certainly be a while, though, and with winter right on us, it doesn't look good."

"I'm thinking we should scale down anyway," Stephen said. "If there's enough ore close by just for our own needs, it should last. What we should do is keep going till winter shuts us down, make a few shipments as we can, then just adjust production. I know that'll mean fewer workers, and that'll be hard on some of them. You have any suggestions?"

"If it was summer, folks could find other work, but this time of year, we'll just have to dig in and get by, looks like. If we had some capital, we could gear down, like you said, and get through till spring, when those who don't want to stay could leave and find other work. Like always, it comes down to money, I'm afraid."

"And there's the question of ownership of the works. I suppose Cabot's heirs, if he has any, technically own it now."

"That doesn't bother me at all," the prospector declared. "I say we form a citizen's group here and take over the business sort of by default. As well as whatever money he had left here. Nobody's going to challenge that, with prospects so thin anyway. Cabot was counting on monopolizing the entire region's iron, but in reality, we're just an obscure outpost."

"Well, I'll leave that up to you and whoever you decide to bring into a group. But maybe I can help some with the money, just to tide us over, you know. I've a bit saved." He was thinking of the gold from that chest his friend Tom Logan had divided among the two of them and Ned Drake. There'd be a certain justice in using Cabot's stolen money to help the people here through the winter.

~ * ~

Hiram Garst rode with an exhilaration at being free that almost overcame his chagrin at not having a weapon and only a few coins. He'd have to remedy that at first opportunity. He could get more money from Eddins and purchase a gun at Saltville, but he didn't like the idea of being defenseless here on the road. And he couldn't imagine that everyone in the village would honor his release.

No, that devil Bone, or Chiles or whoever he was, could well follow him and shoot him from behind without an ounce of remorse. Or as a lone traveler he could be ambushed easily by bandits, as he so well knew. Well, he had his knife, for what that was worth. Maybe he could slip up on a lone camper from behind tonight and disarm him. There should still be men going to Ketchum's Mill, unaware that the ironworks would be closing soon.

Which brought up the question of how he'd make a living, with his benefactor dead. He'd unfortunately gambled away most of the money he'd made as manager of the works, and what little was left wouldn't last long. And just how much could he extract from Eddins?

So then he'd also rob whoever he could get a gun from, of anything he might have on him. That and whatever he could get in Saltville should tide him over.

But staying in the region would get him caught, he knew, remembering the cleanup of the MacNaughton clan out of Saltville. *No, best to head for new territory.* He thought briefly that it might have been better to go over the mountains further into Kentucky, but he missed the allure of bigger towns.

There was Charleston, if he could traverse the whole southeastern part of the country. And the coastal towns in Virginia, with their shipping industry. Or really, any place he chose.

Right now, the object was to arm himself, add whatever he could to his personal treasury, and get out of the immediate area. Again he remembered that some of the villagers hadn't wanted Mason and Davis to let him go either, and he feared pursuit unless he kept riding fast.

He wasn't about to let that happen.

~ * ~

Young Abe Holloway was completing the errand to Saltville to summon Samuel Eddins, supposedly at Reginald Cabot's request. He hadn't been told of Stephen's survival, or of the plans to try Eddins, Garst and Cabot. When questioned by the lawyer as to the nature of Cabot's request, Holloway hadn't been able to answer, because he didn't know. The men at Ketchum's Mill had felt it best he be kept in the dark, unable to let anything slip.

Now he accompanied the somewhat disgruntled Eddins on horseback toward the village, making good time on the improved road. The lawyer hadn't wanted to make the trip, with snow a real possibility, but he reasoned that his employer—*partner*—as he liked to think of Cabot, must have come up with another money-making scheme he needed help with.

They'd been on the road several days when they met Hiram Garst riding toward them. Holloway didn't think it odd that the man was on the road, since he knew Cabot was back to run his operation. *Prob'ly sent th' man off on 'nother of his business deals,* he reasoned.

Eddins, on the other hand, found it extremely strange that Garst would be leaving the village with winter at hand. And just why couldn't *he* have been sent to summon him? Something was wrong, and the lawyer's survival instincts were alerted.

Sure enough, Garst stopped to talk excitedly to the lawyer about the happenings in Ketchum's Mill.

"Mr. Cabot's dead," he blurted out to begin with. "And the whole place has gone bloodthirsty. They put me on trial, but they hadn't any proof of anything, so they let me go. And this you won't believe: Stephen Davis is alive. Hurt bad, but recovering. He sat in on the trial and backed that Carson fellow—only his name is really Jedediah Mason—in acquitting me. Now, I know something of Mason from Philadelphia, and I'm sure you do too, so add him being there to the rest, and that place just wasn't healthy for me." He paused for breath, then asked the obvious question:

"So what're you doing on the road? Cabot send for you?"

"He did, but if what you're saying is true, this looks like some kind of a trap, doesn't it?"

Abe Holloway had listened to this hurried account with shock, and only then began to realize these men could be a distinct danger to him. Garst didn't appear to be armed, but he knew Eddins was. He decided to try to talk his way clear of whatever might happen. He was frankly scared but determined not to show it.

"Well then, Mr. Eddins, I'd say you'd be th' man t'take over th' ironworks, bein's you done all th' paperwork. Wouldn't you say so, Mr. Garst?" As a precaution, the young man backed his horse a few steps, and his hand was near his pistol.

Eddins thought about that for a moment: *could* he step in and take over? Carry out the plans he and Cabot had come up with? Manage the monopoly of the entire region's iron supply?

Or would he be riding right into a hornet's nest, the villagers inflamed by whatever had gotten Cabot killed. He needed to know more.

"How did Cabot die?" he asked Garst. That'd be the key: how much did they know about the man?

"Well, seems he had an eye for Davis' widow—only she wasn't a widow—and went up there a little drunk to claim her. I just got this in bits and pieces, since they'd grabbed me at the works, but either Davis or that ugly Bone—and his name's really Chiles, Mason's bodyguard, shot him when he tried to force himself on her. Don't know how much of that's true, though. Lot of talk, gossip, different versions of what happened.

"I see. Why'd they arrest you? And who headed this all up?"

"Ketchum was elected constable, and they thought they had evidence I'd done some dirty work for Cabot..." At this point, Garst became aware of Abe Holloway's intently taking in every word. "Nothing to it, of course, and some of them saw that clear. Like I said, this Mason, and Davis even..." Eddins was thinking:

Well, if Mason didn't know anything solid against Cabot, what's to keep me from a legitimate claim on the works? With him dead, and Garst gone, looks like I can...

As if reading Eddins' mind, Hiram Garst realized he'd have to tell him the real situation. Or maybe not...why not let him ride into the village and take his chances? It wasn't any concern of Garst's, really. This boy hadn't heard anything damaging; they both could go on, none the wiser.

Then Garst thought about the distribution center in Saltville. With Eddins' help, he could well cash in on whatever funds were there, maybe sell off iron stock, and the two of them would be well set up. He couldn't very well do that by himself, since the lawyer knew all the necessary details of who owed what, where assets were, and...

"You need to know, Mr. Eddins, that Mason and Chiles told everybody what they suspected Cabot of: being the center of a whole illegal operation in Philadelphia. That's why they tracked him down here in the first place. You may know Mason's a sort of vigilante up there, working with the police to stop commercial thefts." As he talked, Garst was working his horse around so that Abe Holloway would be between him and Eddins. This boy was both a danger to them, and his guns would be a help, if he could handle this right. "So I'd say you'd be suspected, being so close to Cabot…"

Yes, Mason, the nasty fly in the ointment. No, I could never succeed with him right there with whatever he's managed to find out. No, I guess it's time to run; cash out what I can in Saltville and get away from here ahead of him and Chiles. He considered the best way to rid himself and Garst of young Holloway. Maybe he could hold his gun on him while the assassin took his weapons…

The boy was looking from Eddins to Garst, who had somehow boxed him between them. In a flash of insight, he realized he had just a chance, and must take it. They could ride him down otherwise…

He drew his pistol, cocked it and aimed at Eddins, trying to keep his eye also on Garst, who was sidling his horse closer.

"Reckon you'd best take out yer gun slow, Mr. Eddins, an' drop it on th' ground. Garst, you ride on now, an' no harm done." His nerves were on high, but he tried to keep his hand steady, and started to back his horse out of line with Garst.

But Garst was fast. He leaped off his horse, knife in hand, and grabbed Holloway's leg, slashing it deeply. The boy's gun went off, missing the lawyer, who then deliberately drew his pistol and cocked it as the boy tried to fend off the assassin. He reached for his own knife and succeeded in getting in a few ineffective jabs at his attacker. But Garst was adept at this kind of fighting and, hauling the young man off his horse, slashed his throat in one deadly sweep. Blood spurted.

Garst calmly stood back, then bent and retrieved Holloway's pistol, powder horn and shot pouch, and reloaded as a shaking Samuel Eddins tried to keep his eyes off the grisly spectacle.

"Damn, did you have to do that, Garst? He was just a boy… couldn't we have just let him go?"

"And have the whole damn village after us? With Mason and those bloodthirsty settlers? And maybe even Davis, we wouldn't have a chance. No, only way was to clean up the loose ends, Eddins. That's always how Cabot handled it, and how I've learned to. Now," he reached, took Holloway's rifle and the reins of his horse, and mounted his own. "We've got some work to do in Saltville, then we'd best find ourselves another place to be.

"Oh, and put that gun away before you shoot yourself in the foot or something."

~ * ~

Campbell and Eppsworth had heard the gunshot, having come to within less than a quarter mile behind Garst, who'd ridden far and fast. They knew he'd try to steal a firearm somehow, and certainly, as Stephen had suspected, team up with Eddins in Saltville. Their job was to see to it that the assassin left the country. Or, if he tried any violence, remove him from the face of the earth.

Now they rode cautiously forward toward the sound they'd heard. A turn of the road showed it to be empty, but somebody had to be close. The slightest blue haze remained from the gunpowder, and then they saw something lying in the road. Motioning for Eppsworth to cover him, Campbell rode ahead, searching the bare trees on the sides of the road as he did so.

He dismounted, turned the body over. Seeing Abe Holloway with his throat cut, blood still gushing from there and a slashed leg, Campbell knew immediately what'd happened: Garst had gotten close enough to knife the boy, whose shot had certainly missed. Holloway hadn't been a fighter, and the veteran felt a flash of anger at their having sent him on this errand.

But where was Garst? And Eddins? This was about the right place for the lawyer and the boy to be, on their way to the village. Yes, and that would explain it: Eddins must have drawn down on the young man, covered him while the assassin attacked him. He motioned Eppsworth forward, studying the multiple hoofprints, realizing what the new situation was.

"Garst's killed th' boy, Todd, fer his guns. An' from th' tracks, looks like he's teamed up with Eddins, or somebody, headed on back t'Saltville. An' I'll wager it was Eddins. Reckon we oughta git after 'em, see they don't git away."

"Guess so, Harvey. I was for lettin' th' snake go, but now I reckon we've gotta be th' law now, ain't we?" Staring at the mangled body before them.

"Looks that way." He straightened. "All right, they couldn't be far ahead, 'less they figgered somebody might've heard th' shot, and are ridin' hard." The men dragged the body off the road, mounted and rode rapidly ahead. Even if the killers started fast, as they were sure Garst had, their tiring horses would mean they'd have to slow soon. A steady pace would close the distance between them, the two ex-soldiers knew.

Thirty-one

Hiram Garst and Samuel Eddins maintained their lead on their pursuers, unaware of them, but taking no chances. They were also able to swap out the horses, having Holloway's mount. As darkness fell, they resolved to camp well off the road, fearing the discovery of the young man's body. No one but a Ketchum's Mill settler would connect them to the killing, but that was exactly what Garst feared.

Still, it should take several days for word to get back to the village and any kind of concerted pursuit to be mounted. That should allow the two of them to liquidate the stores of iron and steel at Saltville and be away with the money.

Eddins didn't trust the assassin, but he'd worked with Cabot long enough to know such men were necessary. He reasoned that this man needed his skills also, in securing some sort of livelihood for them. While Eddins could start a law practice almost anywhere, building a client base would take time. And he rather preferred the easy and quicker money Cabot's enterprises had generated.

The idea of traveling back to Philadelphia had a certain appeal, since the rest of the circle was still there and presumably functioning. Eddins was part of that, and could fit back in, he was sure. So could Garst.

But with Mason and Chiles after them, that was the last place they'd be safe. So it would have to be new territory, and the two men discussed it around their campfire that night.

"I like the idea of Charleston," Garst ventured. "From what I hear, there's a lot of money there, culture, trade, shipping, and the plantations. You know anything about the place?"

"Not really. I never thought about coming south, but it seems a good idea. There's also Richmond and Williamsburg, both closer. And the Virginia coastal towns, Norfolk, and Baltimore on up. But of course Charleston is further from any likelihood that anyone would recognize us."

Echoing Eddins' earlier thought, Garst suggested starting a venture much like the one in the capital, recruiting a network of robbers to funnel money to the two of them.

"You know all the legalities, how to hide money and all, I'm sure. I could find the men, and we could make it work anywhere, but the bigger the city the better." Garst was tired of the backwoods, and envisioned the opulent offerings available in any town of size.

"We'd have to travel across Virginia and North Carolina, and it's the wrong time of year," Eddins pointed out. A cold wind had risen, and clouds blotted the stars. "Unless we head south right now, we could get snowed in."

"Then let's do that...few days in Saltville, get what we can out of the stores there, and strike out for warmer places. If we should get caught out, we could hole up for the winter, preferably in a decent town."

"We'd have to go east first, since there are more mountains to cross, south. These hills flatten out once over the Blue Ridge. I'd say we'd be ahead of the weather if we can get over that."

So that was the plan they agreed upon. After a meal of the provisions Eddins had with him, he sought out a place some distance from the fire, stretched out for sleep. Garst, from long habit, moved even further off into the brush before rolling in his blankets. The tied horses munched on the grain the lawyer and Holloway had brought for the trip, and quiet settled over the camp.

Eddins had trouble going to sleep, the spectre of Garst slashing the boy's throat a grim reminder that the man he traveled with had no scruples about killing. Well, the life he—they—had chosen required that, he supposed. And at least the young man hadn't any family. He'd been hired at Saltville to be Cabot's errand boy at the ironworks and had picked up other odd jobs before that.

And those bumpkins sent him to take me right into their trap. Well, I can be thankful for Garst, scary as the man is. But he'd keep his primed pistol on him at all times, just the same.

~ * ~

"They got Holloway's hoss now, so they'll have kept on futher'n they could've, other," Campbell observed. "But they'll hafta camp somewheres, an' that's where we'll get 'em."

Eppsworth expressed a concern to his friend he'd harbored for many months.

"Harvey, just how c'n we go 'bout killin' these snakes, an' still be good Christians? Been troublin' me some, y'know? Bible says plain, no killin'. 'Course in th' war it was different...had to d'fend ourselves. But that's a lotta why I was 'ginst hangin' th' man."

"Hard one, all right. But a lot in th' Book 'bout defendin' y'self too, in th' Old Testament. Seems like God, He intended His folks t'be safe 'gainst enemies, an' they hadda deal right rough with 'em."

"But Jesus says we gotta turn th' other cheek," the younger man pointed out.

"Yeah, I reckon. But Abe back there, he got hisself killed not defendin' hisself quick 'nough." They rode in silence a while. "Naw, I've wondered 'bout th' same thing, Todd. Take Stephen Davis. Him an' Killy took out them MacNaughton boys on back, an' when t'other one grabbed McKnight's girl, Stephen shot him dead. Now, I don't find a thing wrong in th' way that went, but I wuz glad I didn't hafta do it."

"Me, too. But now we're th' only ones knows what happened t' Abe, an' if we *don't* git them two, they're gonna git on outta th' country, an' no tellin' who all they'll kill, an' whatever other devilment they'll do."

"Reckon we'll just hafta ask God to fergive us, Todd, but meantime, maybe He's got it figgered for us t'take care of things, make 'em as right as we can."

"Wal, I'm some worried too, 'bout how th' others gonna take it, us just shootin' these fellers dead."

"You mean you're 'fraid th' preacher's daughter Marina won't take to it, don'tcha?"

"Reckon that's a big part of it, yeah. I been tryin' t'measure up to that'n ever since they come. Dunno what to expect, we come on back, tell what we done."

"Maybe we won't tell. Or just we tell Stephen. That man won't breathe a word to th' others."

"Don't wanta lie about it, but mebbe you're right. Just wish we could handle it 'nother way than a cold killin'. They come after us, I'm all right with that, but just slippin' up on 'em in their sleep, that's 'nuther thing."

"Well, don'tcha underestimate that Garst. Man's a stone killer. We knew it before, an' he's got to Abe, 'thout no gun, an' cut him t'death. Give that snake enny chance, he'll kill us both 'thout battin' an eye."

"What about Eddins? He prob'ly ain't killed nobody hisself."

"No, mebbe not. But I figger he hadda helt a gun on Abe, helped some way. An' Mason and Chiles, they know he's been in th' middle of all that other stuff from b'fore..."

"An' got off. Slick lawyer, he'd git off again, we let him go, wouldn't he?"

"Likely. Anyways, we'll keep our sights on Garst, but don't give Eddins a chance, either. Garst's told him ever'thing, sure, an' he knows he'll git hung if th' folks git their hands on him. He'll fight like a bear, be sure of that."

~ * ~

Stephen Davis rested a few days at the inn at the insistence of Belle Ketchum and Anna, and continued to mend. He speculated on the success of the two ex-soldiers in their pursuit of Garst, privately convinced a situation would arise in which the two men would have to kill the assassin. He was sorry he hadn't been up to the task himself, but had complete confidence in the two. While Garst had obviously survived in his evil trade for years, he was on the run, and temporarily, at least, without weapons.

Of course, that could change in an instant, if the man could rob a traveler, perhaps camp with him and steal his gun. Well, that's why he'd sent Campbell and Eppsworth, to see that sort of thing didn't happen.

But then there was Eddins, who just might meet Garst on the road. Given the time since young Holloway had left to summon the lawyer, that could well occur. He expressed that fear to Killebrew Ketchum.

"Wal, Stephen, I reckon Ab'll be all right, if Harvy an' Todd are close by. If not, yer right, thet snake Garst c'd do some bad. He'd shore tell Eddins whut's happened here, an' th' lawyer'll turn tail." The miller thought about this for a few minutes.

"Seems we left a hole in our plans, all right," Stephen reflected. "Does Mason have anything to say about this?"

"He's been gittin' ready t'leave out, 'fore th' weather gits bad. Ain't talked with him none, m'self. Him an' Archie been goin' over th' ironworks stuff close, stayin' late at th' place, tryin' t'figger out jist whut t'do 'bout all that."

Yes, the dead-end iron venture. Well, it'll just have to sort itself out. Don't see how we can help all these newer men make it through the winter, except on the barest of rations.

That situation had already begun to change, with a few of the ironworkers heading over the mountains further into Kentucky, a few planning to go back toward Saltville, despite the assurances of support. Nolan's plans to operate the works at a reduced rate left many without prospects, but as always, these pioneers would manage. Newer cabins had gone up further up the side streams and with trapping, hunting, and whatever they and their supporters could manage, it appeared most of these settlers could survive.

Stephen chafed at his inactivity, as he had ever since his injuries. With the ironworks activities coming to a near halt, there wasn't much ahead for him but maintaining his own place, but he'd never before been forced just to sit and wait. The only good part was, if the Garst/Eddins situation could be resolved, he could at least see closure to the threat of violence here, and life could settle into whatever rhythm was possible.

But there was the growing concern that he'd added his voice to the decision to let the assassin Garst go free, albeit it with able men on his trail. It all added up to a depressing time for him.

Anna tended her husband well, as did Belle and her staff, even to the extent that he became a bit crabby at all the attention. What he wanted most of all was to get on back home and put his hand to whatever work he could manage in his condition.

To this end, he tried to mount his horse, with Ketchum's help, but found he couldn't stay on without the strength of his bad leg.

"Just tie me across his back," he instructed Anna, who put her foot down at this request and refused to do it.

"You'll break something open, Stephen. If you're set on going home, let me rig the travois again. The horse didn't like that before, but if it'll stop your complaining we'll get you there."

So this man of action submitted to being hauled up the trail again, the mile to his turnoff, and dragged up the steep way to the cabin. George Weller had insisted on accompanying his friend, and literally carried him into the house.

"Thanks, George. Sorry to put you out, but I was about to go crazy down at the village." Stephen sank gratefully into the padded chair he'd occupied since being able to get out of bed weeks before.

"Nothin' to it, Stephen. You done lost a lotta weight; ain't moren' a sack of 'taters. Now, I'll be cuttin' some more farwood 'fore I go."

"Not necessary; Mason and Chiles got in a lot while they were here." Stephen had bidden the Philadelphia investigator farewell on leaving the village, but Chiles was nowhere to be seen. In fact, he hadn't been around lately, the craftsman reflected.

"Gone hunting," Mason had told him. "Wanted to be by himself for a while, he told me. Didn't like the way we handled the Garst thing at all. I'm anxious to be away as soon as he gets back, but I couldn't begrudge him a little time off."

Stephen busied himself with carving kitchen utensils for Anna, making small pieces of furniture, anything he could do that didn't require standing or much moving about. He figured he'd be mobile about the time he ran out of such projects. Anna had returned to teaching at the school and would do so until the weather made the trip too difficult.

~ * ~

It was on the second night after Garst had killed Holloway that the ex-soldiers caught up with the outlaws. They'd made camp well off the road, but the damp breeze carried a trace of smoke from their fire to their stalkers, and they stopped to confer.

"Now, Garst'll keep away from th' fire, Todd, an' mebbe even roll some blankets t'make it look like he's there with Eddins. We gotta find him first, er he'll likely git away, er git a shot at us, even dark as 'tis. You got better ears than me, way mine buzzes, all that cannon fire f'm th' war. You slip way out an' around, an' I'll watch. Could still be at th' fire, an' if he is, I'll git him clean first, 'fore he knows we're here."

"That'll take some time, so don't look for me t'git around ennytime soon. Not gonna be easy spottin' him, but give me long 'nough, I'll hear somethin', if it ain't moren' him snorin'." Eppsworth tied his horse with Campbell's, well back where Eddins' and Garst's horses wouldn't hear or smell them. Then the two advanced cautiously toward the faint smoke, taking care not to rustle the fallen wet leaves.

Eddins' nerves were on high. Garst had convinced him that surely Davis had sent men to follow them, and with the discovery of Holloway's body they could be close. As a result, both men stuffed leaves into rolled blankets with their hats in place and left them by the fire, while they found two positions well back in the woods.

They did tie the three horses close to the camp, knowing their absence would give their plan away.

"What if men do come?" Eddins asked the assassin. He envisioned faceless avengers encircling them, sworn to slaughter them.

"Then we'll shoot them. Should be enough light from the fire if they come close, and they will. Davis is the only one I'm worried about, and he can't ride yet." Garst didn't have much concern for the men from the village, even Chiles. He was undoubtedly Mason's bodyguard, but that didn't mean he was to be overly feared. It was actually hard to reconcile the vacant-eyed image the man had presented in his role at the village with any idea of a dangerous killer. At least he consoled himself with that thought. *But they'll have sent somebody, or maybe a whole bunch of them.*

When Campbell slipped up close to the campfire, Eppsworth stayed well back, at first covering him, then starting his circuit of the place. The older man settled himself to watch, soon noting that neither shape near the fire moved, and he knew why...not only had Garst slept away in the brush, Eddins had, too.

That gave him a dilemma: his partner might run onto both men and be at a distinct disadvantage. And if Campbell started in a circle the other way to help, he and Eppsworth might shoot at each other. But no use staying here with two dummies, he reasoned, and so slipped back and started a very slow stalk. He eyed every shadow from the flickering fire, paused at each step to listen, focused on every hiding place.

He expected the men to be farther beyond the fire; they'd assume searchers would come from the road. Or possibly the wily Garst would be closer, with the idea of cutting off any stalkers from behind as they approached the campfire. *Best t'expect anything, then.*

Todd Eppsworth had done enough scouting in the army to know some of the tricks of the business and reasoned along much the same lines as Campbell. The fact that both had survived the war meant they'd become adept at this sort of thing. He too, let his eyes search out every hidden spot as he advanced one cautious step at a time on the leaves sodden from a recent shower.

A half hour passed, with only perhaps a fourth of the circle searched by each man. That left the back half, and raised the odds of the hunters' discovering their quarry sooner. At about the same time, both the ex-soldiers sat against tree trunks and rested, giving their nerves a chance to settle and their tense muscles to relax for a few minutes. Both knew they had to keep calm—no place for an excited missed shot.

Campbell reflected that the two should have arranged some sort of signal to keep from shooting at each other, but it was too late now. And, of course, that might alert their targets. Eppsworth would know Garst hadn't been at the campfire, since he'd heard nothing. And he'd reason Campbell would circle the other way eventually. *Wal, if I come on 'em first, I'll just hafta yell out to him soon's I shoot Garst. Be hard t'tell, out away f'm th' fire, but it's th' best I c'n do.*

The heavy clouds completely masked a partial moon, casting the entire forest in a heavy, misty gloom. Visibility was low, and each man knew he'd almost stumble on the outlaws before he saw them. They might even have covered themselves with leaves as camouflage, something both stalkers had done as soldiers. The one thing both knew was that Garst would know all the ways to make himself invisible.

So it was that Eppsworth came upon the first mound he sensed was a sleeping man. And yes, wet leaves barely covered the shape. He stopped completely, slowing his breathing, watching for movement. It came with a slight turning and an arm moving a little. The young man searched for the second man, but saw nothing. *Garst, he'll be off a ways f'm Eddins, even this far f'm camp. Or is this Garst? No way t'tell. Lawyer's shorter, but with those leaves piled, can't guess.*

He knew if he fired, the other man would very likely be on him in an instant, and at least the powder smoke would give his position away. Or if the man were awake, he might even see the flash itself. *No, have to use the knife, an' that's gonna be a bunch harder.*

Eppsworth still harbored his misgivings about killing a man in cold blood, but after seeing the slaughtered Abe Holloway's body, he steeled himself for what had to be done. He had only the one arm, so would have to pin the man with his knee to keep him from firing a pistol. He thought back...Garst was right-handed, but he couldn't remember about the lawyer.

He waited, hoping the man would turn over or otherwise reveal more of himself so he could launch his attack without getting himself shot. *No hurry here: got all th' time I'll need, an' nobody knows I'm here.* He slowly turned his head for a close scrutiny of the woods around him. Wouldn't do to alert the second man, more so if that happened to be Garst. So he'd wait, sure that Campbell was working his way toward him, maybe closer to the center of the circle or farther out, but getting nearer.

Campbell had zigzagged his course to cover more of the circle he reasoned the men would choose. They wouldn't be that far from the campfire, fearing the loss of their horses. So he'd find them eventually, unless Eppsworth did first. And the one-armed man wouldn't be able to tangle with two men, one an accomplished killer.

And after what seemed half the night, he did come upon the same leaf-covered shape, alone in a little depression where a tree had uprooted many years ago. He searched the area for the second man, but found no trace. Then he caught the slightest movement beyond the mound and tensed, his pistol out front. He focused hard on the spot, and eventually made out a crouching man. *So, one's sleepin' an' t'other's watchin'? Then that'll be Eddins asleep, an' Garst takin' th' first watch, most likely. Won't figger it's so dangerous on near mornin'.*

Just then the dim figure put out a hand and waved at him. The hand was empty, and he realized it belonged to Todd Eppsworth. *Damn...might'near shot th' boy. No, that'd brought Garst, if he's th' one out there somewhere.*

He waved in return, and indicated that he would attack the sleeping figure. With only one arm, Eppsworth would have a hard time fending off the aroused man. Campbell signaled for his partner to watch for the second man. And he recalled the younger man's reluctance to take another life, no matter its necessity. For his own part, Campbell knew he'd have to make his peace with God for this, but that was a necessary action.

He set aside his rifle in aching slow motion, tucked his pistol into his belt, and drew his knife by slow degrees. He could tell he'd come up on the sleeper's left side, so he'd pin that arm with his knee, the other with his left hand, and plunge the knife with his right. The sequence was clear in his mind.

He took a deep breath, let it partially out, and lunged. The sharp roar of a rifle sounded as he landed on the man, and he felt a ball tear his coat. But having attacked under fire countless times in the war, Campbell ignored the shot and sank the knife again and again into the man struggling under his weight.

Eppsworth fired his rifle at the flash that had come from farther out and heard a grunt. He rolled quickly aside, and so dodged the return pistol fire. He did not shoot a second time, fearing an attack with his guns empty. He heard a crashing in the brush and followed the sound, keeping back, pistol extended.

That's prob'ly Garst, an' I b'lieve I've at least nicked him. Harvey'll be along right quick, so I dass'nt git too close. Man's shorely got 'nuther pistol, an' I wouldn't doubt he c'n reload in th' dark, same's us.

Sure enough, Campbell caught up in seconds, and the two men separated a few yards and followed the diminishing sound of the man ahead of them, hurriedly making his way in a circle to get back to the horses. By the time the stalkers realized his intent, he'd covered much of the ground. He was running headlong now, counting on outdistancing his pursuers.

They ran too, but stopped frequently to hear where their quarry was. He was well ahead, and Campbell ran faster, right for the distant flicker of the fire, calling for Eppsworth to cover him. They both crashed through underbrush, heedless of scratches, whipping branches, desperate to reach the outlaw before he could jump on a horse and escape.

Garst, for it was he who'd seen Campbell slipping up on Eddins, came in sight of the tethered horses. No time to saddle one, with two men after him and the pain from a flesh wound hindering his actions. He'd have to slash the rope, leap onto his horse bareback, just save himself...

No, wait. Surely there aren't but the two...I can pick them off by the fire. Take everything with me. He retreated, willed his labored breathing to slow, checked to find he was losing only a little blood from a shallow side wound, and reloaded both his rifle and pistol. At least one man would rush to the horses, and he'd be an easy shot. He braced the rifle against a tree, just in time to see Campbell pause well back, a dim shape barely outlined by the fire.

Hiram Garst, the accomplished, invincible assassin, cocked his rifle and drew a bead on the indistinct shape, partially exposed behind a tree. *Even if the other man holds back and I can't kill him, too, I'll have time to get away.*

He was back in control. And he'd destroy these backwoodsmen who dared try to ambush him. He stilled his heaving breath, willed his hands quiet, put pressure on the trigger.

But a strong arm suddenly snaked around his throat from behind, and a long blade pierced his side, ripping sideways, slashing. Garst dropped the rifle, scrabbling at the arm choking the life out of him. He twisted, then despite the pain, reached a hand for his own knife.

And found himself looking into the hard eyes of Leighton Chiles, whose arm had released him for the instant it took for him to slash the assassin's throat. He clutched at the spurting blood, staggered, fell.

"Don't shoot me, Harvey!" Chiles called. "You get the other one?" Campbell had taken cover behind the tree at sound of the scuffle.

"Did that. But who're you?" Then Chiles stepped closer to the fire, hands empty. "Oh, Mr. Chiles." He moved into the firelight. "Didn't think Garst c'd see me, but maybe he did." He came closer, looked at the bloody form on the ground. "Thanks kindly, sir, seems like we was up 'ginst 'nother old soldier here, full of tricks." Epsworth joined the men, seeing at a glance what had happened.

"Yes, but one old soldier just wasn't a match for three of us, I guess," Chiles observed.

Thirty-two

The three men rode back into Ketchum's Mill in a light, falling snow. They dismounted at the mill to report to the constable what had occurred. Ketchum sent Carver MacNaughton for Mason and Nolan at the ironworks, so the principals would all learn the news at once. He noted the somber expressions the men wore and knew their account would have a bad side to it. More so since young Abe Holloway was not with them, nor Eddins.

"Wisht Stephen wuz here too, but I kin let him know later. You men git on over by th' fire an' warm y'selves." Belle and her girls were busy at the inn, but the constable poured each man a mug from the kettle at the mill fireplace.

After a half hour, Carver returned with the others, and they ranged around the fire to hear the news. The dusting of snow melted off each man as he absorbed the welcome heat. Winter was finally upon them.

To a man, they all looked at Leighton Chiles as the unofficial leader of the expedition. His long face was even more somber than usual.

"Men, I hate to be the one to say we did wrong, but letting Garst go was a mistake. He apparently met young Ab Holloway and Eddins on the road, and with the lawyer's help, he managed to kill Holloway and take his weapons." He let that announcement soak in, and saw the shock on the faces of Ketchum, Nolan, Mason and MacNaughton. "Harvey and Todd were just a few minutes too late to stop it, and I hadn't caught up yet. It pains me no end that we let another innocent man die at the hands of that snake."

Chiles knew he was placing the blame on his employer and the others, including Stephen Davis, who'd agreed to the deal with the assassin in order to clean out the criminal ring in Philadelphia. Just then he didn't care what they thought.

"I suppose I'm to blame partly too, since I let him get a head start. But I knew in my bones he'd do something like that, so I rode hard to catch up. Didn't quite make it. They'd ridden hard too, trying to get away, but Harvey and Todd had slipped up on their camp and should have been able to take them without trouble.

"But Garst was a wily one and they'd slept away from the fire, and apparently Eddins was asleep while Garst stood the first watch. He tried to kill Harvey while he was taking care of Eddins, then ran for the horses. Todd did wing him, even there in the dark.

"But instead of getting away, which he had time to do, he hid, and was just drawing a bead on Harvey back at their fire when I got him. The man was out to do the most harm he could, and I have absolutely no regrets about killing him. Losing one good man was more than enough. We buried all three alongside the Saltville road, with a shovel from the O'Neils."

There was complete silence then, only the fire crackling and the wind outside intruding on the thoughts of the men. Mason, as the one who'd urged the strongest that they spare Garst, felt a complete fool, and the loss of Holloway weighed heavily on him. Chiles rose, retrieved his hat and coat.

"Now, I'll be the one to ride up to Davis' place and tell Stephen, so he'll know soonest." His eyes hardened. "I will say this: Harvey and Todd are the best men here." With that he stepped out into the falling snow.

Leighton Chiles was angry. Angry at his employer for his softness in dealing with the criminals, the killers, the entire situation. He respected Mason, but couldn't agree with his methods when the truth had been so plain. He kept thinking of young Holloway, a lad who'd set out to find his destiny in this new land, cut down almost casually by evil he shouldn't have been exposed to.

As he often did, Chiles compared himself to a wild animal: one who must strike first if he is to survive the predators that surround him. No, he was a reasoning being, but that reason included action where it was necessary, and like Davis, he'd had to do what needed doing and leave the hesitation to others.

So it was that the man was deep in thought as he rode up to the porch of the cabin up the hollow. It was evening, and a warm candle-glow came from within. He hailed the house.

The door opened, and Stephen welcomed him inside. The fire was blazing, and the comfort of the room invaded Chiles' being with a sudden but complete warmth. *Dear God, I wish for a place like this.*

Anna also greeted Mason's associate, inviting him to supper. He accepted with his usual good manners, and she returned to the kitchen to lay out the meal. Stephen offered whiskey, and the two men sat before the fire, sipping the product of old Daughtry, whose skill at this art had improved greatly with demand.

"I take it you've news," Stephen invited.

"I do, and I suppose it's good news, depending on how you take it."

"That sounds a bit ominous, but I suppose life will continue to be near-equal parts of both kinds."

"Agreed. Well, the good news is that Garst and Eddins are dead and buried. The bad news is, so is Abe Holloway. They got the jump on him before Harvey and Todd could reach him."

This hit Stephen hard. As general all-around handyman, Holloway had been a favorite in the village. He knew then he should never have agreed to sending the assassin off, even unarmed. Chiles was watching him for his reaction, which was one of sadness mixed with anger, some of it at himself.

"And in our effort to establish law and order here, we've lost one of our best young men. Damn it, Chiles, I should've just shot Garst as soon as you told us he'd tried to kill Mason."

"I wanted to, but I let my employer talk me out of it, Stephen. I know most of us wanted to avoid lowering ourselves to his level, but we overdid it, I'm afraid." His morose face seemed sadder in the firelight, the furrows deeper. "I guess any way we'd handled it would have been wrong, in some respects."

"That boy, though: I sent Harvey and Todd after Garst too late. You must know, not being able to ride, to handle these things myself is torture, Leighton."

"I can imagine. You'd handled things here quite well, till that bastard Cabot pulled that unspeakable attack on you. I see you're getting around a bit better, but overall, how are you?"

"I'll mend. Enforced captivity here this winter anyway, and by spring I should be as recovered as a man in my shape's ever going to be."

Anna announced supper, and Stephen was able to hobble into the kitchen using only a cane. Chiles stayed at his elbow in case he stumbled, but that didn't happen. The master of the house sank into a cushioned hickory chair, adjusting the sore places as best he could. He deferred to Anna to say grace, which she did.

"Well, Mr. Chiles, we're always glad to have you here. I'm assuming that in your absence you've been instrumental in putting an end to the...troubles that have unfortunately plagued us here."

"You are a perceptive lady," he replied. "I've told Stephen what happened, but again to put it simply: Garst and Eddins are dead, but so I'm afraid, is Abe Holloway."

"Oh, no! That young man, with his life before him. Oh, that's so bad. Stephen was worried about a confrontation on the Saltville road, and I suppose that's what happened." She let her thoughts go back to the young man. "We will keep Abe in our prayers."

"Surely. But I don't mind telling you both that I'm somewhat disillusioned at the way it all got...well, out of hand. As a Biblical reference, I think we should have slain the Goliaths earlier, all of them."

"Hindsight, but perhaps you're right." She thought a long moment. "And now I've a woman's curiosity. What are your plans for the future, if I may ask?"

"Well, that's part of my problem. I could just go on back to the old life with Mr. Mason, and his work in the capital. But truthfully, I'm a bit jaded at the prospect. I just might entertain the possibility of starting over somewhere, build a new life. I do find I enjoy the company of ex-soldiers like Harvey, Todd, and of course you, Stephen. There's a certain bond among us, which I'm certain you've recognized.

"And well, I don't see much future in going ahead with my life as it's been since the war. A man gets to thinking he might want a wife and children someday. I'm sure brooding about what happened to young Holloway has influenced my thinking, but then I'm reminded there could indeed be a life ahead. He was robbed of his chance, but it makes one think."

"You'd make some woman a fine husband, Mr. Chiles," Anna assured him. "Though I'd say the prospects are a bit limited here, just now."

"Well, I'd want to take land, build a house, have some stability to offer. But I do like the people here, and living here just this short time has made Philadelphia seem far less desirable."

"Mr. Mason would miss your services sorely," Stephen observed. "But a man must live his own destiny. I got started in the wrong direction after the war, and it's taken God's intervention to get me on the right path, with this good lady's help." He took Anna's hand fondly.

~ * ~

Jedediah Mason rode toward Saltville on a clear but cold winter day, in the company of two former ironworkers, reflecting on the way things had turned out. Cabot was dead, and that was the good part.

That he'd done so much damage before Chiles had shot him filled the investigator with remorse. He should have let his assistant deal with the man directly, as he'd wanted. And young Holloway dead in the bargain...a bad bargain.

And now Chiles had chosen to stay the winter on Troublesome Creek, for some reason only he knew. Just tired of the business, was the way he'd put it, wishing Mason the best in his profession. He'd miss the man's good sense, his competence, his nerve.

Well, it's over. Best get on back to Letitia and my life in the city. Not cut out for this wilderness existence, anyway. Have to find another good man to work with; time to wipe out the rest of the ring, now.

It would be weeks of travel, on into the worst of winter, and it wouldn't be easy. But then it was never easy, and never would be, his line of work. Mason regretted most the crippling of Stephen Davis, as fine a man as he'd ever met. Along with the loss of Holloway. And Lester Cummings, an astute entrepreneur. *Damn Reginald Cabot...a canker, a human scourge.*

And come right down to it, eliminating such destroyers was what kept him in the game, so to speak. Knowing he was necessary to help put away those who preyed on honest people, Mason accepted his role, his work, along with the disappointments, the blunders, the hard-won achievements.

It was as good a life as was due him, he reasoned.

~ * ~

Carver MacNaughton was forging hunting knives, which were in constant demand in the settlement. Stephen and Ketchum had taught him the basics of hardening and tempering steel, and of case-hardening, that absorbing of carbon into hot iron to make the steel. Carver realized he was learning something even many smiths were ignorant of, and he felt a surge of pride in completing a well-made knife. Besides the hunters here, the women all wanted kitchen knives, and Ketchum hadn't been able to produce them fast enough. So he'd imparted these advanced secrets to his apprentice, who had progressed quickly from the basics of nail and chain-making.

Carver resolved to forge a set of knives for young Alice McKnight, who'd just turned sixteen. The young man planned a courtship of the girl as soon as he was better established, maybe had a smithy of his own if the place could support one. Or even if Ketchum turned the shop over to him, which was more likely. The mill took most of the older man's time and attention, along with the light duties of constable.

Carver often reflected on his life as it would have been had not Anna Davis taken him in hand. He remembered clearly her snatching him up, gun and all, and hurling him against that wall, effectively ending his career as outlaw mercifully early. That he could envision eventually asking the stern Reverend McKnight for his daughter's hand was a measure of the change he'd undergone.

Maybe that was what God intended, as the missionary men Harvey and Todd believed. He surely wasn't about to argue with that, the way it'd turned out so far. He thought about Todd's courting Alice's sister Marina with a sense of the rightness of it.

His housemates were his closest friends, and he imagined the three of them, eventually settled here with wives and children.

The thought made Carver MacNaughton glow like the fire in his forge.

Epilogue

It was spring again, and Troublesome Creek roared over its rapids with the snowmelt and the spring branches running full. Anna Davis walked heavily, but with a joy that changed her habitually serious face. Stephen had mended well over the winter, and could ride, hunt, work the soil again. He still ached in places, but she'd regularly massage him with the liniments she knew, and those from Belle Ketchum and the other women.

Leighton Chiles had found himself a remote spring-fed hollow farther up the creek, and homesteaded it. With the help of big George Wellerby, he'd put up a cabin, working on the days of sun through the winter. Chiles became an accomplished hunter, and regularly brought deer, turkeys, grouse and rabbits to the village. Belle Ketchum had practically adopted the homely man, who was considered something of a hero along the creek. She saw to it he had hot food, often sending him upcreek laden with what she termed "too much fer th' folks at th' inn to eat." He was grateful for her generosity, but did his best to repay it, either with coin or those donations of wild game.

Chiles and the Davises became close friends, and the man often helped Stephen with farm chores. It was generally agreed the two veterans were easily the best rifle shots in the region. They often hunted together, and the friendly marksmanship competitions between them became the stuff of legend.

~ * ~

In June, Anna Davis went into labor. Stephen rode hard for Tildy Driscoll, even after his wife's assuring him it would take hours. He found her at home, stammered out his message. She dropped everything, caught up a basket of herbs, cures and necessaries, and mounted the horse he'd saddled for her.

Stephen wanted to gallop up the creek trail, fearing all sorts of catastrophe, but Tildy assured him they had plenty of time.

"First babies'er always late," she stated. "You'll be stompin' around for hours, worryin' about her and th' baby. Shouldn't be any trouble…she's a healthy girl."

Once arrived, Tildy put Stephen to boiling water in which to immerse cloths to soften the pelvic muscles. Anna's water had broken around noon, but no contractions had started.

"Those be about dark, I 'spect," the imperturbable Tildy opined. "Then most of th' night, I'd say, 'fore th' child comes. Most men don't wanta stay around, but you can if you want, Stephen. I imagine Anna'd like to know you're close, though you can't help any."

Despite his wife's and the midwife's assurances, Stephen hovered fearfully close, particularly when the contractions started, sure enough, just before dark. He held Anna's hand, wiped her perspiring brow. She smiled at him, knowing this would get harder and more painful, but grateful for his presence. She knew practically every man would find something else to do at birthing time, and yes, it was a tradition that the wife handle this on her own, with help from another woman only if possible. But this child would belong to the two of them, more so if Stephen were there when it was born.

And Stephen Davis, the veteran sharpshooter, master woodworker, builder, millwright, blacksmith and something of the leader of this frontier settlement, was reduced to almost babbling in his ministrations to his wife. He fretted constantly, in contrast to the quietly efficient Tildy Driscoll, who'd done this many dozens of times.

Repeatedly he asked what else he could do.

"Jist keep her comp'ny, I'd say. Or you c'd go do somethin' else, if y'want. Not gonna happen fer a while, yet."

"No, I'll stay. Anna, you need water? Anything?" sponging her perspiring face yet again with the cool cloth.

"Just you. I'm learning what the term 'labor' really means, and it's good you want to stay." She forced a smile, just as another painful contraction began. It came sooner after the last one, and Tildy noted this, checked the dilation.

"Won't be as long as I figgered," she told them. "Jist you try to stay calm between 'em now, Anna, till I say push. Then's when you'll really work."

Stephen was imagining every disaster that could happen to his wife, and to the unborn child. He'd never witnessed a birth, never imagined what it was like. But here was his strong, capable wife, brave, equal to any situation, and she, like he, was totally at the mercy of this natural occurrence. He didn't need to remember Anna's faith to keep praying for her safety, and for her—and his—God to take care of her and the baby.

Not long afterwards, the midwife urged Anna.

"Now you gotta push, girl, with every c'ntraction. Help git this baby out. It'll hurt more, but t'won't be long now."

And hurt it did. Anna couldn't control the groans, shrieks of pain that accompanied each exertion. Stephen stayed at her head, gripping her hands, mopping her glistening brow.

Then, at a contraction no different from the rest, Tildy suddenly held a small, squirming bluish shape. She wrapped it in a sheet, held it to her shoulder, where it emitted a healthy howl. The woman's face glowed. Stephen stared.

Tildy placed the child on Anna's chest, and the mother's arms cradled it.

"Healthy girl, I'm proud to say," the midwife announced, as she went about tying off the umbilical cord. The baby, registering her mother's heartbeat and breathing, quieted for a moment. All Stephen could do was stand there, feeling entirely useless, marveling at this new creature he and Anna had produced.

Afterwards, the exhausted mother slept, the child held close, making small sounds. Stephen foolishly counted her toes and fingers, finding her completely normal. The blue coloring had been replaced with a healthy pink, and arms and legs moved of themselves.

"I'll stay th' night," Tildy announced, "but she'll be all right. Not much blood, and ever'thing went jist right." She bustled off after cleaning up, depositing sheets and towels into a kettle of hot water.

Anna had cooked food ahead of time, and although he hadn't wanted any, Tildy now got healthy servings for Stephen and herself.

"Best keep yer strength up, Stephen. Anna'll need a lotta help fer a few days, though I'd warrant she'll be up by mornin'. Little thing like deliverin' a baby won't slow her down none."

Outside the stars were paling into dawn. The horses stirred and a distant owl sounded, on its hunt. The trickle of the spring branch was faint, as it fell over the stone ledges toward Troublesome Creek.

Meet Charles McRaven

Charles McRaven is the author of several books, both novels and craft-oriented how-tos. He is a restoration contractor, stonemason, log cabin builder, blacksmith, and minister. A former Journalism professor and historian, he lives with his wife Linda, a former picture editor at *National Geographic*, in central Virginia.

Other Works From The Pen Of

Charles McRaven

Prequel:** **A Piece of Ground - the story of a troubled pioneer veteran seeking land, a livelihood and peace.

Letter to Our Readers

Enjoy this book?

You can make a difference

As an independent publisher, Wings ePress, Inc. does not have the financial clout of the large New York Publishers. We can't afford large magazine spreads or subway posters to tell people about our quality books.

But, we do have something much more effective and powerful than ads. We have a large base of loyal readers.

Honest Reviews help bring the attention of new readers to our books.

If you enjoyed this book, we would appreciate it if you would spend a few minutes posting a review on the site where you purchased this book or on the Wings ePress, Inc. webpages at: https://wingsepress. com/

Visit Our Website

For The Full Inventory
Of Quality Books:

Wings ePress.Inc
https://wingsepress.com/

Quality trade paperbacks and downloads
in multiple formats,
in genres ranging from light romantic comedy
to general fiction and horror.
Wings has something for every reader's taste.
Visit the website, then bookmark it.
We add new titles each month!

Wings ePress Inc.

3000 N. Rock Road

Newton, KS 67114